Also by Jayne Ann Krentz

Absolutely, Positively
Deep Waters
Eye of the Beholder
Family Man
Flash
The Golden Chance
Grand Passion
Hidden Talents
Perfect Partners
Sharp Edges
Silver Linings
Sweet Fortune
Trust Me
Wildest Hearts

Written under the name Jayne Castle
Amaryllis
Orchid
Zinnia

JAYNE ANN KRENTZ
WRITING AS

Jayne Castle

Zinnia

Pocket Books
New York London Toronto Sydney

Pocket Books
A Division of Simon & Schuster, Inc.
1230 Avenue of the Americas
New York, NY 10020

This book is a work of fiction. Names, characters, places, and incidents either are products of the author's imagination or are used fictitiously. Any resemblance to actual events or locales or persons, living or dead, is entirely coincidental.

First Pocket Books paperback edition July 1997

POCKET and colophon are registered trademarks of Simon & Schuster, Inc.

For information about special discounts for bulk purchases, please contact Simon & Schuster Special Sales at 1-866-506-1949 or business@simonandschuster.com

The Simon & Schuster Speakers Bureau can bring authors to your live event. For more information or to book an event contact the Simon & Schuster Speakers Bureau at 1-866-248-3049 or visit our website at www.simonspeakers.com.

Illustration by Craig White

Manufactured in the United States of America

10 9 8 7 6 5

ISBN 978-0-6715-6901-3

Zinnia

Chapter
1

* * * * * * * * * *

There is nothing complicated about our little arrangement, Mr. Batt. I plan to marry soon. Therefore, I require a wife." Nick Chastain folded his hands on the gleaming surface of the massive obsidian-wood desk. "You will find one for me."

Hobart Batt, attired in dapper evening wear, perched on the edge of his chair with the nervous air of a small mouse-wren. He swallowed visibly and tugged at the collar of his pleated shirt with soft, well manicured fingers. He blinked rapidly as he met Nick's half-shuttered gaze.

"I'm afraid I don't quite understand, Mr. Chastain," he said.

Nick suppressed a sigh. Intimidation was a useful tool, but it had to be used with surgical precision. Apply too much and the patient collapsed into babbling hysteria. Use too little and the response was unsatisfactory.

With the intuitive knowledge that he had acquired from years of practice and experience, he knew he was pushing the limit with Hobart. He also knew that if he

1

eased up on the pressure, Batt might regain his nerve and become defiant.

Decisions, decisions.

"Let me put it in more straightforward terms, Mr. Batt. You lost ten thousand dollars downstairs in my casino tonight."

"Yes, sir, I'm aware of that." Hobart rubbed his palms on his knees. "I have no idea how it happened. I rarely gamble. I came here with some friends and they encouraged me to play cards. I seemed to be doing rather well for a while and then, suddenly, everything went wrong. I tried to recover but things only got worse."

"I understand." Nick tried to project sympathy and deep concern in his smile.

Hobart's eyes widened. He flinched and shrank back in his chair.

So much for the smile, Nick thought. He abandoned the effort. He never had been good at sympathy and deep concern.

Hobart's expression became one of entreaty. "I simply don't have that kind of money, Mr. Chastain. I . . . I suppose I could sell my house, but I still owe the bank a great deal on the mortgage and I—"

"There is no need for such a drastic move. You don't seem to get the picture here, Mr. Batt. I'm offering to make a deal. Find me a suitable wife and I'll consider the debt repaid."

"A wife?" Hobart stared at him. "You want me to find you a wife?"

Nick forced himself to keep a tight rein on his patience. "What's so strange about that? You're a syn-psych counselor at Synergistic Connections, one of the most exclusive marriage agencies in New Seattle. I'm not asking you to do anything that you don't do on a daily basis for your clients."

"But . . . but, that's just the point." Hobart

plucked a snowy white handkerchief from his pocket and mopped his damp brow. "A professional match isn't worth ten thousand dollars."

"It is to me."

Suspicion flickered in Hobart's jumpy gaze. "Why would you be willing to let me repay you with my professional services?"

"I hear you're very good." Nick did not mention that he knew that Hobart had matched his friend, Lucas Trent, an off-the-scale illusion-talent, with Amaryllis Lark, a full-spectrum prism, a few months earlier.

The fact that Trent and Amaryllis had found each other on their own was beside the point so far as Nick was concerned. Hobart had confirmed the supposedly impossible match independently, which meant that as a syn-psych counselor he was one of the best. Nick wanted the best. After all, marriage was a lifetime commitment here on St. Helens. Divorce was virtually impossible.

The institution of marriage and the value of strong families were enshrined in law and reinforced with the full weight of the social structures that had been established by the First Generation colonists from Earth.

Two hundred years earlier, the Founders had been stranded on the lush green world of St. Helens after the energy gate known as the Curtain had closed. When it had become obvious that the Curtain might never reopen and that there was no hope of rescue, the colonists had gathered their philosophers, religious authorities, sociologists, and anthropologists together. The group had hammered out the rules and conventions of a society they believed would be able to survive the rigors of isolation in an untamed wilderness. The cornerstone of their carefully crafted civilization was marriage.

Sooner or later almost everyone got married. Although happiness was not the most important goal in marriage, the Founders had understood that well-matched couples would add to the stability of the institution. To that end, they had established match-making agencies staffed with synergistic psychologists to ensure unions that could stand the test of time.

The concept had proven so successful that today non-agency marriages were extremely rare. It was true that a few alliances among the elite were contracted for old-fashioned reasons such as money and power, but the vast majority of the population had the good sense to go through the agencies. Families insisted upon it.

Hobart stared at Nick, perplexed. "I beg your pardon, Mr. Chastain, but if you want a wife, why don't you just walk through the front door of Synergistic Connections and register the same as anyone else?"

Nick leaned back in his chair and propped one elbow on the cushioned arm. He rested his chin on the heel of his hand and allowed the silence in the red-and-gilt chamber to deepen while he considered the situation.

Hobart was proving to be more difficult than he had anticipated. The jovial, well-dressed little man who had entered the casino three hours ago looked crushed and crumpled now. But Hobart was still able to reason clearly enough to be wary of the bargain Nick had offered. Hobart was scared, but he was not stupid.

It was time to take a closer look at the matrix. Nick drew a breath and released part of it as though he were preparing to throw a knife or pull a trigger. He had no prism to help him focus his psychic energy, but after years of grim determination he had achieved enough control to use his raw paranormal abilities in a crude manner for a few seconds at a time.

4

He was a matrix-talent, gifted, or cursed, depending on one's point of view, with a rare form of psychic energy that gave him the ability to intuitively perform what was technically known as Synergistic Matrix Analysis. In lay terms, it meant that he could see connections, weigh possibilities, estimate odds, and deduce synergistic relationships where others saw only random events or complete chaos.

Matrix-talents were uncommon and most were not especially strong. They tended to rank below class-five on the paranormal scale that had been developed by the experts.

Very powerful matrix-talents such as Nick were virtually unknown—the stuff of psychic vampire legends.

Research on matrix-talents was limited, not only because the number of people who manifested the unusual form of paranormal energy was so small, but also because most of them refused to be studied. Matrix-talents were a suspicious lot. Some people claimed they were downright paranoid.

The development of a wide variety of psychic powers in the descendants of the colonists had first been observed some fifty years after the closing of the Curtain. As with everything else on St. Helens, the phenomena was governed by synergistic principles.

To work the talent effectively, efficiently, and with a degree of reliability, people who possessed paranormal abilities required the assistance of individuals known as prisms.

Prisms were unique in that their paranormal gifts were limited to the ability to project a psychic crystal. The prism crystal constructs they created on the metaphysical plane were used by those who possessed psychic talent to focus and control their talent.

The combined use of both kinds of psychic power, talent and prism, required willing cooperation from both of the people involved. The necessity of mutual agreement between prism and talent was thought to be nature's way of ensuring that talents didn't become predatory. Just another example of the laws of synergism in practice.

The need for a prism in order to use his power to the fullest extent annoyed Nick, as it did most strong talents. But the laws of synergy prevailed. You couldn't fight Mother Nature.

Writers of popular fiction and successful filmmakers routinely thrilled audiences with tales of so-called psychic vampires, off-the-chart talents who could overpower innocent prisms and harness their focusing abilities for dark ends.

But scientists scoffed at the notion that any talent, no matter how strong, could be used for more than the briefest of moments without the willing assistance of a prism. Even if, hypothetically speaking, it were possible for a prism to be overpowered, they said, the prism could simply switch off.

Low-level prisms who attempted to focus a much higher power talent were subject to an unpleasant but temporary form of burnout.

The laws of supply and demand being what they were, trained, professional, full-spectrum prisms tended to earn handsome salaries working for firms that supplied their services to clients possessed of various kinds of psychic talent.

Nick did not like to hire professional prisms and, for their part, most prisms did not want to work with matrix-talents. There was something about that particular form of energy that made the focus link between talent and prism extremely uncomfortable for both parties. Most prisms and almost everyone else on the planet considered matrix-talents weird.

There were wide variations in the way paranormal powers manifested themselves in the population. New types of psychic talent were identified and documented on a regular basis. But matrix-talents remained the least understood.

The synergistic psychologists theorized that for some unknown reason matrix-talents had enormous difficulty coming to terms with the paranormal side of their natures. In a society where most types of psychic abilities were accepted as normal and natural so long as they remained within a certain range of power, matrix-talents, even weak ones, were seen as different. An off-the-chart version, such as Nick knew himself to be, was considered a theoretical impossibility.

In addition to being labeled weird, matrix-talents were widely viewed as delicate. They often wound up in the sheltered worlds of academia and esoteric think tanks.

Some ended up in institutions of an entirely different kind, namely the locked wards of syn-psych hospitals. A matrix-talent's ability to see patterns in anything and everything could lead to obsession, paranoia, and suicidal despair.

Nick had concluded long ago that control was the key to surviving with strong matrix-talent. He practiced self-mastery the way others practiced eating and breathing.

Nick prepared to shove energy out onto the metaphysical plane. Without the aid of a prism, a brief glimpse of the pattern of the matrix was all he would be able to catch. But that was all he needed in order to figure out how to apply the right kind of pressure to Batt.

He braced himself for the transient sense of disorientation as his mind instinctively quested for a prism that could be used to focus the power.

The probe for a prism was useless, of course. There were none in the gilded chamber and the focus link only worked at close quarters.

Nick smiled at the syn-psych counselor. Hobart would never know that he had been the target of a short synergistic matrix analysis. Psychic power left no trace on the physical plane. Only a detector-talent could have picked up the energy waves and there were none in the vicinity.

Nick felt the familiar, mildly disturbing vertigo that always accompanied the quest for a prism. He knew the sensation would vanish when a link failed to form. He continued to smile at the uneasy-looking Hobart.

A whisper of light, bright, curiously intense energy brushed across the metaphysical plane. *Not his talent. A prism response.*

Nick froze.

Impossible.

The shock of unexpected contact made him feel as if he had just stepped out of the second-story window of the red chamber. A cold sensation seized his gut.

And then heat, a blazing, fiercely intimate, sensual heat swept through him.

Nick stopped breathing altogether for the space of several pounding heartbeats. But his mind automatically went about the business of securing a link with the prism it had discovered.

On the metaphysical plane, a glittering construct began to form.

This could not be happening.

Nick jerked his gaze toward the door on the far side of the chamber. No one had entered the room. There was no one around who could project a prism, let alone one this powerful.

Such perfect clarity. He could pour power through this prism forever and never burn it out.

He felt as if he had just downed a full bottle of strong moontree brandy. He was intoxicated. Enthralled. He could feel his blood heat.

Whoever had created this incredible prism possessed an ability that was beyond anything he had ever encountered. It was more than full-spectrum. It could handle his talent and he knew that he was off-the-charts.

The euphoria that seized him belatedly triggered alarm bells. He tried to dampen both the exuberant sensation and an exquisitely painful erection.

He knew one thing with absolute certainty. The prism was a woman. He could feel the essence of her femininity all the way to the bone.

This was not good. He forced himself to take a deep breath. He was not in full control here.

Something extremely odd was occurring. The link between talent and prism was supposed to be neutral and asexual. But there was nothing neutral or asexual about this link. The sense of intimacy threatened to engulf him.

An old, very private demon stirred in the depths of his mind.

No. His hand tightened into a fist. He was not going mad. He could not be going crazy. Chaos would not feel like this.

Nick sucked in another deep shaky breath. There were few things that he feared, but the chaos of insanity was at the top of the very short list. Usually he kept the secret terror buried in a bottomless pit in the farthest reaches of his mind. But tonight he could feel a tendril snaking out of the depths to sink its claws into his stomach.

"Uh, Mr. Chastain?"

He was vaguely aware that Hobart Batt was staring at him with renewed alarm, but he could not deal with him now. He was standing at a metaphysical cross-roads that he did not comprehend. Maybe this was it. Maybe he had gone over the edge. Maybe he was having psychic hallucinations.

Anguish and rage roared through him. He would not lose control of his mind. Death was preferable to insanity. He had made that decision long ago.

Five hells. He had been so certain that he could control his psychic powers. But maybe that's what all matrix-talents told themselves just before they went off the deep end.

Maybe his father really had committed suicide in that damned jungle thirty-five years ago.

"Mr. Chastain?" Hobart blinked several times. "Is something wrong?"

With an effort of will, Nick unclenched his fist. He would not let the madness show. He could control that much, at least.

"No. There's nothing wrong," he said between clenched teeth.

He would not go out like this, Nick vowed. He would not let anyone see him lose it. He might be plunging headfirst into chaos, but damned if he would let it show.

But how could chaos be so beautiful? So entrancing? So perfect?

Out on the metaphysical plane, the prism started to disappear. Whoever had created it was dissolving it as quickly as possible.

"No," Nick whispered. *"No."*

Another kind of terror seized him. As much as he feared the mental ward, he feared even more the prospect of losing the incredible prism.

Against all reason he made a mental grab for the glittering psychic construct. Fumbling wildly, he tried to imprison it with his own talent. The experts said it could not be done. It was only in novels that powerful talents could become psychic-vampires capable of holding a prism captive. But in that moment Nick was willing to try anything to hold on to this amazing creation.

He exerted every ounce of will and psychic energy he possessed. Power flooded the psychic plane in rippling waves of energy, surrounding the prism.

He had it.

The prism no longer continued to fade. Nick secured it with manacles of raw energy. It was his. He could not believe his prize. Awe swept through him.

"Mr. Chastain?" Hobart blinked several times and got to his feet. "Mr. Chastain, are you all right?"

Nick ignored the interruption. He was fully occupied holding on to his precious captive. The prism suddenly glittered with a furious energy, as if the person who had crafted it had realized the peril. But it did not vanish. It could not vanish. He held it fast in psychic chains.

He poured talent through the crystal construct, exulting in the rush of raw power. He had never been able to use his talent at full strength this way. It felt incredibly good, incredibly satisfying.

He could go on like this all night, not using his talent for any particular purpose, simply enjoying the process of exercising it. His fears of impending insanity vanished. This link felt right.

Without warning the focus shifted ever so slightly. The facets of the prism twisted and realigned themselves. The energy waves that Nick was forcing through it were suddenly skewed.

Psychic pain crashed through him. He realized that the woman who had created the prism had to be in similar agony.

What in the name of the five hells was he doing? Rational thought finally cut through the whirlpool of sexual and psychic hunger.

He was no vampire.

He forced himself to cut off the flow of talent. The prism winked out of existence.

The reality of the physical plane settled around him.

"Don't worry, Mr. Chastain." Hobart was halfway to the door. "I'll fetch help."

"Sit down." Nick closed his eyes and tried to steady his breathing.

"You're having an attack of some sort. I really think I should call someone."

Nick narrowed his gaze. "Sit. Down."

Hobart's hands trembled. He made his way slowly back to his chair and sat down.

"There's nothing wrong." Nick pulled himself together and glanced surreptitiously around the chamber.

Everything appeared to be normal. He certainly did not feel crazy. He wondered if these things started with brief flashes of madness and slowly grew worse over time.

No, damn it, he was not going insane. He felt fine. Never better, in fact, if he discounted the lingering ache of sexual desire. His memory was perfectly clear. His brain was sharp. He could summon his matrix-honed powers of logic and reason and self-control without effort.

No problem.

He analyzed the situation quickly. Obviously his psychic probe had accidentally brushed up against a very, very powerful prism. Whoever she was, she was so strong that she could link with him even though she was not in the immediate vicinity.

Furthermore, she was an extremely rare type of prism, one that could tune itself perfectly to matrix energy waves.

She had to be somewhere nearby, Nick thought. Right here inside the casino. No prism could be strong enough to reach him from the street outside.

Nick shoved his fingers through his hair and forced himself to analyze the logic of the matrix. They weren't supposed to exist, but he knew for a fact that there were a few off-the-scale talents. He was one of them. He also knew that there were some prisms whose powers went beyond full-spectrum, even though the experts denied it. A few months ago his friend Lucas Trent, a super-powerful illusion-talent, had found himself just such a prism named Amaryllis Lark.

Tonight, Nick knew, he had discovered another. He had to find her.

The casino security system was first-class, he reminded himself. One of the cameras would have caught the mysterious prism when she entered the building. The thought that he had her face on tape brought a wave of relief.

One way or another he would discover her identity. Things were under control.

In the meantime, he had to deal with the business of getting himself married. Nick clamped down the iron restraints of his willpower and looked at Hobart.

"Mr. Batt, you force me to tell you some details of my situation that I would have preferred to keep confidential."

Hobart looked more nervous than ever. "Details?"

"You have asked me why I don't simply go downtown to the offices of Synergistic Connections and register like other people. There are some reasons why it would not do me any good to go the normal route."

"I see." Hobart coughed slightly. "What reasons would those be, Mr. Chastain?"

Nick smiled humorlessly. "For starters, you may have noticed that I own and operate a casino. How many of New Seattle's fine, upstanding families would want one of their daughters to marry a man in my profession?"

Hobart flushed. "I admit your, uh, choice of occupation would not be acceptable in some circles. But, uh, unless you intend to confine your search for a bride to the daughters of the most socially prominent families—"

"I do, Mr. Chastain. I most certainly do intend to marry a woman from one of New Seattle's most elite families."

"Oh, my."

"I have a few other small problems, Mr. Batt. I trust you will view them as challenges."

Hobart closed his eyes. "Yes, Mr. Chastain?"

"I'm an untested, unclassified talent," Nick said gently.

Hobart did not open his eyes. "Would you consider getting yourself rated?"

"No."

Hobart groaned and opened his eyes. "Synergistic Connections only handles classified talents and prisms. Psychic-power-level compatibility between two people is just as important to a successful marriage as other types of compatibility."

"You'll have to work without a rating for me."

Hobart's hand fluttered. "But it will be extremely difficult to find anyone who will marry an untested talent." He brightened. "Unless, of course, you know for certain that you possess only a minimal amount of power."

"I'm afraid I'm not a weak talent."

"I see." Hobart gripped the arms of his chair. A hunted expression appeared in his eyes. "Precisely what sort of talent do you possess, Mr. Chastain?"

"I'm a matrix."

Hobart collapsed in despair. "A powerful, untested matrix-talent who wishes to marry into prominent circles. Impossible. It can't be done. No offense, sir, but no one in the better social classes will want you in the family."

"I find that money can often smooth the way in those circles just as it does at every other social level." Nick paused. "I have a great deal of money, Batt."

Hobart licked dry lips. "You said there were other problems?"

"Challenges, Hobart. Not problems. A marriage counselor must think positive. The last of the challenges I expect you to overcome is that I'm a bastard."

"I'm well aware of that—" Hobart broke off abruptly. He turned an unpleasant shade of pink. "I see. You meant it literally?"

"Yes. My parents were never married. My father was a Chastain. He died before I was born. I'm related by blood to the Chastains of Chastain, Inc. here in New Seattle but they like to pretend that I don't exist. I have no respectable family connections at all."

"Good grief."

There was no need to say anything more on the subject, Nick thought. They both knew that the stigma of being a bastard was a serious handicap for anyone searching for a spouse from a decent family at any level of society. It was a nearly insurmountable obstacle for a man who hoped to marry into the highest circles.

But being a bastard was also highly motivating, Nick thought grimly. No one could appreciate the value of respectability as much as someone who did not have it. He was determined that his future children would never face the subtle as well as not so subtle barriers that society placed in the way of those who could not claim a respectable family lineage. His offspring would have all the advantages he could give them and those advantages started with a suitable marriage.

Nick smiled faintly. "You see why I require your professional expertise, Mr. Batt."

"What you ask of me is impossible, Mr. Chastain. How can I possibly find you a nice young woman from one of the better families?"

"I'm sure you'll manage. I have complete confidence in you and my money."

"You think you can buy your way into high society?" Hobart sputtered.

"Yes, that is exactly what I think. It will no doubt cheer you to know that I don't plan to occupy my present low-class niche for long. I have a plan, you see. I won't go into all of the details, but, trust me, within five years I will be so damned respectable that it will take your breath away."

"A plan," Hobart repeated cautiously.

"Yes. And you, Hobart, have a very important role to play in my plan."

Chapter
2

* * * * * * * * * *

Zinnia Spring leaned heavily against the door marked LADIES and staggered into the women's room. One glance told her that the facility was as tasteless and garish as the rest of the casino. This particular room had apparently been designed to resemble some man's fantasy notion of the boudoir of an expensive but extremely tacky mistress.

A row of gilded stall doors saluted her. Inside the cubicles she could see pink and white marble commodes. On one side of a mirrored wall, fluted gold sinks and faucets in the shape of exotic birds were set in pink and white marble counters. A thick fuchsia carpet covered the floor of the sitting area which was dominated by a gilded pink velvet sofa.

It was enough to make any self-respecting interior designer wince in horror, Zinnia thought. But she was feeling too traumatized at that moment to waste too much energy condemning the decor.

She was relieved to see that she had the restroom to herself.

Her head was still throbbing from the paranormal

assault she had just undergone. Her pulse raced. She could feel the back of her blouse sticking to her perspiration-dampened skin. But at least she was no longer focus-linked to the bastard, whoever he was.

She was still not certain whether he had deliberately released her or if she had managed to break free on her own when she had tried to skew the focus. Everything had been so chaotic during those few seconds of contact that she could not recall them in a coherent fashion.

She gripped the edge of one of the fluted gold sinks and studied herself in the mirror. Aside from the residue of panic in her eyes, she looked amazingly normal. She felt as if she had been caught in a hurricane, but her hair wasn't even mussed. Her trademark flame-red suit still looked crisp and professional. The scarf around her throat was as stylishly knotted as it had been before she arrived at the casino.

She closed her eyes and took a series of deep breaths. Whoever he was, he was powerful. Definitely a matrix. She could recognize one anywhere.

But matrix-talents were not supposed to be that strong. She ought to know. She was something of an expert on the subject. The ones she had encountered in the course of her part-time job at Psynergy, Inc. had all been under class-five in her estimation. This man had been off-the-charts.

And it most definitely had been a man. She shuddered again at the memory of the intense masculinity that had accompanied the focus link. The sensation of sexual intimacy had been unnerving. She had never experienced such an overwhelming rush of physical excitement during a mind link. Or in any other situation, for that matter, she thought grimly.

Lately, she had secretly begun to question whether or not she was capable of strong sexual desires.

Well, at least that issue had been put to rest, she

thought. She was, indeed, capable of passion. But this was not quite what she had in mind when she read one of Orchid Adams's psychic vampire novels late at night.

This was impossible. Powerful matrix-talents were said to be as rare as First Generation relics. In other words, the experts doubted that any even existed.

Zinnia opened her eyes. She reached for one of the little paper cups stacked in a gold dispenser and turned on the gilded water faucet.

The cup trembled in her fingers as she took a long swallow. At least her head had finally stopped whirling. Her heartbeat was slowing to something close to normal. The disturbing sense of sexual excitement was fading. As far as she could tell there had been no permanent damage done.

She frowned. The psychic agony she had experienced had only occurred when she had struggled to free her mind from the link. She hoped her assailant had suffered some during the process, too. Served him right.

No sense trying to rationalize the situation, she thought. There was only one explanation for what had just happened to her.

She had been jumped by a genuine psychic vampire.

As far as most people were concerned, there were no such things as psychic vampires. They were supposed to exist only in novels and legend.

A few months ago, however, everyone who worked for Psynergy, Inc. had learned of Amaryllis Lark's frightening experience with a real-life psychic vampire. Clementine Malone, the owner of the agency, had made certain that all her employees were warned that vampires were out there even though the experts scoffed at the notion. The information had been kept from the media for the very simple reason that no one would have believed the tale.

The one person who could have proven the existence of psychic vampires was presently locked up in a hospital for the criminally insane. Irene Dunley, a staid middle-aged secretary, had gone crazy when her ferocious power was extinguished during a savage confrontation between herself, Amaryllis, and Lucas Trent.

Zinnia studied her reflection as she took another sip of water. She felt much better now. Almost normal.

Maybe she was overreacting. She was very tense tonight because of the Morris Fenwick situation. Perhaps her imagination had run amok during those seconds of psychic disorientation.

It was comforting to think that she had accidentally brushed up against a class-five or lower matrix-talent who had been surreptitiously attempting to use his paranormal power to cheat at cards. Casinos routinely employed detector-talents to ensure that customers didn't use psychic tricks to defraud the house, but someone could have slipped past security.

She sighed. There was no point trying to deceive herself. She had not simply tripped against a mid-level matrix, she had stumbled over an off-the-chart matrix vampire. Her prism talent was very unusual in that she could only work well with matrix-talents, but she was definitely full-spectrum in terms of raw power. She was able to estimate the level of a talent all the way to class-ten. And beyond, apparently, she thought ruefully, because whoever this guy was, he had been much higher than a ten.

It must have been one of the men at the gin-poker table. She had walked very close to the feverish crowd of gamblers gathered there. She had heard that the game was played for high stakes here at Chastain's Palace. Some very desperate, very powerful matrix-talent had no doubt tried to use his power to cheat. It had been her bad luck to be in the vicinity when the psychic probe struck.

He had probably been just as astounded as herself by the contact, but that had not stopped him from trying to grab the prism she had created.

Everyone knew that matrix-talents were a little weird at the weak end of the spectrum. Apparently they were very dangerous at the high end.

She would stay clear of the gin-poker table when she left the restroom. It was a synergistic fact that the strength of any focus link diminished swiftly with even a few feet of distance between talent and prism.

Zinnia considered the situation. There was nothing she could do about what had just happened. She had no proof that she had been attacked by a psychic vampire. The casino security would laugh if she tried to explain. The only people who would believe her were her friends at Psynergy, Inc.

She finished the water and tossed the cup aside. Casino security personnel would scorn her tale of psychic vampirism, but she had a hunch Nick Chastain's thugs would be interested to know that a powerful talent was trying to manipulate the gin-poker game.

A semblance of a plan took shape. She had been wondering how to distract Chastain's people long enough to get inside his office.

With renewed determination, she shoved open the door of the ladies' room and walked back out into the gaudy, glittering casino. It was nearly one o'clock in the morning. The gaming floor was crowded with elegantly dressed men and women. They hovered over the tables, excitement and desperation pouring off their bodies in waves. Cocktail servers dressed in spangled costumes circulated through the crowds with trays of drinks.

Zinnia turned and walked briskly down a carpeted hall. She went past the ornate black-and-gold mirrored elevators and found a door that opened onto the emergency stairs.

With a quick glance around to make sure that no one had noticed her, she stepped into the concrete stairwell and closed the door. Hitching her shoulder bag higher, she hurried up the steps.

On the second floor she found a door marked PRIVATE. She took a deep breath, gripped the knob and prayed it would not be locked.

It wasn't. She stepped out into a dimly lit mirrored hall carpeted in crimson and studded with gilded pillars. The decor made her wrinkle her nose in distaste. She had not yet met Nick Chastain but she had seen enough of his lamentably bad taste to know that she was not going to like him very much. They obviously had nothing in common.

"Can I help, ma'am?"

The low growl of a voice came from behind her. Zinnia whirled around and found herself facing a short, wide, massively built man who looked completely out of place in his formal black evening clothes. His shaved head gleamed in the glow of the torchier lamps. Pale eyes glinted from beneath brows that had been plucked to a thin arched line. The pointed black goatee looked ludicrous on his broad face, but Zinnia decided not to advise him of that fact.

She drew herself up with what she hoped was an authoritative air. "I'm looking for Mr. Chastain."

"Got an appointment?"

Zinnia favored the guard with a superior smile. "Yes, of course. He's expecting me."

The man's bald head glinted as he glanced at the closed door at the end of the hall. "Mr. Chastain is busy at the moment. He asked not to be disturbed. If you'll have a seat in the reception area, I'll tell the receptionist to let him know you're here."

Zinnia tapped the toe of one red high-heeled shoe and glanced at her watch. "I haven't got much time. Look, I'm unarmed." She removed her slim shoulder bag and held it open so that the guard could see the small wallet, comb and lipstick inside. "I'm absolutely no threat to Mr. Chastain. I really must speak with him immediately."

"Why?"

"If you must know, I'm a prism consultant from Psynergy, Inc. Mr. Chastain asked my firm to run an outside check on gaming-floor security. I've concluded the project and I'm ready to make my report."

"I wasn't told nothing about no outside consultant."

Two more heavily muscled men dressed in ill-fitting formal black jackets materialized behind the short, wide guard. They were obviously on alert, but they remained discreetly in the background.

Zinnia gave the bald guard a cool smile. "As I said, it was a security matter."

"I'm in charge of security around here."

"Could have fooled me. I thought perhaps you were Chastain's interior designer." Zinnia spun around and lunged for the closed door at the end of the hall.

She could only hope that the guards would hesitate to use force against a guest who presented no clear threat. Chastain wouldn't want to have to explain the mangled body of an innocent casino patron in his tastelessly decorated hall. Bad for public relations.

"Five hells." The wide man showed a surprising turn of speed as he lurched into pursuit. "Come back here."

Zinnia reached the closed door, seized hold of the knob, twisted, and shoved hard.

The guard's paw closed over her shoulder just as the door slammed open to reveal a crimson, black, and gilt chamber that was even more outrageous than the ladies' restroom.

There were two men inside the chamber. Both turned toward her.

The well-dressed little man seated in front of the

gleaming black desk looked harmless. The one lounging in the black-and-gold throne did not.

"Sorry for the interruption, boss," the guard said. "I'll take care of it."

Zinnia flung out her hands and grabbed the edges of the door frame as the guard started to pull her back out into the hall. She glowered at the man behind the desk.

"Mr. Chastain, I presume," she said loudly.

Nick Chastain looked at her with cold, curious eyes. In that gaze Zinnia saw a slashing intelligence, awesome self-control, and the promise of power. A strange shiver of awareness went through her.

"Is there a problem here, Mr. Feather?" Nick asked in a soft low voice.

"No, problem, boss." Feather's hand tightened on Zinnia's shoulder. "Just a little misunderstanding." He started to peel Zinnia away from the door.

"Hold it." Zinnia tightened her grip on the frame. "Mr. Chastain, I suggest we talk right now. Unless, of course, you want every cop in New Seattle here in this casino tonight."

Nick raised one black brow. He considered her for a long moment. Zinnia could sense everyone around her holding his breath. She made herself inhale. She would not be intimidated by a casino owner with bad taste.

Nick smiled. Zinnia almost lost her nerve.

"Very well." Nick glanced at the nervous man perched in the chair. "You may go, Mr. Batt. I'll be in touch."

"Yes, Mr. Chastain." Batt leaped to his feet and hurried toward the door with the air of a man who has just received a temporary reprieve from some unpleasant fate.

Zinnia gave him a sympathetic look as she ducked from under Feather's heavy hand and stepped out of the way. Batt skittered past her and fled down the hall.

Feather closed the door quietly. Zinnia found herself alone at last with Nick Chastain.

"What can I do for you, Miss . . . ah, I don't believe I caught the name."

"Spring. Zinnia Spring. And I'll tell you exactly what you can do for me, Mr. Chastain. You can produce Morris Fenwick. Immediately. If you don't release him at once, I'm going straight to the police. I'll have you charged with kidnapping."

Chapter
3

* * * * * * * * * *

"Are you telling me that Morris Fenwick has disappeared?" Nick concealed his rage and frustration behind a calm emotionless mask of polite interest. It was not easy.

"Don't play the innocent, Mr. Chastain. Mr. Fenwick is a client of mine. He told me that he was negotiating with you for the sale of an old journal that he had discovered. He said you wanted it badly."

"I do," Nick said very softly.

Zinnia Spring's fingers clenched more tightly around the strap of her shoulder bag.

So much for the expression of polite interest, Nick thought. His determination to get his hands on the journal was obviously leaking through the mask. He watched Zinnia narrow her very fine, very unusual, very clear eyes. He had never seen eyes quite that color. For some reason the odd silvery blue fascinated him.

"Morris also told me that he had informed you that he had another potential customer for the journal," she said pointedly.

"He did."

"And now poor Morris has vanished."

"Define *vanish* for me, Miss Spring."

She glared. "I can't find him. We had an appointment this afternoon at his shop, but when I got there the door was locked. Morris never forgets appointments. He's a mid-range matrix-talent. You know how they are. Obsessive about details."

"Obsessive? You've had a lot of experience with matrix-talents, then?"

She shrugged. "More than most people. But, as I'm sure you're well aware, no one's had a *lot* of experience with them. They're not only quite rare, they're reclusive, secretive, and a little odd. They don't like to be studied."

"Just because most of them won't consent to be guinea rat-pigs in some university research lab doesn't mean they're odd." This was ludicrous. Nick could not believe that he was allowing her to goad him like this. He breathed deeply, centering himself. "It just means they value their privacy."

"Mr. Chastain, I am not here to debate the oddness of matrix-talents. I'm here to retrieve Morris Fenwick. Hand him over."

"Tell me, Miss Spring, what, precisely, caused you to leap to the conclusion that I've got him stashed away somewhere in the casino?"

"I suspect that you were afraid poor Morris would try to drive up the price of the journal by starting a bidding war between you and his other client. So you grabbed him with the goal of intimidating him into accepting your offer."

"An interesting assumption."

Her mouth tightened and so did her elegantly sculpted jaw. "Poor Morris knew that journal was extremely valuable to certain parties. He told me that he had it hidden in a safe place until he could complete the negotiations and close the sale."

"Do you always call him 'poor Morris'?"

She frowned. "Morris is delicate. Most matrix-talents are. They don't function well under stress."

Nick was torn between disbelief and disgust. "In your considered opinion?"

"I told you, I've had more experience with matrix-talents than most of the experts. Morris is a gentle soul who is consumed by a passion for antiquarian books. He will become frantic if you apply the sort of pressure tactics to him that you were obviously using on that poor Mr. Batt who just left."

Nick managed, barely, not to grind his teeth. "Let me get this straight. You think I kidnapped Fenwick because I was afraid I couldn't outbid my competition. Presumably I'm holding him hostage until he turns over the journal."

"We won't call it kidnapping if you release him at once," she said smoothly.

"You're too kind." Nick got to his feet and stalked around the vast desk. He watched Zinnia's face as he moved toward her. She tensed but held her ground. The bright, fierce challenge in her eyes intrigued him.

He knew who she was, of course. He had recognized the name and the face immediately. A year and a half ago she had been notorious throughout the city-state for three days. The trashy newspaper, *Synsation,* had labeled her the "Scarlet Lady."

Nick detested the tabloids, but he kept track of them because he devoured information from all sources. His primary objective was to watch for photos and stories featuring those from the city's elite social circles who had the misfortune to show up on the front pages of the scandal sheets. He never knew when a tidbit from a gossipy piece involving one of the upper-class families might come in handy.

Eighteen months ago Zinnia Spring had been photographed walking out of the bedroom of a wealthy, influential businessman named Rexford Eaton. Eaton was not only the head of one of the city-state's most prominent families, he was also married. The resulting scandal had been a three-day sensation for *Synsation*.

The damning photograph of Zinnia in a dashing crimson-red suit not unlike the one she wore tonight had been featured in a place of honor on the front page.

Nick recalled the photo and the accompanying story, not only because it had involved Rexford Eaton but because something about the unsavory details of the affair had failed to ring true. His matrix-tuned mind had detected hints of wrongness between the lines. But that was hardly a surprise, given the low level of *Synsation*'s journalistic integrity.

He had been absently impressed by the way the "Scarlet Lady" had handled the pushy reporters and gossip columnists who had hounded her for those three days. He had followed the story and he knew that she had refused all interviews with an arrogant disdain that he had admired.

Tonight he was even more impressed. He was accustomed to one of three basic reactions from those who found their way into this chamber: wary respect, extreme caution, or desperate appeal. He did not get a lot of visitors who dared to issue an outright challenge. It took guts.

He was well aware of his own reputation. He had worked hard to build it, first in the wild jungle frontier of the Western Islands and later here in the so-called civilized city-state of New Seattle. A reputation was one of the few things a man in his position could depend upon.

He wondered if Zinnia had worn the scarlet suit to underline the impact of her demands or to shore up her own nerve. Whatever the case, that particular shade of bright, bold, unabashed red looked good on her, even though it clashed with the darker, more menacing red of the carpet and curtains around her.

The well-cut, snug-fitting little suit managed to appear both professional and stylish even as it issued a subtle challenge. It skimmed over gently shaped breasts and emphasized a small waist. It also hinted at the appealing curve of a full rounded derrière.

The way she wore the suit interested Nick far more than the color or the style. Zinnia held herself with a graceful hauteur that said a lot about her fortitude and will. This would be one stubborn woman, he decided. Definitely difficult.

Definitely intriguing.

The feeling of rightness that surged through him was annoying. It also made him wary. One of the problems with being a strong matrix-talent was that he was far more sensitive than most to small nuances and subtle details in everything around him. For better or worse, he noticed things that most people ignored.

Even when he was not actively trying to use his talent, some part of his mind was always observing, assessing, and analyzing. He intuitively searched for patterns, looking for factors which felt wrong or out of place or which generated warning signals. He was always watching for the specters of chaos and disruption.

His acute senses had kept him alive in the jungles of the Western Islands and helped him amass a fortune as a casino owner. But lately Nick had discovered that the constant search for the pattern in the matrix had a downside. After years of watching for the shadow of that which was wrong or dangerous, he found himself hungering for that which felt right.

And Zinnia Spring felt inexplicably right.

It made no sense. She had just accused him of kidnapping.

He tried to make himself step back into that remote, detached place where he could study and assess without reacting to what he saw. He made himself look at Zinnia with the calculating intuition that was such an essential part of his nature.

She was striking but not beautiful. He liked the way her straight nose, high forehead, and well-defined cheekbones came together in a package that could only be called aristocratic. The dark sweep of her hair curved sleekly at chin length.

By any standard, there were far more stunning women dealing gin-poker at the tables downstairs. There were several working the bar at the very moment who could make heads turn from a block away. And the new redheaded lounge singer was considered spectacular by every man and a few of the ladies in the casino.

Unfortunately, one of the curses of a strong matrix-talent was that a man who possessed it found himself looking at lovely women in a decidedly skewed manner. Nick could appreciate superficial feminine beauty as well as the next healthy heterosexual male, but the physical attraction that resulted was also superficial. The older he got, the more unsatisfying relationships based on that attraction proved to be.

He wanted something else, something more, something deeper, something infused with meaning. He wanted something he did not understand and could not name.

The unfulfilled yearning had grown stronger during the past few years. It had played havoc with his sex life, which, he reflected glumly, had become virtually nonexistent in recent months. He wondered if all matrix-talents were burdened with this unpleasant side effect of their paranormal power or if he was just especially ill-fated.

He pushed the intruding thoughts aside and indicated the chair that Hobart Batt had recently vacated. "Please sit down, Miss Spring. Obviously we have a lot to discuss."

She glanced at the chair, hesitated, and then walked defiantly over to it, sat down, and crossed her legs. One red high-heel shoe swung impatiently. "The only thing I want to talk about is Morris Fenwick."

"Strangely enough, that's the subject that interests me most at the moment, also." He leaned back against the desk and planted his hands on the elaborately carved edge. "Let's start by straightening out a minor misunderstanding. I don't know where Fenwick is."

She eyed him with a trace of uncertainty. "I don't believe you."

"It's the truth. I swear it. I may not fit your image of a respectable businessman, Miss Spring, but if you know anything at all about me, you must be aware that my word is considered good enough to take to the bank."

"You're the only one who would have had any reason to kidnap Morris."

"Fenwick, himself, told you that there is someone else who is interested in the Chastain journal."

Zinnia frowned. "Yes, but he said that you were the one who seemed most obsessive about it. He said that you claimed that it was written by a relative."

"My father, Bartholomew Chastain. The journal is the record of his last expedition into the uncharted islands of the Western Seas."

She studied him carefully. "That would be the Third Chastain Expedition. The one in which the crew is said to have mysteriously vanished."

"Yes."

She looked distinctly wary now. He could see that she was swiftly slotting him into a mental file labeled KOOKS, ECCENTRICS, AND OTHER ASSORTED WEIRDOS.

"There isn't much information on the Third," she

pointed out diplomatically. "According to the official sources, it never took place. Morris told me that the University of New Portland records show that it was canceled. And everyone agrees that no Third Expedition ever filed a report."

"I know," Nick said. "Twenty years ago a crackpot named Newton DeForest turned the story of the Third Expedition into a tabloid legend by claiming that the team was abducted by aliens."

She cleared her throat cautiously. "I take it you, uh, don't subscribe to that particular theory?"

"No, Miss Spring, I do not."

"But you do believe that the journal Morris discovered is actually Bartholomew Chastain's personal record of the venture?"

"Fenwick told me he was very certain that he had found my father's journal. I want it and money is no object."

"Morris told me that you said you would top any offer he received for that journal, whatever it is."

"I will," he said very softly. "Fenwick and I have an understanding."

Zinnia tensed in her chair. Her red heel stopped swinging. "Morris told me that he planned to sell the journal to you. He just wanted to get the best possible price. He contacted another client just to test the market. Get a feel for price. That's all there was to it. If you had just been patient, he would have eventually sold it to you. Produce him and I'll leave and we can all forget this ever happened."

"For the last time, Miss Spring, I did not kidnap him. Believe it or not, it's not my style."

"Your style?"

"Contrary to what you may be thinking, a man in my position prefers to conduct his business affairs in a normal manner." Nick smiled. "Besides, the bottom line is that I can afford anything I want. There's no reason for me to take the risk of committing a crime that could get me thrown in prison for thirty or forty years."

A stubborn look appeared in her eyes. "All I know is that Morris is gone. His shop is closed. He doesn't answer his phone. No one has seen him all day."

"One day is not a long time," Nick said gently. "He could have simply left town to buy books in New Vancouver or New Portland."

"No, I told you, we had an appointment. Morris would have called to cancel if he had intended to leave town. I wouldn't be so concerned if it weren't for this business with the journal."

"Why exactly are you so interested in Morris Fenwick's continued good health?"

"I told you, he's a client."

He recalled bits and pieces of the *Synsation* articles he had read during the Eaton scandal. "You're an interior designer, aren't you?"

She gave him a cool look. "I see you know who I am."

"I read the papers."

"Only the tabloids, apparently."

"I collect information where I find it," he explained.

"If you get your information from the gossip columns, my advice is not to rely on it. But that's your problem. Yes, I'm an interior designer but I'm also a full-spectrum prism. I do some part-time work for a firm called Psynergy, Inc."

That caught him by surprise. "The focus consulting agency?"

"That's right. Psynergy, Inc. grabbed a lot of headlines a few months ago when one of our prisms helped solve the murder of a very well-known university professor."

"I'm aware of the case. A friend of mine was involved."

Shock lit her eyes. "Do you mean Lucas Trent?"

"Yes."

"You're a friend of Mr. Trent's?"

For some reason her undisguised astonishment amused him. "Is that so hard to believe?"

"I can verify all this, you know," she warned.

"I know." He glanced at the phone. "I can call Trent at home now if you like and have him vouch for me. Save you the trouble."

"It's one o'clock in the morning."

"So Trent may grumble a bit."

Zinnia glanced thoughtfully at the phone and then pursed her lips. "Never mind, I'll check your story later."

"My story? You're beginning to sound like a cop, Miss Spring. Maybe it's time you showed me some identification."

She stared at him, clearly startled. "I'm not with the police. I told you, I have a business of my own and I do some part-time work for Psynergy, Inc."

Nick was pleased with the progress he was making. The tables had finally started to turn. He had her on the defensive now. "I take it you focused for Morris Fenwick?"

"Yes. It's difficult for matrix-talents to work with most prisms. I'm one of the few who doesn't mind focusing for them." She gave a small elegant shrug. "So my boss gives me all the matrix assignments. That's how I met poor Morris. I help him authenticate some of the really rare stuff he buys."

A nagging unease trickled across Nick's acute senses. "Did you help him discover the Chastain journal?"

"No. As a matter of fact, he found it strictly by accident when he was called in by the heirs of an old reclusive collector who recently died in New Portland. Morris came across the journal when he evaluated the man's private library. He said he didn't require my help to authenticate it. He knew it would be valuable to certain people. Naturally, being a matrix, he promptly hid it."

"Naturally," Nick muttered. "So you never actually saw the Chastain journal?"

"No."

"And now both the journal and Fenwick are missing. It would appear we have a problem on our hands."

She widened her eyes. "We?"

"If Fenwick has really disappeared, Miss Spring, I assure you, I want to find him far more than you do."

She searched his face for a few tense seconds. Then she exhaled slowly and leaned back in her chair. She drummed her fingers on the arms.

"Damn." She sounded morosely resigned to the inevitable. "I think I believe you."

"I can't tell you what that means to me. Perhaps now we can move forward. But before we do, I have a question for you."

She cocked a brow. "What is it?"

He watched closely. "You said you don't mind working with matrix-talents."

"No. Their psychic energy is different, not quite like the energy of other talents, but what the heck, I'm a little different, too."

He frowned. "You said you were a prism."

"I am. Full-spectrum, in fact. But for some reason, I can only focus well with matrix-talents. Creating a prism for any other kind of talent is extremely stressful for me and I can't hold the focus for long."

"I see."

"Look, I didn't come here to discuss my part-time job. We need to concentrate on poor Morris. If you didn't grab him, who did?"

He considered that for the first time. "Assuming anyone grabbed him as you put it, the next suspect in line would seem to be the mysterious other client. The one he was using to drive up the journal's price. Did he mention the name of the other bidder?"

"No. Matrix-talents are so bloody secretive." She narrowed her eyes. "But even if I knew the name of your competitor, I don't think I'd tell you. I'm not sure I trust you completely, Mr. Chastain. I'm going to have to think about this for a while."

"Is that so? Well, think about this, Miss Spring. I did not kidnap Morris Fenwick. And since I had nothing to do with his disappearance and since he's got my journal, it's only logical that I've got the strongest motive for finding him."

"I suppose you do have a vested interest."

He could not believe that he was allowing her to annoy him. He shoved himself away from the desk and walked around to stand behind it. It was time to take control of the matrix.

"You can relax, Miss Spring. I'll locate Fenwick for you."

"Hold on here, Mr. Chastain." Zinnia got swiftly to her feet. "I'm not at all sure I want your help in this."

"That's unfortunate because you're going to get it. I want the journal and Fenwick is apparently the only one who knows where it is. I intend to find him."

"I came here tonight because I thought you had snatched poor Morris. But if you say you haven't got him—"

He looked at her. "I not only said it, I gave you my word on it."

She blinked and took a step back. Then her chin came up. "Well, that's that. There's nothing more you can do." She slung the strap of her purse over her shoulder. "I'll be on my way. Sorry to have bothered you, Mr. Chastain."

"You're suddenly very eager to leave, Miss Spring."

"I've got things to do and places to go," she said with breezy disdain.

"At one o'clock in the morning? You must have an interesting personal life."

"My private life is none of your business." She reached the door and turned. "The important thing now is to make certain that Morris is safe. I'm going to contact the police."

Nick silently ran through the possibilities and probabilities of such a move. He had a reasonably good relationship with the cops in New Seattle, but he definitely did not want them involved in the search for the journal. "You'll have to wait awhile before you contact the police."

Renewed suspicion flared in her eyes. "Why?"

"For one thing, they won't take a missing-persons report on an adult, especially a matrix-talent adult, for at least forty-eight hours. You won't get any action out of them until the day after tomorrow. Second, if Fenwick is in trouble, going to the cops could scare the kidnapper into doing something desperate. Something that might make Fenwick's situation worse than it already is."

"Oh, my God." Alarm flashed across Zinnia's vibrant face. "I hadn't thought of that. What are we going to do?"

Now, finally it was *we*. Much better, Nick thought. At least she was not going to run straight to the cops tonight. "Give me a chance to make a few inquiries."

"Inquiries?"

"In my business I get to know a lot of people," he said, deliberately vague. "All kinds of people. I may be able to turn up some rumors on the street."

She hesitated. "You think some of your, uh, *associates* might know something about poor Morris?"

He didn't care for the emphasis she placed on the word *associates*. She obviously assumed he consorted with a less-than-socially-acceptable crowd. The assumption wasn't that far off the mark. He was planning to change all that, but he figured this was not the time or place to explain his grand scheme to become respectable.

"Kidnapping is not a simple crime," he explained in what he hoped was a calm, reasonable tone. "It requires planning and coordination. There's usually more than one person involved and that means that, sooner or later, there will be rumors and leaks."

"But it could be days before one of the kidnappers lets some vital piece of information slip. Who knows what they'll do to poor Morris in the meantime? If he does tell them where the journal is, they may kill him once they've got their hands on it."

"Assuming he's been kidnapped in the first place."

"The more I think about this, the more I'm convinced that's exactly what's happened."

Nick almost smiled. "Careful, Miss Spring. Common wisdom has it that matrix-talents are the ones who have a tendency to succumb to conspiracy theories. But you're doing a damned good job of it."

Bright color bloomed in her cheeks. She glowered at him as she reached for the doorknob. "Speaking of matrix-talents. You may be interested to know that a very big matrix, possibly a class-ten in my professional opinion, is working one of your gin-poker tables."

For an instant everything in Nick's world, including the blood in his veins stilled. He stared at Zinnia.

"How do you know that?" he asked so quietly that he was almost surprised she heard him. *"Tell me."*

She was suddenly very busy opening the door. "I accidentally brushed up against him on the metaphysical plane. He was questing for a prism. I sensed him and started to respond. It was an instinctive thing. I stopped as soon as I realized what had happened."

"How long ago was this?"

"I ran into him, so to speak, just before I came up here." She looked briefly amused. "Calm down, Mr. Chastain. I'm sure your security people will catch him before he cleans out the casino bank."

He flattened his palms on the desk. "Are you certain?"

"About the matrix downstairs? Oh, yes. I know they're rare, but no prism could mistake a matrix. By the way, you might want to tell your security personnel to be careful. I've never encountered a really strong matrix-talent before but I have a hunch that this one could be dangerous if cornered or provoked."

She went out the door and closed it hastily behind her.

Nick sank slowly down onto his chair.

She was the one.

Zinnia was the powerful prism he had collided with and briefly captured when he tried to use his talent to assess Hobart Batt. She had picked him up even though she had been one whole floor below him at the time.

His finely tuned brain failed to function properly for at least thirty seconds. He felt as if the matrix of his world had just been thoroughly scrambled.

With an heroic effort of will, he pulled himself together and punched the intercom button on the gilded phone.

Feather answered immediately. "I'm here, boss."

"Follow Miss Spring. Discreetly. Make sure she gets home safely. And make a note of the address."

"Sure, boss."

Nick put the phone down very gently and leaned back in his chair. He flexed his hands on the curved arms as he tried to reorient himself in the newly altered matrix.

Zinnia Spring had walked through his door wearing a red suit and red high heels and now everything had changed.

He brooded over the altered matrix for a long time.

Fifteen minutes later the phone rang. The private line. Nick picked up the receiver and heard the muffled sound of street noises.

40

"What is it, Feather?"

"Sorry to bother you, boss, but I don't think she's headed home. Want me to stay on her?"

"Where are you?"

"Second Gen Hill. She's driving real slow."

"Second Generation Hill?" Nick surged to his feet. "That's where Fenwick's book shop is located."

"Looks like she's going to park on a side street."

"Five hells. Keep an eye on her but don't do anything until I get there." Nick slammed down the phone.

He knew exactly what she was going to do. Zinnia was going to break into the book shop to see if she could find any clues to Morris Fenwick's fate.

Nick crossed the gilded red chamber toward the door. He glanced at the black-and-gold watch on his wrist. Breaking and entering would not be routine for a woman like Zinnia. With any luck he would get to Fenwick's shop before she worked up the nerve to try her hand at it.

Then again, his luck had been nothing less than bizarre all evening.

Chapter

4

* * * * * * * * * *

This was probably not a good idea. Unfortunately, she did not have a better one. She knew something was wrong. Morris Fenwick was an eccentric, neurotic, mid-range matrix-talent, but he was a client. And he was delicate. She could not help worrying about him.

Zinnia took one more look at the shadowed alley. The mingled light of the twin moons, Chelan and Yakima, gleamed dully on the lid of a large trash container. The rest of the narrow bricked passageway lay in dense shadow.

She took a grip on the unlocked window. If she did not do this right now, she would lose her nerve. She could not go home tonight until she had taken a look around the shop. She had to be sure that Morris was not lying dead or injured inside.

A strong sense of foreboding had settled on her after she left the casino. No surprise, she thought. She was not used to this kind of excitement. It was not every evening that she got jumped by a genuine psychic vampire and then went on to have a jolly little interview with the reclusive owner of the most notorious casinos in town. No doubt about it, her social life was a lot more exciting lately than it had been in a very long time.

She shoved hard on the sill. The window opened with a moan. The musty odor of old books wafted past her. This was not technically breaking and entering, she decided. After all, she had found this window unlocked.

She eased first one leg and then the other over the ledge and dropped lightly to the floor. She was in Morris's back room. The place where he stored his less valuable stock.

The darkness was absolute. She took a tentative step forward and immediately stubbed her toe against something hard. Stifling a groan, she switched on the small flashlight she had retrieved from the glove compartment of her car.

The narrow beam of light revealed a maze of boxes stacked on the floor. Each was stuffed with books. She raised the light and used it to scan her surroundings. The storeroom was crammed from floor to ceiling with volumes of all shapes, sizes, and descriptions. The shelves that lined the walls sagged beneath the weight of aging tomes.

The stillness was even more disconcerting than the darkness. The light beam wavered a little. Zinnia realized her pulse was racing.

The sense of dread intensified. She glanced at the open window. It would only take a couple of minutes to get back to the safety of her car. Another few minutes and she would be at the door of her loft apartment. The knowledge was tempting.

But she could not leave yet.

If only Aunt Willy and Uncle Stanley could see her now, she thought ruefully. They would faint with shock. They still had not recovered from the dizzyingly swift decline in the Spring family fortunes which had followed the death of her parents four years earlier. Nor had they even begun to rally from the humiliation they had been forced to endure eighteen months ago when she had gotten herself involved in what had become known as the Eaton scandal.

Only her younger brother, Leo, would be likely to appreciate tonight's adventure. She suddenly wished he was with her.

She made her way through the storeroom and cautiously opened the door on the far side. The smell was a lot worse in the main room. She realized it must have been shut up for some time.

The blinds were pulled closed on the windows that faced the street. The darkness was very dense.

She paused on the threshold and flicked the flashlight around the interior of the high-ceilinged shop. The sight that greeted her made her jaw drop.

"Dear God."

Chaos reigned. She gazed, stunned at the mess. Books had been pulled from the shelves and dumped on the floor. The glass counter top had been smashed. The surface of Morris's heavy old-fashioned Later Expansion Period desk was strewn with papers. The contents of the drawers were scattered every which way. The aging swivel chair lay on its side.

She took a step back. Every instinct she possessed was screaming at her to get out of the shop. She had to find a phone so that she could summon the police, she told herself. That was reason enough to leave.

Then she remembered that the nearest phone was the one on Morris's desk. She picked it out with the flashlight beam.

With an effort of will she made herself start toward the instrument. She was halfway across the room when she saw the crumpled form at the edge of the circle of light. The too-still figure lay at the foot of the tall rolling ladder that was used to access the highest shelves in the shop.

"Morris." She started forward. "No. Please, God, no."

"For what it's worth, my advice is not to touch him."

She gasped and spun around at the sound of Nick Chastain's dark disturbing voice. Her heart pounded as she aimed the light at the doorway of the storeroom.

Nick stood cloaked in the shadows. He wore an enigmatic mask on his cold ascetic features that was about as comforting as the expression of one of the proverbial Guardians at the gates of the Five Hells.

In that moment of acute awareness, she knew that he possessed strong psychic abilities of some kind. Even without a focus link, she could sense the metaphysical as well as the physical power in him. Math-talent or game-theory-talent, she thought. That would fit with his choice of career.

She realized that he must have entered the shop through the same unlocked window that she had used a short while earlier. For a minute she was too disoriented from the horror of her discovery to comprehend the significance of his presence.

Then it hit her. Nick Chastain had followed her.

The flashlight trembled again as she pinned Nick in the beam. She struggled to keep her hand from shaking.

"What are you doing here?" she demanded.

"I would have thought that was obvious. We both have a serious interest in Morris Fenwick. And apparently we aren't the only ones." Nick ignored the glare of the flashlight to glance at the body on the floor.

Nothing flickered in his gaze as he studied Fenwick's motionless figure. Perhaps encountering dead bodies was not that much out of the ordinary for him, Zinnia thought. She realized she was hovering on the edge of hysteria.

"I think—" She broke off and tried again. "I think he's—"

"Dead?" Nick moved out of the light. He went to stand looking down at the pathetic shape on the floor. "Yes, I think we can safely assume that much. Looks like someone smashed in his skull with a heavy object. Most likely that stone figure."

Zinnia jerked the flashlight to follow him. The beam gleamed briefly on his collar-length black hair, which was brushed straight back from a peak above his high forehead.

She moved the light downward. A familiar face carved in pale marble lay on the floor near the toe of one of Nick's very pricey black leather shoes. She swallowed when she spotted the reddish-brown stain on one corner of the statue.

"It's the bust of Patricia Thorncroft North that Morris always kept on the counter," she whispered.

"North?" Nick's brows rose slightly. "The philosopher who discovered the Three Principles of Synergy?"

"Yes. Morris specialized in the early theoretical works on synergy. He has, I mean he *had,* a fine collection of North's writings." Zinnia knew she was babbling. She had to get control of herself. "The police. I was about to call them."

"I'll do it." Nick turned away from the body and crossed through the rubble to the desk. "Why don't you see if you can find the light switch?"

Belatedly Zinnia realized that she was still holding the flashlight. There was no longer any need to conceal her presence, she thought. Morris was dead and the police would soon be on their way. She walked to the wall and found the switch that activated the old fashioned jelly-ice lamps.

Their soft warm glow spilled across the wreckage that had been Morris's book shop. Zinnia did not look at the crumpled body near the ladder.

When she turned she saw Nick reach for the phone. For the first time she noticed that he was wearing a pair of thin black driving gloves. She stared, riveted by the sight of his powerful long-fingered hands, as he punched in the emergency number.

He glanced at her, an expression of polite interest in his green-and-gold eyes. "Something wrong?"

She would not let him reduce her to a trembling mass of jelly-ice. She was a Spring. The family coffers might be empty and the tabloids may have labeled her the "Scarlet Lady," but she still had sufficient pride to face down the owner of a gambling casino.

"I just wondered why you bothered to wear a pair of gloves here tonight," she said. "No offense, but it gives the impression that you came prepared for something illegal."

"Yes, it does, doesn't it? At least one of us was prepared. Unfortunately, you've probably left your prints all over the windowsill and everything else you've touched so far."

His sarcasm outraged her. "I have no intention of denying that I was here tonight. Why would I lie to the police?"

"If you can't think of a reasonable answer to that question, there's no point getting into an in-depth discussion of the subject." Nick broke off to speak into the phone. "Give me Detective Anselm, please."

Zinnia listened as Nick spoke briefly with the person on the other end of the line. There was a marked note of casual familiarity in his voice. This was obviously not the first time he had dealt with the police. Given his line of work, that was probably not surprising, she thought.

"Yes, we'll both wait until you get here," Nick concluded. He replaced the receiver with his black-gloved hand and looked at Zinnia. "Anselm said he'd be here in a few minutes."

She relaxed slightly. The authorities were on their way. It would all be over soon.

"Poor Morris." She tried to think of something constructive to do. "I wonder if I should call his wife."

Nick's gaze sharpened. "Fenwick is married?"

"Yes, I think her name is Polly. The two of them haven't lived together for several years. Morris told me once that Polly moved out a long time ago because she thought he was getting too weird."

"I see."

"A very sad situation. They couldn't get a divorce, of course, so all they could do was separate. Morris blamed himself. Everyone knows matrix-talents are difficult to match properly."

"So I'm told," Nick muttered.

"Morris said that when they were dating, he and Polly had gone to an agency where the syn-psych counselors warned them that it wasn't a good match, just barely passable. But they went ahead and got married, anyway." Zinnia closed her eyes. "Good lord, I'm rambling, aren't I?"

"Let the police notify Mrs. Fenwick," Nick suggested with surprising gentleness. "It's their job."

"Yes. Poor Morris."

"Do you think you could stop calling him 'poor Morris'?"

"He was irritable and eccentric and secretive, and he was forever concocting conspiracy theories the way matrix-talents are inclined to do, but I got to know him. I was fond of him. At heart he was just a harmless little man who loved old books. I can't imagine anyone killing him. Unless—"

"Unless what?"

She glanced around uneasily. "I wonder if this is connected to the Chastain journal."

"Not likely." Nick surveyed the room with a single

assessing glance. "For one thing, as far as I know, I'm the only one who wanted the journal badly enough to do something this drastic."

She felt as if she had just stepped into an empty elevator shaft. "My God, are you saying that you would have *murdered* someone in order to get your hands on the journal?"

His mouth curved with deep cynical amusement, as if he had expected her to make the accusation.

"Only as a last resort," he said.

"If that's a joke, it's in extremely poor taste."

"I'm noted for my lousy taste. But that's another matter. Bottom line here is that I prefer to pay for what I want and Fenwick knew that. He had assured me that he would let me top any offer he got and I believed him. As I told you, we had an understanding."

"A gentlemen's agreement, you mean?"

"I'm flattered that you classify me as a gentleman, Miss Spring. I had the distinct impression that you thought I was one of the lower life forms."

Guilt assailed her. She knew that she had been very rude. "I'm sorry. I certainly did not mean to imply that I thought you were a, uh, lower form of life."

"It's difficult to accuse a man of kidnapping without insulting him in the process," he observed.

"Yes, I suppose so." She was thoroughly mortified now. "I beg your pardon. I'm afraid that I jumped to some unfortunate conclusions."

He inclined his head in a graceful manner. "Apology accepted. If you want to know the truth, I found your concern for Fenwick rather touching. Not many people would go that far for a business client. Especially one who was an irritable, eccentric, secretive matrix."

The satisfaction in his words disturbed Zinnia. It occurred to her that Nick Chastain was a man who probably preferred to hold the high cards in any situation. Making her feel guilty and coaxing an apology from her were subtle ways of shifting the balance of power in their relationship.

This was a man who knew how to manipulate and intimidate others and did not hesitate to do so when it suited his purposes.

Fortunately their association was fated to be extremely brief, Zinnia thought. She knew that if she had any sense she should be profoundly relieved by that fact. And she was relieved. Definitely. No two ways about it. The last thing she wanted to do was get mixed up with Nick Chastain. She had problems enough in her life.

So why was she feeling a small wistful twinge of regret at the thought that she would probably never see him again after tonight, she wondered. Too much stress. That was the key. Her emotions were all over the board at the moment. After all, she had just stumbled into a murder scene.

She took a firm grip on over-stressed nerves. "Whoever did this must have been looking for something."

"Maybe. But I don't think it was the journal. It would have been too valuable to hide here in his main sales room. He was a matrix. He would have concealed it in a more clever fashion."

She peered at him, wondering why he seemed so certain of his conclusions. The evidence of a frantic search was all around them. "There's an old saying that things hidden in plain view are less likely to be discovered."

His mouth twisted with polite disdain. "No matrix would subscribe to that dumb theory."

She thought about it. "You're right. Matrix-talents are too secretive by nature to trust the plain view concept." She looked around. "Morris had other valuable books in his collection besides the journal.

Two original North monographs, for example. Perhaps the murderer was after them."

Nick studied the ransacked room and then shook his head once. "I doubt it. This place was torn apart in a random fashion. Whoever did it wasn't searching for valuable books."

"How can you be certain of that?"

He shrugged. "I can see at least two volumes of the third edition of the *Founders' Encyclopedia* on the floor. Each of them is worth at least five hundred dollars to a collector. No one who knew anything about the antiquarian book trade would have left them behind."

"Oh." Impressed, Zinnia switched her gaze back to Nick's face. He was watching her intently. Their eyes locked and for a moment she could not summon the will to look away.

The world grew very still around her. She felt the hair stir on the back of her neck. A prickling sensation coursed down her spine. It was as though every sense she possessed, physical and psychic, was poised on the cusp of acute awareness. The feeling was just a hairsbreadth shy of painful.

"What is it?" Nick asked in his soft heart-of-a-cavern voice.

"I hadn't realized that you knew so much about rare books."

"There's a lot that you don't know about me, Miss Spring." He smiled faintly. "And there's a great deal that I don't know about you. That makes us even."

She shivered. The small whispers of awareness continued to make her uneasy. She'd never experienced a reaction quite like this around any man. Then again, she had never been in a situation quite like this, she reminded herself. For some reason, her life had been so humdrum that she had never before found herself in a room with a dead client and a mysterious man who put on gloves before he walked into the middle of a murder scene.

She was relieved to hear a siren in the distance. "Why did you follow me?"

"I didn't. I had Feather follow you. He called me on the car phone when he realized what you were about to do."

That bit of information incensed her. "What business was it of yours, Mr. Chastain?"

"I think that, under the circumstances, my concern was reasonable. After all, you took the risk of confronting me in order to accuse me of kidnapping. There are very few people who would have done that. It indicated a certain degree of unpredictability and recklessness on your part. How could I know what you might do next?"

"Why should you care what I did next?"

"You're involved with the journal. I'm interested in anyone who's connected to it in any way."

"Did you follow me because you thought I might lead you to it?"

"No." He looked mildly surprised. "It never crossed my mind that you would know its whereabouts. Fenwick made it clear that he had it stashed safely away and that he was the only one who knew where it was. Since he was a matrix, it would probably take another matrix to find it."

"So you had me followed just to see what I would do next?"

"Something like that."

"Of all the nerve." The wail of a siren was louder now. It made her feel increasingly bold. "I suppose you realize that was an invasion of my privacy?"

"Would you rather be standing here all by yourself with Fenwick's body while you wait for the cops?"

He had a point. It would have been a lonely vigil. "No, not really."

She decided there was no point mentioning that

there were a number of other people besides himself who would have made more comfortable companions in such a situation. He might take such a remark as yet another insult. Something told her that she had pushed her luck far enough tonight. Nick Chastain did not seem the type to tolerate insults well.

"Tell me," Nick said quietly, "Have you given any thought to how this is all going to look in the morning papers?"

She stared at him as the full import of what he was saying sank in. For the first time she realized that this might not end once the police arrived. Memories of the nasty tabloid headlines she had endured a year and a half ago flashed through her mind.

"Damn."

The cold amusement burned again, briefly, in his eyes. "My sentiments exactly."

"Well, it won't amount to much of a story for the *New Seattle Times*," she said. "After all, murder isn't exactly front-page news unless there's an unusual slant."

"Something tells me that as far as the *Times* is concerned, this particular murder will definitely have an interesting slant." He paused. "You're the Scarlet Lady from the Eaton scandal and I'm the owner of Chastain's Palace."

"Damn," she said again.

"I think we can safely assume that the *New Seattle Times* is going to splash Fenwick's death across the front page. And that's nothing compared to what the tabloids will do."

Zinnia became aware of a dull ache at the back of her neck. She closed her eyes and absently massaged her nape. "They'll have a field day, especially, *Synsation.* The only thing that could make it worse, I suppose, would be an indication that drugs were involved. At least we know that's not the case."

"Why do you say that?"

She frowned. "This is poor Morris Fenwick we're talking about here. There's no way anyone, not even a tabloid journalist, could link his death to drugs."

"I take it you're a glass-half-full kind of person," Nick said. "That's okay. I've never understood optimistic types, but I've always found them to be amusing."

Chapter
5

* * * * * * * * * *

Zinnia groaned aloud when she read the morning headlines in the *New Seattle Times:*

Murder Victim Discovered by
Casino Owner and Designer

Possible Drug Link

The body of an antiquarian bookman, Morris Fenwick, was discovered late last night by a local casino owner, Nick Chastain, and his companion, Miss Zinnia Spring. The motive for the murder is unclear, but police suspect that the killer was after money for drugs.

Sources in the department speculated that the perpetrator was searching for cash or valuables on the premises of Fenwick's Books when he was surprised by the owner of the shop. Mr. Fenwick was apparently killed by a blow to the head. The shop was left in a shambles.

"The place was ripped apart," stated Detective Paul Anselm of the NSPD. "Looks like the guy was enraged because he couldn't find any money. We're having a real problem with a new street drug called crazy-fog. A lot of burglaries lately have occurred because the users want quick cash to buy the stuff."

Zinnia braced herself with a cup of strong coff-tea before she went downstairs to the street to buy a copy of *Synsation*. Once she was outside on the sidewalk she was able to read the lead headline from twenty paces.

Casino Owner Chastain and the Scarlet Lady Involved in Crazy-Fog Murder

An old file photo of herself was positioned next to a long-range shot of Nick walking out the front door of Chastain's Palace. The story that followed was full of so-called details which amounted to little more than idle speculation. The piece concluded with a quick rundown of background information on Nick and herself.

. . . Both were unavailable for comment. Nick Chastain is the publicity-shy owner of Chastain's Palace, a popular casino in Founders' Square. Miss Spring is the daughter of the late Edward and Genevieve Spring. Readers will recall that Mr. and Mrs. Spring were lost at sea four years ago when their racing yacht went down in a sudden storm. Shortly after the tragic events, Spring Industries was reported to be experiencing financial difficulties. The company later went into bankruptcy.

Eighteen months ago, Miss Spring, an interior designer, figured prominently in a scandal involving one of her clients, Rexford Eaton, President of Eaton Shipping.

"So much for the virtues of optimism," Zinnia muttered to herself as she walked back through the door of her loft.

The phone rang. It was not the first time. It had been ringing all morning. Zinnia tossed the copy of *Synsation* into the trash can as she waited for the answering machine to pick up the call.

It was her Aunt Wilhelmina this time, which made a change from the endless messages that had been left by reporters.

"Zinnia? What in the world is going on? I've just seen the morning papers. I am shocked. I cannot believe that you have become involved with that dreadful casino owner. You're a Spring. We do not associate with his sort. And how could you put yourself into a situation involving murder and drugs?"

Zinnia yanked her red trench coat off the whimsical Early Exploration Period coat tree and headed for the door. She was in no mood to discuss the night's events with her aunt but she owed Clementine Malone an explanation.

A screaming yellow van with the words READ SYNSATION FOR THE LATEST SENSATION painted in purple on the side rounded the corner at the end of the block just as she drove out of the underground garage.

Zinnia accelerated rapidly and swept past the vehicle. Out of the corner of her eye, she saw a photographer inside the van lift his camera for a shot of her fleeing car.

She was tempted to give him the universally recognized single-digit salute, but she resisted. Aunt Willy would not have approved.

* * *

Byron Smyth-Jones—Psynergy, Inc.'s executive secretary, receptionist, and all-around gofer—was at his command post behind the front desk when Zinnia arrived fifteen minutes later.

Byron had recently abandoned the popular Western Islands look for the newer and decidedly more avant-garde Alien Artifact style. Both had been inspired by the New Seattle Art Museum's exhibition of the mysterious and very ancient alien relics that Lucas Trent had discovered deep in an island jungle.

No one knew what to make of the strange artifacts because there was no trace of any other intelligent life on St. Helens. As far as the descendents of the Earth colonists could discern, they had the planet to themselves. The handful of mysterious relics were the only existing evidence that once, a long time ago, someone else had discovered St. Helens.

The Western Islands look had consisted of designer versions of the hard-wearing boots and khaki clothing favored by the rugged folk who prospected and mined the fuel source called jelly-ice. The attire had sometimes appeared a little silly on trendy urban types such as Byron, but at least it had looked as though it had been designed for real human beings. The Alien Artifact style, on the other hand, was over the top in Zinnia's professional opinion.

Today Byron was a vision in tight-fitting acid-green pants and a matching shirt patterned with images of the artifacts. He wore a heavy necklace made out of plastic designed to resemble the strange silver-colored alloy the aliens had used for their tools. His blond hair was razored to within a quarter of an inch around his entire skull. The toes of his black-and-green knee-high patent leather boots were so pointed Zinnia wondered how he managed to walk.

"Sex, murder, and crazy-fog. How exciting can life get?" Byron chuckled gleefully as he put down the copy of *Synsation*. "How did you ever come to meet Nick Chastain? I want to hear every single juicy detail, Zinnia. Never in a million years would I have guessed that the two of you were involved in a relationship. You've been hiding things from your good buddy, Byron. I'm devastated."

Zinnia glowered at him. "For the record, Mr. Chastain and I are not involved in a relationship."

"The *Times* called you Chastain's *companion,* a loaded word if ever there was one." He stabbed a finger at the tabloid lying on the desk. "And *Synsation* clearly states that you two are a couple. So, which is it?"

"Neither. Is Clementine in yet?"

"I'm here, Zinnia." Clementine stuck her head around the door of her office. "I nearly had a seizure when I opened the paper. You okay?"

"Yes, I'm fine." Zinnia relaxed slightly. The sight of her part-time boss was somehow reassuring.

Clementine Malone could be brusque and acerbic, and she had a very short fuse, but she was also savvy, good-hearted, and loyal to her employees.

Unlike Byron, Clementine was not swayed by every passing gust of the fashion wind. Year in and year out she stuck with studded black leather and steel accessories. Her brush-cut, stark white hair was a brilliant contrast to her dark eyes.

"I tried to call you but there was no answer," Clementine said. "Kept getting the machine so I hung up and didn't leave a message."

Zinnia grimaced. "The phone started ringing before I even got out of bed. I haven't answered it all morning."

Clementine eyed her thoughtfully. "Mind telling me how in five hells you wound up in the company of Nick Chastain last night?"

"It's a long story. When I still couldn't reach Morris

Fenwick late yesterday evening, I sort of panicked. I leaped to the conclusion that Mr. Chastain had, uh, gotten hold of him."

"Gotten hold of him?"

Zinnia groaned. "If you must know, I decided that Chastain had kidnapped him in order to try to intimidate him into turning over that journal that Morris had discovered. So I finally went to see him."

"Who? Fenwick?"

"No, Nick Chastain."

Byron uttered a soft low whistle. "Holy synergy."

Clementine's eyes narrowed. "Let me get this straight. You actually confronted Chastain in his own casino and accused him of snatching Fenwick?"

"I'm afraid so."

Byron cleared his throat. "I hate to ask this, but does Chastain know that you work here part-time?"

"Yes, he does." Zinnia glanced at him. "Why?"

Byron shuddered. "Just wanted to know if we should be prepared for a visit from some of his security personnel."

"Oh, for heaven's sake, Byron." Zinnia frowned. "Don't be ridiculous."

"You accused him of kidnapping?" Clementine fell back against the door. "Say it ain't so, Zin. Tell me that you're just having a little cruel fun at poor old Clem's expense."

For some obscure reason, Zinnia felt obliged to defend Nick. "He was actually quite decent about the whole thing. I don't think he's the type to hold a grudge."

"Decent?" Clementine pushed herself away from the door. "Not hold a grudge? For your information, Nick Chastain has a reputation in this city-state. No one screws Chastain and gets away with it. Nor does he take insults well. And he absolutely hates publicity, especially the kind he got in this morning's papers."

"How do you know so much about him?" Zinnia asked.

Clementine made a face. "Everybody who knows anything knows something about Chastain's reputation. Gracie filled me in on some of the lesser-known tidbits, such as his dislike of publicity."

Gracie Proud, owner of Proud Prisms, was Clementine's permanent partner. Same-sex alliances were treated just as seriously by society and the law as heterosexual marriages. Gracie and Clementine had been matched by a professional match-making agency several years ago and had been blissfully happy ever since, in spite of the fact that they were fierce business rivals. Gracie was always a fountain of inside information, rumors, and gossip, much of which tended to be extremely accurate.

Zinnia drew herself up. "It certainly wasn't my fault that Mr. Chastain chose to have me followed after I left the casino last night and that the guy who did the following called him when he saw me go into Fenwick's Books."

Byron gazed at her, goggle-eyed. "Nick Chastain had you followed?"

"He had a business arrangement with poor Morris. He wanted to see what was going on and therefore happened to be on the scene when I discovered the body."

"He actually had you followed," Byron repeated in a voice infused with delicious horror. "There was nothing about that in the papers."

"He was just making certain that I got home safely."

"Oh, yeah, right," Clementine muttered. "This gets worse by the minute. The owner of Chastain's Palace has you followed after you leave the casino and you think it's just business as usual."

"It probably is for Chastain," Byron said.

Zinnia had had enough. "Look, I can't hang around here all morning just to entertain the two of you. If you need me, I'll be at home, working. I'll be screening my calls with my answering machine, so stay on the line if you want to talk to me."

Clementine gave her a level look. "If you have any more problems with Nick Chastain, call me. I don't know what the hell I can do about it, but I'll think of something."

Zinnia smiled wryly. "Thanks, Clementine, but I really don't think there's any need to worry about Mr. Chastain. My biggest problem at the moment is my family."

"Hey, everybody's biggest problem is family," Byron said cheerfully.

Chapter
6

* * * * * * * * *

"Zin? Are you there? It's me, Leo. I just saw the papers. Talk to me, big sister. What's going on? Are you really seeing that Chastain guy? Aunt Willy and Uncle Stanley are having fits and cousin Maribeth is making an appointment with a therapist. She says she can't take this kind of stress."

Zinnia put down the letter she had been about to open and picked up the phone. "Leo? I'm here. Hang on a second." She stabbed various buttons in a random manner until the answering machine clicked off with a last beep of protest. "Sorry about that. I've been screening my calls."

"I don't blame you. Unfortunately when no one in the family could get hold of you, they all decided to call me. I had to go out and buy a paper to see what was happening with my own sister. What's this about you and the owner of Chastain's Palace finding a murdered man last night? I assume the reporters got everything screwed up, as usual?"

"Not entirely." Zinnia leaned back in her chair and

stared at the stack of mail that she had just started to open.

It was good to hear her brother's voice. Leo was the one person she could depend on to remain calm and rational in the face of a family crisis. He was in his senior year at the University of New Seattle. A class-nine psychometric-talent with an intuitive feel for the age and past history of old objects, he was majoring in Synergistic Historical Analysis.

As far as Zinnia was concerned, Leo was destined for a career in academia. He had a passion for his studies and she was certain that he would leave his mark on his field. The rest of the family was already starting to fret about that very possibility.

For four generations, the Spring fortunes had been firmly founded in the world of business. The bankruptcy which had followed the death of Edward Spring had stunned the family. Everyone except Zinnia was obsessed with the notion that Leo should assume the responsibility of rebuilding Spring Industries. Zinnia was determined to protect him from the mounting pressure.

"One of my focus clients was killed yesterday," she explained. "I found the body late last night. Mr. Chastain happened to be with me at the time. We both had to give statements to the police."

"Chastain just happened to be there, huh? Somehow, I don't think that's going to wash with the family. This is your brother speaking, Zin. Tell me what's going on."

"It's complicated. Mr. Chastain was involved in negotiations with my client, Morris Fenwick." She gave Leo a quick summary of events. "So, you see," she concluded. "We had a mutual interest in poor Morris."

"Hmm."

"What's that supposed to mean?"

"I'm not sure," Leo admitted. "But I think I

understand why Aunt Willy and the others are in hysterics. Especially after what happened eighteen months ago when that bastard, Eaton, set you up to take the fall as his mistress."

"I assure you, Nick Chastain and Rexford Eaton have absolutely nothing in common."

That was nothing less than the truth, she thought. Rexford Eaton, patron of the arts, major contributor to the Founders' Values political party and all-around very-important person, had hired her to design new interiors for the Eaton estate.

At the time, she had been fervently grateful for the lucrative commission. The death of her parents, followed by the downfall of Spring Industries had put her and Leo in bad financial straits. The fortunes of the rest of the extended Spring family had gone down with the business so there was no one she could turn to for help.

She had poured all of her energy into building Zinnia Spring Interiors into a viable design firm. She had been thrilled when she had secured the Eaton project, not just because it paid well, but because it gave her an entree into the closed world of the high-end design market. She knew that if she satisfied the Eatons, they would tell others in their exclusive circle.

But less than two weeks after she had begun work on the Eaton estate, she had found herself on the front page of *Synsation* as well as several other tabloids. When she saw the photo of herself emerging from a bedroom of the Eaton estate into a garden with Rexford Eaton at her side, she realized that she had been set up. No one believed that she and Eaton had been examining wallpaper samples inside that bedroom.

It had taken her a while to put all of the pieces of the puzzle together.

Rexford and his elegant wife, Bethany, had conspired to use her as a cover for the *ménage-à-trois* affair that they had been conducting with Daria Gardener, a powerful politician in the Founders' Values political party.

Following the trail of rumors deliberately leaked by one of Gardener's political rivals, reporters had begun asking pointed questions. The Eatons and Daria Gardener had crafted a scheme to throw a chunk of raw meat to the wolf-dogs of the press in an effort to put them off the scent. Zinnia was the dish they had served up on a silver platter.

It had all gone off like clockwork. Bethany Eaton had staged a tastefully tearful scene as the wronged spouse when the tabloids portrayed Zinnia as her husband's mistress.

On the surface, it appeared to be just one more unfortunate tale of a philandering husband caught with his passing fancy who just happened to be the daughter of a once-prominent city-state family. No one suspected the three-way arrangement with Daria Gardener.

An affair was regrettable but survivable. A threesome involving one of the most prominent couples in society and an important politician, on the other hand, would have done serious damage to both the Eatons and Gardener. None of the three lovers would have made it through such a scandal unscathed.

In the end Zinnia was the only one who had been hurt. Daria Gardener was never once mentioned in the press. There was quiet sympathy for Bethany Eaton who bore up nobly. As for Rexford, most people just shook their heads when they read about his affair.

Straying husbands were not all that uncommon, especially among the elite where people were not always matched by an agency. It was an open secret that the very wealthy sometimes entered into marriages for reasons of property and money rather than with the goal of a happy, stable relationship. With divorce an impossibility, there had been no question but that the Eaton marriage would make it through the unpleasantness.

The whole thing had been forgotten by the press within three days.

But three days of sensationalistic journalism, it turned out, was long enough to cost Zinnia much of the design business that she had labored so hard to build after the fall of Spring Industries.

Three days had also been long enough to shred her own personal reputation. When she had finally accepted that she could not outrun the label of the "Scarlet Lady," she had defiantly adopted the color as her business trademark.

To her family's horror and chagrin, she now had a closet full of red. Coats, suits, pants, jackets, skirts, dresses, the garments spanned the red spectrum from bright vermilion to deep dark cherry-berry. There were some obvious limitations, Zinnia conceded, but on the positive side, accessorizing was a snap.

She had lost her shot at the exclusive high-end market after the scandal, but during the past eighteen months she had slowly begun to attract the attention of the up-and-coming entrepreneurial crowd. She was determined to hang on to her new market niche.

"Aunt Willy and cousin Maribeth are frothing at the mouth," Leo said. "I think their biggest fear is that Luttrell will cancel his next date with you."

"Between you and me, it wouldn't break my heart. Duncan's a nice man and I enjoy his company but that's about as far as it goes."

"You're forgetting the very high F factor here, Zin."

"*F* factor?"

"Family factor," Leo explained. "Duncan Luttrell doubled his net worth overnight when he pulled off the recent expansion of his company. When he releases his new generation of software, he'll probably triple his bottom line. I have a feeling that Aunt Willy, Uncle Stanley, and the others will soon start hinting that it's as easy to fall in love with a wealthy man as it is a poor one."

"So what?" Zinnia flipped through some bills and a couple of catalogs. "If they get pushy, I'll play my ace card."

"Yeah, yeah, I know." Leo's voice took on a comically pathetic, melodramatic whine. "You would never dream of contracting an unmatched marriage and the best agency in town, Synergistic Connections, declared you to be unmatchable."

"You got it," she retorted cheerfully. "Statistically improbable, but it does happen. Hey, what can you do?"

"Take it from me, Zin, your unmatchable status won't stop Aunt Willy and the gang."

"How could the members of my very own family even dream of asking me to risk an unmatched marriage?" Zinnia smiled to herself as she reached for the letter opener. "Besides, what decent, sensible man would want to marry a woman who has been declared unmatchable?"

"You know what I think?" Leo retorted. "I think you secretly like the fact that the agency said it couldn't find you a match."

"How can you possibly suggest such a thing?" Zinnia slit open an envelope and found another bill inside. "Being declared unmatchable is a fate worse than death. Everyone knows that."

"Except you, apparently."

Zinnia smiled to herself. Four years earlier, shortly before her parents had been lost at sea, she had thought she might be falling in love. His name had been Sterling Dean. He had been a handsome vice-president at Spring Industries and it had seemed to Zinnia that they had a lot in common. They had both registered at Synergistic Connections to confirm that their mutual choice was a good one.

To everyone's amazement and the acute dismay of the syn-psych counselor, Zinnia had emerged from the testing process with the dubious distinction of being one of an extremely small number of people declared to be unmatchable. Something to do with her paranormal psychological profile, the experts said. She was different in some subtle ways that made it impossible to successfully match her with Sterling Dean or anyone else who was listed on the registry at that time.

Zinnia had not even begun to adjust to the shock of being told that she might never marry when the news of her parents' deaths had arrived. After that, she'd been too busy dealing with grief, the crumbling Spring empire and the family's future to worry about her official status as an eternal spinster.

Family and friends who had learned about her agency results viewed her with mingled shock, fascination, and pity. But lately Zinnia had begun to see distinct advantages in her situation. In a society where enormous pressure was applied to everyone to marry, she had a free pass.

The conventional wisdom was that what she actually possessed was a ticket to loneliness, but she did not spend much time thinking about it these days. She was too busy trying to make a living.

"Aunt Willy says you told her that you enjoy Luttrell's company and that he's got a nice sense of humor," Leo pointed out.

"I do and he does." She did not add that a week ago Duncan had gone so far as to hint that he might be open to the notion of a non-agency marriage.

Duncan was the president of SynIce, a high-profile computer firm. He had introduced himself to Zinnia six weeks ago at an art exhibition. They had fallen into conversation when they had found themselves standing, equally baffled, in front of a painting from the Neo-Second Generation school. They had each taken a long look at the meaningless blobs of paint, caught each other's eye, and immediately succumbed to laughter.

They had promptly adjourned to the museum cafe to share a cup of coff-tea and a conversation about art.

When Duncan had phoned a few days later to invite her to the theater, she had accepted. Aunt Willy had gone into ecstasy. Zinnia was well aware that visions of recouping the family fortunes through marriage were dancing in the heads of her nearest and dearest.

"You're always saying how important a sense of humor is in a man," Leo reminded her.

"Absolutely crucial," she assured him. "After growing up with Dad, how could I live with anyone who didn't know how to laugh?"

"I know. As a businessman, Dad was a complete washout, but he was a great father. I still miss him and Mom, Zin."

"Me, too." A pang of wistfulness went through Zinnia as she recalled her father's robust zest for life.

Edward Spring had been a great-hearted man of huge enthusiasms. His wife, Genevieve, had shared her husband's boundless optimism and gentle nature. Zinnia and Leo had grown up in a home that had been filled with warmth and laughter. Unfortunately, neither of their parents had had a head for business. Under Edward and Genevieve's management, Spring Industries had been driven straight into the ground.

"I guess it's just as well that you're not carrying a torch for Luttrell," Leo said. "The tabloids as good as implied that you're Nick Chastain's mistress."

"It will be old news by tomorrow," Zinnia assured him. She picked up a pen and fiddled with it. "The Spring name doesn't have the interest level that it did a year and a half ago."

"Maybe not, but Chastain's name will sure sell newspapers."

She tossed aside the pen and sat forward. "You know what's really maddening about this whole situation?"

"Yeah. The fact that the papers are trying to slice and dice your reputation again."

"No, it's that everyone seems to have forgotten that poor Morris Fenwick was murdered last night."

"Unfortunately, Chastain is a lot more interesting than Morris Fenwick," Leo said. "And so are you, for that matter."

"It's not right. The newspapers and everyone else should be focused on finding Fenwick's killer."

"The cops will get him," Leo said off-handedly. "Whoever it was will probably be picked up in a drug bust sooner or later."

"Maybe." Zinnia hesitated. "Leo, if I wanted to consult an expert in the Western Seas expeditions, especially one that was conducted about thirty-five years ago, who would I see?"

"Any particular expedition?"

"Yes. Don't laugh, but I'd like to find out more about the Third Chastain Expedition."

"The Third?" Leo laughed. "You're kidding. That's just an old fairy tale. It never even took place. The university that sponsored it had to cancel the venture at the last minute. Seems the expedition master walked off into a jungle and committed suicide a few days before the team was scheduled to set out."

"Was his body ever found?"

"No. We're talking about a jungle, Zinnia. You don't usually find bodies in jungles unless you know exactly where to look. And I guess no one did in this case."

"There's the DeForest theory about the fate of the Third," Zinnia reminded him tentatively. "It came out several years ago."

Leo gave a snort of laughter. "Yeah. And the only place that it got published was in the tabloids. No real scholar would even give it the time of day. Demented DeForest's crackpot story about aliens abducting an expedition team was a tremendous embarrassment to the University of New Seattle. It cost him tenure and his job."

"Demented DeForest?" Zinnia repeated.

"That's what they call him in serious academic circles. I think his first name is Newton or something. He was a professor in the Department of Synergistic Historical Analysis until he went off the deep end and started writing about aliens and lost expeditions."

"Are you telling me that there are no experts on the Third Chastain Expedition that I can contact?"

"None. Like I said, there was no Third."

"But what about Bartholomew Chastain? He existed. He supposedly kept a journal. Morris thought he'd discovered it."

"Oh, sure, Chastain was for real and his first two expeditions were highly successful. He probably did leave some journals of his early trips. Professional explorers always keep diaries of some kind. But there couldn't have been a record of the Third Expedition because that one never took place." Leo paused. "The only thing that might exist—"

"Yes?"

"I suppose Chastain might have begun a journal for the Third at the time the plans were made for it. He might have recorded the preparations and plans before he killed himself."

"Maybe that's what Morris found," Zinnia mused. "What happened to Professor DeForest?"

"He was forced to retire, as I told you. I think someone mentioned that there was some family money. He inherited an old estate. Far as I know, he's still living there."

"And he's the only authority on the Third Expedition?"

"Let's put it this way, he's the guy who invented the legend. I wouldn't go so far as to call him an authority."

"I see." Zinnia tapped the end of a pencil against the desk.

"Hey, Zin?"

"Yes?"

Leo's voice took on a more somber note. "Do you think Nick Chastain will bother you?"

"What do you mean, bother me?"

"From what I've heard, he's kind of mysterious. Very reclusive. No one knows much about him."

"I think that's the way he likes it," Zinnia said. "What's more, I'm sure he intends to stay as mysterious and reclusive as possible. Which means that he'll keep well clear of me. The last thing he'd want to do is draw more attention to himself by extending his association with the infamous Scarlet Lady."

"Hmm."

"Think about it," she said, warming to her own logic. "If he were to start bothering me, as you put it, he'd only risk more public exposure. There would be more speculation. His picture might show up in the papers again. It's the last thing he'd want."

"Yeah, I guess."

"Trust me, he'll stay out of sight. He knows that so long as he doesn't add jelly-ice to the fire, the story will die."

"What about you?" Leo still sounded worried.

"I can avoid the reporters until they give up and go away. It's family members who are going to be difficult, not Mr. Chastain."

"If you say so."

"Don't worry, I've heard the last of him."

Zinnia said goodbye and hung up the phone. When

it rang almost immediately, she jumped in her chair.
She glared at it and waited for the answering machine
to pick up the call.

*"This is Nick Chastain. I assume you're there,
screening calls, Zinnia. I would very much like to
speak with you."*

She froze. Even through the answering machine, the
sound of his voice sent a tingle of awareness across
her nerve endings just as it had the previous night.
Apparently her strange reaction to him had not been
merely a product of the darkness and the unsettling
circumstances.

Nick ceased speaking but he did not hang up. He
just waited.

She hesitated a few seconds but in the end she could
not stand it.

"Damn." She composed herself and reached for the
receiver as gingerly as if it were a live spider-frog.

"Yes, Mr. Chastain?"

"Please call me, Nick. After what we went through
together last night I think we should be on a first-
name basis, don't you?"

The thread of humor in his words bore no resemblance to Duncan Luttrell's easy laughter, she
thought. Nick's amusement came from some dark
remote realm, a place where humor was in extremely
short supply, and what there was of it had gotten
twisted and stunted from lack of sunlight.

"What a surprise." She tried to infuse a blasé tone
into her words. "I just told my brother that you were
unlikely to call because you would be busy putting as
much distance between the two of us as possible. I got
the idea that you prefer to keep a very low profile, Mr.
Chastain."

He ignored that. "I assume you're being pestered by
reporters?"

"There were some phone calls this morning which I ignored and I think the *Synsation* news van is still parked outside my apartment but it's nothing I can't handle. What about you?"

"I employ people to do useful tasks such as keeping the press away from me."

"Yes, of course." Zinnia got to her feet. Dragging the telephone cord behind her, she went to the window to look down at the *Synsation* van. "How convenient."

"I can arrange to send someone to your apartment to do the same for you."

Zinnia had a sudden vision of the hulking Feather stationed downstairs in the lobby. The manager and her neighbors would never forgive her.

"For heaven's sake, don't do that." She frowned at the distinct hint of panic in her voice. She cleared her throat. "I mean, thank you very much, but that won't be necessary. The reporters will go away when they get bored."

"Maybe. But that could take a while."

"You know something? If those journalists paid half this much attention to Morris's murder, the police might be a little more motivated to do a really thorough investigation."

"I'm sure the cops are giving it their best."

"I'm not so sure about that." Zinnia turned and stalked back to her airy little Early Exploration Period desk. "I think that Detective Anselm is content to wait until a likely suspect wanders into his office and confesses."

"Anselm's a good man. He'll pursue any leads he uncovers."

"I hope you're right, but I'm afraid he's going to put the case on the back burner because it looks like just another money-for-drugs robbery."

There was a short silence on the other end of the line.

"Do you still believe there's more to it?" Nick finally asked without any inflection at all in his voice.

"I was awake for hours thinking about it." She sank slowly back down onto her chair. "Don't you find it awfully coincidental that poor Morris got killed just as he was making final arrangements to sell the Chastain journal?"

"There you go with the conspiracy theories again. Are you sure there's no matrix-talent gene in your family?"

"This is not amusing, Mr. Chastain." She frowned. "I wonder where he hid the journal."

"You're not the only one who would like to know what happened to it."

The grim determination in his words did nothing to calm her restless nerves. "It may not turn up for a long time. Don't forget, Morris was a matrix. Very big on puzzles and secrets. No one can hide things as well as a matrix."

"And no one can find things that are hidden as well as a matrix," Nick said.

"True. You know the old saying, it takes a matrix-talent thief to catch a matrix-talent thief. Perhaps you could hire one to help you locate the journal. A matrix-talent, I mean, not a real thief."

"I'll look into the possibility." Nick paused. "If I do turn up a matrix-talent who can assist me in locating the journal I'll need to hire a prism who can focus for him. Would you be available?"

The thought of getting involved with Nick Chastain again brought back visions of the long empty elevator shaft she'd imagined last night. Her stomach did flip-flops as she saw herself stepping out into midair.

"I don't know." That sounded weak, even to her. "I'd have to look at my schedule. I've been very busy with my interior design business lately. I'm not taking on a lot of focus work these days. Morris was something of an exception." It was getting worse. She was on the brink of sounding like a blithering idiot.

What was it about Nick Chastain that set her senses on edge and stirred the hair at the nape of her neck, she wondered. Other than the fact that he was dangerous, mysterious, and reclusive and the two of them had discovered a body together, of course.

"Has it occurred to you that if your hunch is right and there's more to Fenwick's murder than Detective Anselm thinks there is, locating the journal would be a major step toward finding the killer?" Nick asked.

She suddenly wished that she could see his eyes. Not that she would have been able to read much in those green-and-gold depths, she thought. Nick wore his enigmatic mask as easily as he wore his expensively tailored clothes.

"I thought you said you didn't think that anyone else except yourself wanted the journal badly enough to kill for it," she said very carefully. "Have you changed your mind?"

"This is your conspiracy theory, not mine. All I want is the journal. I was merely pointing out that if you happen to be right, then we have a mutual interest in locating it. It's safe to say that the police won't go in the direction your theory is taking you. Anselm seemed convinced of the drug-robbery motive."

Zinnia propped her elbow on the desk and rested her forehead in her hand. "To tell you the truth, I don't know what to think at the moment."

"I suggest you don't take too long to make up your mind. I'm going to start making inquiries immediately. There's no time to waste. This kind of trail grows cold very quickly."

"Yes, I imagine it does."

"Do you want to work together on this or shall I handle it on my own?"

She twisted the telephone cord in her fingers. He

was applying pressure. It was subtle but unmistakable. "You're suggesting that we should join forces?"

"Why not? We both have compelling reasons to search for the journal. Together we would be able to accomplish more than we could separately."

Zinnia drummed her fingers on the desk. "It would be impossible to keep our association a secret."

"That's true. There is a risk that the tabloids would get interested in us all over again."

"Well?" She was annoyed by his obvious lack of concern. "That's the last thing you'd want, isn't it?"

"I can live with it if there's a good reason to do so. What about you?"

"I'd hate it." She flopped back in her chair and released a long breath. "But I've had to put up with having my name smeared across the front pages so often that it's beginning to seem routine. I can handle it."

There was another of the unsettling silences on the other end of the line. "You think that having your name linked with mine amounts to a smear?"

Great. She'd managed to insult him again.

"I didn't mean to imply that. I only meant that there's no really terrific way to appear in the tabloids. No matter whose name is involved."

"Never mind," he interrupted. "Since we can't avoid the inevitable, I suggest we give the gossips a logical reason for the two of us to be seen together."

Zinnia's instincts went on full alert. "What sort of reason?"

"As it happens, I'm in the market for an interior designer."

She seized the phone cord in a death grip. "I beg your pardon?"

"You heard me. I'm planning to marry in the near future. I want to redecorate."

For some reason, that news caused Zinnia to tighten her hand even more violently around the cord. He was going to marry. So what? Almost everyone got married sooner or later. Even mysterious casino proprietors. She was probably the one exception in the city if you discounted a few assorted incarcerated felons and the inmates of some asylums.

"I see."

"I have a feeling that my future wife won't care for the casino look."

"You live in a casino," Zinnia pointed out grimly. "I doubt very seriously that you'll be able to conceal that fact from her for long. The clang of the slot machines will be a dead giveaway."

"I don't expect my bride to live here above the casino. I've bought a house. A large one on a hill overlooking the city and the bay."

"Oh." She was not certain what to say. "When's the wedding?"

"I don't know yet. I've only recently begun the registration process."

"You're going through an agency?"

"You sound surprised. Doesn't everyone with common sense go through an agency?"

"Sure. Naturally. In most cases." Lord, she was babbling again. "But there are exceptions."

"I don't intend to be an exception. Contracting a non-agency marriage is a huge risk. I'm not a gambling man."

She blinked. "You're not?"

"I may make my living off the synergistic laws of probabilities and chance, but I don't take stupid risks. Not with something as permanent as marriage."

"Very wise," she agreed hastily.

There was a discreet pause.

"Are you registered?" he asked softly.

She swallowed. It was a perfectly normal question, especially given her age. She was getting precariously close to thirty. "I was registered four years ago. But the agency declared me unmatchable."

Dead silence greeted that information.

"I see," Nick said eventually. "Unusual."

That was the understatement of the decade. Zinnia almost smiled. "Very. But it happens."

"You don't sound too broken up about it."

"Life goes on."

"Full-spectrums are said to be difficult to please," Nick observed.

"That's not our fault," she retorted. "We've got high standards. It goes with the territory. But in my case, the problem was complicated by the fact that I'm not exactly a normal full-spectrum prism."

"Ah, yes. You told me that you could only focus comfortably with matrix-talents."

"Uh-huh. Apparently that fact makes for a peculiar reading on the MPPI," Zinnia said.

"MPPI?"

"The Multipsychic Paranormal Personality Inventory. It's the standard syn-psych test that all the match-making agencies use. You'll have to take the exam sooner or later, if you're registered. Didn't your counselor tell you about it?"

"I've just started the registration process. I haven't had a chance to discuss all the details with my counselor yet."

"I see. You'll start with a questionnaire and then you'll do the MPPI." For some reason Zinnia's curiosity would not let go of the matter. "Which agency are you using?"

"My counselor is from Synergistic Connections."

"Good firm. That's where I was registered." She was more convinced than ever now that Nick possessed a strong psychic ability of some kind. Synergistic Connections was one of the few marriage agencies in town that worked with full-spectrum prisms and high-class talents. "Very expensive."

"I can afford their services," he said.

She winced. "Yes, I suppose you can."

"As I was saying, I want my house redecorated for my future bride. I could tell people that I've employed you to design the interiors. It would provide a credible reason for us to be seen in each other's company on a frequent basis."

For some reason her brain seemed to be functioning as if it were mired in hardening amber. "Uh—"

"We can pool our resources and information." Nick paused. "I'm quite prepared to pay your usual fees, of course."

That remark broke through the congealing amber as nothing else could have done. Zinnia was incensed. "How dare you bring money into this? I guess I should have expected that from a man who owns a casino. I've got news for you, Mr. Chastain. The only thing that matters here is justice for poor Morris."

"Of course," he said quickly. Too quickly.

"All you want is that journal. For some reason you've decided I might have some useful information that you can use to find it."

"Now, Zinnia, I was only putting forth a reasonable proposition, one that will benefit both of us."

"The hell you were. You're trying to manipulate me, Mr. Chastain. I don't like being manipulated."

"Think about it, that's all I ask." He was the essence of reasonableness now. "Give me a call when you've had a chance to consider my plan."

"Don't hold your breath." She slammed down the phone before he could try another tactic.

Chapter
7

* * * * * * * * * *

He had her hooked, Nick thought as he hung up the phone. Now all he had to do was reel her in quickly and carefully. She would call back by the end of the day. She would not be able to resist.

True, she had gotten a little stubborn, even a trifle annoyed with him there at the tail end of the conversation, but when she'd had a chance to cool down and think it over, she would call.

Nick was satisfied with his analysis of the matrix that now included Zinnia Spring. She was the loyal type. To a fault, in his opinion. She was under the impression that she had a responsibility to find Fenwick's killer. He had offered her a chance to do just that.

She would call. Soon.

In the meantime, he had another problem to sort out.

He stood and walked to one of the mirrored panels on the wall of the lushly decorated chamber. He pushed a hidden switch with the toe of his shoe. The panel slid open to reveal the functional state-of-the-art office where he did the real work required to manage the casino and his extensive investments.

When the section of mirrored wall closed behind him, he went to the desk and opened a small concealed drawer. He wondered what Zinnia would say if she could see the hidden office and the secret drawer. *Typical matrix-talent. Obsessive. Secretive. Probably paranoid.*

The truth was, in his business, it paid to be cautious and careful. Besides, there was an old saying to the effect that even paranoid matrix-talents had enemies.

He removed the two small white cards he had retrieved from Morris Fenwick's address file. He had waited until Zinnia's back was turned the previous night before he had taken them. He suspected she would have disapproved of him removing anything from the crime scene.

He studied the neatly typed address cards. One contained his own name and the number of his private phone line. It had been no surprise to discover it in Fenwick's file. He had given his number to the book dealer, himself. But with Fenwick dead it seemed only prudent to remove the record from the file. The fewer people who had access to his private phone number, the better.

What he had not anticipated was the name on the address card that had been filed directly behind the one that contained his own private phone number. Orrin Chastain. President of Chastain, Inc. Brother of Bartholomew Chastain.

Nick's uncle.

He knew for a fact that Orrin had no interest in rare books. There was only one reason why his name would have been in Fenwick's files. Orrin was after the Chastain journal.

The discreetly embossed name on the plate in front of the formidable-looking receptionist read Mrs.

HELEN THOMPSON. She took one look at Nick and managed to appear both disapproving and polite at the same time. A neat trick, Nick thought.

"Do you have an appointment with Mr. Chastain?" she asked, coughing discreetly. "Mr. Chastain?"

"No." Nick glanced at the closed door of Orrin's office. "But he'll see me, Helen. Don't worry about it."

"I'm afraid he's in conference this morning." Helen's expression was tight with reproof. "He does not wish to be disturbed."

Nick smiled. "But, I'm family, Helen. Of course he'll see me."

He started around her desk without waiting for a response.

"Wait." Helen surged to her feet when she saw that Nick was halfway to the closed door. "Come back here, Mr. Chastain. Where do you think you're going?"

"Hold his calls, Helen. This won't take long." Nick opened the door and walked into his uncle's office.

Unlike Chastain's Palace, Chastain, Inc. had been decorated with Restraint and Good Taste. Everything was done in muted shades of beige and gray. It was a model of corporate elegance. In fact, it had been featured in a recent issue of *Architectural Synergy* magazine. Nick had read the entire article. He was studying Good Taste these days. It was part of his five-year plan to become respectable.

"You know, Uncle Orrin, this place could use a touch of red."

Orrin was seated at his desk, speaking into the phone. At Nick's words, he swung around, scowling.

"Get back to me on that as soon as you get the numbers from Riker, understand? Fine. Do it." Orrin dumped the phone back into its cradle and glared at Nick. "I see you've managed to drag the Chastain name into the papers. The least you could have done was stay clear of Chastain, Inc. until the worst of the fuss blows over. We don't need that kind of publicity."

"How long have you been looking for the journal, Uncle Orrin?" Nick sank down into one of the gray leather chairs. Orrin hated to be reminded of their biological relationship, so Nick made it a point to drop the word *"uncle"* into the conversation as often as possible whenever he visited.

In truth, there was not much of a family resemblance. Nick had been told that he looked very much like his father, Bartholomew. Orrin, on the other hand, had the light brown hair, hazel eyes, and sturdy build that characterized much of the rest of the Chastain gene pool.

Orrin ripped off his glasses and tossed them carelessly onto the desk. "What in five hells are you talking about?"

"You were dealing with that antiquarian book dealer, Morris Fenwick, who was murdered last night. You have no interest in rare books in general, so you must have been after the Chastain journal."

"That's a goddamned lie."

"I found your name and private phone number in Fenwick's address file last night."

Orrin's jaw clenched. "You went through a dead man's address files?"

"I had a little time to kill while my companion and I waited for the cops. Don't worry, I removed the card with your phone number on it."

Orrin's face reddened with anger. "You're a disgrace to your name."

"I believe you've mentioned that once or twice."

Nick's young unwed mother, Sally, had made certain that her son carried his father's name. That fact was a festering sore in the sides of the legitimate Chastains. They saw it as a blatantly encroaching move on Sally's part, an attempt to try to grab a share of the Chastain fortune.

Gruff, taciturn, good-hearted Andy Aoki had raised Nick after Sally's car had plunged off a jungle mountain road. Andy had owned the tavern in Port LaConner where Sally had worked. She had left her infant son with Andy the day she headed for Serendipity to find out what had happened to Bartholomew Chastain. She had never returned.

Nick had grown up in the tavern. He had learned a lot from Andy including how to stop a bar brawl, how to survive in the jungle, and the elements of honor and self-control.

Andy was the only parent Nick had ever known. When he was thirteen he had told him that he wanted to change his last name to Aoki.

> Andy gave him a long thoughtful look and then slowly shook his head. "Your mama wanted you to be a Chastain, son. And so did your pa. You need to honor their memory by respecting that."
>
> "I'd rather honor you," Nick said, meaning every word.
>
> Andy's eyes lit with a rare warmth. "You've already given me more than you'll ever know, son. It's enough. Keep your name."

Andy had died a little more than three years ago, a casualty of the Western Islands Action. He had been shot dead by one of the invading pirates while defending his tavern. At the time, Nick had been deep in the jungles together with Lucas Trent and Rafe Stonebraker, hunting more of the invaders.

Andy had died behind his cash register. The rifle at his side had been fired until it was empty. Nick had managed to shove his grief into a dark corner of his mind but he doubted if it would ever disappear entirely.

After he had tracked down Andy's killer, Nick had

finally gotten around to sorting through the contents of the cluttered storeroom behind the tavern. The old storage shed had been crammed with memories of a life that had spanned eighty-one years. Nick had found faded photos of Andy's long-dead wife, records of his early jelly-ice prospecting trips, business receipts, copies of Nick's school records, and childhood artwork.

He also found the small metal box that had belonged to his mother. The discovery had come as a stunning surprise. Andy had told him that all of her possessions had been destroyed in a fire that had consumed her house around the time of her death. But before she had left on the fatal trip to Serendipity, Sally had apparently hidden the metal box in Andy's back room without telling him what she had done.

Inside the box Nick had found only one item, the last letter that Bartholomew Chastain had written to Sally before he set out on the Third Expedition.

Nick still couldn't decide which irritated his Chastain relatives more, Sally's defiant attempt to force them to acknowledge her son, or the fact that he had made his fortune on his own and had no interest in their wealth.

The Chastains were accustomed to controlling people with money. Nick's failure to ask anything of them made him, in their eyes, uncontrollable and therefore dangerous. Nick understood. He was, after all, a Chastain, himself. He figured that his own need to be in command of any given situation was probably stronger than that of all the other members of the clan put together.

"I didn't come here to reminisce about the past, delightful as that no doubt would be," Nick said. "I want to know about your interest in the Chastain journal."

"What about it? If my brother's private journal exists, it belongs in the family." Orrin's mouth tightened. "The *legitimate* branch of the family."

"I've done a lot of thinking since last night. No offense, Orrin, but it's difficult to believe that you've suddenly developed a keen interest in family history, especially the part my father played in it."

"Just what in hell is that supposed to mean?"

Nick smiled. "We both know that it was the fact that my father died out in the islands that made it possible for you to take over the reins of the family empire, wasn't it?"

"Bastard," Orrin hissed.

"Yes, but that's old history. As I was saying, if Bartholomew Chastain had lived, you wouldn't be sitting where you are today. What's more, he would have married my mother and I would have become the heir apparent to Chastain, Inc. Funny how things work out, isn't it?"

"Bartholomew would never have married your mother." Orrin's face worked furiously. "He knew his duty. He would never have given the Chastain name to some cheap hooker he met in a Western Islands bar."

The blood suddenly pounded in Nick's ears. He was on his feet before he had time to think. He rounded the corner of the desk and seized a fistful of Orrin's expensive shirt.

"My mother was not a hooker," he said very, very softly. "Don't ever call her that. Do you hear me, Uncle Orrin? Don't ever call my mother a hooker or, so help me, you and everyone else on the *legitimate* side of the Chastain family will pay."

Orrin's mouth opened and closed. His eyes bulged. "I'll have my secretary summon security."

"My parents planned to marry when my father returned from his last expedition. But Bartholomew Chastain didn't make it back alive." Nick leaned closer. "No one knows exactly what happened, but we all know who benefited, don't we?"

Orrin's mouth opened and closed twice more before he managed to put a coherent sentence together. "How dare you imply that I might have had anything to do with Bart's death or that I was glad he never returned. That's a goddamned lie."

"Is it?"

"Face the facts, Nick. There never was a Third Chastain Expedition. It's just a legend. The most likely explanation for Bart's disappearance is that he walked off into the jungle one afternoon and committed suicide. He was a matrix. Everyone knows they're not real stable."

"If you believe that there was no Third Expedition, why are you after his journal?"

"Look, I'm not saying that Bart didn't leave a personal diary of some kind," Orrin snapped. "God knows, he was obsessive about keeping notes on everything. But it couldn't be a record of the Third Expedition because that venture never took place."

The roaring in Nick's ears diminished. He noticed that his hand was clenched much too tightly around the fine fabric of Orrin's shirt front. Disgusted with the loss of self-control, he released his grip and took a step back.

A glint of gold caught his eye. He glanced at Orrin's expensive cuff links. They were each elegantly embossed with a large *C* and the initial *O*. Every man in the Chastain family received a pair of gold cuff links when he came of age. Nick wondered what had become of his father's set. Damned if he would ask Orrin.

He met his uncle's eyes. "So we come back to the basic question," he said softly. "Why would you be willing to pay a lot of money for my father's journal?"

"Because it's a family heirloom." Orrin straightened his tie and collar. "If you had any sense of responsibility toward the family you'd understand that. Now get out of here before I have you thrown out."

"I'm on my way." Nick walked to the door. He paused briefly just before he opened it. "I almost forgot to ask, how are things going with Glendower? Any luck convincing him to pour money into Chastain, Inc.?"

Orrin stared at him with stunned shock. Then a slow flush rose in his face. "What do you know about Glendower?"

Nick shrugged. "I'm aware that Chastain, Inc. is in bad shape since the acquisition of Meltin-Lowe. You paid far too much for the company, didn't you? Meltin-Lowe turned out to be a very deep hole. Now you're in trouble. You need cash so you're wooing potential investors. I believe Glendower is the third one you've talked to in the past six weeks."

"That is none of your business, damn it."

"Relax, I'm family, remember?" Nick smiled. "But a word of warning, Uncle. I know you've got a cash-flow problem, but if you're after Bartholomew Chastain's journal because you believe those old rumors about the treasure, save your time and energy. The legend that my father discovered a fortune in fire crystal is just that, a legend. Old Demented DeForest invented that part of the story just like he did the part about aliens abducting the expedition team."

Without waiting for a response, Nick let himself out of the office. He closed the door very quietly.

Helen bristled when she saw him.

"Have a nice day." Nick smiled as he went past her desk.

She flinched.

He walked down the plush corridor to the elevator. When the doors slid open he stepped inside and glanced at his watch. Perhaps Zinnia had called by now. Impatience and a strange sense of eagerness pulsed through him.

A few minutes later, he walked out of the imposing entrance of the Chastain building and into a light misty rain. He strode quickly to where his dark green Synchron was parked at the curb.

He reached for the phone as soon as he was behind the steering bar.

"I'm on my way back to the casino, Feather." Nick eased the sleek Synchron into the light traffic. "Any messages?"

"I put out the word that you were willing to pay five grand for any information about the Chastain journal, just like you said, boss. But nothing so far."

"Double the reward." Nick absently calculated the distances that separated the Synchron from the other vehicles on the street. He factored in the effects of the rain, the wet pavement, and the speed of the blue compact ahead of him. Something was not quite right in the matrix. He changed lanes.

The driver of the blue compact suddenly slammed on his brakes, narrowly avoiding a rear-end collision with another vehicle. Tires screeched. Horns blared. Nick accelerated smoothly past the near-accident.

He drove the same way he did everything else, with an instinctive awareness of all of the elements in the matrix in which he moved. He always knew exactly where he was in relation to the objects around him. His timing was nearly always perfect. It was one of the side effects of his psychic talent.

"Any other messages?" he asked.

"Nothing important," Feather said.

Nick tightened his grip on the phone. "Has Miss Spring called yet?"

"No, boss."

"I'll be there in a few minutes." He punched the disconnect button on the phone.

She would call. He was good at this sort of thing. He knew she would call.

But he could feel something shifting again in the matrix. Zinnia was proving to be unpredictable.

Chapter
8

* * * * * * * * * *

Zinnia poured coff-tea into the dainty antique Early Explorations Period cup. "Don't worry, Aunt Willy, the *Synsation* van is the only one left out in front. In another day or so it will be gone. This kind of news loses its impact fast."

"It's outrageous." Wilhelmina accepted the cup and saucer with the arrogant grace that had been bred into her bones. "One would think that the police would do something about those dreadful little insects who dare to call themselves journalists. In my day they showed a proper degree of respect for privacy. Now, nothing is sacred, not even one's personal life."

Zinnia regarded her with irritation and admiration. Wilhelmina was a commanding presence in any setting. Seated here amid Zinnia's collection of airy, whimsical Early Explorations Period furnishings, she was a monument to family authority. Zinnia had to concede that Willy was the reigning matriarch of the Spring clan.

A large woman of statuesque proportions, Wilhelmina transcended any common notions of beauty.

She was endowed with the sort of strong, indomitable features that would have done credit to a statue of a First Generation Founder.

The decline and fall of the Spring family fortunes in recent years had only served to shore up Wilhelmina's aura of unbending determination. She was a woman with a mission. She would not rest until she had seen the bottom line of the family finances and the social position of the Springs restored to their former impressive levels.

"And as for you, Zinnia, whatever were you about last night? How did you come to be in the company of a common gambler?"

"Actually, Mr. Chastain is rather uncommon and I got the impression that he doesn't gamble." Zinnia pursed her lips. "I wouldn't put it past him to take a few calculated risks, though."

"Of course he's a gambler. He owns a casino, for heaven's sake."

"Yes, but I don't think he plays any of the games." Zinnia sipped her coff-tea. "Mr. Chastain prefers to be in control of things."

"Be that as it may, the man is little more than a gangster. Hardly what one would call respectable. You had no business being seen with him." Wilhelmina's eyes snapped. "And whatever possessed you to become involved in a murder investigation?"

"I'm not involved, Aunt Willy. I'm just one of the two people who found the body. Mr. Fenwick was a client of mine."

"And that's another thing. You know I don't approve of your part-time job with Psynergy, Inc."

"I need the money," Zinnia said bluntly. "I've explained that to you. My interior design business fell off rather drastically after the Eaton scandal. I'm only now beginning to rebuild."

Wilhelmina looked pained. "It seems we've had to endure one catastrophe after another since we lost

Edward and Genevieve. And most of the disasters have been at your hands, young woman."

Zinnia said nothing. She merely raised her brows.

Wilhelmina put her cup firmly down on the saucer. "Which brings me to the crux of the matter. We must stop the downward spiral of events. You are the only one in a position to save this family."

"The family will survive, Aunt Willy. No one's starving. You and Uncle Stanley seem to be managing off the annuities Great Uncle Richmond left for you. Cousin Maribeth is making ends meet with the profits from her boutique. Leo will graduate soon and I'm sure he'll be offered a research assistant position at the university. We're all going to make it."

"There is a difference between mere survival and assuming one's proper position in the world," Wilhelmina retorted. "Speaking of Leo. You've been a bad influence on him, Zinnia. You have not encouraged him to take an interest in business."

"Leo was born for academia, not the business world." It was an old argument, one that bored Zinnia, but her aunt would never admit defeat.

Wilhelmina regarded her with the sort of gaze that was meant to instill backbone in those she considered to be lacking in that quality. "Sometimes events demand that one make sacrifices for the sake of the family. I'm sure you know what I mean."

"Indeed, I do." Zinnia gave her a glowing smile. "You'll be pleased to know that Duncan Luttrell phoned just before you arrived. He asked me to have dinner with him tonight."

"Mr. Luttrell called?" Wilhelmina looked as if she hardly dared to believe her ears. "In spite of those horrid stories in the tabloids linking your name with Chastain?"

"Yes. He was very sympathetic."

"Thank God."

"Don't get your hopes up, Aunt Willy. Remember, I'm unmatchable."

"Let me be frank here, Zinnia. Everyone knows that in certain circles marriages are occasionally contracted without the assistance of a marriage agency. Especially when there are important family considerations."

"But surely you wouldn't want me to take such a risk, Aunt Willy. Even assuming I could persuade some man to take a chance on me. I mean, it's my whole future we're talking about. I can't imagine anything worse than being shackled for life to a man I couldn't love and who didn't love me. Why, it would be a living hell."

"Skip the melodrama, dear. It may interest you to know that before the Founders established the institution of the match-making agency, our ancestors on Earth routinely married without the guidance of synpsych counselors."

Zinnia burst into laughter, nearly spilling her tea. "That's just an old myth, Aunt Willy, and we both know it. No civilization that was advanced enough to colonize other planets would run their private lives in such a primitive fashion."

Zinnia waited until after her aunt had left before she tried Newton DeForest's number again. It was the third time she'd attempted to phone him that day. No one had answered her earlier calls.

She counted the rings. After the fifth, she reluctantly started to replace the receiver.

"Hello?" The man on the other end of the line sounded remarkably cheerful and a little breathless.

"Professor DeForest?"

"Yes. Sorry, I was out in the garden when the phone rang. Who is this?"

"My name is Zinnia Spring, sir. I'm sorry to bother you, but I'm doing some research on the islands of the

Western Seas and I understand you're an authority on Chastain's Third Expedition. Would it be possible to talk to you about it?"

There was a pause. "What was your name?"

"Zinnia Spring."

"Are you an academic, then, Miss Spring?" DeForest sounded suddenly hopeful.

"I'm afraid not. I'm an interior designer."

"Oh." There was a short pause while he assimilated that piece of news. "Why in the world would an interior designer be interested in Chastain's Third?"

"It's a personal interest, Professor DeForest. A hobby, you might say. I'm fascinated with the legend and I want to learn as much as I can." She allowed a delicate pause. "I'm told that you are the leading authority on the Third, sir."

"I suppose I could spare some time tomorrow."

Zinnia seized a pen. "That's wonderful. May I have your address?"

At eight-thirty that evening Zinnia smiled at Duncan Luttrell across a snowy white tablecloth. "I can't tell you how much I appreciate this. I've been trapped in my apartment most of the day. I left once, early this morning, and was almost cornered by a crew from one of the tabloids."

"You're safe here at the Founders' Club. The staff knows how to keep reporters at bay." Duncan grinned. "I won't claim that the food is still the best in New Seattle because Chastain's Palace stole the chef six months ago, but the privacy's great."

"I appreciate it." Zinnia glanced around at the paneled confines of the dining room.

She had deliberately chosen a refined, rose-orchid-red gown with a discreet neckline and long sleeves to suit the somber elegance of her surroundings. The Founders' Club was a prime example of the heavy Gothic style popular during the Later Expansion

Period. Arched doorways, carved stonework, and a sense of brooding age were the key elements. The atmosphere provided a suitable backdrop for the wealthy movers and shakers of New Seattle who were members of the club.

A sense of wistfulness went through Zinnia. "My father used to belong to this club."

"I know. So did mine." Duncan looked up as the wine steward came to a halt beside the table. "A bottle of the 'ninety-seven Chateau Sequim blue, please."

"Yes, Mr. Luttrell." The steward vanished quietly.

Zinnia relaxed for the first time that day. Duncan had a soothing effect on her. Having dinner with him was a lot like dining out with her brother. No pressure, just a sense of pleasant companionship.

Duncan was good-looking in an open, rugged sort of way. He had a strong muscular build that seemed at odds with his career in the high-tech world of computers. He wore his light brown hair cut short in a conservative style that suited his position as the head of his own firm. His brown eyes lit easily with laughter.

After the waiter had taken their order, Duncan turned back to Zinnia with a commiserating expression.

"I know how irritating the tabloids can be," he said. "After Dad took his own life last year, the press hounded me for days. I refused all comment and they eventually went away."

"My technique precisely."

The waiter returned with the wine. Zinnia waited until Duncan concluded the tasting ritual and approved the vintage.

When they were alone again, Zinnia took an appreciative sip of the fine blue wine. She rarely got to drink the expensive stuff these days. The bottle she had at home in the icerator was a cheap green.

"I think the worst of it is over. When you picked me up tonight, the *Synsation* van was gone."

"A good sign." Duncan smiled. "So long as you and Chastain don't feed the fires of gossip, the whole thing will dry up and blow away."

Zinnia winced. "Don't worry. I definitely don't want to throw any more bones to the gossip columnists. And it's safe to say that Nick Chastain feels exactly the same."

"I understand how you happened to stumble over Morris Fenwick's body. You're the type who would worry about a missing client. What I don't quite get is why Chastain was with you when you found Fenwick. The stories in the papers did not make that clear."

Zinnia hesitated a split second while she decided how much to tell Duncan. For some obscure reason she felt a responsibility to protect Nick's privacy and she knew intuitively that he would not want her to discuss the Chastain journal. She opted for a limited version of the truth.

"You'll never believe it, but apparently Nick Chastain collects rare books."

Duncan chuckled. "You're right. Hard to believe a casino owner with a taste for antiquarian books."

"I know. But he was one of Morris's clients and I was aware that they had been in negotiations. When Morris failed to keep an appointment, I contacted Chastain to see if he knew what had happened to him."

Duncan frowned. "You actually went to see Chastain?"

"I couldn't think of anything else to do. He was as concerned as I was. We both went to the book shop to see what was going on and found poor Morris together. Mr. Chastain called the police."

Duncan looked thoughtful. "Mind if I give you a little friendly advice?"

Zinnia held up one hand. "Stop. I have a hunch

you're going to tell me the same thing I've already heard from everyone else. You want to warn me to stay clear of Nick Chastain. Right?"

Duncan smiled, but the expression in his eyes remained serious. "Right. I'm no expert on the subject, but I've heard enough to know that Chastain is not the kind of guy whose attention you want to attract."

"Don't worry, I'm in complete agreement."

A short silence descended.

Duncan picked up his wine glass and swirled the contents with a reflective air. "When you went to see Chastain did you get into his office?"

Zinnia helped herself to a bit of pâté and a cracker. "Uh-huh."

Duncan leaned forward and lowered his voice. "So, is it true what they say about his incredibly bad taste?"

Zinnia grinned as she crunched down on the cracker. "Every single word."

> She could not see him but she sensed his presence. He was there in the darkness, waiting for her. She knew she should turn and run from him while she still could. But some invisible force tugged at her, drawing her into the endless night. If she entered that darkness with him there would be no turning back. She would be trapped with him in the terrifying emptiness that seemed to extend forever.
>
> She heard the muffled sound of her own heart beating. The sound grew louder, ringing loudly in her ears. The thunder of blood.

Zinnia came awake with a great startled gasp. Her nightgown was clinging to her sweat-dampened body.

Only a dream. A nightmare.

But the thunder did not cease.

It took her a few seconds to realize that what she was hearing was the telephone, not her pounding heart.

She glanced at the clock beside the bed. Midnight. No one called at midnight unless something was terribly wrong.

She picked up the receiver with a trembling hand. "Yes?"

"Miss Spring? This is Polly Fenwick. Morris Fenwick's wife?"

"Yes. Hello, Mrs. Fenwick."

"Did I wake you?"

"It's all right." Zinnia collapsed back against the pillows. "I'm so very sorry about Morris."

"That's why I called."

Zinnia frowned as the anxiety in Polly Fenwick's voice finally seeped through the phone. "Are you all right, Mrs. Fenwick?"

"I've been going through his things. There was a note. With instructions, you know."

"Instructions?"

"Very specific. Morris was that way. Very specific. I followed the instructions to the letter. I found a book that he had hidden. It looks like a diary or a journal of some kind."

Zinnia stilled. "A journal?"

"According to Morris's note, it's quite valuable. But his instructions are to dispose of it as fast as possible. He thinks it may be dangerous to possess it. I'm to sell it to Mr. Chastain. You, know, the man who owns that casino in Founders' Square?"

"Yes. Yes, I know." Zinnia was having trouble following the rushed explanation. Part of her mind was still churning with the images embedded in the nightmare. "Excuse me, Mrs. Fenwick, but are you saying that you have this journal in your possession?"

"Yes. Didn't I make that clear? But Morris's note says I must get rid of it quickly. Apparently he thought someone might come looking for it if any-thing happened to him."

"What, exactly, does the note say?"

"I just told you, I'm to conclude the sale of the journal the moment I discover it."

"You want to sell the journal now? Tonight?"

"Yes. I don't mind telling you that Morris's note has made me very nervous. I'm sorry to bother you like this, but it definitely says here that I'm to call you. It says you'll contact Mr. Chastain for me. Will you do that?"

"Me?"

"Please, Miss Spring. My stomach is terribly upset as it is. I just couldn't call that dreadful man person-ally. The very thought of dealing with him terrifies me. Why, he's not much better than a gangster."

Shades of Aunt Willy. Zinnia closed her eyes. "All right. I'll call Mr. Chastain for you."

"Thank you so much, Miss Spring." Gratitude and relief bubbled in Polly's voice. "We mustn't be seen together, though. I thought we could meet at Curtain Park in an hour."

"You're sure you want to do this tonight?"

"Definitely. I won't sleep until this matter has been taken care of, Miss Spring. You will come with Mr. Chastain, won't you? I'd be too frightened to go through with the sale if you weren't there. Morris said in his note that I could trust you."

"All right. But I can't guarantee that I'll be able to get in touch with him tonight. He operates a gambling casino, Mrs. Fenwick. There's no telling what he's doing at this hour of the night."

"Please try. I'm so nervous about all this. Morris was always a little paranoid, but this note is very insistent, even for him."

"I'll call the casino and see what happens."

Zinnia hung up the phone and switched on the bedside lamp. She got out of bed and found her purse.

Inside she discovered the tacky red-and-silver business card Nick had given her.

Nick Chastain was not the type to be sitting beside a phone, waiting for it to ring, she thought, as she punched in the number of his direct line. She wondered what she ought to do next if he could not be reached.

Nick answered on the first ring.

Just as if he had, indeed, been sitting beside the phone, Zinnia thought.

Chapter
9

* * * * * * * * * *

She had finally called.

It was a good working demonstration of the old adage about being careful what you asked for because you just might get it, Nick thought grimly.

She had finally called, all right. Not because she wanted his help but because Polly Fenwick had asked her to act as an intermediary in the sale of the journal.

Now here he was, alone at last with Zinnia Spring, and what was he doing with her? Sitting in a car in a dark park at one-forty-six in the morning waiting for a stranger.

Nick was not in a good mood. He never was when things were not proceeding according to plan.

"Tell me." He turned off the Synchron headlamps and dourly studied the stretch of heavily wooded park that surrounded the car. "At what point did it strike you that these meeting arrangements were just a little out of the ordinary?"

Zinnia shot him a sidelong glare. He was intensely aware of her sitting beside him. She was dressed in a pair of snug-fitting jeans and a sweater that was the lush red of ripe cherry-berries. Her hair had been hastily pulled back into a ponytail. She wore no makeup.

He knew she was annoyed with him. He had picked her up in front of her apartment less than fifteen minutes ago and he sensed that she was already regretting her decision to assist in the transaction. It was his own fault.

The atmosphere inside the close confines of the car seethed with tension, mostly his own. There was not much he could do about it. He was fighting two inner battles simultaneously and the effort required nearly all of his self-control.

On the one hand, he was struggling to resist the instinctive use of a few quick bursts of his talent in order to assess the risk factors in the matrix. He knew that if he did not rein in his power, Zinnia would pick up the telltale traces of energy on the metaphysical plane. She might recognize him as the same matrix-talent who had reached out to her last night when she walked through the casino. Nick had not yet thought of a graceful way to explain that incident so he thought it best not to raise the issue yet.

The second skirmish he waged was against his own brooding frustration. As far as he was concerned, when Zinnia had finally condescended to call him, she had done so for all the wrong reasons. It was not his carefully set lures that had drawn her back into the pattern of his matrix. It was her sense of responsibility to a dead client that had brought her back to him. He had a strong suspicion that once she had fulfilled her duty tonight, he would again lose his tenuous hold on her.

"What's that crack supposed to mean?" Zinnia asked.

"I don't know about you, but secret meetings in secluded locations with complete strangers are not the way I usually do business."

"That does it. I've had enough of this nonsense." She turned abruptly in her seat to confront him. "What's wrong with you? I thought you wanted to get your hands on the journal."

"I do."

"In another few minutes it will be yours. But you're acting as if I've dragged you out in the middle of the night for no good reason."

"I can't believe you agreed to meet with a stranger at this hour."

"She's not exactly a stranger. She's Morris's widow. I explained that."

"Why in five hells did you choose the park?"

Zinnia's mouth tightened. "I didn't pick the location. Mrs. Fenwick suggested it."

Her quick uneasy glance out the window told Nick that in spite of her bravado, she was having a few qualms, too. *About time,* he thought with morose satisfaction.

Curtain Park was not an inviting place at this time of the night. The thickly wooded stretch of greenery occupied a section of land near the bay. During the day the paths were full of joggers, picnickers, and tourists from New Vancouver and New Portland. But at night it was empty.

The closest object of interest was a large unlovely monument to the First Generation discoverers of semi-liquid full-spectrum crystal quartz. *Jelly-ice,* as the stuff was commonly called, had eventually enabled the descendents of the stranded colonists to build a new technology to replace the Earth-based one that had disintegrated within months after the Curtain had closed.

Nick flexed his fingers around the steering bar. "Tell me again how Polly Fenwick just happened to come across the journal tonight."

"She said she found a note that led her to it and instructed her to sell it to you as quickly as possible.

Morris apparently advised her to contact me to handle the sale. I think Mrs. Fenwick is scared to death of you. Lord knows why."

Nick glanced at her, but even in the shadows he could see that her expression was perfectly sincere. "Right. She's so terrified of me that she asks to meet with me at this hour in a badly lit section of the city's biggest park?"

Zinnia spread her hands. "She said the note from Morris told her to unload the journal as quickly as possible and to keep the deal a secret. He was adamant that no one was to know she'd even found it. Look, I'm sorry if you disapprove of the way I handled things. Mrs. Fenwick woke me out of a sound sleep. I was a little confused and disoriented when she suggested the meeting place."

"I think we can agree on that."

"She asked me to get in touch with you, so I did." Zinnia tapped her hand against the back of the seat. "Would you rather I hadn't called you?"

"You should have discussed the situation with me before the decision was made."

"Nobody forced you to come out here tonight. If you're too jumpy to go through with the transaction, we can call it off. Polly and I can get in touch with the other bidder, whoever he is. Maybe he won't be so darn picky."

Nick remembered the card with his uncle's name on it that he had taken from Fenwick's address file. "Is that a threat?"

"I'm merely laying out your options," she said a bit too airily.

"Thoughtful of you."

"I can't figure out why you're so angry. I thought you'd be pleased that the journal has reappeared so quickly."

"Amazingly quickly."

She frowned. "What's that supposed to mean?"

"Forget it." Nick saw the dimmed lights of a slow-moving car angle across the narrow park access road. "We'll finish this argument later. We've got company."

Zinnia turned her head to peer at the approaching vehicle. "That must be Polly. No one else would be here at this hour."

"With the possible exception of a few drug dealers or serial killers."

"Do you always whine when things don't go your way?"

"Always." Nick watched the car come to an uncertain halt a short distance away. "Stay here. I'll handle this."

"I don't think that's going to work. I told you, Polly Fenwick sounded very uneasy about having to deal with you all by yourself. That's why I'm here, remember?"

Nick almost smiled in spite of his foul mood. "Does she think you'll be able to stop me if I decide to take the journal without paying for it?"

Zinnia folded her arms under her breasts. "Morris told her that she could trust me to deal with this."

"Trust you to deal with me, do you mean?"

Zinnia shrugged and said nothing, but her eyes did not waver.

For some reason Nick's mood lightened a little. "Just how do you plan to handle me if things get tricky?"

She ignored him to peer instead at the other car. "How can we be sure that's Mrs. Fenwick?"

"Finally, a sensible, one might even say, astute, question. I guess I'd better go see." He cracked open the door. It slid smoothly up into the roof. He had removed the interior lamp earlier. No light came on to illuminate the inside of the Synchron.

"Nick, wait." Zinnia leaned across the seat. Her eyes were very wide in the shadows. "Don't—"

"Don't what?"

She hesitated. "Don't do anything stupid."

He smiled. "I appreciate the advice, but I'm afraid it's a little too late. Stay in the car. If anything goes wrong, don't even think about getting involved. Just get the hell out of here."

"Now you're starting to make me nervous."

"It's about time."

Leaving the Synchron's door open in case he needed to return to the vehicle in a hurry, he went forward to lounge against the gleaming fender.

He waited. He was good at waiting. Behind him he heard Zinnia slide across the console into the driver's seat.

"What's going on?" she asked urgently.

"Nothing."

At that moment the door of the other vehicle slowly opened. In the glow of the interior light Nick saw two people, a middle-aged man and woman. Even from here he could see the anxiety in their faces.

Amateurs. That was reassuring.

"I'm sure that's Mrs. Fenwick." Zinnia sounded vastly relieved. "I saw a picture of her in Morris's shop."

"Mr. Chastain?" Polly Fenwick's voice was high and shrill with tension.

Nick did not move. "I'm Chastain."

"Miss Spring is supposed to be here. She promised me she would come with you. I really don't know if I should go any further with this if she isn't here. Morris was very explicit in his note."

"Miss Spring is in the car," Nick said.

Zinnia leaned out the open door. "It's all right, Mrs. Fenwick. I'm Zinnia Spring."

"Oh, thank goodness." Polly got stiffly out of the car. She clutched a package to her full bosom. "Morris said I could trust you, Miss Spring."

The man who had accompanied Polly opened the
door on his side of the car. He got out and stood
glaring at Nick over the roof. "Let's get on with it.
Did you bring the money?"

"I've got it," Nick said. "Locked in the trunk. I'm
the only one who knows the combination. Who are
you?"

"This is my good friend, Omar," Polly said quickly.
"Omar Booker. I was afraid to come alone tonight."

"Did you bring cash?" Omar demanded with a
boldness clearly rooted in fear and desperation. "The
deal was for cash, you know."

Even without the aid of his talent, Nick sensed that
there was no real danger in the matrix tonight. He
relaxed for the first time since he had gotten the call
from Zinnia. Polly and Omar were terrified. They
wanted the money very badly but they were scared.
That was fine by him. He knew how to manipulate
nervous people.

"I brought cash," he said.

"The deal was for fifty thousand," Omar reminded
him shrilly.

"I know." He would have paid a hundred thousand,
two hundred thousand. He would have paid any
amount for the journal. But there was no need to
inform Polly and Omar of that fact.

The moonlight revealed Omar's suspicious scowl.
"How did you get so much cash together in such a
short time?"

"I own a casino," Nick reminded him softly. "I
don't have problems with cash. Or with very many
other things, either."

"Nick, stop it." Zinnia's voice was sharp with
disapproval. "You're scaring the daylights out of
them."

"I'm not doing anything," Nick muttered.

"You're trying to intimidate them." She got out of

the car. "Come on over here, Mrs. Fenwick. Mr. Chastain will be happy to give you the money. Turn over the journal and we'll all go home and get some sleep."

Polly hesitated. She glanced nervously back at Omar. He squared his shoulders in a determined fashion and came around the front of the car to join her. He switched on a flashlight and the pair crossed the grass to where the Synchron was parked.

"Get the money out of the trunk, Nick." Zinnia gave him a small encouraging shove. "Go on. We don't want to hang around here all night."

Nick eyed her as he straightened away from the fender. "Has anyone ever told you that you've got a tendency to be pushy?"

"It's been mentioned."

"I'll bet it has." Nick went to the trunk and deactivated the specially designed jelly-ice lock. No matrix ever trusted standard locks. He raised the lid and reached inside for the attaché case that held the cash.

Zinnia turned to Polly. "There's no need to be concerned, Mrs. Fenwick. Mr. Chastain fully intends to pay for the journal."

"I'm sorry for all the secrecy," Polly said. "It's just that Morris's note made me very nervous. Of course, he may have exaggerated. He was a matrix-talent and you know what they're like."

"I know," Zinnia assured her. "They tend to be delicate and overanxious."

Nick slammed the lid of the trunk much harder than necessary.

"Everyone knows that matrix-talents are paranoid." Omar watched Nick come forward with the attaché case. "Poor Polly suffered for years with Morris's odd fits and starts. Finally had to get out of the house."

"It's been a miserable existence," Polly said. "The thing about being separated is that you aren't really free to get on with your life. I don't know what I would have done without Omar. He's been so kind and loyal."

"I understand." Zinnia looked at Nick. "You can give Polly the money now."

Omar frowned. "Hold on, we want to see it, first. Got to make sure it's all there."

"Whatever you say." Nick set the case on the ground, unlocked it, and opened it.

Omar aimed the flashlight at the neatly bundled packets of crisp bills inside. His jaw fell open. "Good lord. Will you look at that, Polly."

Polly stared. "That's a great deal of money, Mr. Chastain. I hadn't realized . . . I mean, Morris told me that you would pay that much but I never dreamed—" She broke off.

"You asked for fifty grand." Nick closed the case and snapped it shut. "This is fifty grand. Now let me see the journal."

"What?" Polly raised her eyes to his face in a bewildered manner.

"The Chastain journal," Zinnia prompted gently. "You can turn it over to Mr. Chastain now."

"Oh, yes. Of course." Polly shoved the package she had been holding into Nick's hand as if it were a jellycracker with a lit fuse. "Take it. It's yours. I certainly have no use for it."

Nick tightened his fingers around the package. His father's journal. He could feel the shape of a leather-bound volume inside, but he could not quite believe that he finally had the thing in his possession.

He was aware of Zinnia watching him intently as he slowly, carefully unwrapped his prize. Omar held the flashlight so that they could all see the journal.

The tough, expensive green specter snakeskin that

111

had been used to bind the volume had stood up well over the years. It had begun to acquire the unique patina that the skin took on with age, but it did not appear to be badly faded or worn. The journal was only thirty-five years old, Nick reminded himself. Green specter snakeskin could last for a century or more.

"Hurry," Omar said. "We don't want to hang around here any longer than necessary."

Nick ignored him. He opened the journal. Although he was prepared for it, the sight of his father's name on the first page struck him with unexpected force.

Record of the Third Expedition
to the Islands of the Western Seas.
Expedition Master: Bartholomew Nicholas Chastain

Nick was chagrined to see that his hand shook a little as he turned the first few pages. The entries in the journal had been written in black ink, which was slightly faded but still quite legible. The handwriting was strong, clear, and decisive.

"Well?" Zinnia asked. "Is that what you wanted, Nick?"

"Yes." Nick closed the journal very carefully. He felt a little dazed. "Yes, it's what I wanted."

"Then, if you don't mind, Polly and I will be on our way." Omar picked up the attaché case with both hands.

Polly gave Zinnia a relieved smile. "Thank you, Miss Spring. It was very nice of you to help me with all this. I feel much better now that it's over."

"Good night," Zinnia said. "And good luck."

Nick said nothing. He gripped the journal and watched Omar and Polly hurry back to the other car.

Zinnia stood quietly beside him as the pair got into the vehicle and drove off down the park road.

"Time to go home," Zinnia said finally.

Nick shook off the dazed sensation with an effort of will. "Yes."

"Are you all right?"

"I'm fine." He opened the passenger door for her.

"You're acting a little strange."

The sharp claw of panic slashed across his senses. Had she guessed that he was a matrix? In the next breath he realized that she was concerned, not nervous. "It's hard to believe I've finally got the journal. I wasn't even sure it actually existed."

Zinnia's eyes were luminous in the moonlight. "I understand."

He closed her door and went back around to the driver's side. He put the journal carefully into the back seat and got behind the steering bar. He sat quietly for a long moment, composing his mind.

"Thank you," he said at last.

Zinnia smiled. "When was the last time you had to thank someone for doing you a favor, Mr. Chastain?"

"I offered a reward for the journal. You're entitled to it. I'll see that you get it."

"You have a real knack for ruining the moment. I don't want your money, Mr. Chastain."

He realized that he had offended her. He gazed steadily ahead through the windshield. "I got the journal. Polly and Omar got fifty thousand dollars. You're the only one who didn't get anything out of this. Why did you get involved?"

"It came under the heading of unfinished business." Zinnia settled back in her seat. "And it's still not finished."

Something in her tone of voice put him on full alert. "What does that mean?"

"Morris's killer is still on the loose."

"Five hells. It isn't your job to find him." Nick turned to face her. "Leave it to the cops."

She rested her head against the back of the seat and stared out into the darkened park. "What if the police are looking in the wrong place?"

"Stay out of it, Zinnia."

"Morris was a matrix."

He flexed his fingers impatiently. "I'm aware of that. It's got nothing to do with solving his murder."

"But it does, you see. People, cops included, tend to dismiss matrix-talents. No one understands them."

"I know," he said stiffly. "But has it occurred to you that matrix-talents may prefer it that way?"

"Everyone says they're paranoid, reclusive, secretive," Zinnia continued as if she had not heard him. "Some people think they're borderline crazy. But I've worked with enough of them to know that they're quite sane."

Nick stared hard at her moonlit profile. "They are?"

"Yes, but they live their lives under a constant and very unique kind of stress. No one who isn't a matrix or who hasn't focused for one can possibly comprehend the incredible struggle they go through to control their psychic energy."

"No kidding." He was disgusted by the unmistakable note of sympathy in her voice.

"It's a very different, very powerful form of paranormal energy. Matrix-talents obsess on patterns of any kind. They can get lost in them for hours on end. The problem is that their instinct to see the underlying design in everything, the need to make connections, sometimes causes them to see patterns where most people think that none exist."

"In other words, they become paranoid."

"Who knows? Maybe they simply see deeper and more clearly." She shrugged. "Or maybe they are inclined toward paranoia. There simply has not been enough research done on them or on the handful of prisms such as myself who seem to be able to work with them."

Nick hesitated. Curiosity finally overrode his good sense. "How did you learn that you could focus for matrix-talents?"

"I had a friend in college who was a matrix. She and I practiced together for hours. Interestingly enough, the more we worked together, the more relaxed she became with her talent."

Nick spread his fingers and gripped the back of the seat. "She didn't go super-paranoid?"

"No." Zinnia smiled slightly. "Okay, she's a bit more suspicious than most people. And she does tend to overanalyze everything, but, then, so do a lot of non-matrix-talents. She's doing just fine, though. She's working in a think tank which has a prism on staff who can focus fairly well for her. She's happily married and expecting a baby."

Nick could feel the tension gathering in him. "What class is she?"

"Linda is a class-four or -five."

"Mid-range." His excitement faded.

"There are almost no high-class matrix-talents," Zinnia reminded him. "In fact, the one I picked up briefly in your casino was the only one I've ever encountered who was stronger than Linda. By the way, did your security people find him?"

"No. But there were no big winners last night. Whoever he was, he didn't break the bank."

"Lucky for you. Just the same, I wish your people had caught him."

"Why?"

She glanced hastily at her watch. "It's the general principle of the thing," she said with patently false unconcern. "It's very late. You'd better take me home."

"About Fenwick's murder," Nick said deliberately. "Promise me you'll let the police deal with it."

"There's not much else I can do."

"Don't give me that. I can almost feel you making plans. What are you thinking?"

"Nothing."

"Five hells." Nick reached out and caught her chin with his hand. He forced her to look directly at him. "Tell me."

"Well, it just occurred to me that now that Morris is dead, Polly and Omar are free to marry."

Nick stared at her, astounded. "Polly and Omar? Wait a second. You don't actually believe that they had anything to do with Fenwick's murder, do you?"

"Why not?" She sounded aggrieved by his lack of support. "They couldn't marry as long as poor Morris was alive."

"Polly and Omar are obviously involved in a long-standing affair. Why would they suddenly decide to murder Fenwick after all this time?"

"I don't know." Zinnia's jaw was set in stubborn lines. "But you have to admit, it's a possibility."

"An extremely remote one. I'd estimate the odds at about the same as those of the Curtain reopening in our lifetime. Damn it, Zinnia, I do not want you messing around in a murder investigation, do you understand?"

She tilted her head, gazing at him as if he were not making sense. "Why are you getting worked up over this? Whatever I decide to do, it's none of your business."

"Do you want to know why I was furious when you phoned me an hour ago?"

"You told me why. It was because I made arrangements for us to purchase the journal in a dark, deserted park."

"That was just the icing on the cake," he said through his teeth. "I was pissed long before you even picked up the phone."

She watched him with an unwavering gaze. "Why?"

"Because. You. Never. Called."

She stared at him. "But I did call."

"Only because Polly asked you to get in touch with me."

"Let me get this straight. You expected me to call earlier? Before I heard from Polly?"

"We were going to talk about searching for the journal and the killer together, remember?"

"Like heck we were," she shot back. "You were just trying to manipulate me with all that gooey blather about joining forces. You wanted whatever information I might have had concerning the whereabouts of the journal but you had no real intention of helping me find Morris's killer."

"That's not true. Talk about suspicious paranoia. You're giving a pretty good demonstration of it right now." He was going to lose her. He had nothing he could use to hold on to her now. Desperation tore through him.

"Damn it, Chastain, if you wanted to talk to me, why didn't you pick up the phone?"

"I'd already done that." He felt his jaw clench. "It was your turn."

Zinnia threw up her hands. "I can't believe we're arguing like this. We sound like a couple quarreling after a bad date."

"I'd glad you finally noticed." He reached for her. "That's exactly what this feels like. A bad date."

"Hold it right there." She braced both hands against his shoulders. "What do you think you're doing?"

"I'm going to kiss you."

"Why?"

"Damned if I know."

"Good." She glowered ferociously. "I like you much better when you don't pretend to have all the answers."

117

"Believe me, if I had all the answers, I wouldn't be sitting here arguing with you like this. I'd be back in my office doing something more constructive."

"Such as?"

"Such as making money." He hauled her halfway across the console and into his arms.

Chapter
10

* * * * * * * * * *

The storm of passion stunned her. The deluge came
thundering out of nowhere, sweeping her up in a
magnificent wave. She found herself whirling down
into the depths of an uncharted sea.

Zinnia could almost feel the energy crackling in the
front seat of the Synchron. She wondered vaguely why
there were no actual sparks.

Nick's mouth was infinitely compelling, infinitely
demanding, infinitely satisfying. She tasted his need,
savored his hunger, gloried in his desire for her. He
even smelled good, she decided. Enticingly masculine. She could tell that he used soap but did not
bother with cologne. She liked that. She liked that
very much. She had never been a fan of perfumed
men.

"Oh, my God." She gave a small, choked cry of
excitement and wrapped her arms very tightly around
his neck. "I didn't realize . . . I didn't know—"

"Maybe you didn't." Nick shifted, pressing her
back against the seat. "But I've been wanting to do
this since the minute you walked into my office."

"Must have been the red dress."

"I've always liked red." His eyes gleamed in the shadows as he bent his head to kiss her throat.

She felt a sultry heat pool in her lower body. Her fingers sank deep into his shoulders. The feel of sleek muscle and bone beneath his shirt sent another shimmer of anticipation through her.

She had always known deep inside that something had been lacking in the handful of previous relationships she had experienced. But she had never been able to identify the elusive, missing element. Tonight, she decided in a rush of exultant satisfaction, she was finally getting a real clue.

Flickers of awareness coursed along her nerve endings. *That* had never happened before during a kiss. It took her a few seconds to realize that the heat of Nick's body had set fire to all of her senses, even those that functioned on the metaphysical plane.

Obviously the paranormal side of her nature was as shaken and unsettled by the embrace as the physical side.

Nick crushed her up against the seat back, using his weight to hold her there. A strange, wholly inexplicable desire to create a prism unfurled within her. Startled, she resisted the psychic probing.

She was almost certain that Nick was a talent. At such close quarters, he might pick up her energy waves. It would be embarrassing. Sex, after all, was supposed to be confined to the physical plane. She had never heard of it affecting the psychic senses.

This was not normal. Definitely not normal.

But, then, she had been told by experts that her type of psychic energy was not entirely normal.

Nick moved his mouth to hers. She felt the edge of his teeth and immediately decided that an analysis of events on the metaphysical plane would have to wait. There was no time to contemplate the peculiar sensations that rippled through her. She was too thrilled, too curious, too dazzled to ponder such esoteric considerations.

"This is going to be good." Nick's voice was hoarse. His hand drifted down to cover her breast. "Very good."

"Nick."

Out of the corner of her eye, Zinnia noticed that steam was condensing on the inside of the Synchron's windows. A part of her brain was still thinking clearly enough to be amazed by her own reaction to the explosion of sexual tension. She was chagrined to realize that she hadn't even recognized the volatile nature of the atmosphere that had been swirling in the front seat of the car until Nick reached for her.

Apparently he had figured it out right away.

But she had an excellent excuse for her delay in grasping the reality of the situation, she told herself. She had never experienced anything like it before in her life.

She nestled deeper into Nick's embrace, intensely aware of the hard, unyielding shape of his erection against her leg.

He was big. Very big. Maybe abnormally so. But certainly interesting.

Gingerly, she put her hand on his thigh, learning the broad outline of him through the taut fabric of his black trousers. His answering groan was encouraging.

She threaded the fingers of her other hand through the hair that covered the nape of his neck. She could have sworn that his groan became a low growl.

He slid one hand down her spine and curved his fingers around her hip. Another shiver that was both physical and metaphysical shot through her. *This was not supposed to happen.*

"Impossible," she muttered against his throat.

"No," Nick said. "Highly improbable, but not

impossible. I haven't done this in the front seat of a car since I was eighteen, but I think I can remember how."

"That's not what I meant." She flinched as another burst of psychic awareness echoed the tug of physical desire. "There's something strange going on here."

"It's just the console. Let's move to the back. It will be more comfortable there."

He was talking about sex, she thought. Here she was, wondering if the psychic side of her nature had gone on the fritz and had begun producing metaphysical sexual hallucinations while Nick was calmly suggesting they get more comfortable.

A disorienting panic flared deep within her. It was strong enough to dampen a large measure of her earlier enthusiasm.

She opened her eyes and planted her hands against his strong chest.

"Wait." She was breathless. "That's enough. We've got to stop. Right now."

Nick stilled. Slowly he raised his head to look down at her. "Why?"

The appalling simplicity of the question left her speechless for a few seconds. She had no idea of how to explain the peculiar sensations she had been experiencing. "Uh, well—"

"You've had your antipregnancy vaccination like everyone else, I assume?"

"Yes," she sputtered, suddenly embarrassed by the pragmatic question. "Yes, of course."

His mouth curved slightly. "So have I. We're perfectly safe." He started to lower his head.

"That's not the point," she managed. "I'm trying to tell you that this has gone far enough. I said you could kiss me. That's all. For heaven's sake, we barely know each other. And one-night stands are not my style."

He raised his head and studied her for a long moment. There was a shattering intensity in his gaze that stopped the breath in her lungs. Zinnia could have sworn that a new kind of energy now hummed in the close confines of the car. This was not the sparkling, exciting zing of sexual attraction, physical or metaphysical. It was something much more dangerous.

"What, exactly," Nick said with great precision, "is your style?"

It occurred to Zinnia that she was in a somewhat precarious position. She was alone in an isolated park with one of the most notorious men in the city. Aunt Willy's words came back to her. *The man is little more than a gangster.*

"Don't you dare try to intimidate me, Nick Chastain. I came out here tonight to help you get that damned journal. I did you a very big favor. I suspect it annoys you to be in someone's debt, but that's the way things are. You owe me. I'm calling in the marker."

He stilled. The familiar enigmatic mask slipped into place on his austere features. "What do you want?"

"I want you to behave in a civilized manner."

The mask dissolved as quickly as it had formed. Amusement glittered in his eyes. "I love it when you talk dirty."

She blinked. "I beg your pardon?"

His smile was barely discernible. "Never mind. You're right, I do owe you. And I would like to repay the debt."

She eyed him warily. "How?"

He curled his finger around one trailing tendril of her hair. "Would you have dinner with me?"

"Dinner?" She could not seem to get her thoughts into logical order. "When?"

"Tomorrow night?" He glanced at his watch. "Make that tonight."

"I have a focus assignment tonight."

"The following night?"

"You're serious about this, aren't you?"

His gaze did not waver. "Very."

"But you don't need my assistance now. You've got the journal."

"Forget the journal. Will you have dinner with me?"

"You don't need to repay me. I take back what I said about your being in my debt."

"Fine. I don't owe you. I still want to have dinner with you."

She hesitated. "I'm not sure if it would be a good idea. The tabloids seem to have lost interest in us. If we're seen together again in public it might start a new wave of speculation."

"I don't give a damn about the tabloids or the gossip columns." He brushed his thumb across her lower lip.

She was horrified to realize that his touch made her lower lip tremble ever so slightly. She swallowed and took a deep breath.

"Excuse me, but I was under the impression that you were very concerned about your privacy," she said.

"You mean you heard that I'm reclusive? Secretive?"

"Among other things. Are you telling me that's not the truth?"

"I'm telling you that I want to have dinner with you. I'll put up with the gossip and the speculation in order to do so. All I want from you is an answer. Yes, or no?"

It was not the most gallant or gracious invitation she'd ever had, but at least he was not trying to manipulate her this time, she thought. He was simply asking her out on a date. Sort of.

Having to make a request, knowing he had no way to enforce the answer he wanted, was no doubt a completely foreign experience for Nick Chastain. She almost felt sorry for him.

Almost.

A dinner date with him would not be wise, she told herself. It would alarm her family, worry her friends at Psynergy, Inc., and quite possibly draw unwanted attention from the tabloids.

But a few sparks of the invisible, beguiling energy that had sizzled between them a moment ago still snapped in the air around her. She had waited all of her adult life to feel that delicious kind of energy, she thought.

And Nick had asked, not threatened or manipulated.

"Yes," she said. "I would like to have dinner with you."

"I called it the Lost Expedition." Newton DeForest cradled the trailing end of a green vine in one heavily gloved hand and clipped it with a pair of gardening shears. "Bartholomew Chastain had made two earlier expeditions to map the islands of the Western Seas. Both had been extremely successful. The teams found deposits of previously unknown ores and minerals. They brought back specimens of a vast array of new plant and animal life. But Chastain's last expedition simply vanished in the jungles of some uncharted island."

"But why aren't there any official records of the expedition?" Zinnia watched uneasily as crimson liquid seeped from the cut vine. The severed plant looked as if it were bleeding.

Leo's information had been correct in one respect, she thought. Newton DeForest was definitely strange. He had invited her into his garden while they talked and she had readily agreed. She loved plants and longed for the day when she could afford to buy a house with space for a garden.

But nothing in DeForest's garden looked quite right to her. There was a grotesque quality to the foliage. Leaves appeared oddly shaped. The colors of the occasional blooms did not look wholesome. Vines were twisted in an unnatural fashion.

The extensively planted grounds of the DeForest estate existed in a perpetual gloom created by a thick canopy of broad leaves and gnarled vines. Once Zinnia got past the trellised gate, she found herself enveloped in an artificial twilight.

Within a few steps she realized that she was disoriented. That bothered her more than the wrongness of the shapes and colors of the foliage. Her sense of direction was usually fairly reliable. She knew that she was not far from the main house but she could no longer see the aging, tumbledown stone structure. She was not certain how to get back to it. She had already lost sight of the trellised garden gate.

She was surrounded by walls of dense dark green. They towered several feet overhead. Corridors formed of seemingly impenetrable masses of leaves twisted their way into the interior of the estate. She stood with Newton in a narrow crooked passageway formed by thick creeping vines. There was a carpet of luminous green moss underfoot. It gave off a faint eerie sheen.

Nothing was normal in this garden, she decided. And that included the gardener.

Newton seemed pleasant enough, even if he was distinctly odd. She wished that he had thought to offer her a cup of coff-tea. She could have used it. What with all the excitement in Curtain Park during the night, she had completely forgotten about her appointment with Professor DeForest until she had awakened an hour ago. In her rush to make the meeting on time she had missed breakfast, coff-tea, and the morning paper—all the little rituals that got the day started.

Newton was a plump, jovial, red-cheeked elf of a man with a neatly trimmed beard and a comfortable paunch. He wore a leather gardener's apron festooned with tool and implement pockets over his plaid shirt and denim trousers. Tiny round glasses perched on his nose. A cap covered his balding head.

He was obviously enamored of his subject, the legendary Third Chastain Expedition. From the way in which he was holding forth, Zinnia suspected that Newton missed the captive audience he had once enjoyed in the classroom. She did not mind his chattiness in the least. She was prepared to listen.

The journal was now safely in Nick's hands, but Morris Fenwick's killer was still at large. If she stuck to her suspicion that Morris had not been murdered for dope money, then the journal was the only other lead she had. She needed to know more about the Third Expedition.

"Ah, yes. Why aren't there any official records of the Lost Expedition?" Newton gave her a sly approving glance as he clipped another vine. "Your question is an excellent one, indeed. I spent years looking for documents and papers that would prove my theories."

Zinnia watched, fascinated, as more blood-red juice dripped from the cut vine. "Did you find any hard evidence?"

"Nothing that satisfied the naysayers and the scoffers." Newton sighed as he surveyed an ugly purple flower. "There was some early paperwork indicating that a Third Chastain Expedition had been planned at one time. But official records state that it was never carried out because Chastain wandered off into the jungle and killed himself a few days before the team was scheduled to depart."

"But you believe that the expedition did take place?"

"Oh, yes." Newton said. "I'm quite sure of it.

Twenty years ago I managed to find a couple of old jelly-ice miners who happened to be in Serendipity the week the team gathered there. They remembered the five men of the Chastain Expedition."

"Serendipity?"

"That was the jumping-off point. The last outpost of civilization, you might say. It was just a small mining camp located on one of the outer islands. It was later abandoned by the company. The jungle grew back very quickly. There's nothing left there today. I made a trip out to the Western Islands several years ago to take a look for myself."

"What happened to your two witnesses? Why didn't they ever come forward?"

"Another good question." Newton prodded the closed petals of a sickly yellow flower with the tip of his shears. The bloom opened with a snap to reveal a nest of sharp spines at the center. "The answer is that by the time I was ready to publish my work, they were both dead."

"Killed, do you mean?"

Newton looked sly. "Oh, the authorities claimed the deaths were not mysterious. One man was an alcoholic. He wound up facedown in a gutter in Founders' Square. The other had a drug problem. He was killed by another addict whom he apparently tried to rob. Utter nonsense."

"What do you think happened to them?"

"The were killed by the aliens." Newton gave her a knowing look. "Not directly, of course. The creatures most likely placed some poor dupe under mind control and then ordered him to get rid of the witnesses."

Zinnia winced. "I see." She thought about asking Newton why the aliens hadn't had him killed, too, since he was the one who was onto their nefarious scheme, but she refrained. He might not want to continue talking to her if she confronted him with too much logic. "There must have been other people who recalled the expedition."

"I managed to find a few others who recalled that it had been *planned,* but as far as they know, it was canceled at the last minute because of Chastain's suicide. Everyone I talked to who was involved, from the university officials to the folks who lived in the islands, believes the expedition never left Serendipity."

"What about the families of the five men who formed the expedition team? They must have been a bit suspicious when their relatives failed to return."

"Chastain was written off as a suicide by his family. The other four men had no close relatives. No one noticed that they had simply disappeared."

Zinnia frowned. "Isn't that a little strange?"

"Not really. Chastain handpicked his teams, himself. His first requirement was that every individual be experienced in jungle survival. That limited his pool of potential candidates to the usual assortment of loners, bastards, and riffraff who tend to wind up in the islands and who are willing to sign on for expedition work. Not many would take that sort of job, in those days."

"Why not? It sounds rather exciting."

Newton chuckled. "Not nearly as exciting as prospecting for jelly-ice. After all, a man can get rich if he locates a deposit of ice. Expedition work, on the other hand, is a salaried job. Anything valuable that is discovered becomes the property of whoever has funded the venture."

"In this case that would have been the University of New Portland, right?"

"Correct. And, as I said, their records show they canceled the expedition after Chastain disappeared."

"Hmm." Zinnia bent closer to a severed vine to examine the red juice that dripped from it.

"No, no, Miss Spring, you don't want to touch that little blood-creeper." Newton batted her hand away with a playful pat. "Not until the wound has sealed."

Zinnia glanced at him. "Wound?"

"Figure of speech." Newton's merry eyes danced behind his round spectacles. "As you can see, the vine appears to bleed when it's cut. The liquid is rather toxic. Leaves a nasty burn."

"Oh." Zinnia quickly shoved her hands into the pockets of her jeans as she followed Newton down another green passageway. "So, you're convinced that the expedition team was abducted by aliens?"

"It's the only reasonable explanation for the disappearance of those five men together with all of the records that would have proven that the team left on schedule," Newton said. "I admit that my work has caught the attention of one or two kooks over the years, thanks to the tabloids. Some of the fools have come up with their own theories, but they're all nonsense."

"What are some of the other theories?"

"Several years ago one of the tabloids published a fanciful piece which claimed that the last Chastain expedition had discovered a treasure of some kind. Perhaps a huge deposit of fire crystal. The author suggested that the five members of the team had made a pact to conceal the location of the crystal and then faked their own disappearance."

"So that they wouldn't have to turn the discovery over to the university officials?"

"Yes." Newton chuckled. "Ridiculous theory, of course. If those five men had been secretly mining a vast quantity of fire crystal all these years, someone would have noticed. Fire crystal is so rare that if a lot of it suddenly came on the market, it would cause quite a stir."

"True." Zinnia could not argue that point. "Still,

the idea that the team found a treasure worth hiding is intriguing."

"Bah. Five men could not have kept such a secret for long." Newton waved his shears at her. "Those men were abducted by aliens, Miss Spring. And then those same aliens plotted to remove all traces of the Third Expedition so that no one would figure out what had happened."

"It seems a little unlikely," Zinnia suggested as gently as possible.

"Not unlikely at all. Don't forget, we have proof that aliens have visited this planet in the past."

"You're talking about the relics Lucas Trent found."

"Indeed," Newton said.

"But the experts say they're extremely ancient. Whoever left them behind has been gone for a thousand years or more."

"That doesn't mean they didn't come back thirty-five years ago to kidnap Chastain and his men."

"But why would they choose those five people?" Zinnia asked.

"We may never know the answer to that, my dear. They are aliens, after all. Who can tell how their minds work?" Newton frowned. "You may want to stand back from that snap-tongue."

"Snap-tongue?" Zinnia glanced down at a large, fleshy, throat-shaped leaf.

"A clever little plant, if I do say so. It can take off a finger or two if you aren't careful. Watch this." Newton plucked a small plastic bag from his pocket and opened it to remove a strip of raw meat. He tossed the meat toward the snap-tongue plant.

When the tidbit sailed past the leaf, a long, fleshy, tongue-like extension unfurled. It snagged the passing meal and bundled it swiftly downward into the sticky fibrous heart of the plant.

Zinnia grimaced as the meat vanished down a green gullet. "I see what you mean."

"The key to making it through my maze without any little accidents is to not touch anything," Newton said happily.

Zinnia halted abruptly. "We're in a maze?"

"Indeed. Hadn't you realized that yet?" Newton chuckled indulgently. "A matrix-talent friend designed it for me. It's constructed in such a way that anyone who enters it is funneled directly to the center. Once there, the visitor won't find his way out unless he knows the key."

Zinnia glanced warily around. "Which you do know, I trust?"

"Indeed, indeed. It's my maze, after all." Newton tapped a seemingly impenetrable wall of leaves. "Come along. Let's see some action."

"I beg your pardon?"

"I was speaking to my naughty little spike-trap here," Newton explained. "Usually it's a bit more active at this time of day but I suppose the slight frost this morning has slowed it down somewhat."

"Slowed it down?" Zinnia took a step back.

"I'll demonstrate." Newton touched the tip of his gardening shears to the impassive green wall one more time. "If I can wake it up, that is. Ah, there we go. About time, sleepy-head."

Zinnia heard a soft, sibilant rustling. In the next instant a mass of long sharp thorns burst forth through the green leaves. She realized that any creature unlucky enough to have brushed up against the wall of green would have been impaled.

"Interesting." She swallowed heavily.

"I've been working on this hybrid for some years now." Newton looked pleased with himself. "In its natural habitat a spike-trap is rather small. The thorns can only pin insects or small birds. But my experiments have produced this version which could easily fell a medium-sized rabbit-mouse."

Zinnia eyed the massed thorns. "And do serious damage to anything larger."

"Indeed, indeed." Newton beamed. "As I said, the trick to enjoying my garden is to avoid touching anything unless you know exactly what you're doing."

"I'll keep that in mind." Zinnia made certain that she was standing in the very center of the green passageway. "Have you ever heard any rumors about Chastain's last expedition journal?"

"Journal?" Newton paused reflectively. "There must have been one, of course. After all, Chastain kept a journal for the first two expeditions. He was very meticulous in such matters. But the journal for the Third was no doubt lost when the aliens snatched him."

Zinnia had a feeling that Nick would not appreciate her informing Demented DeForest that the journal of the Third Expedition had turned up recently. She was reluctant to admit it, but it was obvious that she was wasting her time with the professor.

"You've been very helpful, sir. Thank you for answering my questions. I really should be on my way now."

"Oh, you mustn't leave before you've seen the heart of my maze, my dear. It's a very special place, if I do say so, myself."

"What's at the center?" she asked uneasily.

"My water plant grotto, of course." Newton chortled as he ambled off down a dark green passage. "Come along, my dear. I'll show it to you. I'm very proud of my aquatic specimens."

Zinnia's palms suddenly felt damp. She dried them on her jeans. "I don't have a lot of time, Professor."

"Oh, you'll have time for this, my dear." Newton disappeared around a corner. "I love to show off my grotto. Besides, you can't get back to the house without me."

"Professor DeForest, wait—"

"This way, Miss Spring." Newton's voice grew fainter.

Zinnia looked back the way she had come and realized she was completely lost. She could not identify which of the twisting corridors of green foliage had brought her to her present position. There was no choice but to follow Newton.

"Professor DeForest, I really can't stay long," she said in what she hoped was a firm voice.

"I understand, my dear." His voice grew fainter.

Zinnia took one last glance over her shoulder. It was hopeless. She would never be able to find her way out without Newton.

"Hold on, Professor, I'm coming. I can't wait to see your grotto."

She hurried around a corner and nearly collided with Newton.

"Ah, there you are." His eyes crinkled with cheery pleasure. "This way." He turned and trundled down another path. "Remember, don't touch anything."

"Believe me, I won't." Zinnia followed reluctantly. "How do you find your way through this maze?"

"Quite simple, my dear." He glanced back at her with his twinkling blue eyes. "I know my garden. Be careful of that Curtain plant. You wouldn't want to be standing too near when it closes."

Zinnia edged around a heavy, drooping cascade of leaves. She thought she heard water bubbling somewhere in the distance. An unpleasant smell of rotting vegetation wafted past her nose.

"Here we are, my dear," Newton said as he turned one last corner. "Lovely, isn't it? I spend so many enjoyable hours sitting on that stone bench over there."

Zinnia walked cautiously around the corner and saw a rocky grotto covered in slimy green moss. A pool of dark water swirled around the opening of a stony cavern and disappeared into the black interior.

Large evil-looking plants hunkered around the perimeter of the pool like so many hungry predators waiting for prey. Zinnia supposed that, given the general theme of the garden, that was not an overly imaginative image.

Greasy-looking vines trailed across the entrance of the grotto. More vegetation floated on the surface of the dark pool. Zinnia glimpsed something large and tuberous inside the cave.

"Most unusual," she said.

Newton glowed with an almost paternal pride. "Thank you, my dear. I have devoted years to my plants. They are all unique. So nice to be able to show them off once in a while."

Zinnia was about to suggest once again, in a tactful manner, that she had to leave. She paused when a thought struck her. "Professor, you must have made some notes in the course of your research."

"Indeed, indeed. A great many. Haven't looked at them for years. They're filed away in the special place where I store all of the mementos of my career in academia."

"Where is that?"

"Beneath the house in the family crypt, of course." Newton gave her a wistful smile. "The perfect place for that sort of thing. My career in academia, after all, is as dead as my relatives. And, frankly, between you and me, my dear, I much preferred my career to my family. Nasty lot."

A vision of Aunt Willy popped into Zinnia's mind. "I can sympathize with that feeling, Professor. I have one last question."

"What's that, Miss Spring?"

"You said that the University of New Portland officials were quite willing to believe that Bartholomew Chastain committed suicide."

"They accepted the story without a qualm."

"Why is that? Did Chastain have a history of psychological problems?"

"No. But he was rumored to be a matrix-talent. Everyone knows how odd they are."

It was after ten when Zinnia stepped out of the elevator and started down the hall to her loft apartment. She was exhausted. The late focus assignment had gone on much too long, as was often the case with matrix-talents. They had a tendency to lose themselves in the patterns they generated on the metaphysical plane. When that happened they enjoyed themselves so much that Zinnia hated to interrupt them. Unfortunately for them, Psynergy, Inc. billed by the hour.

This evening the client, a matrix working in the field of biological synergism, had obsessed on an elaborate array of biosyn statistics. When Zinnia had gently reminded her of the passing time, the researcher had brushed the interruption aside. She had promised that the lab would cover the cost.

Clementine would be pleased at the high bill the matrix had run up, Zinnia thought as she let herself into her loft. But right now, bed sounded far more exciting than a bonus in her paycheck. It had been a very long day.

She yawned as she reached for the light switch.

A shadow shifted in the darkness near the fireplace. Zinnia stopped yawning and prepared to start screaming.

"Tell me," Nick said from the heavy Later Expansion Period reading chair. "What in five hells made you think you would get away with it?"

"What?" She was so stunned, she could barely

speak. Her hand fell away from the light switch, leaving the loft in darkness. "What do you mean?"

"It's a very well-done forgery, I'll give you that much." Nick's eyes gleamed in the shadows. "But it's a fake from first page to last."

"What are you talking about?"

"The journal, of course." His voice was infinitely soft, infinitely dangerous. "The one you so generously arranged for me to buy from Polly and Omar last night. It's a complete fraud."

Zinnia took a step forward and paused. She was too dazed to think very clearly. "How do you know that?"

"How do I know? This is how I know."

Power slammed across the metaphysical plane, a great raw surge of it.

Matrix-talent seeking a prism.

Demanding a prism.

Hunting a prism.

Summoning a prism.

Zinnia stopped breathing when she felt the questing presence of the psychic probe. There was something disturbingly familiar about it. Something that called to her as no other talent ever had. Instinctively she responded with a crystal-clear prism.

A torrent of dazzling power crashed through it, emerging in great waves of controlled psychic energy.

She knew this talent. She knew this man.

"It was you," Zinnia whispered. "You're the vampire."

Chapter
11

* * * * * * * * * *

She switched off the focus. And then she turned on the lights.

For some reason the simple mundane action caught Nick off guard. Instinctively he suppressed the fiery storm of power that he had generated on the metaphysical plane. The prism Zinnia had created winked out of existence.

"Great. Just great." Zinnia threw up her hands. "The end of a perfect day. I missed breakfast because I had to spend the morning with a loony professor and a bunch of blood-sucking plants. I missed dinner because I had to spend the evening boring myself silly holding the focus for a statistician. I walk in the front door, asking no more out of life than a glass of wine and a sandwich, and what do I find? A psychic vampire in the living room. It's too much. I quit."

She gave Nick a withering look as she stalked across the open loft into the kitchen. She yanked open the icerator and jerked out a bottle of green wine.

Nick rapidly reassessed matters as he watched her reach into a drawer and rummage around for a corkscrew. Things were not going as he had planned. He hated it when that happened.

Ever since he had realized that the journal was a forgery, he had been obsessing on this confrontation with Zinnia. His rage at having been played for a fool was bad enough. The frustration he felt at having once again failed in his quest was even worse. But it was the knowledge that Zinnia had betrayed him that was gnawing at his guts.

She had set him up. There was no other logical explanation.

He did not understand the anguish that had welled up inside when he had forced himself to face the truth earlier that afternoon. He had not allowed anything or anyone to affect him this strongly for a long, long time.

It infuriated him to know that he was reacting so intensely to what he should have foreseen as a possibility right from the start. He should never have trusted Zinnia.

Nevertheless, in spite of the facts, more than anything else at that moment he wanted her to defend herself.

Earlier, as he had brooded in his hidden office, he had envisioned a dozen different scenarios for this meeting. All of them had involved Zinnia desperately struggling to convince him that she had been duped by Polly and Omar. He wanted her to plead, to declare her innocence even though logic told him that she must have been in on the scam up to her elegant ears.

"Where is the real journal?" he asked very softly. "Did you sell it to someone else? Or did you keep it for yourself? Did you buy into that old tabloid legend about my father's team discovering a fortune in fire crystal? Do you think the journal can lead you to it? If so, you're not nearly as intelligent as I had assumed."

"Gosh, I'd hate to sink any lower in your opinion than I already have."

"No one betrays me and gets away with it, Zinnia."

"Don't waste your time trying to intimidate me tonight, Chastain." She came around the end of the counter with a long-stemmed glass of wine in her hand, walked to the antique sofa near the window, and sank down on it with a heartfelt sigh. Propping herself in one corner, she stretched out her legs on the cushions. "I'm too tired to be scared."

"Better work up the energy for it because I'm not playing games."

She took a slow meditative sip of wine and regarded him over the rim of the glass. "If that journal you bought off Polly and Omar last night is a fake, then I'm as much in the dark as you are."

"You made all the arrangements for the transaction." The steady clarity of her gaze made him seethe. "You had to be in on it. The only thing I don't understand is why in five hells you thought you'd get away with it."

She folded one hand behind her head. "Do you really believe this nonsense or is it just matrix paranoia talking?"

"I am not paranoid," Nick said through his teeth. "But I am very good at detecting patterns, even without the aid of a prism. Not that it takes a matrix-talent to see the connections in this situation. A small child with a pencil could connect the dots."

"Then I suggest you go find a small child with a pencil because you're not doing a very good job on your own." She took another sip of wine, leaned her head back against her folded arm, and closed her eyes. "Lord, am I tired. I hate statistics."

Fury swept through Nick. He shoved himself up out of the chair and crossed the room to the sofa. "Look at me, damn it."

She opened her eyes. "I'm not in the mood for this, Mr. Chastain."

He reached down and snatched the wine glass out of her hand. "Did you really think I'd be blinded by a few kisses and the promise of good sex?"

"What promise? The only thing I agreed to was dinner." She raised her brows in mocking inquiry. "Speaking of which, I assume this performance means that the invitation for tomorrow night has been canceled?"

Nick heard a sharp crack. Liquid flowed over his hand. He glanced down and was stunned to see that he'd snapped the fragile stem of the wine glass. He stared, shocked by the evidence of his loss of control. Blood and green wine dripped from his fingers onto the wooden floor.

"Oh, for heaven's sake. Now look what you've done." Zinnia got to her feet and started back toward the kitchen. "Come over to the sink. I'll get you cleaned up and then you can go back to your cave."

Anger and despair washed through him. *"Zinnia."*

He reached for her with his mind the way a drowning man lunges for a lifeline. He felt the familiar floating sense of disorientation as he sent out a psychic probe. Relief rushed through him when he sensed her response. He wished he was sitting down. The overwhelming impact of intense intimacy nearly drove him to his knees.

Zinnia said nothing as she turned on the water faucet, but she offered him a prism on the metaphysical plane. It was crystal clear, very powerful. This time he took a few seconds to study it. He sensed that it could focus the full range of his talent. Never in his life had he ever been able to use his psychic gifts to the maximum.

He could not resist. He sent talent crashing eagerly through the prism. The metaphysical construct did not waver. It channeled the full thrust of raw psychic power and converted it into finely tuned waves of energy. It was energy that could be used the way he used his hands or his ears or his eyes. Energy that was as natural and controllable as any of his other senses.

He no longer had to grope for or deduce the patterns in the world around him. From the slightly irregular edges of the mosaic tiles on the kitchen walls to the myriad tiny sparkles on the surface of the water that poured from the faucet, the intricate designs of the surrounding matrix took on a whole new dimension on the metaphysical plane. Several dimensions, in fact. He could have studied them for hours, analyzing the connections, extrapolating the possibilities, assessing probabilities.

But he made no attempt to use the energy waves. He simply watched the great, glittering cascade of psychic power with his inner eye and marveled. He was drunk with the beauty and excitement of his own fully focused talent.

"You're dripping all over my hardwood floors," Zinnia said.

The normal nature of a good focus link was such that both prism and talent could indulge in a casual conversation or perform a routine task while they worked their combined psychic energy. It came under the heading of being able to chew gum and walk at the same time.

But tonight Nick had a hard time concentrating on Zinnia's words. In addition to the wonder of indulging his own psychic senses to the hilt, he was in the grip of sexual desire so strong that he literally ached with it. He doubted if he could have chewed gum at that moment, let alone walk.

After a brief struggle, however, he managed to subdue the heady sensation long enough to get himself as far as Zinnia's kitchen sink.

"Don't you feel it?" he asked.

"What? The focus link? Sure." She reached for his

hand and held it under the running water. "You're very strong, aren't you?"

"Yes." He had meant the feeling of intense intimacy, not the power of the link. Perhaps she didn't experience the connection the way he did. The possibility that the shattering sense of closeness was only happening on his side triggered a wave of melancholy. "I don't know what class. The official paranormal spectrum scale isn't accurate for matrix-talents."

"Speaking as a full-spectrum prism who's had a fair amount of experience with matrix-talents, I can tell you that you're way over a ten." She met his eyes. "As I'm sure you're well aware."

There was no point trying to pretend that he was normal. "I guess so." He leaned back against the counter and savored the flow of his own power on the metaphysical plane while Zinnia rinsed his hand.

He watched, enthralled, as she cradled his fingers in hers. Her hand was beautiful. A model of exquisite evolutionary forces. He could trace the whole history of human development in the pattern of the delicate bones beneath her incredibly soft skin.

"I assume you've never been tested?" Zinnia asked crisply.

"No." He was fascinated by the pattern of the pooling water in the bottom of the sink. "Some researcher probably would have leaked the results. Wouldn't have been good for business."

She smiled wryly. "I don't doubt that. Being a matrix is questionable enough in the eyes of most people. Being an off-the-chart matrix is the stuff of psychic vampire novels."

"Yes." He pushed more power through the prism and deliberately used it to study the intricate design of the drops of water that splashed onto the tile around the sink. He could see an entire mathematical universe in them.

"Speaking of which," Zinnia continued. "I've read

every psychic vampire romance Orchid Adams has ever written but you're the first genuine PV I've ever worked with. If Clementine finds out about this, she'll want me to charge extra."

He jerked his eyes up to meet hers. She couldn't possibly be joking. "Reading novels about mythical monster matrix-talents and rolling dice at a casino run by one are two entirely different things," he said.

"True. Most people would be extremely wary of gambling in a place where the owner was capable of tampering with the laws of chance."

"Don't have to tamper with them," he muttered. "They naturally favor the house. Just ask any synergistic probability theorist."

He took a deep breath and was able to reassert some of his normal control. Thankfully, the slightly inebriated sensation was fading. He was still moving power through the prism at full charge, but he was no longer quite so enthralled with himself. The disturbing sense of intimacy persisted, however. He had a fierce erection.

"I believe you." She turned off the faucet and handed him a paper towel. "I'm sorry the journal was a fraud, Nick. But I had nothing to do with it. I was only trying to help. I don't appreciate your attitude tonight. I don't like people trying to intimidate me."

The prism began to fade. Nick realized that she was cutting the flow of her own power. "No, wait." Instinctively he tried to surround the prism with chaotic waves of unfocused talent.

"Don't you dare try to jump me the way you did the other night in the casino." Zinnia glowered. "I don't know which one of us is the stronger but I'm in no mood to find out tonight."

"And you say I'm intimidating." He wrapped the paper towel around his hand and reluctantly stopped projecting his talent. He watched wistfully as the beautiful prism winked out on the metaphysical plane. "I'm sorry about what happened the other night. You took me by surprise."

"I took *you* by surprise? How do you think I felt?"

"It won't happen again," he promised.

"It better not."

He looked at her. "What was it you did to the prism when you tried to get free?"

She hesitated. "To tell you the truth, I'm not quite sure. It was instinctive. I didn't think about it."

"You twisted the focus somehow."

She shrugged. "Maybe it's the flipside of being able to focus for matrix-talents in the first place. A built-in defense mechanism."

"Why aren't you afraid of me?"

She smiled as she turned away to pour more wine. "Because I know you aren't crazy."

"How can you be sure of that?"

"Probably has something to do with the fact that my own type of psychic energy is weird. I told you, I'm not a normal prism. I can only work comfortably with matrix-talents, so out of necessity, I've become something of an expert on them. Maybe the only real expert in the world. Thanks to Psynergy, Inc., I've had an opportunity to work with more matrix-talents in the past year or so than most researchers see in a lifetime."

"You didn't answer my question. What makes you think I'm not crazy?"

She handed him a glass of wine. "It's hard to explain. I can feel things when I work with a matrix. Things most prisms aren't able to detect when they work with one. I once tried to hold a focus for a matrix who was certifiably bonkers. Believe me, I can tell the difference. He was only about a class-three but he scared the living daylights out of me."

"How? Did he try to take control of the prism?"

"Yes, but he was much too weak to do it. That wasn't the scary part. The frightening stuff was the talent, itself. It was—" She frowned. "Not normal. I don't know how else to describe it."

He held her eyes. "You think I'm normal?"

"I don't know if I'd go that far. There is nothing real normal about you, Nick. But you certainly aren't a wacko."

He took a sip of the weak green wine. "You'd know, huh?"

"Oh, yes. I'd know." She watched him intently. "Your father was a matrix, wasn't he?"

"Yes."

"Are you obsessed with finding his journal because you want to know if his talent drove him to suicide? Are you afraid the same fate awaits you?"

She was too damn perceptive. It was dangerous to continue any kind of association with her, let alone risk the intimacy of either a mental or sexual liaison. But she was part of the matrix now. He saw no escape. He did not even want to escape.

Perhaps she was his fate.

But he was not ready to face her blunt questions head-on. It would force him to confront some things he preferred to sidestep.

"How did you learn that my father was a matrix?" he asked instead.

"Professor Loony mentioned that the reason no one questioned Bartholomew Chastain's suicide was because it was strongly suspected that he was a matrix and people have so many misconceptions about matrix-talents."

"Professor Loony?"

Zinnia made a face. "Newton DeForest. Retired history professor. Maniacal gardener."

"You went to see Demented DeForest?" Nick was disgusted. "Why the hell did you do that? I told you he was just an old crackpot."

"I'm not going to argue with that assessment. DeForest is about as stable as a deposit of jelly-ice.

You should see his garden." She shuddered. "He's a horti-talent who specializes in carnivorous plant hybrids. A matrix friend helped him design a maze full of them. It's positively gruesome."

"What in five hells were you doing in DeForest's garden?"

"I still think Morris's murder may be connected to the journal. My brother, Leo, is studying synergistic historical analysis. He told me that DeForest is the only person who ever actually researched the Third Expedition. I had an appointment to talk to DeForest today."

"Damn." Nick set the wine glass down on the tile counter with enough force to make it ring. "You should have told me that you were going to talk to him."

"You made it clear that you were only interested in the journal." She smiled coolly. "Of course, that was before you realized I was a cunning scam artist and that I had masterminded a diabolical scheme to set you up for a major con job."

"Stop it, Zinnia. Please."

"Do I take it that your curiosity about poor Morris's death has been renewed now that you know the journal is still missing?" she asked bluntly.

"Yes." He took a step toward her. "You could damn well say that my interest in the matter has been renewed. Furthermore, for your information, I'm the leading authority on the Third Expedition, not Newton DeForest."

"Is that right? How come no one, including my brother who's really into history, knows that interesting little fact?"

"Because I've never bothered to publish. I have no reason to share what I've learned with the rest of the world."

"Every matrix I've ever met makes a fetish out of secrecy."

He opted to ignore that goad. After all, she was right. "I've spent the past three years collecting every scrap of information I could find. I know every single theory, legend, and rumor. I've talked to everyone I could find who was in the Western Islands thirty-five years ago. If you want to know anything about the subject, ask me."

A speculative look appeared in her eyes. "DeForest told me that none of the men on your father's team had much in the way of family ties."

"He's right." Nick picked up the wine glass and took another swallow. "Loners, misfits. But all good jungle men. That's one of the things that doesn't make sense. If an accident occurred on the trail, one or two of them should have survived."

"You're assuming that the expedition did leave the jumping-off point."

"It left," he said softly.

"How can you be so sure?"

"I'm certain."

She sighed. "Okay, back to the other issue. You said the team members were loners and misfits. But your father was hardly alone in the world. He was the heir to the Chastain business empire."

"My father was the exception." Nick hesitated. "Andy Aoki told me once that he thought that it was the Chastain family that drove my father out to the islands. Apparently they put a lot of pressure on him to take over the reins of Chastain, Inc. That was the last thing he wanted to do so he got as far away from the clan as he could."

"Andy Aoki?"

"The man who raised me after my parents died."

"You lost your mother, too?"

"Before I was six months old. She left me with Andy the day she went to Serendipity to look for answers concerning my father's disappearance. She never came back. The six-track she was driving went over a cliff during a storm."

"How terrible for you," Zinnia said very softly. "To lose both parents."

"To be truthful, I don't remember my mother. And my father disappeared before I was even born." Nick gave her a level look. "Andy was a good man. He was a father to me in every way that counted."

"I believe you." Zinnia was silent for a moment. "It was probably Bartholomew Chastain's talent that led him to take up expedition work. The lure of analyzing and mapping the unknown would have obvious appeal to a strong matrix."

"I suppose so." Nick considered that. "Depends on the matrix, I think."

"Did you ever consider expedition work?"

"No. I did a little jelly-ice prospecting to get a stake together but once I had the money I needed to open the casino, I quit the jungle work. I have . . . other interests."

"Synergistic probability theory, I presume." She eyed him shrewdly. "That would fit with your career choice."

He shot her a sidelong glance. "I don't run a casino because I'm into gaming theory."

"Why do you run one?"

"Because, among other things, it's a good way to make lots and lots of money."

"Succinctly put. And what do you plan to buy with all the money?"

"Respectability." *And everything that goes with it,* he added silently.

Her eyes widened. "I beg your pardon?"

"You heard me. I've got a plan."

She gave him a look of reluctant fascination. "Amazing. What is this plan?"

"I'll tell you about it over dinner."

"Hold on here, Chastain." She put up a palm. "Things have changed in this little matrix. You can't just accuse me of fraud one moment and then expect me to go out to dinner with you the next. I've got some pride, you know. Plus which, I'm still pissed."

The phone on the wall rang before Nick could decide how to deal with that.

Zinnia grabbed the receiver. "Hello? Oh, hi, Duncan. No, it's okay. I worked late tonight."

Nick did not like the way her voice softened and warmed. Whoever Duncan was, he was more than a casual friend. A relative, he thought optimistically.

"I meant to call you this evening, anyway." Zinnia lounged against the counter in a casual pose that said volumes about the easy nature of her relationship with the man on the other end of the line. "I wanted to thank you for dinner."

Not a relative. Nick sipped morosely at his wine. He recognized the feeling of possessiveness that was uncurling within him but he did not fully comprehend it. Possessiveness implied jealousy. Jealousy was a byproduct of desire that was not properly controlled. He hadn't even gone to bed with Zinnia Spring yet. How could he be feeling anything as strong as jealousy?

He was still suffering aftereffects from the focus link, he decided. He would have to be careful. Very, very careful.

"I had a really bizarre day, as a matter of fact," Zinnia said into the phone. "I'll tell you all about it the next time I see you. Thanks. Yes, I promise. I'll check my calendar in the morning. Good night, Duncan."

Nick watched her hang up the phone. "Good friend?"

"A friend. His name is Duncan Luttrell."

Nick made the connection swiftly. "SynIce?"

"Do you know him?"

"Not personally." Nick summoned up an image of a big, good-looking, confident man. "But I know who he is. He gets a lot of business press. And I've seen him at Chastain's Palace a few times. Strictly a recreational gambler. Doesn't get into deep play." But Luttrell usually won when he played, Nick reflected. Even when the stakes were penny-ante.

"Duncan would never gamble heavily." Zinnia's smile was a little too sweet. "He likes money, too, just as you do, but he prefers to earn it the old-fashioned way."

"Meaning he works for it and I don't?"

"I'm sure running a casino requires all sorts of executive ability. But I suspect your corporate style is somewhat different than Duncan's."

Amazingly, Nick managed to hang on to his temper. "Are you and Luttrell serious?"

"You mean, are we having an affair? No." She grimaced. "My relatives would dearly love us to get more closely involved. Aunt Willy reminded me just this morning that in certain social circles, marriages are sometimes made for what she likes to call family considerations."

"You mean, she wants you to marry for money and position."

"Let's just say she'd like to see the Spring family restored to what she considers its proper station in the world."

"But you're digging in your heels." Nick felt his spirits rise. His best ally in this new battle was Zinnia's own stubbornness.

"With the exception of my brother, none of my relatives is particularly concerned with whether or not Duncan and I would be happy together. They see marriage to him as a way to recoup the family fortunes."

"How does Luttrell feel?"

"I don't know," she said. "I've never asked him.

But he's a smart man. No intelligent person would consider marrying a woman who has been declared unmatchable."

"He'd probably be real happy to consider an affair," Nick muttered.

She blushed. "Maybe. But that's not any of your business, is it? I'm sure you're not interested in my personal plans. All you care about is the Chastain journal."

"And all you care about is finding Morris Fenwick's murderer. It seems to me, we're back to Plan *A.*"

"Plan *A?*"

"The one where you and I work together."

"Together?" Her mouth kicked up at the corner. "Surely you jest, Mr. Chastain. I thought you had concluded that I was a conniving little scam artist. Why on St. Helens would you want to work with me?"

Nick felt the heat rise in his face. He wondered if he was turning red. "I've changed my mind. I don't think you were in on the scam."

"Really? Tell me, what brought about that grand cognition? Did you utilize your phenomenal matrix-talent to deduce that I'm innocent? Or was it my naive charm and big blue eyes."

"Silvery," he corrected, without thinking.

She blinked. "What?"

He felt like a fool. "Your eyes aren't really blue. They're sort of silvery."

She raised her gaze to the ceiling. "Trust a matrix to fuss over details."

"Look, I admit that I was annoyed when I realized that I'd been conned. It was logical to assume that you'd been involved."

"Logical, my Aunt Willy's left foot. All that happened was that you finally calmed down long enough tonight to use some common sense. You've no doubt realized that I'm not stupid enough to risk cheating the notorious Nick Chastain out of fifty thousand dollars and then hang around my apartment waiting for him to find me."

"I figure Polly and Omar pulled a fast one on both of us."

"Brilliant deduction." She contemplated him with narrowed eyes. "So tell me why you want to work with me?"

"Simple. We can help each other."

"Hah. Don't give me that. You don't have any real interest in finding Morris's killer. All you want is the journal." She smiled grimly. "I know perfectly well why you suddenly want us to be partners."

He folded his arms. "Is that so? Why?"

"Simple. You're afraid that I'll cause problems for you if I continue my investigation on my own. My blundering around could interfere with your own strategy. And now that I know you're a matrix-talent, it follows that you do have a strategy."

"I don't want you poking around on your own because it could be dangerous," he said patiently.

"That's not what's worrying you. The real problem so far as you're concerned is that I'm a loose cannon. An uncontrolled element in the matrix. You want to keep tabs on me and you've decided that the easiest way to do that is to pretend we're partners."

"It wouldn't be a pretense."

"Oh? What's in this for me, *partner?*"

"I told you that first night, I've got connections on the street."

"No offense, Nick, but I don't see you sharing information very readily. Not your style."

"Because I'm a matrix and all matrix-talents are secretive?"

She raised her wine glass in a salute. "That's one good reason."

He tapped a finger on his forearm while he considered the challenge. Then he reached for the phone and punched in a familiar number.

It was answered on the first ring.

"That you, boss?" Feather was not given to polite preliminaries.

"Yes. What have you got on Polly Fenwick and Omar Booker?"

"Looks like they moved fast last night. Must have had their bags packed and in the car when they met you in the park. Their house is locked up tight. Yesterday they told the neighbors they were going on vacation."

"Keep on it. They've probably left the city-state. Ask our friends in New Vancouver and New Portland to keep an eye out for them."

"Right, boss."

Nick hung up the phone and glanced at Zinnia as he punched in another number. "Polly and Omar were packed and ready to leave town before they met us last night. Looks like they had a plan, too."

She frowned. "They either knew the journal was a forgery or Morris's last instructions really did scare them."

"Yes." Nick broke off as the second call was answered. "Stonebraker? This is Chastain. I need a favor."

"I don't do favors, you know that." Rafe Stonebraker's voice was that of a man who lived in shadows. It was laced with a bleak, cynical ennui. "I have bills to pay, same as everyone else. And you, of all people, can well afford my services. What are you looking for?"

"The name of a very, very good forger."

"How good?"

"Good enough to create a fake copy of Bartholomew Chastain's journal from the Third Expedition."

"When you say good enough, do you mean good enough to fool you?"

"For a while, yes. It took me almost an hour of close analysis to be certain that I had just paid fifty grand for a fake. And I doubt that I would ever have figured it out if I had been something other than . . . what I am."

"A matrix?"

Nick was aware of Zinnia watching him. "Yes."

"You're right." Rafe sounded marginally more interested in the problem now. "There are very few craftsmen of that caliber. Fewer still who would take on that kind of project. I'll get back to you in a day or two with a name."

"Thanks." Nick hung up the phone again and met Zinnia's eyes. "That was a friend. He'll find the forger for us. When I get a name, I'll share it with you. Satisfied?"

"Maybe." She confronted him with a calculating expression. "What do you want from me?"

Everything. The realization took away his breath. He sucked in air and forced himself to sound calm and in control. "Cooperation. No more going off on your own. We talk before we make our moves."

She appeared to think that over for a few seconds. Then she nodded once. "Okay, it's a deal."

He felt something inside himself untwist and relax slightly. "Like I said, we're back to Plan *A*. As far as everyone else is concerned, you're my new interior designer. And to answer your earlier question, yes. The invitation to dinner tomorrow night still stands."

Zinnia smiled slightly. "Your place or mine?"

He glanced around the bright, airy loft. "I like your place better."

"Let's make it yours," she said softly.

"You want to eat above a casino?" He didn't want to entertain her there. The casino represented the past he intended to leave behind soon.

"Not the casino," Zinnia said. "Your new home. The one I'm supposedly going to redecorate for your future bride."

Chapter

12

* * * * * * * * * *

You've got to be kidding." Leo swept the crowded coff-tea house with a worried glance, as though he feared that some of the students or faculty clustered around the small tables might eavesdrop. Then he turned back to Zinnia. "You're going to be his *what?*"

"His interior designer." Zinnia grinned. "Don't get excited. It's not quite the same thing as being his mistress."

"This is not a joke, Zin."

"No. Actually, it's just a pretense."

"You're talking about a little game of pretend with the guy who just happens to operate the most exclusive casino in town. Are you out of your mind? Chastain is dangerous."

"He may be able to turn up information that will point to Morris's killer. Something that I can take to the cops to get their attention."

Zinnia had been braced for a negative reaction to her plans, but Leo seemed more upset about them than she had anticipated.

When had her gangly little brother turned into a

strong handsome man, she wondered. Leo had their
mother's clear, thoughtful blue eyes and their father's
lithe build. His dark brown hair was drawn back from
his face and tied with a black cord in a style left over
from the waning Western Islands look.

Zinnia was grateful that he hadn't gone in for the
garish colors and outlandish designs of the new Alien
Artifact fashions as had so many of the other students
on campus. In truth, he was already starting to look
like a budding young professor of Synergistic Historical Analysis in his cuffed khaki trousers, unpressed
button-down shirt, and slouchy tweed jacket.

It seemed only yesterday that he had stood beside
her at the memorial service that had been held for
their parents. With their stoic-faced relatives ranged
behind them, they had held each other's hands and
fought back tears. Perhaps it was then that Leo had
begun to emerge into manhood, Zinnia thought.

She certainly had not been the same since that
bleak day. The stress of dealing with the personal
tragedy as well as the very disastrous, very public
bankruptcy of Spring Industries had changed both of
them.

"I admit he's got a reputation," she said. "But I
think it's somewhat exaggerated. In fact, I think he
deliberately promotes it because he believes it's good
for business."

"The rumors about him aren't all fantasy." Leo's
fingers tightened around his double tall coff-tea latté
glass. "Listen, after the story about you and Chastain
finding Fenwick's body broke in the newspapers I
started hearing things."

"What sort of things?"

"Remember John Garrett?"

"Sure. Garrett Electronics. John used to be a friend
of yours back in the old days." The *old days* was
mutually understood by both of them to refer to the
era before the loss of their parents.

"John and I ran into each other again in a History of Synergistic Theory class this semester. He took me aside yesterday. Told me he'd seen the headlines about you and Chastain. He wanted to warn me."

"About what?"

"About what kind of guy Chastain is." Leo leaned a little farther across the tiny table. "Seems like John's cousin, Randy, lost a lot of money in Chastain's Palace a few months ago. Randy had to go to his father for cash to settle the debt."

"That would be John's uncle?"

"Right. At any rate, old man Randolph Garrett was furious. Mostly because he didn't have the cash. He didn't want anyone to know he was having financial problems. Some kind of merger was in process. At any rate, John said that borrowing to pay off Randy's debt would have brought the kind of attention from the business news media that could have jeopardized the deal."

"What happened?"

"Randy's father went to see Chastain who said that things could be worked out." Leo glanced around once more and then lowered his voice. "Get this, Chastain told him that the gambling debt would be wiped off the books provided Garrett sold him a certain piece of property up in the hills above the city."

"So? That seems perfectly reasonable to me. Generous, even."

Leo gave her an exasperated look. "The property was the original Garrett estate. The one John Jeremy Garrett, himself, built three generations ago. It's a piece of the Garrett family history. They would never have parted with it willingly. Chastain must have known that."

"Did Randy's father sell the property to Chastain?"

"He had no choice. John told me that the other

branches of the Garrett clan were furious when they found out that the estate had been sold off. It was supposed to pass down through Randy's side of the family."

"You just told me that Randy's father was in financial difficulty. If that was true, the estate would likely have been sold, in any event. We had to sell our family home four years ago. These things happen." It worried Zinnia that she was trying to defend Nick Chastain or at least excuse his actions. Not a good sign, she thought. Not good at all.

"John said the Garrett estate would have been the last thing to go. And even if it had been sold, the family would never have agreed to sell it to someone like Chastain."

Zinnia chuckled. She couldn't help herself. "Horrors. A casino owner in the neighborhood. Who will they let in next?"

Leo's mouth tightened. "Don't you get it? It's an example of how Chastain works. He obviously wanted that estate. He knew he'd never convince the Garretts to sell it to him, so he manipulated Randy into a big loss at the casino."

"Are you accusing Nick of cheating his customers?"

"He wouldn't have to resort to cheating." Leo flopped back in his chair. "John said Randy is kind of wild. Give him a few drinks, feed him all the gambling chips he wants, and the end result would be a foregone conclusion. Chastain must have known that."

Yes, Zinnia thought, Chastain would have known that.

"He's a matrix," she said quietly.

"Chastain? Five hells." Leo's mouth twisted with acute disgust. "I should have guessed. That explains a few things."

"Such as?"

"Such as your trying to see his good side when it's

obvious to everyone else that he doesn't have one. You know how you are when it comes to matrix-talents. You always feel sorry for them. God knows why."

"Don't worry about me feeling sorry for Nick Chastain. I'm well aware of the fact that he can take care of himself. I promise I'll watch my step."

"Zin, I don't want you fooling around in a murder investigation."

"If I find anything I'll go straight to the cops. Now, enough about that. How are things going with you?"

Leo frowned at the change of subject. He raised one shoulder in a small shrug. "Okay."

"That doesn't sound like okay to me."

Leo groaned. "Uncle Stanley came to see me yesterday. Took me to lunch. Said he wanted to talk to me man-to-man."

"Oh, dear. Same song and dance?"

"Yeah. Asked me when I was going to give up the academic world and start concentrating on preparing myself for the real world of business. Went into his usual routine."

"You mean he pointed out that there was no serious money in teaching?"

"Yeah. Reminded me that the Spring family roots were in business. Said you were being difficult about fulfilling your responsibilities to the clan. That if you refused to contract a suitable marriage, there would be no one left but me to restore the family fortunes. Blah, blah, blah."

"Don't listen to him, Leo." Zinnia reached across the table to touch his sleeve. "You're going to be a brilliant synergistic historian. It's what you were born to do. You've got a powerful psychometric-talent and an aptitude for research. It would be a crime to give up your dreams."

Leo's mouth twisted. "And besides, we both know

I'd never make it big in the business world. Spread sheets, bottom lines, and five-year financial forecasts bore the socks off me. But the family is going to keep pushing both of us, Zin."

"We'll stand firm."

"Easier said than done."

"I know." Zinnia sighed. "I know. But we've made it this far. We can hold out for the duration."

"Don't count on it."

Zinnia and Leo exchanged troubled glances. When push came to shove on St. Helens, family almost always won.

"What is it, Feather?" Nick did not look up from the computer screen on his desk.

Feather's voice emerged from the intercom only slightly more gravelly than usual. "Hobart Batt is here, boss."

Nick stared at the screen full of financial data in front of him. He should have been pleased that Batt had apparently moved quickly to start the match-making process, but for some reason, he felt a chill in his gut.

"Damn," he said softly. "I forgot about him. Give me a couple of minutes, then send him into the red chamber, Feather."

"Sure, boss."

"By the way, Feather?"

"Yeah?"

"When I'm through with Batt, ask Rathbone to come see me for a few minutes."

"You want to talk to the head chef, boss? Something wrong in the Palace dining rooms?"

"No. It's a private matter."

"Private?" Feather sounded confused.

"Tell him to bring some sample menus for a picnic for two."

"A picnic?" Feather was beyond confused now. He was beginning to sound uneasy. "You going on a picnic, boss?"

"A classy picnic. The kind you see in movies. You know, where they serve a bottle of good wine and pâté and tiny little sandwiches."

"I never been on any picnics like that."

"Neither have I. But I'm sure Rathbone can handle it. Any chef who can get the tri-city-state award of excellence four years in a row and who could please the Founders' Club members for a decade should be able to put together a decent picnic."

"I'll tell him you want to see him, boss." The intercom went silent.

Nick reluctantly blanked the computer screen and got to his feet. He went to the wall and pushed the button that opened the secret panel. It slid aside with the hushed mechanical whir of a hidden motor to reveal the gilded red-and-black chamber.

Batt could not have come up with any matches yet, Nick assured himself. There were forms to be filled out. A battery of syn-psych tests to take. Everyone knew that the marriage registration process was a lengthy thorough-going business. No reputable syn-psych counselor could produce a match after a single interview.

It was too soon.

What the hell was he thinking, he wondered as he walked toward the gleaming obsidian-wood desk. He wanted Batt to move quickly. Why the cold chill?

It didn't take a matrix to answer that, he decided grimly. He took his seat behind the ornate desk. For all his planning and unwavering intentions, he didn't want to think about his future wife now that he was involved, however tenuously, with Zinnia.

The door opened. Feather's gleaming skull reflected the soft glow of the jelly lamps. He ushered Hobart, who was nattily attired in a fashionable, well-cut gray suit and a pink bow tie, into the room.

"Come in, Hobart." Nick did not rise. "Please sit down. I assume you're here on business?"

Hobart cleared his throat and walked nervously to the chair in front of the desk. "I brought a questionnaire. You'll have to fill it out before I can proceed."

"Of course. Let me see it."

Hobart perched primly on the edge of the chair and opened his briefcase. "It asks for details about your personal preferences, your hobbies and uh—" He glanced around the chamber with ill-concealed dismay and swallowed heavily. "Your tastes."

"Don't look so worried, Hobart." Nick smiled as he took the questionnaire. "I'm sure you'll find me a lady who won't mind my tastes. And I have no hobbies."

"No hobbies?"

"I don't have time for unimportant pursuits." Nick glanced through the thick questionnaire. "Running a casino keeps me fully occupied."

"I see." Hobart drew himself up. "Mr. Chastain, we really must discuss your business occupation and your unusual psychic talent."

"What's to discuss?"

"You must understand that both are serious impediments to a successful match, especially since you have insisted upon limiting your selection to registrants from a certain social class."

"Don't worry about it, Hobart." Nick closed the questionnaire. "I'm sure you'll find someone suitable for me."

"There is one other thing, sir."

"Yes?"

Hobart took a deep breath. "You mentioned that you were an untested talent."

Nick raised his brows. "What of it?"

"Sir, I work for a very reputable marriage agency.

Synergistic Connections adheres to a code of ethics. We simply cannot attempt a match unless both parties have been rated and assigned a position on the paranormal power spectrum."

"In that case, I'm afraid you'll have to handle this match off the record, Hobart. It will be our little secret."

"How am I supposed to convince a respectable lady to consider a match with an untested matrix-talent? It just isn't done. No family would permit such an alliance. No woman in her right mind would even think of taking such a risk."

"You're forgetting my one great asset, Hobart."

Hobart looked wary. "What is that, sir?"

"I'm rich."

Chapter
13

* * * * * * * * * *

Zinnia stood in the courtyard and surveyed the imposing structure in front of her. "As we interior designers say in situations such as this, it's got great bones."

This was the home that Nick had chosen for his bride, she thought. The place where he and the future Mrs. Chastain would raise a family. She did not want to admire the mansion. For some obscure reason, she longed to find fault with the soaring columns, graceful steps, and spacious gardens. But the designer in her was too honest. The old Garrett estate was beautiful.

The house and well-planted grounds occupied an acre of prime-view land above the city. The main building was a large two-storey stone affair in the Neo-Early Exploration Period style. The architect had captured the exuberant spirit of the earlier era while managing to avoid the frothy excesses. The result was elegant restrained exuberance. This was a house that was imbued with a sense of the future, Zinnia thought. A house infused with optimism and hope.

An elegant colonnaded porch surrounded the entire

mansion. The windows were tall and well-proportioned to match the high-ceilinged rooms inside. There was a subtle symmetry to the design that was not generally found either in the original buildings of the Early Exploration Period or in the Later Revival Period.

"Good bones?" Nick removed a huge picnic hamper from the trunk of the Synchron. "If that's a polite way of telling me the place is a little run-down, save your breath. I already know there's a lot of work to be done. The good news is, I've got the money to do it."

"Unlike the Garretts?"

Nick quirked a brow as he walked toward her with the hamper. "So you do recognize the place."

"Any architect or designer would." She glanced at him out of the corner of her eye. "I also know how you got the Garrett family to sell it to you."

"I didn't force the sale," he said coldly. "And I paid full market value. The Garretts came out of the deal with enough cash to finance a merger that was very important to the corporation at the time."

"Uh-huh."

Nick started up the front steps. "Don't kid yourself. Old Randolph Garrett, Senior, put out the word that he was forced to sell in order to rescue young Randy from my clutches. But the truth was, Garrett was secretly thrilled to have an excuse to get rid of the place. The property descended through his side of the family. He had the responsibility for maintaining it. It was a steady drain on his finances at a time when he couldn't afford it."

"I see. You must have been one of the few people in the entire city-state who was willing and able to buy it. Most folks couldn't afford the upkeep, let alone a major remodel."

"I can afford both." Nick set down the hamper to activate the old jelly-ice lock on the door. "And I want the remodeling done right."

"I'm surprised the Historical Preservation Society didn't try to get their hands on the house. I would have thought they'd have paid big bucks for John Jeremy Garrett's personal estate."

"I beat them to it." Nick opened the door to reveal a spacious circular hall tiled in pale green rainstone. "And for the record, from now on, it's the new Chastain estate."

No one could have missed the naked possessiveness in his voice, Zinnia thought. She studied the spacious graceful rooms as she followed him through the empty mansion.

"It's not exactly your style, Nick."

"Don't worry, by the time I gild the columns with some fake gold paint, put down lots of red and black carpeting, cover the windows with red velvet drapes and hang a lot of scarlet and gold wallpaper, it will look like home."

"You wouldn't."

Nick turned to glance at her over his shoulder. He said nothing but his eyes gleamed.

Zinnia put up her hands, palms out. "Okay, okay, it was a joke. You shouldn't tease a professional interior designer that way."

"I thought you liked red." His gaze traveled slowly down her body, taking in the gauzy, ankle-length, sunrise-red dress she wore. "You sure look good in it."

She felt herself grow very warm beneath his blatantly sexy gaze. "It's my trademark. And it's okay for clothes. But a whole house done in red would look like a bordello or a, uh—"

"Casino?" he suggested.

"Well, yes. And you distinctly told me that you didn't want your future bride to live in a casino."

"No," he said. "I don't." He set the hamper down on the floor. "As you can see, I really do need an interior designer. Someone who knows the Neo-Early Exploration Period style. I want the place restored properly. Like one of those places you see in *Architectural Synergy* magazine. How about it?"

She surveyed the vast, empty, great room in which they stood. "Are you offering me the job for real?"

"Why not?" Nick walked to the bank of windows that overlooked the city. He kept his back to Zinnia as he gazed into the late evening sun that was sinking swiftly into the bay. "Nothing says we can't continue on with our partnership after we finish this business with the journal."

"I'll think about it."

"You do that."

He was serious, she thought. "This house is very important to you, isn't it?"

"It's my future," he said simply.

"What about your past?"

"My past is the casino. I'm going to sell it."

That startled her. "Why?"

"It's part of my plan."

"Your plan to buy respectability, you mean?"

"I told you, I only got into the gambling business because it was a way to make a lot of money." Nick turned slowly around to face her. "I've invested the profits in a variety of places during the past three years. Stocks and bonds. Western Islands shipping. I've provided some venture capital for some new businesses that have gone big. The usual."

"All very respectable."

His smile held cold satisfaction. "Exactly. My children will have all the benefits of respectability. They won't have to live with gossip and sly glances. My daughters will never face humiliation at society's hands. My sons won't know what it is to have the doors of opportunity closed in their faces simply because they can't claim a socially acceptable family."

"You mean they won't have to struggle the way you did?" she asked softly.

His eyes were fierce with unshakable determination. "I will make certain that they don't have to go through what I did to achieve success. My family will have every advantage I can give them."

"I see." She was suddenly aware of a slight chill in the room. She folded her arms beneath her breasts. "Tell me, what's the rest of this grand plan? How do you go about buying respectability?"

"Simple. You purchase a membership in the Founders' Club and attend its annual charity ball." He broke off. A look of speculation appeared in his gaze. "Which just happens to take place in a few days."

"Yes, I know. Go on. What else do you do to get respectable?"

He shrugged. "You give big bucks to the New Seattle Art Museum and to the Theater Guild. You contribute to the right political campaigns. You buy a house like this one and you pay someone who knows what she's doing to restore it."

"And you marry into the right family," Zinnia concluded.

"That's about it. Like I said, all you need is money and a plan. I've got both."

She looked into his eyes for a long time. He did not look away. "I wish you luck," she said, meaning every word.

"Luck has nothing to do with it."

"Of course." She managed a bright professional smile. "Well, this is supposed to be a business dinner, so let's do some business, partner. I wanted to ask you how you knew for certain that the journal Polly and Omar sold you was a fraud."

He eyed her thoughtfully for a long moment. "I'll show you after we eat." He walked to the picnic hamper and opened it.

She watched curiously as he spread a blanket on the

169

floor and began to unpack a variety of tempting packages. He arranged a pâté, a cold pasta salad, tiny sandwiches, fruit, and a tart on top of the hamper.

"I'm impressed." She walked to the blanket and sat down, curling her legs beneath her gauzy dress. "Did you make all this?"

"What do you think?" Nick lit the two jelly-ice candles that he had taken from the hamper.

Zinnia sampled a tiny sandwich and grinned. "I think you hired an excellent chef."

"The best. Rathbone. Formerly of the Founders' Club. He supervises the dining rooms at the Palace."

"Lucky you."

Nick looked up from pouring the wine. "I keep telling you, luck is not a factor."

"Spoken like a true matrix."

Zinnia was amazed at how quickly the next hour slipped past. By the time she and Nick had polished off the outrageously expensive bottle of blue wine and eaten the last bit of the flaky pear-berry pastry, night had descended. The twin moons, Yakima and Chelan, rose above the horizon and cast a golden glow over the bay. The light of the two jelly-ice candles flickered warmly.

"Now I'll show you how I knew the journal was a fraud." Nick pulled another package out of the hamper.

Zinnia recognized it. "That's the fake that Polly and Omar sold to you."

"Yes." He unwrapped the brown paper and put the volume down on the blanket. Then he reached back into the hamper and removed a faded envelope.

"What's that?"

"The letter my father wrote to my mother the night before the Third Expedition left for uncharted territory."

She stared at him with mingled disbelief and excitement. "You've got a letter?"

"Yes. After Andy died I went through his old storeroom and found it. My mother must have hidden it there all those years ago before she left for Serendipity. I think she may have sensed that it was valuable. It refers to the fact that the expedition was preparing to leave on schedule. My father was looking forward to it. He was focused on the future. He was not talking of suicide."

"My God, Nick. No wonder you've been so sure that the expedition actually took place. Why didn't you tell anyone?"

He looked up, his eyes very cold. "Because someone went to a hell of a lot of trouble to make it appear that it didn't take place. Until I know why, I'm not going to reveal the existence of this letter. It's the only hard evidence I've got."

She watched as Nick carefully, reverently unfolded the letter. It occurred to her that the handwritten note was probably the only link he had with his mother and father. Another wave of empathy went through her.

"I take it you did a handwriting analysis?" she asked, struggling to sound businesslike. Nick would not appreciate it if she started crying, she thought.

"Yes. With the aid of my talent. I have some control over it when I use it in short bursts." He opened the journal and placed it next to the letter. "Take a look."

She peered at the bold firm handwriting on the first page of the journal and then glanced at the letter. "It looks identical to me."

"It's a very good forgery. But give me a prism and then take another look."

Zinnia hesitated, remembering the strong sense of intimacy she experienced whenever she held the focus for him. But she'd heard that one of the side effects of focusing with a strong talent was that a prism could observe a small portion of what the talent sensed. She was just curious enough now to risk the connection.

"All right." She braced herself.

She didn't have long to wait. Waves of power surged toward the prism she projected onto the metaphysical plane. They crashed through the glittering lens and emerged as controlled energy on the other side.

A feeling of intense intimacy swept through her. But it did not jolt her this time. It was becoming familiar, she thought. Comfortable. Right.

Not good.

"Ready?" Nick watched her face.

"Sure. Go ahead. Show me." It annoyed her that he seemed oblivious to the personal nature of their link. Perhaps he felt nothing.

"Look at the handwriting on the letter," Nick instructed.

She looked down at the note. The candlelight created intricate patterns of shadows as it illuminated the single sheet of paper.

My dearest Sally:

I'm writing this from Serendipity, our jumping-off point. The six of us leave at dawn. This is the last time I'll have a means of sending a letter until we return in three months. It's late but I can't sleep. I should be going over the details of our plans but I'm thinking of you, instead. I'll miss your laughter and your warmth and all that we have found together. You cannot know how important you are to me. When I'm with you, I am no longer alone. And now that I know you're carrying my baby, I feel as if I've finally found my future.

I wish you had not waited until the morning I left Port LaConner to tell me that you were pregnant. If you had let me know earlier we could have been married before this expedition. But in the end, it won't matter. I'll be back in three months and then we'll make it official.

You gave me more than you will ever know when you agreed to marry me. Spend the next three months planning the wedding. This will be my last expedition. When I return I want to settle down in the islands with my new family. In the meantime, know that you are my true love. I will keep you in my heart forever.

> *All my love,*
> *Bart*

P.S.: Why do I get the feeling it will be a boy?

Zinnia blinked back tears.

"See the pattern of the words?" Nick said. "The shapes of the letters?"

She forced herself to concentrate on the handwriting, not the poignant message of love. There was, indeed, a pattern to the words. A kind of internal rhythm that seemed quite clear now that she viewed it with the assistance of a matrix-talent. Each letter was a tiny work of art with unique nuances and characteristics. She would never have detected the subtle differences with normal vision.

"Yes," she whispered. "I see what you mean."

"Now look at the journal."

She read a few sentences.

. . . I have instructed Sanderford to keep his eye on the jelly-ice fuel capsules but I no longer trust him. He's careless. I'm starting to wonder if he's got a drug problem . . .

"See the differences?" Nick asked.

Zinnia studied the words more closely. "Yes. There's a slight alteration in the rhythm or something."

173

"The design is wrong. It's out of sync. Unbalanced. The connections aren't right."

She could not see all those fine distinctions, but she did not doubt that Nick did. "The differences could be explained by the fact that this is a journal entry, not a personal letter."

Nick gave a decisive shake of his head. "The individual letters would still look the same. Handwriting doesn't change."

"No." She took a closer look. The seepage of matrix-talent that she picked up through the focus link was sufficient to allow her to see the tiny differences between the writing in the journal and that in the letter. "Something about the loops is off and the angle of the slant is not quite the same."

"Exactly." Without warning, Nick cut off the flow of talent. "Without a prism to help me focus, it took me a lot longer to be certain that I was looking at a forgery. But there's no doubt about it."

"How many entries are there in the journal?"

"Only eight. All of them are dated before the expedition was supposed to leave Serendipity. Each is shorter than the last. The tone of each one is increasingly paranoid and depressed. In the last entry the writer says that he can't go on much longer. He just wants to walk off into the jungle and be absorbed by what he calls the great green matrix."

"In other words, you're supposed to believe that your father really did commit suicide before the expedition took place."

"Yes."

Nick had shut down his formidable psychic power, but the sensation of intimacy did not vanish. It pulsed across Zinnia's nerve endings, insistent and compelling. She uncurled her legs and restlessly shifted position on the blanket.

"Someone went to a great deal of effort to deceive you with that fake journal," she said.

"And expense," Nick added. He closed the volume and rewrapped it. "This kind of craftsmanship doesn't come cheap."

"How much would an expert forger charge for something that detailed?"

His smile was chilling. "Probably about as much as I paid for it. Fifty grand."

Zinnia's heart twisted as she watched the care with which he refolded his father's letter. Once more she tried to beat back the empathy that threatened to swamp her common sense.

"Well, if you needed any further proof that I'm innocent, you've got it," she said briskly. "I couldn't possibly afford fifty grand for a fake journal."

"I don't need any more proof of your innocence."

"Gee, thanks." Why didn't the intense feeling of intimacy fade? It was messing up the synergistic balance of her entire nervous system. "Where does that leave us?"

Nick's eyes were rare exotic gems in the candlelight. "Here. Together."

On the other hand, why was she trying to fight this incredible attraction, Zinnia wondered. She had waited a long time for passion.

"Are you going to kiss me again?" she asked, deeply curious.

"I want to make love to you."

She smiled. "That's okay, too."

Chapter
14

* * * * * * * * * *

The hunger inside him threatened to explode. He fought it, willing his self-control to win the battle. It worried him that the sensation of touching and being touched in some other dimension had not faded when the focus link was severed. The intimacy of the connection was disturbing enough as it was. He did not know what to make of the fact that tonight the feelings continued even after the psychic joining ended.

He had to be careful, Nick thought. He wanted her, but when he had sex with her he could not sacrifice the part of him that governed his self-control.

On the positive side, if there was one thing he was good at, it was control. He could handle this.

He touched the curve of her hair and smiled slowly. "We're going to be good together."

"I certainly hope so." She drew up her knees and wrapped her arms around them. "I've got certain expectations, you understand."

"Expectations?"

Her eyes glowed with warmth and a shy amusement that caught him by surprise.

"I told you, I've read every psychic vampire romance novel that Orchid Adams has ever written."

Nick stared at her. "Five hells."

"Not that I want to put any pressure on you, of course."

Nick felt a very weird sensation rise inside him. It was big, powerful, all-consuming. He did not recognize it until he nearly choked on it.

And then the laughter roared forth. It cascaded out of him like a very strong orgasm.

He could not shut it down. It squeezed him as if he were a sponge, causing him to double over. He howled until he was breathless.

Through it all, he was aware of Zinnia studying him with deep interest.

Eventually he managed to catch his breath. When the unfamiliar laughter finally exhausted itself, he sprawled on his back on the blanket.

"You are so damn unpredictable," he said.

She hugged her knees. "Is that a bad thing?"

"I don't know. I used to think so, but now I'm not so sure." He reached for her and pulled her down across his chest. The skirts of her sunrise-red dress flowed around him.

The last of his laughter was consumed by the flashfire of need that swept through him. Something else evaporated with it. Something important. He worried briefly that it was the sense of control that he had told himself he must maintain at all costs. But for some obscure reason it no longer seemed quite so important.

He cradled her head between his hands and kissed her with the same fierce energy that he had channeled into his psychic talent moments earlier.

She responded with a sweet passion that took his

breath. Excitement slammed through the matrix, igniting all of his senses.

There was no time for the slow erotic loveplay that he had fantasized about all day.

"I need to be inside you," he said against her soft mouth.

"That sounds . . . interesting." She fumbled with the fastenings of his shirt.

He groaned when he felt her fingers on his bare chest. "Zinnia."

"You feel so good." She dipped her head and brushed her mouth across his bare skin.

He smiled when he saw that her hands were trembling. He buried his face in her hair. "You smell good."

She shifted slightly. The soft firm weight of her thigh settled against his erection. He could tell it was an unintentional move. She had no idea of the impact it had on him.

He thought he would lose it all then, but he managed to hold himself together. He opened the front of her dress and found her breasts. Her nipples budded, firm and proud, against his palms. He heard her sharp intake of breath and a soft half-strangled cry. Her fingers suddenly sank deep into his shoulders. Although they were linked, he could have sworn that iceworks lit up the metaphysical plane.

He surged upward and tumbled her gently onto her back.

"Nick."

His hands shook as he pushed the skirts of her dress up to her waist. He reached between her thighs and discovered that her panties were already damp. He managed to drag the scrap of delicate fabric down her long legs and free of her ankles. She went very still.

He smiled and bent his head to kiss her throat. She sighed and seemed to relax against him.

He was fascinated to discover that her skin felt as soft as it looked in the golden glow of the candles. The dark triangle of curls glittered with moisture. The scent of her body clouded his mind.

He quickly unbuckled his pants and shoved them downward until he could kick them aside.

Zinnia's eyes widened at the sight of his aroused body. "I didn't realize—"

"Touch me," he whispered. He caught her hand and moved it to his rigid penis.

"So strong," she breathed. Hesitantly she encircled him with her fingers. "Hard and strong."

He closed his eyes, set his teeth, and held on to the last shreds of his control with sheer willpower. When she moved her palm, tightening her grasp, he shuddered.

"Don't," he managed. His voice was ragged. "I won't last another second if you do that again."

She released him quickly. "Are you all right?"

He opened his eyes partway and saw that she was genuinely concerned. "Are you kidding? I'm about to disintegrate into a million pieces. I'd rather do it inside you than on the damn blanket."

"Oh."

"That's all you can say? Oh?"

She looked up at him with an uncertainty that he did not understand. Then she smiled tremulously. "What would you like me to say?"

"How about, please make love to me?"

She wrapped her arms around his neck. "Please make love to me, Nick."

"That's better. Much better." He spread her legs widely apart and settled himself between them.

When he glanced down he saw the pink wet folds waiting for him. He stroked the tight swollen nub nestled in the damp curls and felt the shiver that went through her. She was as ready as he was for this.

He could not wait any longer. He parted her, positioned himself, and pushed swiftly into the snug clinging heat of her body.

"Nick."

He did not need her sharp shocked exclamation to bring him to a stunning realization of the truth. But by then it was much too late. He was lodged tightly inside her.

"Why didn't you tell me?" His voice was little more than a hoarse croak.

"The subject did not come up," she said through gritted teeth. "Unlike something else around here." She drew a deep breath. A shiver went through her. "I'll be fine. Just give me a minute."

He did not dare to move. He could feel the perspiration on his back. His shoulders were slick with it. "Damn it, you should have told me."

"Really? Did you make a big announcement to all parties concerned on the occasion of your first time?"

He groaned. "If you make me laugh again, we'll both regret it."

"I think I'm okay now."

"You're sure?"

"I'm sure. Sort of. What about you?"

"Me? I'm feeling a bit faint," he muttered. "I may swoon before this is over."

"The psychic vampire heroes in Orchid Adams's novels never collapse in a faint at the crucial moment."

"Sure, go ahead. Put a little more pressure on me." He began to move carefully within her.

She was still very tight but her body was rapidly adjusting to his. Nick allowed himself to breathe again. He reached down with one hand and trapped the small nub between his thumb and forefinger. He tugged gently.

"Oh, my God." Zinnia clutched at him. Her legs

tightened with unmistakable urgency. "Oh, yes. Nick. Oh, yes, please. *Nick.*"

Somehow he found the strength to hold back until he felt the first stirrings of her impending climax. The delicate tremors reached him on the physical plane first, and without conscious thought he sought their echo in the metaphysical realm. He sent out a probe of talent, searching for her, thirsting for her.

And she was there, waiting for him. She touched him with her psychic energy even as she clung to him there on the floor. The prism appeared, clear and dazzling.

He sent energy crashing through the brilliant lens created by Zinnia's mind even as he thrust deeply into her body. He felt her convulse beneath him and he knew he was lost.

So why did he feel as if he had just been found, he wondered as he hurtled headlong into his climax.

Zinnia opened her eyes a long while later. She gazed up at the dark coved ceiling. Nick had his arm around her, cradling her against his side. Moonlight streamed through the undraped windows. Yakima's and Chelan's twin beams accented the sleek planes and angles of Nick's hard lean body and cast his forbidding features into deep shadow.

She felt good, she realized. Lighthearted. Full of hope. Happy. The aftereffects of lovemaking, she warned herself. They wouldn't last. And neither would this strange unsettling sense of an intimate connection to the man beside her. Surely it would vanish now that both the focus and sexual links had been broken.

Gradually she became aware of the deep silence in the great room. Nick had said nothing since he had shuddered and muttered something unintelligible in the throes of his release. In all fairness, she thought, she had not been exactly chatty, herself, there at the end. She had been consumed by the overwhelming experience of lovemaking.

She tried to think of a conversational gambit that would be suitable for a moment like this.

"Does it strike you that this floor is getting hard?" she asked.

"Why?"

"Probably because it's made out of rainstone. The blanket doesn't offer much in the way of cushioning."

Nick turned his head. His eyes were stark in the flickering shadows. "I wasn't talking about the floor."

"In that case, I've lost the thread of the conversation."

"Why did you wait this long to have an affair?"

She felt her cheeks grow warm. "I thought it was only women who were supposed to ask lots of unnecessary questions at times like this."

"It's not an unnecessary question," he said very evenly.

"No one particular reason. Just a lot of little ones. Are you sure you really want to hear them?"

"Yes. Every single one of them."

"I see." A flicker of wariness made her suddenly cautious. "Well, timing was part of it, I suppose. Four years ago I was involved with a man. His name was Sterling Dean. Vice-president in my family's company. All-around great kisser."

"Great kisser?"

She cleared her throat. "Yes, well, we had a lot in common. We talked about marriage." She paused. "But things didn't work out."

"Because you were declared unmatchable by the marriage agency?"

"That kind of verdict tends to make a man think twice," she said. "And it gave me a lot to think about, too. After all, being unmatchable works both ways. If

I'm not a good match for someone else, it means no one is a good match for me."

He was silent for a moment. "I see what you mean."

"At any rate, shortly after that, my parents were lost at sea. Spring Industries went into bankruptcy. Then I was very busy getting my own business up and running and making sure Leo could stay in school. I was just starting to get on top of things when the Eaton scandal hit."

"And there went your business."

"It fell off drastically and I've been devoting myself to rebuilding it ever since. So, what with one thing and another, I was just too busy to worry about my personal life."

There was more to it than that, she thought, a lot more, but she did not know how to put it into words. It was just beginning to dawn on her that her decision to wait had been influenced to some extent by the nature of her psychic energy. She might never know for certain but she had a suspicion that some part of her had been holding out for the right man, at least the right man on the metaphysical plane.

It was a scary thought because whatever else he was, Nick was not the right man.

"Too busy." He did not sound convinced. There was a distinctly brooding quality in the depths of his voice.

"You seem to be awfully concerned about this." She propped herself up on one elbow. "Do you always grill your dates after the big event?"

"No." His eyes glittered beneath his long black lashes. "I just want to know why you waited, that's all."

She swept her hand out in a wide all-encompassing gesture. "What can I say? Life happened. Sex didn't."

"The Eaton scandal," he said quietly.

"What about it?"

"I always knew there was something about the story in the tabloids that didn't ring true."

"No offense, Nick, but it doesn't take a matrix-talent to figure out that there's something about most of the stories in the tabloids that doesn't ring true."

"Why me?"

She knew what he meant. She looked out the window into the moonlight. "Things felt right tonight." That was truer than he would ever know.

He still did not appear content with her answer. But he picked up her hand, turned it, and kissed the inside of her wrist. His lips were warm on her skin. "I'm glad." His eyes burned beneath the fringe of his lashes.

She could not think of anything to say.

Nick released her hand to glance at his watch. "It's nearly midnight."

"The night is young for a casino owner."

"But not for a lady who has to go to work in the morning. I'd better get you home."

She did not need to be a high-class talent to feel him trying to pull back from the invisible brink. Now that sexual desire had been sated, his super-cautious matrix-instincts were coming to the fore. He was retreating into that more detached, remote sphere where he did not have to cope with the confusion of strong emotions.

Two could play that game.

She summoned up what she hoped was a breezy smile. "You're right. It's late." She started to rebutton her dress. "Speaking of business, any leads on Polly and Omar?"

"No." He gave her an assessing glance as he fastened his shirt. "My people will find them eventually, but I doubt we'll learn anything when we do."

"Why do you say that?"

"The forgery of the journal was a sophisticated,

expensive operation. Feather hasn't turned up anything to indicate that either Polly or Omar had the kind of money or contacts it takes to plan such a scam, let alone finance it." Nick ran his fingers through his hair, shoving it straight back from his forehead. "I'm much more interested in getting hold of the forger."

"No word yet from that man you called?"

"Stonebraker? No." Nick got to his feet and pulled on his pants. "But Rafe works nights. With luck he'll turn up a name by morning."

She watched as he buckled his belt, fascinated by his powerful graceful hands. There was something quintessentially male about the way he went about the simple routine task. Every movement was efficient, economical, sure.

He saw her looking at him and raised his brows. "Something wrong?"

"No." She started to get to her feet and discovered that her legs were not quite steady. She could feel twinges in small muscles which until now had been unaccustomed to serious exercise.

"Are you all right?" Nick caught her arm.

"Yes, of course." She bent down to refold the blanket so that she would not have to meet his eyes. "Just a little stiff."

"The damn floor," he muttered. "Next time we'll use a bed."

She let a couple of heartbeats go by. Then she straightened and turned slowly to face him. "Next time?"

Uncertainty flashed briefly in his eyes. It vanished almost instantly, but Zinnia was curiously reassured by the glimpse of vulnerability.

"You said you weren't into one-night stands," he reminded her gruffly.

"That's true." She felt a little lighter now, more buoyant.

"Neither am I." He picked up the hamper. "And as long as we're working on Fenwick's murder together, I figure we'll be spending a lot of time in each other's company. We're both single. It's obvious there's a physical attraction between us. Why fight it?"

She widened her eyes. "Golly. Are all matrix-talents this romantic when they propose an affair?"

He stopped and turned so quickly to pin her with his intent gaze that she nearly collided with him.

"Are you laughing at me?" he asked.

She smiled. "Yes. If you aren't careful you'll ruin the image of mythical psychic vampire lovers everywhere. You've been doing swell up until this point. Candlelight picnic. View of the city. Wine. Great sex. Don't mess it up now."

"Was it?"

"Was it what?"

"Great sex?"

"Trust me, you met all of my expectations, and as I told you at the start, they were extremely high due to my devoted study of Orchid Adams's novels," she said cheerfully.

He touched her cheek. "You're sure?"

"Well, I'll admit I'm not in a position to make comparisons."

"Keep it that way." He went down on one knee to repack the hamper.

She gave him a few seconds. When he did not say anything more, she cleared her throat meaningfully, planted her hands on her hips, and tapped her toe. "So how was it for you, Mr. Chastain?"

"What?" He looked up, clearly startled.

"You heard me."

"Couldn't you tell?" His eyes darkened to the color of green that was at the heart of the jungle. He got to his feet and brushed his mouth across hers. "I'm still in shock."

"Okay." She mulled that over for a few seconds. "Shock is good. I think."

"Zinnia—"

"You're right," she said brightly, "it really is getting late." She swung around and led the way back through the darkened circular hall.

Nick followed with the hamper. "Zinnia, I'm not good with this kind of thing."

"You know, you really do have an incredible house here." She threw open the front door with a flourish and stepped out onto the colonnaded portico. "It will take a lot of work, but when it's finished—"

"Shut the door," Nick ordered sharply. He was gazing past her into the gardens. "Hurry."

But it was too late. Blinding light flashed in the nearby bushes.

Zinnia blinked. "What in the world?"

"A camera. Damned photographer must have followed us. Wait here." Nick dropped the hamper. He moved so quickly through the doorway that he seemed to flow, rather than run.

"What are you going to do?" Zinnia called after him.

"I'm going to get that film. I'll be back in a few minutes. Stay inside."

"But, Nick, you can't just grab a photographer and take his film," she shouted. "He'll sue or something."

Nick ignored her. He went down the steps and vanished almost instantly into the darkness.

"Just like a PV." Zinnia propped herself against the doorjamb and folded her arms. "One night of good sex and then he disappears." Or maybe it was just like a matrix, she corrected silently.

There was a violent commotion from the vicinity of the gardens where she had seen the flash. She realized that the photographer was running through the foliage back toward the front gates. There was no sign of Nick.

A moment later she saw a figure dart out of the trees that lined the drive. There was just enough moonlight to see the array of camera accoutrements flapping around his torso as he dashed toward the entrance of the estate.

Still no sign of Nick.

Zinnia wondered if he'd gone the wrong way. He would not be pleased when he realized he had missed the intruder, she thought. But it would be better for all concerned if he failed to stop the photographer.

The running man vanished around the bend in the drive. Zinnia listened for the sound of a distant car engine signaling that the intruder had made his getaway. She heard nothing.

Another minute ticked past. Two. Three.

She did not care for the growing silence.

"Nick?"

More silence.

"Where are you?" She unfolded her arms and went down the front steps. "Nick, answer me."

A shadow detached itself from one of the fern-trees at the edge of the courtyard and came toward her.

"I got the film," Nick said.

She frowned. "I do hope you didn't do anything violent to that man. He could cause you a great deal of trouble."

"I don't think he'll be a problem." Moonlight gleamed on Nick's hair as he walked toward her. "He turned over the film without a single argument."

Zinnia sighed. "You can't just go around intimidating people, Nick. Not if you want to be respectable."

His teeth flashed briefly in the shadows. "Shows how much you know."

"What do you mean, there's a photo of me in today's issue of *Synsation?*" Zinnia slammed the door of Psynergy, Inc. and hurried toward the front desk. "That's impossible."

"It's definitely you, Zin." Byron wore an expression of deep awe as he gazed at the photo on the cover of the tabloid. "A whole new you, though. What happened? Did you and Chastain get into a wrestling match or something?"

Clementine stormed out of her office to peer over his shoulder. "Or something." She raised grim worried eyes to Zinnia's face. "So much for my good advice. Don't know why I bother."

Zinnia donned a cloak of aloof dignity. "I told you, Mr. Chastain hired me to do the interiors of the old Garrett estate."

Clementine's steel rings flashed as she pointed at the photo. "Looks to me like he was doing you."

"Don't be crude." Zinnia forgot about her dignity. She snatched up the tabloid and stared at the front-page photo. "Oh, dear."

The picture was excruciatingly clear. It showed her standing in the doorway of the mansion. Nick was directly behind her. She was annoyed to see that in the shot he appeared as darkly enigmatic, and mysterious as always.

Unfortunately, she looked like a woman who had just made wild uninhibited love on the floor. Her sunrise-hued dress was buttoned askew, revealing enough cleavage to send Aunt Wilhelmina into hysterics. Her hair was tousled around her face and her expression could only be described as sultry. The caption under the photo said it all.

Does local casino owner Nick Chastain have designs on his new interior designer, the Scarlet Lady?

Zinnia glanced at the photo credit and saw that the photographer's name was Cedric Dexter. "Nick said he got the film out of the man's camera."

"Photographers who work for *Synsation* are real resourceful," Byron said, not without a note of sympathy. "My guess is this one had two cameras with him. Chastain probably never even saw the second one."

"Nick is not going to be pleased," Zinnia said. "I think his plan to become respectable has just suffered another setback."

Nick tossed the copy of *Synsation* into the wastebasket. He looked at Feather. "Get the editor of that rag on the phone."

"Sure, boss." Feather took a step back toward the door. "Speaking of phone calls, I got a message for you from someone named Stonebraker. He called a few minutes ago, just before you walked in the door."

Anticipation replaced seething irritation. "What's the message?"

"He said to give you a name and an address." Feather removed a notepad from his pocket. "Alfred Wilkes. At two-twenty-three West Old Vashon Street."

Nick hesitated, torn between the urge to deal with the editor of *Synsation* and the arguably more important issue of talking to the master forger.

"Hold the call to the editor." He got to his feet. "He'll keep. I'll take care of him later."

"Right, boss." Feather paused. "You going out to this address?"

"Yes." Nick walked around the edge of his desk and grabbed his jacket off the chair where he had tossed it a few minutes earlier. "I don't know when I'll be back. This could take a while."

Feather eyed him thoughtfully. "Want backup?"

"No, not this time." Nick hooked the jacket over his shoulder and led the way out of the inner office.

The secret panel slid shut. With Feather at his heels, he crossed the gilded chamber and opened the door.

Voices rose in the hall.

"I'm sorry, Sir, Mr. Chastain is busy at the moment. I'll be glad to schedule an appointment."

A young man dressed in a sweater and khaki trousers leaned across the reception desk. His long hair was tied back with a thong. The muscles of his shoulders were bunched with rigid aggressive tension.

"You tell Chastain that if he doesn't see me right now I'll go downstairs to the casino and raise the kind of hell that will bring the cops. You hear me?"

"Sir, I'm afraid I'm going to have to ask security to escort you off the premises," the receptionist said. He nodded to one of the guards. "Immediately."

"I'm not leaving until I see Chastain."

Nick started forward. "What's going on here?"

"I'm sorry, sir." The receptionist turned toward him. "Nothing we can't handle."

The young man's head came up sharply. "Chastain. Goddamnit, who the hell do you think you are to treat my sister as if she were your latest mistress?"

"You must be Leo."

"You got that much right." Leo bounded up onto the reception desk, leaped to the floor on the far side, and launched himself at Nick.

Chapter
15

* * * * * * * * * *

Out of the corner of his eye, Nick saw Feather move to intercept the charging Leo. The guard rounded the desk. The receptionist got to his feet and started to press a concealed button that would bring more assistance.

It all happened in less than two seconds, but to Nick's senses, sharpened by his matrix-talent instincts, every action was a clear distinct event in the total matrix. He sorted it all out and made his decision.

"No," he said softly.

With the exception of Leo, everyone in the hall froze as if they had been trapped in a deposit of jelly-ice.

Leo crashed into Nick, swinging his fist wildly. The force of the impact sent both of them to the thickly carpeted floor.

"Damn you." Leo scrambled awkwardly to his feet. Breathing heavily, he stood looking down at Nick. His face was twisted with rage. His fists were clenched at his side. "I won't let you use her, you bastard. She's taken enough bat-snake shit from guys like you."

Nick rose on one elbow and absently touched the edge of his mouth. When he glanced at his fingers he saw blood. He looked up at Leo.

"You want to talk about this in private?" he asked. "Or would you rather have all these nice people listen to us discuss your sister and her reputation?"

Leo scowled. He glanced hurriedly around and saw the watchful faces of Feather, the guards, and the receptionist. He flushed and turned back to Nick. "Why don't you sic your goons on me?"

"I don't employ goons." Nick got slowly to his feet, careful to keep a pragmatic distance between Leo and himself. "These folks are all highly skilled professionals."

"Yeah, right." Leo looked a little uncertain now. Common sense had obviously started to reassert itself. It was clear that he was no longer sure how to proceed. "What the hell do you think you're doing with my sister?"

Good question, Nick thought. He wished he knew the answer. All he could be sure of this morning was that he did not want to have to do without her. At least not yet. Maybe not for a long time.

The knowledge made him more than uneasy. It worried him as nothing else had for a long time. Last night, after he had surfaced from the pool of desire in which he had been submerged, he had finally recognized the nature of the danger in which he found himself.

Where Zinnia was concerned, he was deep into a new uncharted matrix. He had to be careful. He had to remain in control.

"Let's go into my office." He did not glance back as he turned and led the way into the gilded chamber.

Behind him he felt Leo hesitate and then follow. Feather shifted slightly. Nick shook his head.

"It's okay. I don't think he's going to hit me again. Are you, Leo?"

"Depends," Leo muttered. He walked through the door and gazed around the red, black, and gilded chamber with an expression of acute amazement. "Sheesh. I guess it's sort of obvious that you and Zinnia don't have a lot in common when it comes to taste." He glared at Nick. "Or anything else for that matter."

"Your sister is an adult." Nick pressed the hidden switch to open the secret panel. "Why don't you let her make her own decisions?"

"Most of the time Zinnia is good at figuring out people." Leo stepped warily into the concealed office. "But you're a matrix."

"She told you that?" Nick crossed the room to open the door of the small private bath.

"Yeah."

Nick studied his cut lip in the mirror over the sink. A thin trickle of blood coursed down his chin. He turned on the water. "What does my being a matrix-talent have to do with anything?"

"Are you serious? Being a matrix is bad enough. But on top of everything else, Zinnia's got a soft spot in her heart for matrix-talents." Leo began to pace the room. "She feels sorry for them. Thinks they're delicate and misunderstood. Lord knows why."

Nick looked at his own reflection. The eyes that stared back at him could have belonged to a ghost. Whatever it was he wanted from Zinnia, it was definitely not pity.

He leaned over the sink to rinse the blood from his mouth. "Did your sister tell you that she and I have formed a partnership?"

"Partnership? That's shit synergy and you know it." Leo leveled a finger at him. "Guys like you don't form partnerships, especially not with women like Zinnia. You use people."

Nick finished washing off the blood and snagged a towel. "What do you know about men like me?"

"You're a matrix-talent and you run a casino. That says it all as far as I'm concerned. Look, I came here to tell you to leave my sister alone."

"Why don't you tell her to leave me alone?"

"I tried doing that." Leo grimaced. "But she's made up her mind to find out who killed Morris Fenwick and she believes that you can help her. The problem is that once Zinnia decides to do something, it's almost impossible to talk her out of it. She's got a stubborn streak."

Nick smiled ruefully. "I've noticed."

"You seduced her last night, didn't you? You took her to the old Garrett estate and you took advantage of her."

"I took her to the new Chastain estate, not the old Garrett estate."

"Damn it, I don't care what you call it. I know how you got your hands on that mansion. It will always be the old Garrett estate as far as people in this town are concerned. That's not the point. I'm talking about what you did to my sister."

"Did Zinnia tell you that I seduced her?"

"She won't discuss it." Leo stalked back and forth. "Says it's none of my business. She thinks she can handle you. But I saw today's edition of *Synsation*. And so did just about everyone else in New Seattle. It was pretty obvious what you'd done to her."

"I'm sorry about the picture in the paper." Nick tossed the towel into the hamper. "I tried to prevent it."

"She told me that you took the film out of the photographer's camera, but obviously you didn't. You probably lied to her."

"Why would I do that?"

"Damned if I know." Leo shrugged. "You're a matrix. Who the hell knows how you think? Maybe it suits your purposes to have her name linked with yours. Maybe you've decided it's a way to ensure her cooperation in this so-called partnership. My guess is you need her to help you find that journal you're after."

"Not a bad conspiracy theory." Nick switched off the bathroom light and walked to the desk. "If I didn't know better, I'd think you had a touch of matrix-talent, yourself."

"Look, I want you to leave my sister alone, Chastain. Do you hear me?"

"I hear you." Nick halted in front of the desk and leaned back against the edge. He braced his hands on either side and waited until Leo looked at him. "But you just told me, yourself, that there's no stopping Zinnia once she makes up her mind to do something."

"She was always independent." Leo's mouth tightened into a grim line. "But after our parents died, I swear, she developed a will of iron. She was the one who had to handle the bankruptcy and the bad press that surrounded it. The rest of the family was worse than useless. Aunt Willy and the others fluttered and fretted and carried on as if the loss of the company was more awful than the loss of Mom and Dad."

"I see."

"Most of our relatives went into hiding. They claimed they couldn't handle the humiliation of it all. It was Zinnia who had to deal with the creditors and the reporters and all the wolf-dogs at the door."

"That kind of experience can either make or break a person."

"Yeah, and that wasn't the end of it. A year and a half ago she got dragged into another mess."

"The Eaton scandal."

Leo stopped near a wall and slammed his palm against it. "The Eatons used her to hide the fact that they were involved in a three-way sex thing with a

Founders' Values politician named Daria Gardener. The papers made it look as if Zinnia had been having an affair with Rexford Eaton. It was all a lie."

"The Eatons in a menage-a-trois with Daria Gardener? Interesting." Nick filed that fact away for later analysis. During the last election Gardener had tried to use Chastain's Palace as an example of the sort of business she intended to clean up in New Seattle.

"And now the family has the gall to put pressure on Zinnia to marry money. They don't care about her happiness. All they care about is regaining their position in society."

Nick listened to the old anger spill forth. Leo's rage vibrated in the air. The punch in the jaw a few minutes ago was not just the result of seeing the photo in today's issue of *Synsation.* It was the culmination of several years of a younger brother's simmering frustration over his own inability to protect his sister.

"Leo, I understand what you're telling me. I know you want to take care of Zinnia. So do I. But as you said, she's set on finding Fenwick's killer. That could be a dangerous business."

Leo whirled around. "For God's sake, don't you think I know that?"

"You just admitted that you can't convince her to abandon the project. The next best thing you can do is make sure she's got someone around who can keep an eye on her. Someone who can make sure that she doesn't get in over her head."

Leo shot him a disgusted look. "And that someone is you, I assume?"

"Think about it. As her partner, I'm in the best possible position to look after her. I can control the situation. Take me out of the matrix and you'll have a lot more to worry about than you do already."

There was a short fraught silence while Leo processed that.

"Damn." Leo came to a halt, his hands knotted on

his hips. He looked around as if searching for something to kick. *"Damn."*

Nick assessed the various possibilities and probabilities. He had enough problems without adding the complications of an enraged, suspicious Leo to the list. His best course was to get the younger man on his side and he needed to establish the alliance quickly.

"Someone just gave me the name of the forger who produced the fake copy of my father's journal," Nick said quietly. "I was on my way to talk to him when you showed up. Want to come with me?"

Leo swung around. "Are you serious?"

"Why not? I could use some backup. Just in case."

Twenty minutes later Leo studied a small nondescript house through the Synchron's front window. "How do you know that this Alfred Wilkes is the man who forged the journal?"

"The source of my information on this is highly reliable." Nick opened the door. "You coming?"

"Yeah. I'm coming." Leo looked wary but determined. He got out of the car and stood waiting as Nick came around the front of the vehicle. "The name on the mailbox is Boyd, not Wilkes. You sure this is the right place?"

"I'm sure. Let's go." Nick went up the walk of the house.

"You're going to just knock on the guy's door?" Leo asked, incredulous.

"Got a better suggestion?"

"I guess not. But Wilkes must know who you are. Why would he open the door to you?"

"Maybe because he'll be afraid to not open it." Nick knocked twice and waited.

There was no response.

"See?" Leo looked morosely satisfied. "I told you he wouldn't answer."

"Let's go around back."

"Huh? Wait. What are you going to do?"

Nick did not bother to respond. He walked quickly around the corner, down the narrow space that separated Wilkes's house from its neighbors, and arrived at a small, tidy backyard. Leo followed, looking more uneasy than ever.

He stood watching as Nick studied the door. "Look, if you're thinking of breaking in or something, you can count me out."

"All right. Wait for me in the car." Nick examined the lock as he pulled the thin driving gloves out of his pocket. He was interested to see that the mechanism was much more sophisticated than most jelly-ice house locks.

But it was still child's play for a matrix-talent whose every instinct was to seek out patterns. Even without a prism to focus for him, Nick had no problem with locks. He pulled on the gloves and set to work.

Leo made no move to return to the car. He stood watching, first with sharp concern and acute disapproval and then with gathering curiosity and fascination as Nick made short work of the lock's secrets.

"Where'd you learn how to do that?" he asked as Nick opened the back door.

"I had what some would call a misspent youth."

"Yeah, I'll just bet you did."

Nick stepped into the kitchen. "Feel that?"

"Feel what?" Leo glanced around at the pristine interior. "Something wrong?"

"I don't know yet. Don't touch anything."

"Believe me, I wasn't going to touch a damned thing."

"Good." Nick walked through the house the same way he had once walked through the jungles of the Western Islands, with every sense on full alert. The feeling of wrongness was strong, but there was no outward sign of it.

"Looks like Wilkes is a perfectionist to a fault," Leo

observed in a subdued voice as he glanced into the small bathroom. "A place for everything and everything in its place."

It was true, Nick thought. Each of the rooms in the single-story house was in painstakingly neat condition. He noted absently that there was a pattern to the order of everything from the way in which the books were shelved to the arrangement of the furniture. Taken as a whole, it all formed a coherent matrix that spoke volumes about Alfred Wilkes.

There was no sign of the owner of the house. But the sense of wrongness persisted.

"Maybe he's out grocery shopping," Leo suggested.

"I don't think so." Nick sent out a short surge of talent.

Without a prism he could not hold a focus. But he could use the wild energy long enough to catch some glimpses of the internal workings of the patterns that surrounded him.

For a few seconds the scene around him came into exquisitely sharp focus. The position of every item in the room assumed a deeper significance.

Too neat. Too orderly. The condition of the house was too perfect, even for an obsessive-compulsive perfectionist. Nobody lived in these rooms. This was a forgery of a real house.

Realization came to Nick as his flickering talent dissipated. He looked up. "There's no attic, so there must be a basement. Look for a door."

Leo frowned. "I don't see one."

"It has to be here somewhere."

"Not everyone is into secret rooms that way you are, Chastain."

"Whoever owns this house definitely has another place where he lives and works." Nick walked slowly back through each of the perfect little rooms.

He found no telltale lines in the walls, no secret

doors inside the closets. Together he and Leo pulled up the area rugs, but there was no trapdoor in the floor.

"The rooms where Wilkes really lives have to be here somewhere. Stonebraker is never wrong when it comes to this kind of stuff." Nick reached the kitchen and stood gazing at the various appliances. "Notice anything missing?"

Leo glanced around. "Nope. Looks like a normal kitchen."

"Except for one thing. The icerator isn't humming."

Leo looked at the large white appliance in the far corner. "You're right. Maybe he turned it off."

"Or maybe he uses it for something besides keeping food cold." Nick walked across the kitchen and opened the icerator door.

There were no shelves or containers of food inside. The interior was at room temperature. At the back of the wide appliance was the thin, almost invisible outline of a door.

Nick reached into the icerator and shoved hard against the back panel. It swung open without protest to reveal a flight of steps.

Leo whistled soundlessly. "Five hells. How did you guess?"

"You've seen one hidden entrance, you've seen 'em all. Ready?"

"Yeah. I hate to admit it, but this is getting interesting."

"It does kind of grow on you." Nick stepped into the icerator.

Leo followed quickly.

Halfway down the basement steps, Nick knew that he had found the real house, the place where Alfred Wilkes lived and plied his trade.

There was another complete apartment here, including kitchen, bath, and bedroom. But most of the downstairs suite was devoted to what was obviously a workroom.

And it was a shambles.

Leo whistled softly. "Synergistic hell."

Benches, racks of chemicals, tools, reams of paper, and various instruments were scattered around the room. Drawers stood open, their contents in jumbled disarray. A lamp lay smashed on the floor.

Nick studied the scene closely. Superficially, it bore a striking resemblance to Morris Fenwick's ransacked bookshop. But there was something different about the matrix pattern of this mess. Unlike the other situation, which had struck him as a completely random piece of vandalism, this bore the subtle earmarks of a frantic but deliberate search.

"Someone really tore this place apart." Leo sounded shaken.

"The question is, did he find whatever it was that he was looking for." Nick crouched down to study some papers scattered on the floor.

They were miscellaneous receipts for some expensive office equipment. Forged receipts, he concluded after a closer glance. Probably commissioned by one of Wilkes's clients for use in an embezzlement scheme.

"If Wilkes was a professional forger he must have made a few enemies over the years," Leo noted.

"Yes." Nick rose and began to walk slowly through the disarray, searching for some pattern that would give him a clue to the object of the hasty search.

"I wonder what happened to Wilkes."

"I don't see any signs of a struggle. No blood on the floor. I don't think he was around when this happened."

Leo looked up from an examination of a small printing press. "He probably decided to take a long vacation in one of the other city-states after he finished forging the Chastain journal. If I'd been in his shoes, I'd have gone all the way out to the Western Islands. Maybe a little farther. He must have known that sooner or later you'd come calling."

"Yes." Nick paused beside a desk and surveyed the cluttered surface. "He must have known. He was the cautious, careful type. He'd have left town as soon as he got his money."

A glint of gold on the floor caught his eye as he turned away from the desk. It winked at him from under a table. He bent down and scooped up a small cuff link. An elegantly scrolled letter *C* entwined with a smaller *O* was inscribed on it.

"Find something interesting?" Leo asked from the other side of the room.

"No." Nick dropped the small bit of beautifully wrought gold into his pocket. He would have to pay another call on his uncle to ask him why one of his cuff links had been found in the secret room of a master forger.

"Any idea why someone would have done this?" Leo asked.

Nick glanced at more papers lying on the floor. "I think whoever went through this room was trying to cut off the money trail."

"What do you mean?"

"There's a pattern to the papers that have been pulled out of the drawers and the desk. Most of them relate to routine business matters. Receipts, bills, orders, that kind of thing. Some are real, some are forged."

Leo glanced at the papers. "So?"

"I have a hunch that whoever went through this room was trying to find any records Wilkes might have made regarding the sale of the forged copy of the Chastain journal."

"You mean the man who ordered the fake journal came back because he figured out that Wilkes might have made some incriminating records of the deal?"

"It's one of a couple of possibilities." Nick thought of the cuff link in his pocket. "Money leaves a stain that is just as permanent as blood. Very hard to wash out."

Leo slanted him a sidelong glance. "You sound like you know something about the subject."

"Anyone who runs a large business has to know something about it. A money trail can be dangerous." Nick was suddenly annoyed with himself. "I should have considered that element of the matrix more closely. I've been concentrating on other factors."

"Think the guy who did this found what he was looking for?"

Nick surveyed the room. His attention was caught by the broken lamp. "I don't know. But it's clear he was in a rage when he did it."

"How can you tell?"

Nick gestured toward the smashed lamp. "It didn't fall accidentally. It was hurled against a wall."

"Whoever tore this place apart was real mad, huh?"

"Yes."

"Maybe he was scared, too," Leo offered. "Maybe like the forger, he figured out that you'd come calling."

Zinnia held the phone in one hand and used the other to flip through the latest copy of *Architectural Synergy* as Wilhelmina continued her tirade.

"The entire family is appalled." Wilhelmina's voice rose to a shrill pitch. "Absolutely appalled. How can you shame us like this? What will that nice Duncan Luttrell think when he sees that dreadful picture in that cheap tacky tabloid?"

"You'll be glad to know that Duncan called an hour ago, Aunt Willy. We had a pleasant chat."

"Thank God. Such a nice man. How on St. Helens did you explain that disgusting photo?"

Duncan had been kind, understanding, and very sympathetic. He had, however, offered a gentle warning about the folly of risking one's reputation with a man such as Nick Chastain. Zinnia had resisted the nearly overpowering urge to tell him to mind his own business. She knew that Duncan meant well.

"I told him the same thing I'm telling you. Mr. Chastain has hired me to restore the interiors of his new property. He was showing me the house."

"That isn't his property. It's the old Garrett estate."

Zinnia smiled. "Better start calling it the new Chastain estate."

"Nonsense," Wilhelmina sniffed. "That would imply that it belongs to the legitimate branch of the Chastain family, which it most certainly does not."

"Has anyone told you that you're a snob, Aunt Willy?"

"Someone in the family must maintain standards."

"I know, it's a tough job, but somebody has to do it. Look, I've got to run. I've got an appointment in a few minutes. Goodbye, Aunt Willy."

"I haven't finished, yet—"

Zinnia pretended not to hear Wilhelmina's squawk of protest. She hung up the phone very gently.

She exhaled deeply, tossed the magazine aside, and leaned back in her chair. Morosely she eyed the heavy glass paperweight that sat atop a stack of sketches.

The sketches had been made for a new client who had phoned a few minutes earlier to fire her. The client had been horrified by the photo in *Synsation*.

Business was drying up quickly. She wondered if she ought to accept Nick's offer of a real job. She needed the money and the designer in her was excited at the prospect of redoing the classic interiors of the new Chastain estate.

But the part of her that was falling in love with Nick

found it difficult to accept the fact that another woman would live in the house once it was completed. Better not to pour her heart and soul into that particular project, she decided. Things were dicey enough as it was.

On impulse, she reached for the phone and punched in his private number. Feather answered.

"Yeah?"

"You have a lovely telephone personality, Ms. Feather. So warm and welcoming. Is Mr. Chastain back yet?"

"He just walked in the door with your brother."

"Leo?" Zinnia was so surprised she nearly dropped the phone. "What's he doing there?"

"How the hell should I know?"

"Put him on the phone, please, Feather."

"Mr. Chastain or your brother?"

"My brother," Zinnia snapped.

There was a short pause and then Leo came on the line. He sounded energized. "Hey, Zin, you'll never guess where Nick and I were when you called earlier."

"What's going on, Leo?"

"We went to the forger's house."

Zinnia felt her jaw drop. "The forger who did the fake Chastain journal?"

"Right. Alfred Wilkes. Nick got his name from somebody named Stonebraker and we drove over there. The place had been ransacked. Wilkes was gone but Nick thinks someone searched the place to find any kind of financial paperwork that would have linked him to the forgery."

Zinnia clamped her hand very tightly around the receiver. "Let me get this straight. The two of you went to see this suspected forger together?"

"Yeah."

"Without bothering to tell me your plans?"

There was a short pause before Leo rushed into explanations.

"Things happened kind of fast. Nick said there was no time to lose. It was really weird, Zin. The guy had a secret door built into his icerator." He broke off abruptly. "Hang on, Nick wants to talk to you."

"Good," Zinnia said through set teeth. "Because I have a few things to say to him."

"Hello, Zinnia." Nick's voice was as cool and controlled as always, just as if last night had never happened.

"How dare you go to that forger's house without me?" Anger made her chest suddenly tight. "We're supposed to be partners. That means we consult with each other before we take action. Either we work together on this project or you can forget the whole plan."

"Calm down, Zinnia."

"I will not calm down. I'm furious. Listen to me, Chastain, we had an agreement. You promised to share information with me."

"I had to move quickly. As it was, Wilkes had already skipped. I'll tell you everything over dinner."

"Forget dinner. I've got other things to do tonight." The depths of her rage and anguish stunned her. She realized that both were far more powerful than the situation warranted, but she could not squelch the emotions.

"Zinnia, give me a chance to explain the situation."

"The only thing I want to know is why my brother is involved in this."

"Leo showed up just as I was leaving. He was concerned about the photo in *Synsation.*"

"Oh, no." Zinnia braced her head on her hand and closed her eyes. "He went to see you about it?"

"It was a perfectly normal reaction for a brother. We talked and then I offered to take him with me when I went to Wilkes's house. Which should tell you that I wasn't trying to be secretive. I simply wanted to move fast."

"Would you have bothered to tell me anything about this Alfred Wilkes person if Leo hadn't happened to be there when you decided to talk to him?"

There was an acute silence on the other end of the line.

"I'm getting the impression that you don't trust me." Nick's voice dropped to an exquisitely dangerous whisper.

"You're damned perceptive for a matrix." Zinnia slammed down the phone.

Suddenly it was all too much. She had a vision of pressure building steadily for over four years. Her parents' death, the bankruptcy, the never-ending money problems, the scandals, the marriage-agency verdict declaring her to be unmatchable, her worries about Leo, Aunt Willy's unceasing demands, Morris Fenwick's death.

And now this. The only man she had ever wanted badly enough to have an affair with was acting like the secretive, manipulative matrix-talent that he was.

It was just too much.

She put her head down on her arms and burst into tears.

Chapter

16

* * * * * * * * * *

She had overreacted, Zinnia told herself later that evening while she held the focus for an accountant. It was all right. Perfectly understandable. There was no need to chastise herself for the emotional outburst and the tears. She had been temporarily overcome by events. That sort of thing happened. One could not always control one's emotions, although certain people seemed to think they could do just that.

The important thing was that it would not happen again.

She had herself together now and she would not allow Nick Chastain to destroy her composure so thoroughly a second time. Sleeping with him had obviously been a grave mistake, but she prided herself on learning from her mistakes.

She forced herself to concentrate on the job at hand. Not that it took a great deal of attention. She estimated Martin Quintana to be approximately a class-three matrix. He had been retained by a mid-sized manufacturing corporation to find evidence on a suspected embezzler. To that end he had been poring over voluminous computer printouts of various financial transactions all evening, searching for patterns.

He was humming to himself. In typical matrix fashion he was lost in a design that only he could fully appreciate. Zinnia could glimpse some of the rhythms that Quintana perceived because she was holding the focus for him. But to her the subtle ebb and flow of the endless tide of numbers on the printouts were mere curiosities, not compelling puzzles. Only a matrix would find them fascinating.

She glanced at her watch. It was getting late. Clementine had warned her that Quintana only wanted to pay for three hours' worth of focus time. They were well into the fourth hour. Zinnia was getting stiff from sitting still for so long. She was also hungry. She had missed dinner again.

She cleared her throat politely. "Mr. Quintana?"

He did not seem to hear her. He was busily entering a string of figures into his computer.

"Excuse me, Mr. Quintana, but your time is up. I'll have to ask you to stop now."

"What's that?" He jerked his head around to peer at her over the rims of his reading glasses. "Oh, yes, Miss Spring. Three hours I believe I said."

"Yes. If you want to contract for more time, I'm sure my boss can arrange it."

"No need. Can't justify charging the expense to my client." He lounged back into his chair with a long sigh. "I've got all the information I need to nail the perpetrator of the fraud. Had that an hour ago. I'm afraid I was merely entertaining myself."

"I understand." Zinnia gave him a sympathetic smile. Clementine got annoyed with her because she frequently allowed her matrix clients to fool around in the pattern for a while after the agreed-upon allotment of time. It was hard to tell a matrix who was having a good time that things had to come to a halt. "I'm glad you got what you wanted from the print-outs."

"Oh, yes, it's all there. I take a great deal of satisfaction in my work at times like this." Quintana riffled through the stack of papers. "Money always leaves a trail, you see. It's almost impossible to hide the traces when one knows where to look."

"I see. Well, I'd better be going." Zinnia rose from her chair and picked up her shoulder bag. "Psynergy, Inc. will bill you within a week."

"Of course. I'll see you to your car." Quintana stood and stretched. "Always a pleasure to work with you, Miss Spring. So few prisms can focus properly for a matrix. And even fewer can do it for long periods of time."

"Thanks. Be sure to tell my boss."

"I most certainly will."

He escorted her out the door and walked with her to where her car was parked at the curb. It was the only vehicle left on the street. Zinnia could barely see it through the fog that had coalesced during the past few hours.

She glanced at the darkened windows and doorways and automatically took a firmer grip on her purse. This was a quiet neighborhood of small businesses and shops that was buttoned up tight after closing time.

"Allow me." Quintana gallantly opened the car door. "The fog has grown worse, hasn't it? Do drive carefully, won't you, Miss Spring?"

"I will." She slid behind the steering bar and smiled up at him. "What about you?"

"I'm going to go back inside and write my final report. Then I'll go home. Goodnight, Miss Spring."

"Goodnight, Mr. Quintana."

Zinnia waited until he closed the door and then she made certain that all the locks were set. She activated the ignition and pulled away from the curb.

She tried to remember what she had at home in the icerator. Extended periods of focus work took a considerable amount of energy. Granted, it was psychic energy, but energy was energy. She was starving.

Glumly she recalled the dinner invitation from Nick that she had summarily turned down over the phone that afternoon.

She was several blocks away from Quintana's office when a sputtering sound from the car's engine immediately took her attention off the matter of food. Startled, she surveyed the small number of simple gauges on the dashboard. She had plenty of fuel and nothing appeared to be amiss with the ignition system. Jelly-ice engines were as reliable as the sunrise.

The sputtering grew louder. She felt the car hesitate. She increased the flow of jelly-ice but nothing happened. With one last jerk and a cough, the engine shut down. She hastily turned the steering bar to guide the coasting vehicle to the side of the deserted street.

The sudden silence was more alarming than any noise could have been at that moment. The fog swirled around the car, silently menacing.

She tried to prod the engine back to life, but there was no response. A chill of dread shot through her as she surveyed her surroundings. As luck would have it she was in a section of town that had been slated for redevelopment for some time. But to date little had been done. The few windows that she could see through the mist were boarded up and several of the street lamps were out. She could not see a telephone booth.

The only sign of life was an eerie blue glow in the distance. She gazed at it for a long time. There was something vaguely familiar about that particular shade of blue light.

She considered her options and realized she only had two. She could remain in the locked vehicle until a police cruiser happened by, which could be hours from now, or she could get out and search for a phone booth. Neither choice held much appeal.

She looked at the glowing blue light in the distance again, pondering the sense of familiarity. Then she realized why she recognized it. The light was the same shade of azure blue that the Children of Earth, one of the largest of the Return cults, used to illuminate its temples.

This was just the sort of neighborhood the cult favored, she thought. She had read in the business pages that the Children of Earth had begun acquiring cheap real estate in depressed areas.

She hesitated a while longer and then made up her mind. She opened the door and got out. There was no sign of anyone around. She buttoned her coat, locked the car and pocketed the keys.

She set off briskly through the fog toward the beckoning blue light.

She did not hear the echo of a second set of footsteps behind her until she paused at an intersection. She froze at the hollow sound.

The footsteps halted.

She made herself whirl around and stare into the misty darkness. The dim beam of one of the few functioning street lamps revealed nothing.

She tightened her grip on the strap of her purse and stepped off the curb. The footsteps followed, moving more swiftly now, moving with purpose.

A thick fear rose in her throat. She broke into a run, heading toward the welcoming blue glow. She tried not to think about what she would do if the beacon turned out to be the lights of a billboard.

The footsteps picked up speed. Something about the solid ring of leather on stone told her that it was a man who pursued her. What's more, he was gaining. She knew that if she stayed on the sidewalk, he would likely overtake her.

She forced herself to think. He could not see any better in this fog than she could. He was using her footsteps to track her.

She veered off the sidewalk into what had once been someone's front yard. Her shoes made no sound on the bare ground which had been softened by a recent rain. She plunged into the darkness that separated two dilapidated buildings.

The footsteps paused on the sidewalk. She prayed that she had confused her pursuer.

A moment later, when she emerged into an overgrown backyard, she was relieved to see that the blue glow was much closer now. It illuminated a globe-shaped roof that rose above the empty single-story houses around it. The music of a horn-harp reached her. Definitely a Children of Earth temple. Surely the monks would let her use a phone.

She made her way cautiously across the yard. The last thing she wanted to do now was trip over an old fence or fall into an abandoned pool. She listened intently, but she could not hear any more footsteps. There was no way to know if her pursuer had given up or if he was now moving silently over the damp ground, just as she was.

A frisson of awareness clawed at the nape of her neck with icy fingers just as she started across another backyard. When she glanced over her shoulder she thought she detected a shadow moving in the fog. Panic threatened to engulf her. She broke into a full run, heedless of hidden obstacles.

Panting for breath, she raced around the corner of another abandoned house. The bright blue lights of the temple blazed straight ahead. She could see a number of people dressed in a variety of colorful hooded robes. They were milling casually about on the front steps.

She was safe. Whoever had followed her was hardly likely to try to grab her in front of so many witnesses.

She slowed her pace and tried to catch her breath as she crossed the street. A group of Children of Earth monks dressed in green robes turned to stare as she hurried toward them. She noticed that everyone who wore green had shaved his or her head. Those who were dressed in black wore their hair in long ponytails. The handful of people garbed in yellow wore braids that were coiled on top of their heads. Obviously there was a hierarchy here, she thought. She wondered who outranked whom.

One of the men dressed in green came down the steps to greet her. "Welcome, Seeker. I am called Hiram." He folded his arms and bowed from the waist. "Will you join us for tonight's Curtain Call?"

Zinnia came to a breathless halt and pushed her hair back off her face. "No, not exactly. My car stalled a few blocks from here. May I please use your phone?"

"Of course. The Children of Earth offer assistance to all who seek. Please come inside." Hiram gestured toward the wide doors of the temple.

"Thanks, Hiram. I can't tell you how much I appreciate this."

"The ways of the Curtain are often obscure. Perhaps you have been summoned." Hiram ascended the steps and led her into the dimly lit entry hall of the temple.

"I don't think so." Zinnia wrinkled her nose at the scent of incense. She had never been inside a Return cult temple. Few people who were not members had.

Intelligent people ignored the cults as much as possible, dismissing them as financial shams. The Children of Earth were considered weird at best and diabolical at worst. But those families which had lost offspring to the temples favored legal action to put the Children of Earth out of business.

The outlandish attire of the cult members together with their use of aggressive panhandling to raise funds were enough to irritate the average person. Their ridiculous, wholly unscientific theories about the energy Curtain that had once provided a gateway between Old Earth and St. Helens disgusted scientists and outraged the academic crowd. The mainstream churches were appalled by what they saw as more than a passing flirtation with the occult.

Zinnia discovered that she was willing to be very tolerant tonight in exchange for the use of a telephone.

On the far side of the hushed entry hall she saw two great swaths of azure blue velvet draped across the entrance to the temple's auditorium. She peeked between the folds and caught a glimpse of several tiers of blue seats. They were arranged in a semicircle around an elevated stage. Behind the stage hung a white velvet curtain. It framed a massive painting; an artist's rendition of Old Earth.

Zinnia had seen many similar pictures in textbooks when she was in school. No one could be absolutely certain what the old planet looked like because all of the original pictures and photos had been lost when the First Generation data banks crumbled into dust. The Founders had left sketches and paintings and descriptions, however, which had been reinterpreted by generations of artists. During the past two hundred years since the closing of the Curtain, any number of variations on the theme had appeared.

Judging from the paintings and drawings she had seen, Zinnia supposed that Earth was a pretty enough planet, but she doubted that it could be as beautiful as the lush green world of St. Helens. Like most people, she had no desire to return to the mother world. It was little more than a legend. St. Helens was home.

Only the Return cults obsessed on the possibility that the Curtain would someday reopen. Their members had convinced themselves that Old Earth was a Utopian place, a perfect world fit for perfect people.

"You should consider the possibility that you were deliberately chosen to be summoned here tonight, Miss Spring. The Call of the Curtain often comes in mysterious ways." Hiram's robes swayed gently as he walked beside Zinnia down a thickly carpeted corridor. "Seekers are led here by many different avenues."

"I'm sure they are. I came by way of High View Street, myself. With a couple of detours through some backyards."

Hiram smiled patiently. "Perhaps the fact that your car stalled in our neighborhood will prove to be an example of the Curtain Call in action."

"Anything's possible, I suppose." Zinnia did not want to insult him. "But at the moment the only urge I feel is a need to call someone who can give me a ride home."

"Earth is our true home, Miss Spring." Hiram's expression was infused with the serenity of an inner vision. "But only those who are pure of heart and spirit will return when the Curtain rises once again."

"Uh-huh." The last thing she wanted to do was argue theology with Hiram. "Where is your phone?"

"In here, Miss Spring." He ushered her through another door and into a surprisingly ordinary office. "Help yourself. I must leave to assist with the preparations for this evening's services."

"Thank you, Hiram. You've been very kind."

Hiram folded his hands and bowed low. "May the Curtain rise for you, Miss Spring."

She nodded politely as he backed out the door.

As soon as she was alone, she seized the phone. She had punched in the first two digits of Nick's private line before she realized what she was doing.

"Five hells." She slammed the receiver down. She had no intention of calling Nick. She had planned to call a cab.

Then she thought about the footsteps in the fog. Someone had definitely followed her, and it was quite possible that whoever it was knew that she was searching for information related to the death of Morris Fenwick. That meant that this evening's events were linked to the Chastain journal.

Anything that involved the journal, involved Nick.

"Five hells," she said again. With a groan, she picked up the phone and punched in the number.

Nick answered on the first ring.

A dangerous combination of anger and relief simmered within him as he climbed out of the Synchron in front of the floodlit temple. Beneath both equally intense sensations, he was aware of a cold chill in his gut. Protecting Zinnia had become the most important element in the matrix but he was not doing a good job of it. Then again, she was not making it easy for him.

The dissonant notes of a horn-harp greeted Nick as he started up the broad steps that led to the temple's massive front doors. There was no one standing around outside, he noticed. Apparently the evening service had begun.

The day was not going well, he thought as he stalked into the dim entry hall. Thus far he had exposed Zinnia to the humiliation of a front-page photo in *Synsation,* gotten himself punched in the mouth, discovered more evidence that his uncle was involved in the conspiracy surrounding the Chastain journal, and had Zinnia slam the phone down in his ear.

Now this.

The matrix of his life had been considerably less complex before Zinnia Spring had become a factor in it, he reflected.

A deep sonorous voice issued forth from behind heavy blue velvet curtains.

"Welcome, Seekers. Welcome to all those who seek to purify themselves so that they may be fit to return to the world from whence the Founders came. The Curtain calls and those of you in this chamber tonight have answered. Earth awaits her children."

The horn-harp music swelled. Nick winced.

"Mr. Chastain?" A figure in a green robe detached itself from the shadows near a hallway. "I am Hiram. I presume you are here to assist Miss Spring?"

"Where is she?"

"This way." Hiram's robes swirled gently as he turned to start down the corridor. "We invited her to attend the last Curtain Call of the evening but she declined."

"Can't imagine why."

"Some people take longer than others to answer the Call." Hiram opened a door. "Mr. Chastain is here, Miss Spring."

"Nick." Zinnia leaped up from a chair and started toward him.

For a few hopeful seconds he thought that she would throw herself into his arms. But the expression of bright relief that had leaped in her eyes when she saw him in the doorway vanished quickly. She came to an abrupt halt a short distance away.

He stifled a small sigh of regret. What had he expected, he wondered. The fact that she had called him tonight when she was in trouble did not mean that she was not still furious.

"Are you all right?" he asked brusquely.

"Yes, of course." Zinnia's smile was composed and polite. "Hiram has been very kind."

"Good. Let's get out of here."

"Right." She started toward the door and then stopped. "Uh, Nick?"

"What is it?" He frowned when he saw that Hiram was standing squarely in the opening. There was a large metal collection plate in the monk's hand. "I probably should have seen this coming." He reached for his wallet.

"We who seek to Return to the mother world strive to be generous," Hiram said smoothly. "But we do have certain expenses."

"Yeah." Nick tossed fifty dollars into the plate. "Picking up real estate all over town at bargain rates takes capital, doesn't it?"

Hiram pocketed the fifty, unperturbed. "The Children of Earth must invest in the future."

"Why bother investing here on St. Helens if you're all going back to Earth?" Nick asked.

Zinnia gave him a reproachful look. "Now, Nick, Hiram has been very hospitable."

"I was most happy to help you in your hour of need, Miss Spring," Hiram stepped aside. "You are welcome to join us in our Return to Earth. All it requires is a pure heart and a mind that is open to the truth."

"I'm sure Earth would be a very nice place to visit," Zinnia said politely.

"Yeah, but who'd want to live there?" Nick said as he took her arm.

He could feel the gaze of the green-robed monk on his back as he hauled Zinnia swiftly down the corridor to the entry hall.

"What about my car?" Zinnia said.

"I'll send Feather to take care of it." He glanced at her as they went through the imposing entrance and out onto the front steps. "Now tell me what in five hells happened tonight? Where were you, anyway? And what went wrong with the car?"

"I don't know what happened to the car." She

angled her chin. "And as for where I was, I had a focus assignment."

"You didn't mention it earlier. What did you do? Call up your boss at Psynergy, Inc. and tell her you were suddenly free for the evening?"

"Yes, that's exactly what I did. As it happened, she'd just had a client call to ask for a prism who could work with a matrix."

"Sure she did."

"It's the truth." Zinnia smiled grimly. "And I was available."

"Only because you broke our date."

"We didn't have a date."

"You knew damn well I planned to see you this evening."

"Did I? How strange. Apparently I forgot to note the appointment on my calendar. I don't recall you mentioning a dinner engagement except in passing this afternoon after I found out that you'd gone sneaking off to find the forger."

"I did not sneak off to see Wilkes. I had your brother with me. Look, I didn't come here to argue with you."

"Could have fooled me. Oh, no." Zinnia halted abruptly halfway down the steps. "It's him."

"Who?" Nick glanced at the foot of the steps and saw a familiar figure. "Damn."

A camera flash exploded in the darkness.

"Great shot," Cedric Dexter called cheerfully. He whirled and raced off into the night. His footsteps echoed loudly on the sidewalk.

"I swear, I'm going to have that twerp's job in the morning," Nick vowed.

"Well, I think that answers the evening's most pressing question." Zinnia sounded chagrined.

"What's that?"

"It must have been Dexter's footsteps I heard

earlier in the fog. He was the one who followed me here to the temple. If only I'd realized who it was. I would have told him exactly what I think of him and his lousy photography."

"It wouldn't have done any good. Anyone who works for *Synsation* has the delicate sensibilities of a rhino-phant." Nick tightened his grip on her arm and steered her down the remaining steps.

"Actually, it's a relief to find out that it was Dexter. At least we know what he's after."

"True." Nick opened the Synchron's door and bundled Zinnia inside. "And tomorrow he's going to be after a new job."

"Now, Nick, he's only doing what he's paid to do. You can't go around intimidating people."

He closed the door very deliberately before she could finish the lecture. He would take care of the twerp in the morning. Tonight he had other things to discuss with Zinnia.

He got in behind the steering bar and activated the engine. He pulled away from the curb and did a U-turn in the middle of the street.

"That's sort of illegal, Nick."

"So make a citizen's arrest."

She slanted him a speaking glance.

Nick wondered again how he had stumbled into this crazy unpredictable matrix where Zinnia seemed to establish most of the rules.

There were several beats of silence.

"Thanks for picking me up tonight," Zinnia said after a while.

Nick said nothing. He was fairly certain that any remark he might utter would make the situation worse.

"I called you because I was afraid the whole thing was connected to the journal. I didn't realize that it was only Dexter scaring me to death."

"We can't be sure yet that it wasn't related to the journal."

She glanced at him. "What do you mean?"

"Have you been having trouble with your car lately?"

"No."

"It just quit on you tonight with no warning?"

"That's right." She crossed her arms. "A few sputters and then it stopped cold. Right in the middle of a deserted neighborhood."

"Not like a good jelly-ice engine to up and die without warning. I'll have a mechanic check it out tomorrow."

"Are you saying you think someone sabotaged it?"

"I'm saying it needs to be looked at. Once we have a mechanic's verdict, we'll take it from there."

"Even if someone did fool with it," she said, "that doesn't mean the someone in question wasn't good old Cedric trying to stage another photo op."

"I know. In which case, in addition to losing his job, he'll pay for the repairs."

"Nick, the best thing you can do is forget Dexter and *Synsation.* Trust me on this. I've been through scandals before. The only way to survive them is to ignore them. Eventually they go away. You can't buy respectability with a lawsuit against a tabloid photographer."

"I'll deal with Dexter later. Zinnia, we have to talk."

"Yes." She gazed straight ahead through the windshield. "I suppose we do. What did you discover today when you went to the forger's house?"

He frowned. "That wasn't what I wanted to discuss."

"Do you want our partnership to continue?" she asked much too sweetly.

"Damn it, yes, I want the partnership to continue."

223

He realized he was struggling to hold on to his temper. "But we're also lovers now and that's what I want to talk about tonight."

"I'd rather not," she said primly.

A strange kind of panic seized him. "You were disappointed, weren't you? You waited a long time to have sex and the experience didn't live up to your expectations. Look, I'm sorry. I rushed things. Next time—"

"For heaven's sake, will you stop talking about sex?" She half turned in her seat. Her eyes blazed in the shadows. "Sex has nothing to do with this."

He tried to assimilate that. "It doesn't?"

"Can't you get it through that thick matrix-talent head of yours that I'm not mad because the sex was a disappointment? It was what happened afterward that upset me."

"Afterward?" Nick relaxed slightly. This he could handle. "Right. The photo in this morning's paper. I'm very sorry about that. I thought I had got the film out of Dexter's camera. Obviously it was a decoy roll. I promise I'll take care of him tomorrow."

"For a supposedly brilliant matrix, you're as dumb as a bowl of jelly-ice when it comes to some things. Listen to me, Nick Chastain, it wasn't the photo that annoyed me."

He sighed. "You're angry because I went to see the forger with Leo and didn't take you along."

"Congratulations on the stunning flash of insight."

"I explained that. I had to move quickly. There wasn't time to call you and arrange an appointment with Wilkes."

She drummed her fingers on her jean-clad leg. "Did you find anything of significance?"

"Maybe." He eyed her warily, uncertain of her mood.

"Talk, Chastain."

"I told you that Wilkes had skipped out before we arrived."

"And someone had searched his workshop?"

"Yes. Looking for financial records related to the forgery of the Chastain journal."

She turned her head to study him. "How can you be sure of that?"

He hesitated and then reached into the pocket of his jacket. "Leo and I didn't find any useful financial data, but I did discover this."

He put the cuff link in her palm. It gleamed in the lights of the dash.

"I don't understand." Zinnia examined the small gold link. "Do you think it belongs to Wilkes or to the man who searched his workshop?"

"It belongs to my uncle, Orrin Chastain."

Zinnia sucked in a deep breath. "The head of Chastain, Inc.?"

"Yes."

"What was it doing in the forger's workshop?"

"Good question," Nick said. "I haven't had a chance to ask him. I intend to do so tomorrow. This isn't the first time his name has come up in connection with this mess."

She closed her hand around the cuff link. "You didn't mention that little fact."

He felt a sudden need to explain his silence on the subject. "I didn't say anything because—hell, I don't know why I didn't tell you. But it wasn't because I'm a paranoid matrix. I just wanted to think about the situation for a while, that's all."

She raised one shoulder in a small shrug. "You didn't tell me because it was a family thing. Your first instinct was to protect your uncle until you knew what was going on. Perfectly understandable. I'd have done the same in your place."

He was startled. Then he tightened his hands on the

bar. "Don't make me into a saint over this. Orrin and I can barely stand the sight of each other. There's no love lost between us."

"But you are family."

"Not in his view."

"Never mind. You did what you had to do. I can respect that."

"You can?"

She smiled for the first time since he had collected her from the temple office. "I know it must have been difficult for you to share this information with me. But because you did, I'm willing to let bygones be bygones. You can consider our partnership to be reinstated."

He took a deep breath. "What about our affair?"

"I'm going to have to think about that. To be perfectly honest, I'm not sure if it's a good idea for me to have an affair with you."

He felt as if he had just been run over by a fast-moving glacier. He struggled to breathe. The air was so cold it froze in his lungs.

"I see," he managed after an eternity had passed. "Let me know when you've made up your mind."

"I'll do that." She gave him an unreadable look. "But for the record, I wasn't disappointed last night."

Chapter
17

* * * * * * * * * *

The first thing Zinnia saw when she opened the door of her loft apartment the following morning was the photograph of Nick and herself on the steps of the Children of Earth Temple. It was on the front page of the new copy of *Synsation.*

"Great shot." Leo stood directly behind the paper, holding it up so that she could not miss the picture or the caption.

Has Casino Owner Nick Chastain seen the blue light? Or is this his idea of how to show the Scarlet Lady a good time?

"Cedric Dexter strikes again," Zinnia said with a groan of resignation.

"*Synsation* sales will go through the roof today."

"Oh, lord." Zinnia snatched the paper out of his hand. "Nick is going to be very upset about this."

"Very upset?" Leo chuckled as he walked through the door. "I wouldn't be surprised if he put *Synsation* out of business before the day is over."

"He couldn't possibly do something that drastic."

"Wanna bet? Something tells me Nick could do just about anything he decides to do."

Zinnia's brows rose at the note of masculine admiration in her brother's voice. She closed the door and turned around. "What's this? Since when did you become a fan of Nick Chastain?"

"He's okay." Leo ambled into the kitchen, opened the icerator, and began to rummage around inside. "We had a long talk yesterday."

"Before or after the two of you went merrily off to search Alfred Wilkes's house?"

"Before." Leo removed a carton of fruit juice from the refrigerator. "You know, I've been thinking."

"About what?"

"That's quite an operation Nick has there at Chastain's Palace. Very impressive, when you consider it. A lot of money goes through that place. Too bad for Chastain, Inc. that Nick didn't inherit the family business."

"What do you mean?"

"Uncle Stanley mentioned the other day that there are rumors that Chastain, Inc. is going through a rough patch. The firm apparently needs a major infusion of cash but can't seem to interest any big investors."

"What's Nick got to do with it?"

"Nothing, really." Leo poured the juice into a glass. "It's just that I doubt that Chastain, Inc. would be in trouble if Nick were running the firm. The man has a talent for making money."

"The money is only a means to an end for him." Zinnia tossed the tabloid into the trash. "He's applied himself to making a lot of it because he thinks it will help him achieve his real goal."

Leo finished the last of the juice in a single gulp. "What's that?"

"Respectability."

Leo grimaced. "Tell him respectability is not all its cracked up to be."

"I tried." She reached for the coff-tea pot. "But he wants it for his future offspring. He knows what it's like to live without it and he's determined that his children won't have to go through what he went through as a bastard."

Leo whistled softly. "Hard to argue that one."

She wrinkled her nose. "Besides, he's a matrix. Once they make up their minds, it's almost impossible to change them. They can be incredibly stubborn."

Leo grinned.

"What so funny?"

"I told him pretty much the same thing about you yesterday."

"Thanks a lot."

Leo laughed. "You know, the two of you make quite a pair."

Zinnia stilled. Then she concentrated very hard on her coff-tea.

"Zinnia?" Leo's laughter faded. A speculative look dawned in his eyes. "There's no chance that the two of you might get together on a permanent basis, is there?"

She slammed her coff-tea cup down on the counter. "He's arrogant, inflexible, overcontrolling, secretive, and obsessive about his goals, of which he currently has only two. He wants to get his hands on his father's journal and he wants respectability. What do you think?"

"I just wondered," Leo said dryly.

"And besides, I was officially declared unmatchable, if you will recall."

"You've been hiding behind that long enough. But it's not doing you any good. If anything, it just makes it easier for Aunt Willy and the others to pressure you into an unmatched marriage."

"I know, I know."

"Things change." Leo's expression grew oddly intent. "New people register every day at the agencies. Who knows who's out there now? Mr. Right might be filling out his agency questionnaire even as we speak."

"Not bloody likely."

"Tell your boss that Nick Chastain wants to talk to him. Now." Nick cradled the phone against his shoulder and turned the page of the lengthy Synergistic Connections questionnaire. "If he doesn't want to talk to me, I can make arrangements to see him in person."

The receptionist on the other end of the line swallowed audibly. "Yes, sir. One moment, please."

Nick glanced at the next row of questions while he waited for the editor of *Synsation* to come on the line.

Please list your hobbies.

That was an easy one. He had no hobbies. If something was not sufficiently important to warrant his full attention, he ignored it. He filled in the blank with the word *none*.

"Nick Chastain? Bill Ramsey here." Ramsey's voice was unrelentingly cheerful. "I'm the front-page editor of *Synsation*. What can I do for you?"

"You can fire Cedric Dexter. I want him gone by the end of the day."

"Sorry, no can do." Ramsey chuckled. "Dexter's only been working for me for a month, but he's already proven himself to be the best photographer on the staff."

Nick put down his pen. "Listen to me, Ramsey, I've had it with Dexter's cute tricks. Last night he went too far. He stalked Miss Spring through the fog to get his shot. It was a terrifying experience for her. I want him gone or your trashy little newspaper will be out of business by the end of the month."

"Take it easy, Chastain. We're both businessmen. I

don't tell you how to run your casino. You don't tell me how to run my newspaper."

"You're wrong," Nick said very softly. "I am telling you how to run your newspaper. One more photo of Miss Spring in your rag and *Synsation* is yesterday's news. I can do it, Ramsey. Believe me."

"Look, what say we talk about this man to man? We can make a deal. Give me a solid story. Confirm the rumors about your plans for marriage and the sale of Chastain's Palace and I'll call off my photographer."

"I do not discuss my personal affairs with the tabloids. If you want to stay in business, Ramsey, you will get rid of Dexter sometime in the next ten minutes."

"Be reasonable. I've got a paper to get out here."

Nick hung up the phone before Ramsey finished whining. He went back to the questionnaire and was relieved to see that he was almost through. Who could have guessed that there would be so many idiotic questions? And this was only the first step in the matchmaking process.

How much of your time is devoted to the above listed hobbies?

Nick picked up his pen again and dutifully wrote *none.*

A single knock sounded on the door of the reception chamber.

"What is it, Feather?"

Feather opened the door. "Mr. Batt to see you, boss."

"He's early. I told him I'd have this damned questionnaire filled out by noon."

Before Feather could respond, Hobart Batt, looking particularly stylish in an off-white suit and matching bow tie, bounced through the doorway. He bristled with outrage as he waved the day's edition of *Synsation.*

"This is simply too much, Mr. Chastain. I am a

professional. I cannot be expected to work under these conditions."

"Calm down, I've taken care of the situation."

"Taken care of it?" Hobart's voice rose. "You can't take care of something like this. It's too late to take care of it. This issue of *Synsation* is all over town. Mr. Chastain, you are making my job a thousand times more impossible than it was at the beginning of our association. And that was bad enough."

"There won't be any more photos in *Synsation*."

"Don't you understand?" Hobart almost hopped up and down in his agitation. "You and Miss Spring have been featured in this rag three times in recent days. Every photo of the two of you together makes you less desirable as a prospective spouse."

"I'm sure you'll be able to overcome these slight setbacks."

"These aren't slight setbacks." Hobart slapped the paper down on Nick's desk. "These are disasters."

Nick glanced at the photo of Zinnia and himself on the temple steps. Dexter had done a nice job of framing the shot. He had captured the imposing doorway and the glowing blue dome. There was no doubt about the location.

"Don't worry about it, Batt."

Hobart simmered with righteous indignation. "Mr. Chastain, you were very specific in your requirements for a wife. To be quite crass about it, you wish to marry up in the world. You stated that you wanted a spouse from one of New Seattle's most elite families."

"Listen, Batt—"

"You also told me that you wished to be properly matched. It is going to be difficult enough as it is, given your professional, psychic, and personal attributes. None of which, I might add, do you any credit."

"I never said it would be easy. That's why I have you, Batt."

"I'm doing my best under exceptionally difficult circumstances." Hobart stabbed a finger at the photo. "But how do you expect me to find you a respectable wife if you keep showing up on the front page of *Synsation* in these compromising photos with Miss Spring?"

"There was nothing compromising about that photograph."

"Not compromising?" Hobart gave him an incredulous look. "The two of you on the very steps of one of the most disreputable Return cults in town? Don't be ridiculous. You have no notion of the damage you have done. Bad enough that most people think that you are only one step above the level of a gangster. Now they'll think that you've either got financial dealings with a cult or that you've joined one. And Miss Spring's presence doesn't add what one could call a positive note."

"Leave Miss Spring out of it." Nick planted his hands flat on the desk and shoved himself to his feet. "She has nothing to do with this."

"On the contrary." Hobart drew himself up. "I must tell you that these recent photos in *Synsation* have very likely revived old gossip concerning a scandal in which she was deeply involved a year and a half ago."

"I don't give a damn about that scandal."

"Well, you certainly should. It was linked to the Eatons, a very distinguished family. It is precisely their social circle that you wish to marry into, Mr. Chastain. Everyone in that very exclusive crowd knows about Miss Spring's shameful affair with Rexford Eaton. Mr. Eaton is a married man, you know."

"Miss Spring did not have an affair with Rexford Eaton," Nick said evenly. "I can personally testify to that fact. Anyone who says otherwise is a liar."

Hobart was unfazed. "The facts do not matter, sir. Only the perception. And as far as everyone in that particular social strata is concerned, she did have an affair with Eaton."

"Say one more word about Miss Spring and I will personally separate your head from your shoulders."

"Am I interrupting anything?" Zinnia asked politely from the doorway.

Nick swung around and saw her. The sense of awareness he always experienced in her presence swept through him. She was wearing a rakish little wrap dress with a long sweep of a skirt. The color was lipstick red. Her eyes gleamed with comprehension and something else, something he could not name. But he knew that she had overheard far more than he would have liked.

"Miss Spring." He dampened the outward evidence of his anger with the ease of long practice. "I didn't hear the door open. This is Hobart Batt of Synergistic Connections."

"How do you do, Mr. Batt?" She smiled coolly at Hobart.

Hobart flushed. "Miss Spring." He adjusted the crisp knot of his off-white tie. "A pleasure to meet you."

"Thank you." Zinnia walked forward. "Is Mrs. Lane still with Synergistic Connections? She was the syn-psych counselor who declared me unmatchable when I registered four years ago."

The color deepened in Hobart's face. It did not go well with his suit. "Yes, Mrs. Lane is still with the agency. You cannot imagine how difficult your case was for her. She has never forgotten the experience."

Zinnia propped herself on the corner of Nick's desk. "Neither have I."

"Yes, yes, I'm sure you haven't." Hobart looked deeply embarrassed. "Synergistic Connections prides itself on its extremely high success rate with difficult clients. Your case has become something of a legend in the agency."

"Fancy that." Zinnia swung her neatly shod foot.

"Mrs. Lane has often given staff lectures on the peculiarities of your situation." Hobart was starting to warm to the topic. "As I recall your MPPI profile did not go at all well."

Nick looked from one to the other. "MPPI?"

"The Multipsychic Paranormal Personality Inventory test," Zinnia explained. "I flunked it."

"Now, now, Miss Spring," Hobart said earnestly. "There are no right or wrong answers in such a test, therefore, one cannot say one failed it. The problem was that your psychic profile was so unique that Synergistic Connections was unable to find a suitable match in our files. Mrs. Lane even went into the multiple listing services of all three city-states, but no luck."

Zinnia slanted a wry smile at Nick. "I bombed in New Portland and New Vancouver, too."

"Perhaps you should let us try again," Hobart said with the ever-hopeful tone of the dedicated professional matchmaker. "Who knows? The list of registrants changes constantly. We might have more luck this time."

"Thank you, Mr. Batt." Zinnia gave him an heroically tragic smile. "But I've come to terms with my status as an unmatchable woman. I really don't think I could go through the trauma a second time."

Her air of stoic martyrdom irritated Nick. "I think you've done more than come to terms with it. I get the impression you're starting to enjoy it."

Zinnia ignored him.

"Nonsense," Hobart said briskly. "There is no substitute for a good match. Everyone knows that. Our far-sighted Founders understood that only the institution of marriage could provide the synergistic stability needed for a successful society. History has proven them correct. Marriage is the very cornerstone of our civilization, Miss Spring."

"Spoken like a pro," she murmured.

Hobart brightened. "Your records from four years ago are still in our files. We could always reactivate them at your request."

"And a hefty fee." Zinnia smiled. "Don't bother. And by the way, don't let Mr. Chastain intimidate you. His bark is worse than his bite."

Hobart blinked. He stared at her as if she'd just announced that the Curtain had reopened. Then he coughed a little. "Yes, well, I must be off. I have a full day of appointments." He glowered at Nick. "I don't suppose you've finished filling out your questionnaire?"

"Close enough." Nick scooped up the thick booklet. "Here, take the damn thing." He tossed the questionnaire across the desk.

Hobart caught it awkwardly. "I'll call you when we're ready for the next phase of the registration process." Clutching the questionnaire, he turned and marched out of the room.

Zinnia waited until the door closed. Then she looked at Nick with a speculative expression. "You told me that you've never had your psychic talent tested and rated."

"That's right."

"Mind explaining how you obtained the services of a top-notch agency like Synergistic Connections without an official psychic classification? I know for a fact that agency insists on a rating. They refuse to match untested talents or prisms."

"Batt and I have a private arrangement. I've told him to consider me a class-ten matrix."

"But you're much more than that." Her eyes widened. "Wait a minute. I get it. You're not officially registered with SC, are you? You're trying to find a match outside the system."

Nick decided that comment did not require an

answer. He came around from behind the desk. "I see you got my message."

"Yes." She looked as if she wanted to question him further on the subject of his agency registration, but she apparently changed her mind. "Feather phoned an hour ago to tell me that you located Polly Fenwick and her friend Omar Booker in New Vancouver."

"I'll tell you all about it over lunch."

"Lunch?"

"Why not? It's lunch time."

Polly and Omar had been located early this morning but Nick had told Feather to delay the call to Zinnia so that it would coincide with the noon hour. He saw no need to go into detail about the timing, however. Zinnia would probably get mad all over again.

He took her arm. "We're eating out by the pool."

"It's raining."

"It never rains on my pool."

Chapter
18

* * * * * * * * * *

Nick was right, Zinnia discovered a short time later when she found herself on the roof of Chastain's Palace. She listened to rain beat down on the glass roof that covered the graceful pool and lush garden.

"This is amazing. I never knew this was up here."

"These are my private quarters."

She noticed that he did not use the term *home*. Home for Nick was still an unrealized element in the pattern of the matrix that was his carefully planned future.

He waited until the waiter had retreated out of sight. Then he looked at her across the small table. "I'm sorry you overheard that conversation between Batt and myself."

"I assume your decision to marry up in the world is all part of your scheme for becoming respectable?" Zinnia hid the pain she was feeling behind a forced smile as she examined the selection of salads and cheeses.

She was trying to cope with the wrenching blow Hobart Batt had unwittingly delivered. *How do you expect me to find you a respectable wife if you keep showing up on the front page of Synsation in these compromising photos with Miss Spring?*

She was overreacting again, Zinnia told herself. She must not get emotional. She had known all along that Nick intended to marry. It should come as no surprise to learn that he had some very specific requirements in a wife. He was a matrix, after all. Whoever he selected as a mate would have to fit into his grand design for the future.

"I'd rather not talk about my marriage registration," Nick said in his most remote voice. "I'm still in the preliminary phases."

"Okay." It was not a subject she wanted to discuss, either. She forced another smile as she chose a small cracker and dipped it into the tom-olive spread. "Let's get down to business. Tell me about Polly and Omar."

"In a minute. Did you really mean what you said to Batt?"

"About what?"

He watched her with hooded eyes. "About not wanting to reactivate your old registration with Synergistic Connections?"

"I've got enough problems on my hands. Besides, it would cost a fortune. SC is the most expensive agency in New Seattle. And like I said, why would I want to go through the process a second time? You haven't dealt with real rejection until a professional match-making agency tells you that you're unmatchable."

"You seem to have borne up rather nobly under the crushing blow."

"One can adjust to almost anything," she assured him.

His jaw tightened as if that was not what he wanted to hear. "I have a hunch that Hobart is just looking for an excuse to tell me I'm unmatchable."

"He did seem a trifle disturbed about your prospects." Zinnia munched on the cracker. "Especially given your somewhat stringent requirements. What are you holding over poor Hobart's head to get him to work for you off-the-books like this?"

Nick's gaze gleamed with the essence of pure innocence. "What makes you think I'm holding anything over his head?"

"I know you, Chastain." Zinnia selected some cheese. "It's second nature for you to use intimidation to grease the wheels in all of your operations. What have you got on Mr. Batt?"

Nick shrugged as he forked up a bite of salad. "Batt owes me ten thousand dollars."

Zinnia nearly choked on the cheese. "Ten thousand? I don't believe it. Hobart doesn't look like a gambler. I can't envision him losing that kind of money in a casino. What did you do? Set him up?"

"No." He gave her an amused look. "You don't know much about the synergistic psychology of gambling, do you?"

"I suppose you're an expert."

"Yes," Nick said. "I'm an expert. It goes with the territory. Hobart made the mistake of succumbing to the fever one night. Casino policy with mid- and low-range players is to intervene before they get in too deep."

"Bad for business if word gets out that middle-income people can lose their life savings in Chastain's Palace, I suppose?"

"Very bad."

"But when poor Hobart got in over his head, you didn't intervene, did you?" she accused.

"Don't worry about Batt."

Exasperated, Zinnia put down her fork. "Look, Nick, if you want to become socially acceptable you're going to have to stop using tactics like those to achieve your ends."

"Has anyone ever told you that your girlish naiveté is enchanting?"

"One more crack about my naiveté and I'll push you into the pool. All right, it's obvious that you don't want my good advice. So let's get down to business. Tell me about Polly and Omar."

"Not much to tell." Nick tore off a slice of bread from the fresh-baked loaf. "They're registered under false names in a first-class hotel in New Vancouver. Living the good life on my fifty thousand, from what Feather could determine. I've got a private investigator keeping an eye on them."

"What are you going to do?"

"Nothing for the moment. I still don't think they're involved in the fraud. The man I want is the one who used them to sell me the fake journal. Whoever he is, he's rich enough and sufficiently well connected to be able to afford a master forger like Wilkes."

"So why pay an investigator to keep an eye on Polly and Omar?"

"A simple precaution. I like to keep track of all the factors in the matrix."

"I see." Zinnia pondered that. "Nick, I've been thinking about something you said."

"What was that?"

"You told me it looked as if whoever searched Wilkes's house was after financial records that could be used to trace the sale of the forgery."

"So?"

"I focused for a matrix accountant last night. I was driving home from that assignment, in fact, when my car died."

Nick speared a stalk of chilled aspera-choke. "It didn't die of natural causes. The mechanic told Feather that someone killed it. Loosened the jelly-ice injector."

She sighed. "Mr. Dexter does try one's patience. At any rate, as I was saying, my client made a comment about the way money leaves a trail."

"He's right. It does."

"This morning I thought about what both you and

Mr. Quintana had said. It occurred to me that there must be a trail of financial paperwork connected to the Third Expedition."

"One of the first things I checked when I started looking into this three years ago. The financial records are gone, just like the personnel documents."

"All of them?"

"The expedition was financed by the University of New Portland," he explained patiently. "The financial records from that period were destroyed in a fire that occurred about thirty-five years ago."

She slowly lowered her fork a second time. "Another amazing coincidence, I take it?"

Nick's brows rose. "Being the world's leading expert on matrix-talents, I'm sure you're aware of the fact that for people like me there are no coincidences."

"You think someone deliberately destroyed the university's financial files?"

"Yes. Just as I think someone deliberately burned down my mother's house after he arranged her death on that jungle road."

Zinnia shuddered. "I hate to say it, but I think I'm beginning to see a pattern here."

"Welcome to the wonderful world of Synergistic Matrix Analysis. You're right. There is a pattern. But, then, there always is."

She could hardly believe her own conclusions. "Do you really think it's possible that someone deliberately set out to destroy all traces of the Third Expedition?"

"I think that is exactly what happened. Failing that, he tried to turn it into a legend."

She crumpled her napkin. "But why would anyone go to such great lengths?"

"The only reason that fits is that the expedition discovered something so important or so valuable that the killer was willing to go to a lot of trouble to conceal it."

Zinnia contemplated that briefly. "Whoever he is, I'll bet he's a matrix."

Nick paused with a bite halfway to his mouth. He put it down very carefully and met her eyes. "Is that a serious observation from a self-declared expert on matrix-talents or was it just an off-hand remark?"

"It was serious." She frowned. "I think. There's something about the thoroughness of what's happened that makes me believe a matrix is behind it."

"I agree that there is a systematic pattern." Nick stroked one long finger slowly down the length of the glass that held his iced coff-tea. "And the end result is that history has been rewritten."

He said nothing else but Zinnia felt the questing probe of psychic energy seeking a prism. She hesitated only an instant and then obliged . . .

And experienced the deep tug of satisfaction that came whenever she focused for Nick. It was as if they were meant to focus together, she thought wistfully.

But if Nick was aware of any emotional side effects to the focus link, he concealed the knowledge well. He went to work.

Zinnia watched as a complex matrix construct took shape on the metaphysical plane. She glimpsed an overall design, but she did not understand it until Nick started talking quietly.

"So much paperwork lost," he said. "But there's a pattern to the way the records disappeared. First and foremost, the financial data had to go."

Connections shimmered within the intricate matrix construct.

"He must have concluded that those records would be the most damaging," Zinnia said.

"He was right. He reasons like a businessman. A very good one."

The metaphysical matrix that Nick had created grew increasingly sharp. At the same time it also became more complex. Myriad points spread throughout a finite universe. Zinnia knew that each one represented a thought or an idea, a fact or an impression for Nick. His mind was studying them as a whole, searching for connections and links. She realized that she was catching a rare glimpse into the way a powerful matrix-talent performed pure abstract psychic analysis.

"Someone set out to make the Third Expedition literally disappear into the mists of history," Nick said. "And he's been remarkably successful. Only thirty-five years have passed, but the expedition has already been reduced to the level of a minor legend. Officially, it never even took place. In another few years it will have been forgotten altogether."

"Only you and perhaps a handful of others such as Professor DeForest will even remember the story."

"And we'll have no proof," Nick said softly.

Complex designs within designs emerged throughout the mental construct that he had created.

"What do you see?" Zinnia asked, fascinated and dazzled but unable to interpret the patterns. Only Nick could fully comprehend what had been crafted. He was the master of the matrix, a magician who worked in several dimensions, seeking invisible possibilities and improbable connections.

Nick stirred. "The stain of money."

"What about it?"

"I told Leo that you can never wash it out completely. But someone is trying very hard to do just that in this case. Which means that whoever he is, he knows enough to understand that the money trail will lead back to him."

"So?"

"Only someone who truly understood how money works would know how and what to do to hide the trail." Without any warning, Nick cut the flow of talent. The inward-looking expression vanished from his eyes. The matrix winked out of existence on the metaphysical plane.

"Well?" Zinnia prompted.

"The University of New Portland sponsored the Third Expedition," he said.

"We know that. You said their records indicate that it was canceled before it left Serendipity. What of it?"

"Universities don't usually fund major expeditions with their own money. Too expensive. They go after grants or tap wealthy corporations."

"I think I see where you're going with this," Zinnia said slowly.

"Whoever destroyed the financial records did so because he knows they would point straight back to him. We need to find out who gave the university the money to finance the Third. When I identify him, I'll have the man who killed my father."

"You're sure that your father was murdered?"

"Yes." Nick's hand tightened fiercely around the glass. "Just as my mother was. It's all there in the matrix design. The logic is perfect now. My father didn't commit suicide. He was killed because of the secret he discovered. That secret is in the journal. My mother was a threat because she was asking questions about Bartholomew Chastain's disappearance. Her house was burned in case there were any letters or notes that might have made things awkward for the killer."

"But your father's last letter survived because your mother hid it in Andy Aoki's storeroom when she left you with him. I wonder why she didn't tell Mr. Aoki about it?"

"Probably because she was afraid that if he knew too much, he might be in danger. She wanted to protect him until she found out more about what was going on."

"She must have been a very brave woman," Zinnia said. "No wonder your father fell in love with her."

"Yes." Nick gave her a strange look. "I never knew either of my parents, but lately, for the first time, I've begun to feel as if I have a tangible connection to them. Andy said it would be this way someday."

Zinnia touched his hand. "Nick, if you're right, it wasn't just your father who was killed in the course of the expedition. Professor DeForest told me that five men vanished in the jungle. Do you realize what that means? Someone murdered the entire expedition team and then altered all of the records."

"The sixth man," Nick whispered.

"What?"

"My father's letter clearly says that six men were due to leave in the morning, remember?"

"Yes." Zinnia drew a deep breath. "But DeForest said there were only five."

"I know. I've been assuming that DeForest got the number wrong just like he got so much else wrong. I figured he took a guess. My father's previous two teams had each consisted of five men including himself. But what if old Demented was right for once in his life? What if only five men were scheduled to be on the team but at the last minute a sixth was added?"

"That would mean that whoever murdered Bartholomew Chastain and the other four men was a member of the expedition," Zinnia whispered.

"Yes. And when the killer returned, he tried to rewrite history. Anyone who can destroy records so thoroughly is capable of planting a few false ones."

"Why would your father have accepted a last-minute addition to the team?" Zinnia asked. "You said he always insisted on experienced jungle men. If he only wanted five and he had those five, why take on a sixth?"

Nick's smile was slow and infinitely cold. "I don't know. But I can take a guess. He may have had to accept the sixth man if that man was the one who had underwritten the entire expedition."

"But the university officials would have known

about the sixth man. They would have known that he went out on the expedition." Zinnia waved her hands, exasperated with circles within circles. "Good lord, if that was the case, their records would show that there *was* an expedition. Instead, they show that it was canceled."

Nick shook his head. "If the sixth man was a paranoid matrix-talent who never told the university officials that he intended to join the team, it would all fit."

Zinnia breathed deeply. "A paranoid matrix?"

"I agree with you. This entire affair has the fingerprints of a matrix all over it," Nick said softly. "A matrix who undoubtedly knew or suspected that my father was also a matrix."

"And didn't trust him?"

"Right."

Zinnia thought that through. "Talk about conspiracy theories. If what you're saying is correct, then whoever funded the Third Expedition was also part of it."

"He was there when my father made his discovery, whatever it was. He understood the significance of it. After he killed my father and the other four men, he took the journal. When he returned, he concealed the records of his own involvement so that there was no way he could be traced to the expedition. And then he systematically erased all documents relating to the venture."

"Nick, hang on here. You're going too fast for me. If the killer has had the journal safely hidden for the past thirty-five years, why would the rumors about it have suddenly started up in the past few months?"

"From what I know of the rare-book trade," Nick said, "I'd guess that the journal may have been lost or stolen recently. It was resold to that collector in New Portland who then died."

"And poor Morris Fenwick came across it in the estate sale."

"I told you that whoever searched Morris's shop the

other night was not actually looking for anything," Nick said. "There was no pattern to the way the place had been torn apart."

"Which meant that the killer knew the journal was not there. He just wanted the police to think Morris had been murdered for drug money."

Nick nodded slowly. "The murderer had already commissioned a fake journal from Alfred Wilkes. He planted it so that Polly and Omar would find it and sell it to me. He wanted to put me off the scent."

Zinnia wrapped her hands around her damp iced coff-tea glass. "Whoever he is, he must not have realized that you're a high-class matrix."

"Maybe he thought he could fool me, even if I was a matrix."

"Very arrogant of him. But, then, this entire plan is breathtakingly arrogant."

"Yes."

"Nick, are you sure about all these conclusions? This is a very heavy-duty conspiracy theory, even for a matrix-talent like you."

"I'm as certain as I can be without hard proof. I have to find out who financed my father's last expedition."

"Thirty-five years have gone by," Zinnia said gently. "And the records have been destroyed."

Nick's eyes burned with a fierce light. "Even a matrix-talent would have a hard time getting rid of every single clerk, accountant, and secretary who worked in the budget offices of a large university thirty-five years ago."

Zinnia frowned. "I see what you mean. There must be a few left who would recall the source of the funds for the Third Expedition. Probably retired by now, though."

"We can trace them through their pensions. I'll have Feather make some calls this afternoon."

Zinnia smiled. "You're incredible."

"Is that a compliment or an accusation?"

"Never mind. What do I get to contribute to this new plan?"

"You've made your contribution." Nick picked up her hand and brushed his lips across her palm. "You are my inspiration. If it weren't for you, I would never have been able to put it all together so clearly and quickly."

She thought he was teasing her, but when she met his eyes she realized that he was deadly serious.

"Thanks," she muttered, "but I have higher aspirations. Being your inspiration just isn't enough for an overachiever like me."

"What do you want to do?"

Zinnia leaned back in her chair. "Why don't I talk to Professor DeForest again? Maybe he'll have some other interesting tidbits that you've discounted."

"Waste of time. The guy's got more than one screw loose." Nick reached for the phone that sat on a small table near a lounger.

"What are you going to do now?"

"Tell Feather to start looking for retirees from the University of New Portland's budget office."

"And when you've finished that?"

He gave her a sidelong glance that held a new kind of speculation. "I thought we could go for a swim."

"I don't have a suit."

"There's one in the cabana. Red. You can change while I'm giving instructions to Feather."

Chapter
19

* * * * * * * * * *

The hot red swimsuit fit perfectly.

Naturally.

One of the really annoying things about matrix-talents was that they had a knack for estimating the distance, length, height, or width of just about anything. Show them a diagram of a complex multidimensional mathematical figure and they could quickly tell you the approximate angles of every intersecting line and the volumes of each defined space. Show them a woman and they could estimate her bra size.

Zinnia figured Nick probably had the coordinates of her measurements plotted on a matrix that he had stored somewhere in his very different brain. She wondered wistfully if he studied it occasionally when he was alone at night. Matrix masturbation was no doubt an interesting phenomena.

It was too bad that matrix-talents were not as good at personal relationships as they were with the spatial kind, she thought.

She walked to the edge of the pool and sat down.

For a few minutes she watched Nick do laps. She marveled that he did not cause the water to boil as he sliced through it. The energy he was radiating was palpable.

The sleek muscles of his shoulders glistened wetly. His powerful strokes propelled him forward with the lethal grace of a marauding shark-cuda. He had been raised in the Western Islands, Zinnia reminded herself. He had learned to swim in treacherous seas, not in a safe backyard swimming pool.

Midway through a lap Nick changed course and swam to meet her. When he reached the side, he braced himself in the deep water with one hand on the tile very close to her leg. He used his other hand to shove gleaming wet hair back from his high forehead.

"I see the suit fits." He surveyed her with undisguised satisfaction and something that could have been possessiveness.

"Perfectly."

He smiled. "And just your color."

She gazed down into his face and saw that his eyes still burned with the remnants of the fires of the focus link. "Do you have any other hobbies besides swimming?"

He looked surprised and then slightly baffled by the question. "Swimming isn't a hobby. I do it because it's an efficient way to exercise. I don't have any hobbies."

"I see." Typical obsessive matrix. There was no middle ground for them. Things were either compelling enough to warrant full attention and energy or they weren't worth doing at all.

He watched her closely. "Do you?"

"Have hobbies?" She shook her head ruefully. "Not really. I've been too busy with other things for the past few years. Someday I'd like to have a garden."

"You'll have to move out of that loft apartment if you want to have one."

"I know."

"You'd need a house and some land."

"Yes."

He was silent for a moment. Then, very deliberately, he put his hand on her bare thigh. He stroked slowly downward, briefly cupping her knee. She flinched at the touch of the cool water. Then the heat of his palm warmed her.

When he looked up again she saw that his eyes still burned. This time it wasn't just the smoldering embers of the focus link that blazed in the depths of his gaze.

"Have you made a decision?" he asked.

She knew what he meant. "Yes."

"Is that yes you've made up your mind, or yes you'll have an affair with me?"

"Yes to both."

"Zinnia, my talent may not drive me crazy, but you surely will."

He seemed to explode out of the water. Laughter and exultation flared in his eyes. His hands closed around her waist.

"Wait," she yelped. But it was too late.

He pulled her off the edge and toppled back into the pool with her in his arms.

"Take a breath," he warned.

The shock of hitting the cold water made her gasp. Nick's teeth flashed in a wide grin. He plunged below the surface, drawing her down into the depths with him. The sudden sense of weightlessness made her feel giddy and disoriented.

He swam with her through the silent blue water world, his hold on her sure and confident. Down they went, into the deepest portion of the pool.

When they reached the bottom he tightened his grasp and soared back toward the light. Just when she thought she could not hold her breath a second longer, they broke the surface together.

"Beast." She laughed as she clutched his shoulders. "I'll get even for that. And you'll never know when it's coming."

"I can't wait."

The amusement in his eyes metamorphosed into sexual hunger with a speed that shook her to the core. His mouth closed over hers, searching, demanding, exciting.

When he raised his head a long time later she could feel her fingers trembling. If it had not been for his hands anchoring her against him, she would have floated away.

"I want this to be a real affair," he said.

"I don't see how much more real it can get."

His mouth tightened with impatience. "I mean I don't want to play any more games."

"Games?"

"We're not going to pretend that I've hired you as my interior designer."

She made a face. "Just as well. I don't think anyone was buying the interior-designer story. Not after those photos in *Synsation*. But, Nick, I have to warn you, dating me is probably not a good way to pursue your big plan to gain respectability."

"Don't worry about my respectability. I can buy that the same way I can buy everything else." His eyes darkened. "Except you. No one could buy you, Zinnia."

She touched his throat. "Or you."

"Neither of us is for sale." He smiled with an almost savage satisfaction. "We'll make it official tomorrow night."

"What happens tomorrow night?"

"I'm going to take you to the Founders' Club Ball."

She raised her brows. "Nick Chastain and the Scarlet Lady at the annual charity event of the year? Oh, my. That will certainly liven up the conversation in certain circles."

"Be sure to wear red." He bent his head and took her mouth once more.

She realized what he intended and managed to tear her mouth free long enough to protest. "Nick, for heaven's sake, not here. The waiter may come back at any moment."

"He won't come back until I call him." He held her with one hand and peeled the top of her swimsuit down to her waist in a single motion. He stared at her as if he had never seen another woman in his life. "You are so beautiful."

She knew full well that no objective observer would label her beautiful. But that only made his words all the sweeter. He was a matrix. Beauty was far more complex and multileveled for him than it was for most people. She framed his face with her hands. "So are you."

He lifted her partway out of the water and bent his head to take one taut nipple between his teeth.

She shivered. Water streamed from her hair down her arched back. She sank her nails into Nick and took fierce pleasure in the shudder that went through him. A glorious sensation of wild heady freedom flowed in her veins. She abandoned herself to her own womanly power.

Nick worked the red swimsuit down over her hips. A moment later it floated out of sight. His eyes gleamed as she slipped her fingers beneath the waistband of his suit.

She flattened her palms against his thighs and savored the feel of hard muscle beneath firm skin. Then she pushed the suit downward until it disappeared into the depths. She cradled his rigid erection in her hand.

He drew in his breath. "I told you, you're an inspiration to me."

She stroked gently, fascinated by the size and feel of him. "I take back what I said earlier. Maybe being an inspiration for you is enough for an overachiever like me."

"Come closer." He braced himself and pulled her legs around his waist. An erotic thrill shot through her when she realized that she was completely open to his touch.

He reached between her thighs and found her erect clitoris. He pressed it slowly, deliberately.

Ripples of anticipation gripped her. "I want you."

"You don't know what real wanting is," he said.

"Do you?"

"Yes." He eased a finger inside her. "God, yes, I know all about it. It's what I feel whenever I see you." He pushed upward against the top of her vagina. "Or think about you." He maintained the pressure inside her while he used his thumb on the small stiff nubbin that was a focus of so much sensation. "Or link with you."

Zinnia's eyes flew open. "So you *do* feel it."

He smiled faintly. "You mean this?"

Power crashed across the metaphysical plane, questing for a prism. Zinnia responded as she had the very first time, as she always did to him, instinctively, eagerly, with a sense of rightness. The feeling of intimacy that was somehow sexual and yet far more than that, shimmered through the focus link.

"Yes," she whispered. *"This."*

"The first time it hit me I felt as if I'd stepped off the edge of a cliff." Nick pushed slowly, heavily into her. "I wondered if I'd finally snapped, the way they say high-class matrix-talents do sometimes."

"I thought I'd just met a real psychic vampire." She held her breath as her body stretched to accommodate him.

"I would never hurt you."

But you will, she thought. *When Hobart Batt finds you the perfect wife, the woman who will fit into your grand plan for the future, you will marry her. And when you do, you will hurt me far more than you ever could with your psychic talent.*

Nick thrust fully into her. In that moment she knew that he was not thinking about the nameless, faceless woman he would someday marry. In typical matrix fashion he was completely absorbed in the task at hand.

And that task was making love to her.

She would worry about the future when it crashed down around her, she promised herself.

On the metaphysical plane, vibrant energy pulsed through the crystal-clear prism. Zinnia gloried in the knowledge that, for a little while, whether or not he knew it, Nick was as much in love with her as it was possible for him to be.

Nick absently analyzed the pattern of the rain as it beat down on the glass roof. He felt as if he was still drifting, but it was an illusion. He was no longer in the pool. He and Zinnia were both wrapped in thick towels and stretched out on loungers that had been placed side by side.

Everything was supposed to be under control now. He had achieved his goal. She had agreed to the affair. So why couldn't he get rid of the cold uneasy chill of wrongness that had settled in his gut.

It was as if some element or coordinate was still missing from the design. But he could not figure out what he lacked to complete the matrix. He only knew that it was not yet right.

"Nick?" Zinnia turned her head and smiled at him. Feminine satisfaction gleamed in the depths of her warm languorous eyes. "Something wrong?"

"I was just thinking."

"Always a bad sign with a matrix."

He ignored that. "Why did you agree to the affair?"

"Complaints already?"

"I'm serious."

"You're always serious." She paused. "Or, almost always."

"I just want to know why you decided to go ahead with it."

"Nick, I know you're a matrix and therefore inclined to obsess on details that don't seem to fit into the pattern, but some things you just have to accept."

He gazed steadily at her. "Is it because of what we feel when we link?"

"No." She smiled. "Although I'll admit it's interesting."

"Is it because the sex is great?"

"No, but that's very interesting, too."

"Is it because you got tired of waiting for Mr. Right to show up and decided to experiment with me, instead?"

"No."

"Is it because you feel sorry for matrix-talents in general and since I'm the highest-class matrix you've ever met you feel more than the usual degree of pity?"

"You're starting to slip into paranoia, here, Nick."

He levered himself up and looked down at her. "Tell me why you agreed to have an affair with me."

"For heaven's sake, isn't it obvious?" She rolled off the lounger, tightened her grip on the towel, and started toward the cabana. "I decided to have an affair with you because I'm in love with you."

Nick stopped breathing. By the time he managed to fill his lungs with air, she had vanished into the changing room.

And the patterns in the matrix had tumbled into disarray.

He was still reeling from the shock of Zinnia's words three hours later when he walked into the richly paneled bar of the exclusive Founders' Club.

She loved him.

She didn't know it, but she had completely screwed

up his entire world. He had been struggling to make her simple words fit into the matrix ever since she had flung them at him with such devastating nonchalance.

She probably hadn't intended the words to be taken literally, he told himself for what had to be the seventy-sixth time in three hours. She had probably meant that she loved the sex. After all, she didn't have much in the way of comparisons.

Which meant that she had undoubtedly confused passion with love. An understandable mistake for a woman who had never had another lover.

But even if that was true, he would never forget Zinnia's words of love. They had warmed something inside him that had been cold for a very long time. He did not know what would happen if he doused the cheerful blaze. The thought of confronting the chill again was not an inviting one.

He forced his new problems to the side of his attention when he spotted Orrin Chastain sitting alone in a booth. The older man's shoulders were hunched. A scotch-tini sat on the table in front of him.

Nick crossed the heavily carpeted room to join Orrin. The day was winding down and the club bar was beginning to fill with expensively suited members.

The Founders' Club catered to the business and political elite of New Seattle. The heavy, dark, Later Expansion Period decor provided the discreet ambience needed by those who made the kind of decisions that affected the politics and economy of the entire city-state.

As he walked through the room Nick could hear snippets of muffled conversations. They involved a wide variety of topics, but he knew that at the core of each lay the subject of money. It always came down to money, he reflected.

"Hello, Uncle Orrin."

Orrin looked up, startled, when Nick came to a halt beside the table. Belatedly he squared his shoulders. "What in five hells are you doing here?"

"I want to talk to you." Nick slid into the booth on the side opposite Orrin. "I have a question to ask you."

"How did you get into this club?" Orrin cast a disgruntled glance toward the entrance. "It's supposed to be private. Members only."

Nick smiled humorlessly. "I got in the same way everyone else in here did. I bought my way in."

Orrin's jaw clenched. "I don't believe it."

"Want to see my membership card?"

"Goddamn it, I've got a business meeting here in a few minutes."

"How are the talks with your new potential investor going?"

"I have no intention of discussing the future of Chastain, Inc. with you."

Nick shrugged. "Suit yourself." He reached into his pocket and withdrew the gold cuff link he had found in Wilkes's workshop. "Mind telling me where you lost this?"

Orrin's brows jerked in surprise. "That's mine. I've been looking for it. Where the hell did you find it?"

"It was just lying around."

"Give it to me." Orrin held out his hand in an imperious manner. "That is one of my Chastain cuff links. I thought I was going to have to commission a duplicate to replace that one."

Nick closed his fingers around the cuff link. "What happened to my father's set?"

Orrin's face turned an unpleasant shade of purple. "That is none of your concern. The tradition affects only the legitimate branch of the family. Give me that cuff link. It belongs to me. If you don't hand it over, you're no better than a thief."

"I want to know where you lost it."

"I have no idea," Orrin exploded in muffled tones. "I simply noticed that it was missing a few days ago. I'd like to know how you came across it."

"I found it in the house of a man named Alfred Wilkes." Nick watched Orrin's face carefully but there was no flicker of recognition.

"I don't know anyone named Wilkes. Hand it over at once."

Nick slowly uncurled his fingers. He rose to his feet and dropped the cuff link into Orrin's palm. "Thanks, Uncle. As usual, you've been very helpful. I'll look forward to seeing you tomorrow evening."

Orrin's eyes widened in outrage. "What do you mean?"

"Don't tell me you've forgotten the annual Founders' Club ball?"

"You're going to attend the charity ball?" Orrin looked shocked. "But it's . . . it's a club affair."

"And as I told you, I'm now a member." Nick smiled thinly. "Brace yourself, Orrin, my side of the Chastain clan is going legit. In another few years no one will even remember that there was a bastard in the family tree. It's amazing how easy it is to rewrite history. If you have the money, that is."

"You can't just buy your way into respectable circles," Orrin sputtered.

"Watch me."

"Why, you . . . you—"

Nick ignored him. He started toward the door without a backward glance. He had gone two strides when he saw Duncan Luttrell enter the bar. There was something about the way Luttrell briefly surveyed the crowd that enabled Nick to make several small connections in one portion of the matrix.

He paused, considering the matter briefly. Then he turned and walked back to the booth were Orrin sat.

"Thought you'd left," Orrin muttered.

"A word of advice, Uncle."

"I don't want your damned advice."

Nick indicated the scotch-tini sitting on the table. "If you're going to do a deal with Luttrell, lay off the alcohol before you start negotiating."

"Now what in blazes are you talking about?"

"Luttrell may look and sound like a nice guy who just happened to get lucky in the computer business, but he didn't build SynIce into the company it is by being a good-natured pushover. He's smart. Very, very smart. And he's nobody's fool."

"Luttrell is a good businessman, I'll grant you that." Orrin's gaze narrowed. "He is also a gentleman, unlike some people I could mention. Take your so-called advice and get out of here."

"Whatever you say, Uncle." Nick turned and started back toward the door. He did not know why he had even bothered to issue the warning. Zinnia would no doubt have some silly explanation involving his so-called family values.

Duncan smiled politely when he made to pass Nick. His eyes held cool speculation. "You're Nick Chastain, aren't you?"

"Yes."

"We've never met personally, although I've been into your casino once or twice. An interesting business you've got there."

"Thanks. It's made me rich."

Duncan looked briefly amused by the tasteless answer. "We seem to be hearing and seeing a lot of you lately in the tabloids. I thought you liked privacy."

"I do," Nick said. "But sometimes one has to make sacrifices in order to get what one wants."

"Very true. I understand you're a new member here."

"That's right." Nick wondered if Duncan would make a crack about the club's declining standards.

"You're seeing a friend of mine, I believe," Duncan said instead. "Zinnia Spring."

Nick was stunned by the rush of fierce protectiveness and possessiveness that slammed through him. He fought down an almost irresistible urge to shove Duncan up against the nearest wall and tell him how things really were between himself and Zinnia. *I'm not just seeing her, I'm having an affair with her, you son of a spider-frog. Stay away from her. I don't want you touching her.*

Somehow he managed to keep his expression calm and controlled. "Zinnia and I are very close."

"Look, I'll level with you here, Chastain. She's a very nice lady and she's been through a lot. I wouldn't want to see her hurt."

"Zinnia and I understand each other." Nick walked away before Duncan could give him the rest of the lecture. He had enough problems on his hands. He did not want to add a sense of guilt to the matrix.

"The financial aspect? I don't understand, Miss Spring. I thought I mentioned that the University of New Portland funded the Third Expedition."

Newton DeForest's voice was as cheerful as ever on the other end of the line. Zinnia had a vision of him manicuring the tentacles of one of his grotesque plants while he spoke with her.

"Yes, I know," she said. "But I'm wondering about the university's source of funds. A major expedition costs a lot. Was the Third underwritten by a wealthy donor or a corporation?"

"I see what you mean." DeForest sounded thoughtful. "There was very likely corporate money involved. After all, business has a lot to gain from successful exploration trips. Companies often finance expeditions. But any materials on that subject were no doubt destroyed when the records storage facility burned some thirty-four years ago. The aliens are very clever, you know. Very thorough when it comes to covering their tracks."

"Do you think you might have anything in your personal files? The ones you said you kept in the family crypt?"

"Doubt it," Newton said. "Didn't bother much with the financial side of the story. I've always found money a rather dull subject. The aliens don't use money, you know. They've evolved beyond the need for cash."

"How convenient for them," Zinnia muttered. "Professor, I hate to put you to any more trouble, but would you mind very much just taking a look through your old files? Anything that dealt with the funding of the Third Expedition would be of great interest to me."

"Very well. But don't get your hopes up, Miss Spring. Even if I did find the name of a company that contributed funds for the project, what good would the information do you?"

"I don't know," Zinnia admitted.

She hung up the phone and sat thinking for a long time.

The larger and more complicated the mystery became, the more confusing it was. Or, as Nick would say, the more the elements in the matrix threatened to shift and realign themselves in meaningless patterns.

And the most disturbing factor of all was her relationship with the master of the matrix.

Chapter
20

* * * * * * * * * *

Duncan smiled at Zinnia as he took her into his arms on the crowded dance floor. "You look lovely tonight. I'm only sorry it was Chastain who brought you. At least he let me have one dance."

Zinnia chuckled. They both knew Nick had not given his permission. He had been talking with a business acquaintance when Duncan had appeared at her side and asked for the dance. She had accepted without a second's hesitation even though she had been aware of Nick's frown of disapproval when he saw her take the floor with Duncan.

Start as you mean to go on, she told herself. If she was going to have an affair with an off-the-chart matrix, she had to get the rules straight at the very beginning. And the first rule was that Nick could not make all the rules. He could not control everything and everyone. He would drive them both crazy if he tried.

Zinnia was mildly surprised to discover that she was enjoying herself tonight. It had been a long time since she had last danced. The Founders' Club ballroom was a glittering scene. The jelly-ice chandeliers cast a warm romantic glow over the well-dressed crowd. Through the windows she could see the lights of the city sparkling below on the dark carpet of the night.

She had panicked briefly when she had found herself faced with the problem of coming up with an appropriate dress but Gracie Proud, Clementine's permanent partner, had come to the rescue. Gracie knew fashion almost as well as she knew the focus business. She had sent Zinnia to one of her favorite boutiques.

The long, elegantly simple slip of a dress that Zinnia had discovered in the shop was the color of rare fire crystal. She had stored the memory of the appreciative gleam that had appeared in Nick's eyes when he saw her in it away in her heart. In the years ahead she knew that she would take it out from time to time to cherish it.

"I read in the papers that your recent expansion has given you the platform you need to launch the new generation of SynIce software," she said. "Congratulations. You pulled it off."

"The media blitz is scheduled to start next month." Duncan's mouth tilted wryly. "I'm surprised you even noticed the news about SynIce. Your relationship with Chastain seems to occupy most of the front page these days."

She wrinkled her nose. "Only in the tabloids. And only because a certain Cedric Dexter has apparently decided to use Nick as a means of establishing a reputation as a sleazeoid photographer."

"Seems to be working. From what I can tell, *Synsation* sales are skyrocketing."

"How would you know?"

Duncan grinned. "Are you kidding? I'm one of the first in line to get my copy every morning."

Zinnia blushed. "I'd like to strangle Dexter."

Duncan's smile faded. "It's serious, isn't it? This thing with Chastain?"

"Yes."

"I guess there's not much point in warning you off him again, is there?"

"No."

"Be careful, Zinnia."

"It may be too late for that, too." She smiled. "But don't worry about me, Duncan. I know what I'm doing."

"And you don't give a damn about the gossip." He shook his head slightly. "I should hire you into an executive position at SynIce. You've got more guts than all of my managers put together."

Nick stood in the shadows of a large potted fern-tree and sipped a glass of champagne while he watched Duncan and Zinnia finish their dance. He was brooding again. He couldn't help it. The sensation of wrongness was a whisper of dread that touched all of his senses this evening, including those that functioned on the metaphysical plane.

The confusing part was that he could no longer sort out the legitimate sensory input that his psychically honed instincts were picking up from the rush of tangled sensations that he felt toward Zinnia.

He wanted to protect her from Luttrell, but logic told him there was no cause for concern. After all, she had been seeing Luttrell off and on for a month and a half before he had even met her. If she had been interested in the president of SynIce, she would have done something about it earlier. If there was one thing Zinnia was good at, he reminded himself, it was taking action to achieve her goals.

So why did the sight of her in Luttrell's arms make every single one of his muscles tighten as if in response to a threat? He did not understand the matrix here. This emotional stuff clogged up his thinking processes.

"Good evening, Nicholas."

Only one person in the whole world called him Nicholas. Nick steeled himself and turned to see Orrin's wife, Ella, standing at his shoulder.

"Hello, Aunt Ella."

He knew the greeting would annoy her. Like her husband, Ella hated to be reminded that he had a blood-relationship with the family. She was a small too-thin woman whose once-lovely features had become sharp and tightly drawn over the years. Nick was almost certain that her pinched look was the result of a restless dissatisfaction that ate away constantly at her insides.

His investigations into Chastain family history had produced the information that thirty-five years ago Ella had hoped to marry Bartholomew Chastain. When Bartholomew had left for the Western Islands without showing any interest in either the marriage or his family's business, she had turned her attention to Orrin. Nick suspected that it was Ella's skillful maneuvering that had resulted in Orrin becoming CEO of Chastain, Inc. after Bartholomew disappeared.

Ella had got what she wanted, but as far as Nick could see, she had never been particularly happy about it.

"I was surprised when Orrin told me that you would be here tonight," Ella said crisply. "I hadn't realized that you had been accepted into the Founders' Club."

"I can understand your deep sense of shock." Nick swirled the champagne in his glass. "The decline in standards these days is appalling, isn't it?"

"I assume you intended that to be amusing."

"Not really."

Ella cast a disapproving look at Zinnia, who was still in the middle of the dance floor with Duncan. "If you plan to move in these circles you would do well to be a bit more discriminating in your choice of female companions. Miss Spring has a certain reputation."

Nick swung around so quickly that Ella gasped and took a hasty step back. He lowered his voice to the merest of whispers. "So do I. Among other things, I am known for not tolerating insults to women who have honored me with their company."

Ella blinked once and then recovered quickly. "Don't you dare threaten me, Nicholas."

"I assume you want something or you would not have gone out of your way to talk to me in front of all your socially acceptable friends."

"There's no need for sarcasm. I wish to speak to you about a family matter."

"I thought you didn't consider me to be a member of the family."

Ella's too-snug features became even more tightly drawn. "There is no denying that you are Bartholomew's son. The whole world can see that. You are his living image. Therefore, I think it's time you repaid your obligation to this family."

"Only a Chastain would have the nerve to suggest that I've got an obligation to this family."

"I'm sure you're well aware that Chastain, Inc. is having financial difficulties."

"Yes." He smiled.

Ella's gaze hardened with grim determination. "I won't beat around the bush. Orrin's talks with Mr. Luttrell did not go well."

"You mean Luttrell refused to pour cash into Chastain?"

"Very shortsighted of him, but there you have it. As of this evening, Orrin has exhausted all possibilities. Chastain faces complete ruin. It is your responsibility to step into the breach. You are the only one who possesses sufficient financial capital to save the firm."

Nick nearly choked on the champagne. "My responsibility?"

"As the son of Bartholomew Chastain, it is your duty to invest in the family business. Orrin tells me that the company must have a cash infusion soon or we shall face bankruptcy. I will contact you in a few days to tell you exactly how much money is required."

"You look as if you've just watched the Curtain reopen." Zinnia smiled quizzically at Nick as he drew her out onto the dance floor. "Something wrong?"

"I had an amazing conversation with my aunt a few minutes ago." Nick took her into his arms and moved her into a slow gliding turn. "She informed me that I have a duty to invest in Chastain, Inc."

"Your family's firm?"

"My side of the family has no interest in the company."

"I see." She was amused by the austere passion that he had somehow managed to infuse into that simple declaration.

"What are you smiling at?"

"Nothing."

"Don't give me that." He glowered. "You think it's funny that my aunt wants me to put my money into the company?"

"No. I think it's a sign that the rest of the Chastains are desperate. I know the feeling."

"What in five hells do you mean?"

"If I'd been in your aunt's position, I'd have done the same thing. Unfortunately when Spring Industries went under there was no one in the family who had enough cash to save it."

"As far as the rest of the Chastains are concerned, I'm not in the family." Nick's hand tightened around her waist. "And I don't think that you would have gone down on your knees to anyone. Not even to save Spring Industries."

Zinnia raised her brows. "Did your aunt actually beg?"

"No, not exactly." Nick exhaled deeply. "You could say she stated her demands in no uncertain terms."

"I'm sure it took courage for her to approach you. She probably expected you to laugh in her face."

"You don't know my Aunt Ella." Nick steered her through the crowd of dancers with negligent grace. "She expected me to whip out my checkbook then and there."

"What did you do?"

"Smiled very politely and came over here to pry you out of Luttrell's arms."

"Smiled very politely?" She frowned. "I don't believe that for one moment. You never smile politely. Nick, I really think that you ought to think very carefully about this situation before you make any rash decisions."

"Don't," he warned gently, "try to tell me how to deal with the Chastains."

"I wouldn't dream of it."

"Damn." He had the grace to look chagrined. "I didn't mean to snap at you."

"Maybe we should both just shut up and dance."

"Good idea." He swung her into another slow turn.

Zinnia gave herself over to the music and the many sensory pleasures to be derived from the experience of dancing with a matrix. Nick's instinctive sense of timing and distances meant that they never accidentally bumped into other couples or had to change direction in a hasty awkward manner. When viewed from above the movements on a large ballroom floor always appeared random to her, but she knew that Nick had a feeling for the underlying pattern. The result was a smooth graceful trip around the room.

When the music came to an end, he seemed reluctant to let her leave his arms. He halted at the edge of the crowd and looked at her with intense eyes. "I think we've made our statement for the evening. Everyone here knows that we're a couple. Let's go home."

She felt herself grow warm in direct response to the blatant sexual desire that emanated from him. "Do you know, I used to think you were the subtle type."

"I don't know where you got that idea." He took her arm and started toward the nearest of the long row of double doors that lined one side of the ballroom.

Zinnia noticed a few heads turn to follow their progress toward the lobby. She had been aware of several discreet stares since Nick had escorted her into the ball but no one had actually said anything nasty in her range of hearing.

There were several small conversational groups clustered in the lobby. One or two people who had been friends of Zinnia's parents noticed her and nodded politely. She could see the speculation in their gazes when their attention shifted to Nick.

Nick did not appear to be aware of the attention they received as they crossed the lobby. He guided her toward the cloak room with the cool arrogance that seemed to be built into him.

"Wait here. I'll get your coat." He released Zinnia's arm to deal with the woman at the coat-check booth.

A flicker of movement near the elevators made Zinnia turn to see who was staring at her now.

She found herself looking straight at Rexford Eaton. It was the first time she had encountered him since the day the tabloid photographer had taken the ruinous picture of the two of them emerging from the bedroom.

Rexford was clearly nonplused to see her. He stood with his wife, Bethany, and the third member of their intimate trio, the tall distinguished Daria Gardener.

Zinnia told herself that she should have been prepared for this. After all, the Eatons had been members of the Founders' Club for three generations. And Daria Gardener's climb to the heights of politics had been largely financed by contributions from the people who moved in this world.

Eighteen months had gone by since the scandal had broken across the pages of the tabloids, but Zinnia's anger and disgust boiled up inside as if it had happened yesterday. Damn them all, she thought. They had come out of it unscathed, but she was still trying to recover from the loss of business these three secret lovers had caused her.

Her only consolation in that moment was that all three appeared as stunned to see her as she was to see them. She was particularly pleased to notice the distinct uneasiness that flashed in Rexford's eyes.

Zinnia gave Rexford, Bethany, and Daria her coldest smile and pointedly turned her back.

She found Nick standing right behind her. He had her coat draped over his arm.

"Easy," he said quietly. His eyes went to the threesome. "Run into some old acquaintances?"

"No one important."

"I can see that." He arranged the coat around her shoulders, took her arm, and started toward the bank of elevators.

A premonition of impending disaster descended on Zinnia. It did not require a matrix-talent to deduce that the vector of the path that Nick had chosen would bring them very close to Rexford, Bethany, and Daria.

"Uh, Nick—"

He ignored her.

The elegant threesome seemed to recognize that a predator was moving in their direction. Like a small flock of nervous goat-sheep, they turned to melt discreetly out of the way only to find themselves trapped by the wall and the wine bar. By the time they realized that they had been neatly cornered, Nick and Zinnia were almost upon them.

It might have been amusing to see the nervous alarm in their eyes, Zinnia thought, if it had not been for the fact that she knew Nick had purposefully selected this route to the elevators. He was up to something and that worried her.

"Think respectability," she warned out of the side of her mouth.

"Respectability is ever at the forefront of my thoughts." He studied the threesome with the lazy interest of a lion-pard that has happened upon trapped prey. He paced closer.

Rexford, Bethany, and Daria tried to squeeze discreetly aside but Nick gave them no space. His eyes were filled with dangerous anticipation as he came within a hairsbreadth of brushing against Rexford's shoulder.

"Well, well," Nick said in a soft voice that managed to reach the small crowd standing at the nearby wine bar. "Will you look at this, Zinnia. You know the old saying, two's company but three's a syn-sex show."

Zinnia groaned silently. The devil was loose in the Founders' Club. There would be hell to pay.

Rexford blinked several times. His mouth opened and closed and color rushed into his face. "What is the meaning of that crude remark?"

Bethany's eyes widened in alarm. "For God's sake, Rex, don't make a scene."

"Don't let him goad you, Rex," Daria said with cold authority.

Nick grinned at Rexford. "Which one is the dominatrix, Rex? Or do they take turns with the little whips and chains?"

"Bastard," Rexford managed in a hoarse whisper. "Get out of here."

Daria took charge. She looked at Nick with icy disdain. "I see the Founders' Club has lowered its criteria for the acceptance of new members."

That was too much for Zinnia. She smiled sweetly at Daria. "It certainly has. Otherwise how could one possibly explain the presence of three such avant-garde thinkers such as you and the Eatons?"

Bethany's eyes snapped. "I would advise you to control your tongue, Miss Spring. You're getting enough publicity in the tabloids as it is, these days."

"I've always been rather sorry that the three of you didn't get the kind of attention that I got eighteen months ago," Zinnia murmured.

Rexford took a step toward her, his hands clenched at his sides. "One more word, Miss Spring, and I'll have my lawyers after you. By the time they're finished, you won't have a dime left to your name."

"Don't make threats you can't carry out, Eaton," Nick said gently. "You aren't going to call your lawyers."

Rexford swung toward him, chin outthrust. "I damn well will do just that if the two of you don't leave us alone. Now take yourselves off. This club is for decent, civilized people, not bastard trash from the islands."

Zinnia saw red. "Don't you dare call him trash. Nick Chastain is a gentleman. You, on the other hand, are a hypocritical son-of-a-spider-frog, Rexford Eaton. You had no compunction about throwing me to the press in order to cover up your cozy little arrangement with your wife and Miss Gardener."

Daria's face went rigid. "Speaking of cozy arrangements, Miss Spring, how does it feel to be the current mistress of the notorious Nick Chastain? I assume there are some interesting financial advantages to the position?"

"Nothing compared to the financial advantages a

politician like you receives from sleeping with the
Eatons," Zinnia shot back.

Bethany gasped. "You little tramp. I can't imagine
why they let you or Mr. Chastain attend this ball."

Nick grabbed Zinnia's arm and hauled her back to
his side before she could get her fingers on Daria's
throat.

"Think respectability," he said. But his eyes were
gleaming.

"That does it." Rexford clenched and unclenched
his hands. "I'm calling my lawyers in the morning."

Nick looked at him. "Before you call them, I
suggest you talk to your nephew, Warren. He owes me
over sixty thousand dollars. At this point, it's a
private matter. But I can certainly arrange for the
debt to be made public. I'm sure it would make
interesting reading in the tabloids."

Rexford's face turned an unpleasant purple. "Why,
you . . . you bastard." He took a menacing step forward.

"Rex, no," Daria snapped.

Nick grinned. "You heard her. Down, Rex. By the
way, just how far down do you usually go?"

Rexford gritted his teeth in rage and threw a
roundhouse punch.

"Nick, look out," Zinnia yelled.

Someone at the wine bar screamed.

A familiar figure leaped out of the hallway that led
to the restrooms.

"Totally synergistic," Cedric Dexter said happily.
He raised his camera and grabbed the shot.

The flash exploded just as Nick crumpled dramati-
cally to the floor.

Zinnia gazed steadfastly at the closed doors of the
elevator that was carrying them to the parking garage
twenty floors below. "I can't believe it. A brawl in the
hallowed halls of the Founders' Club."

"Hey, these things happen even in the best places." Nick straightened his black bow tie. "No harm done."

"No harm?" She was nearly speechless. "That picture that Dexter took will be on the front page of *Synsation* tomorrow."

"We've been there before," Nick said. He looked remarkably cheerful.

She shoved her hands into the pockets of her coat. "What about your plans to become respectable?"

He smiled as the elevator glided to a halt. "I keep telling you, respectability is a commodity. I can afford it."

Zinnia watched the doors slide open to reveal the dark confines of the third floor of the underground garage. "For the record, I want it noted that this time, it was not my fault. You started that scene."

"I had help." Nick's eyes were wickedly amused. "I thought we worked well together, partner."

She glanced back at him over her shoulder as she stepped out of the elevator. "You deliberately took that fall. Eaton missed you by a mile."

"Not for lack of trying."

She eyed him thoughtfully. "Is Rexford Eaton's nephew really in hock to your casino?"

"Yes."

"I'll bet you set him up," she accused. "What's more, I'll bet you planned that whole confrontation with Eaton and his wife and Daria Gardener."

"Now, Zinnia, how could I have known we'd run into them tonight?" Nick followed her out of the elevator.

"Maybe you didn't know it would happen tonight. But you knew that sooner or later we'd encounter them if we went to functions like this one. What's more, you knew that Rexford would very likely threaten to sue when it did happen."

"It was a possibility."

"So you arranged to make sure that his nephew was in an embarrassing financial position with your casino before you made your move tonight."

"You're getting pretty good at this conspiracy-theory stuff," he said approvingly.

"It comes from hanging around you."

"The *lights.*" The laughter vanished from Nick's eyes in the space of a heartbeat.

"What?"

"Zinnia, come here." Nick reached for her.

"What's wrong?" At that instant it hit her that all of the lights in this section of the garage were out.

By then it was much too late to retreat to the safety of the elevator.

She heard the rapid footsteps behind her and whirled around to see two men leap from the deep shadows between the parked cars. There was just enough light spilling from the crack between the closing doors of the elevator to see the scarves around their faces and the knives in their hands.

"Don't move," one of them shouted. "Don't nobody move."

"Oh, my God, Nick. Look out."

Nick went past her in a smooth, silent, utterly lethal rush. She saw the two muggers halt in shock and confusion when they realized that one of their victims was attacking.

"He's crazy," one of them shouted.

"Not as crazy as he's gonna be." The other man slashed wildly with his knife.

And then Nick was upon him. Zinnia heard a knife clatter on the concrete garage floor.

"Get him." The second man reeled backward and fetched up hard against the hood of a car.

"It wasn't supposed to go down like this," the first man yelled.

Zinnia watched in horror as the shadows of the

three men merged. She looked around desperately for a weapon. She could barely make out the shape of the metal trash bin stationed beside the elevator.

She seized the lid and dashed toward the struggling men. The dim glow filtering from the far end of the garage enabled her to distinguish Nick from his two assailants.

One of the attackers was on the floor, groaning. Zinnia saw that he was clutching his groin. The other one rolled heavily past her feet and scrambled erect. He lurched backward toward the elevator.

Nick came up off the floor in pursuit.

Zinnia saw something gleam in the shadows. "Nick, he still has his knife."

The man who had been groaning and clutching himself tried to stagger to his feet. He lunged for his fallen knife.

"Forget it," Zinnia said. She swung the lid hard against his head and shoulders. He flopped back down to the floor and lay there, moaning.

She kicked the knife under a car and whirled back around. She heard a sickening thud as Nick shoved his quarry up against the wall. The knife fell from the man's hand.

Nick smashed a fist into the mugger's midsection.

Zinnia heard the sound of shattering glass and a faint hiss.

"Enjoy, sucker. Compliments of the house." The man's voice was slurred but unmistakably triumphant as he slithered to the floor and collapsed.

Nick stood utterly still in the shadows, staring down at the fallen man. He said nothing.

"Nick?"

A great terror unlike anything she had ever known swept over Zinnia. Something was very, very wrong.

"Nick." She dropped the trash-can lid and rushed toward him. "Are you hurt? Did he cut you?"

"No." His whisper was barely audible, impossibly remote. "He didn't cut me."

The elevator doors opened at that moment. Two couples made to step out.

"What the hell happened to the lights?" One of the men demanded.

"Oh, my God," a woman whispered.

All four people stared in shock at the sight of the two men lying on the garage floor.

"What's going on here?" the other woman demanded. "George, call the police."

Zinnia ignored them. She stared at Nick's stark features. In the light that poured from the elevator cab she could see the last traces of a white mist that had enveloped him for a few seconds. It was dissipating rapidly but the stunned horror in his eyes looked as if it would last forever.

"Nick, what is it?" She reached him, grabbed his shoulders and tried to shake him. It was like trying to shake a mountain. "Tell me what's wrong."

"Crazy-fog. He broke the pod in my face just as I hit him. Must have been very pure stuff. I got a huge dose of it."

"Nick, it's all right, you won't die from an overdose of crazy-fog. I'll get you to the hospital."

"No. I won't die." His eyes glowed with dread. "It'll be much, much worse."

"What is it?" She wrapped her arms tightly around him. "What's the stuff doing to you? Tell me. Tell me, damn it."

"I can see the chaos," he said softly. "In another few seconds I'll be in the middle of it. And there is no way back. I'm going insane, Zinnia. Contact Feather. He'll know what to do. He has instructions."

Zinnia nearly choked on her rage and fear. "Instructions for what?"

He caught her hand in his and crushed her fingers. "Promise me you'll call him quickly. Promise me."

"Yes. I'll call him."

"Something I want to tell you."

"Save it." She pushed him toward the elevator. "I'm taking you to the emergency room."

"No. Got to tell you now. While I still can."

"What is it?"

"I love you, Zinnia."

Chapter
21

* * * * * * * * * *

The chaos rolled toward him, a tidal wave of darkness that would consume the matrix of his soul. Zinnia's face was the only point of reference that he had left. He knew he would not have it for long. He wished she would smile just once more. He wanted to hold the memory close as the storm swept over him.

But she was glaring at him.

"Nick, Nick, can you hear me?"

He tried to reach out to touch her face but his hand would not obey the command. His fingers folded into a tight fist instead. He tried to use the fist to fend off the whirling lights but there were too many.

Zinnia's face vanished into the depths of the night. The panic that he had been trying to cage broke free. He lurched toward the place where she had been a second earlier, but she was not there.

"Zinnia." His scream echoed in the winds of chaos. He did not know whether he had uttered it aloud or if the sound he had made was only in his head.

Crazy. He was going crazy. He stared into the depths of the dark waves hurtling down on him and he realized that he was looking at the forces of his own psychic energy whirling out of control.

"Nick, listen to me. Don't you dare slip away from me. Do you hear me?"

Zinnia was yelling at him. Her voice reached him through the thunder of meaningless noise. That was Zinnia for you. Nothing could hold her down for long. When she had a point to make, she made sure it got heard.

"Damn you, Nick, pay attention. Squeeze my hand if you can hear me."

He could not figure out how to give the instruction to his fingers.

"Nick, hang on. The ambulance is here now."

More lights appeared in the storm. Meaningless.

No doctor could save him from the sea of chaos. He tried to anchor himself, but there was nothing that he could hold. The world itself was no longer stable.

The matrix was coming apart, fracturing into millions of bits of meaningless data. No connections. No links. No pattern.

The truly terrifying thing was that in another moment he would no longer be able to frame such a logical coherent thought. He would not be able to contemplate his own madness.

In another few seconds he would be trapped forever in chaos.

"Nick, pay attention. I want you to link with me."

He knew the voice belonged to Zinnia, but he could no longer comprehend the words.

"Link, damn you. Do it now."

Something appeared in the spinning darkness. A stable glowing object. Clear as crystal. He gazed at it with hungry longing. A great need arose within him.

"Focus your talent through the prism, Nick. Don't think about anything else. Just send your power through the prism. I'll keep it safe."

Safe. He would be safe if he could just figure out what the voice was talking about.

The prism shimmered, untouched by the storm that howled around it. Nick fought his way toward the crystal. If he could just touch it, he would be safe.

It was the longest journey of his life. In the midst of it he forgot why he was battling his way through the raging tides of uncontrolled energy. He only knew that he had to get to the prism. It compelled him with a power that could stand against chaos.

"Come to me, Nick. Focus the energy through me. Channel it into the prism."

One more faltering step and he managed to put his hand on the crystal. At last he had something solid to cling to in the spinning darkness that enveloped the metaphysical plane.

The winds of psychic energy shrieked around him, trying to tear him away from the crystal.

Rage blossomed. "No. I am the master of the matrix."

Somewhere in the darkness he heard a faint response.

"Yes, Nick. You are the master of the matrix. You control the energy. It does not control you. Not unless you let it. I've given you a prism. Use it. Use it, damn it."

He would not be torn from his anchor. With savage determination he clung to the prism. He chose the closest wave of ravenous energy and fed it to the glowing crystal.

To his amazement, it obeyed his will. It slammed through the prism and emerged as a band of controlled energy.

He reached for the next crashing wave. It, too, entered the prism as a piece of chaos and was transformed into a controllable band of power.

He grabbed another.

And another.

A new fear replaced the old. What if the prism could not handle so much raw energy.

But the crystal did not waver or weaken as he shoved power through it.

Slowly the chaos faded. The psychic talent that slammed through the crystal and roared across the metaphysical plane was as powerful as ever, but thanks to the prism it was a force that could be controlled.

As long as it was controllable, he would not be swallowed up by chaos. He would not go crazy as long as he kept feeding energy to the prism.

"He seems to have calmed considerably during the past hour," the doctor said. The name tag on her jacket read DR. MILDRED FERGUSON. Her dark brown skin glowed warmly in the lights of the bedside monitors.

The overhead lamps had been turned off in an effort to create a more soothing environment for the patient. Standard procedure in cases of crazy-fog overdose, Dr. Ferguson had explained. Zinnia was not certain that Nick would have noticed, one way or the other. As far as she could tell, he was unaware of anything except the battle for survival that he was waging on the metaphysical plane.

Dr. Ferguson glanced at Zinnia. "We may be through the crisis."

"You aren't certain?"

"Crazy-fog is unpredictable stuff." Dr. Ferguson's brown eyes were kind but troubled. "It just appeared on the streets a few months ago and we don't know much about it yet. We have learned that it affects people in different ways, depending on the syn-psych profile of the patient."

"Nick is a matrix."

"So you said. To be frank, we've never seen a

matrix-talent under the influence of fog, let alone a high-class matrix. We don't know what to expect."

"I understand." It wasn't easy talking to Dr. Ferguson while she held the focus on the metaphysical plane. There was so much power pouring through the prism now that Zinnia could barely concentrate on anything else.

"Miss Spring, as I'm sure you're well aware, people who manifest a talent for Synergistic Matrix Analysis are the least understood by the syn-psych experts."

"I know."

"The lack of information is partly the fault of the talents, themselves, of course. By nature they tend to be secretive and reclusive. They won't allow themselves to be properly studied and tested." Dr. Ferguson sighed. "Unfortunately, that means that when this sort of thing happens, we're left with very little in the way of syn-psych data to guide us."

"How long will the drug be active in his system?"

"Fortunately crazy-fog metabolizes relatively quickly. Most of it will be gone in a few hours." Dr. Ferguson hesitated. "I must warn you that one of the problems in this case was that the dose he received was extremely large and very pure."

"He's back in control on the metaphysical plane. It's taking everything he's got to deal with his psychic energy, but he is managing to handle it."

Dr. Ferguson's dark brows drew together. "You're still holding the focus for him?"

"Yes."

"Very few prisms can work for extended periods of time with a matrix. They're not quite normal."

Zinnia smiled wanly. "I'm not exactly a normal prism."

"Even so, you must be getting close to psychic exhaustion. How much longer can you hold the focus?"

Zinnia tightened her grip on Nick's hand. "As long as he needs it."

He heard voices. Familiar voices. A man and the woman who kept him sane. They were arguing.

"Get out of here, Feather." The woman was furious. "I told the nurse not to let anyone into this room."

"Don't give me orders, lady. I don't work for you. I work for Nick. Why didn't you send for me when it happened?"

"I was too busy getting him to the hospital."

"Bat-snake shit. You coulda told someone to call. Instead, I have to find out from Nelson Burlton on the late-night news."

"Stay away from the bed, damn you." The woman sounded wild now. "If you don't get away from him, I'll scream for help."

"Hey, leggo my arm. What the hell is wrong with you? I got a right to visit my boss in the hospital."

"You're not here to visit him. You're here to kill him."

"Huh? Kill Nick? Five hells. Are you crazy or somethin'?"

"He told me that you had instructions," the woman said grimly. "That you would know what to do in a situation like this."

"Yeah. That's right. I got my instructions."

"The only thing Nick fears is the possibility that he might go insane. He told you that if that ever happened, he wanted you to put him out of his misery, didn't he? But he's not going crazy, Feather. I'm holding the focus for him. He's going to be all right."

"If you think Nick would ask someone to slit his wrists for him, you're the loony one, lady. He'd never put that kind of burden on someone else. If he wanted to commit suicide, he'd do the job, himself."

"Are you telling me that you're not here to kill him?"

"Hell, no. I'm here because I'm his friend and because I'm also his next-in-command. If somethin' happens to him, I'm supposed to take care of things at the casino."

"What do you mean?"

"Lady, Nick, here, employs a coupla hundred people at Chastain's Palace. Folks depend on him. He's got responsibilities."

"And you're the one who's supposed to take care of those responsibilities if he can't, is that it?"

"You got it right, lady. About time."

"Well, nothing is going to happen to him." There was absolute conviction in the woman's voice. "He'll be fine in a few more hours. The doctor says the last of the crazy-fog will have been flushed out of his system by morning."

"Glad to hear that."

"So why don't you leave? I'll call you when he comes out of it."

"You know somethin'? You're as suspicious as he is."

"Leave. Now."

"Okay, okay. You're some piece of work, you know that? Wonder if the boss knows what he's getting into with you."

"Feather?"

"Yeah?"

"Nick says you have contacts on the street."

"So?"

"If you want to make yourself useful," the woman said slowly, "why don't you have your contacts look for the two men who did this. In the confusion, they both got away before the cops arrived."

There was a short silence.

"You saying what I think you're saying, lady?"

"This was no ordinary mugging attempt. Those two men were waiting for us when we got off the elevator. The doctor says the dose of the drug that Nick received was very strong and very pure. If those two junkies already had their fix for the night, why would they bother to rob us?"

"Good point. If they already had the crazy-fog, the only thing they would have been thinking about was getting off on it. Fog-heads don't tend to worry much about the future. All they care about is the next fix."

"The two who attacked us did not fight as if they were on drugs. What's more, I'm sure I heard one of them say something about how Nick would soon go crazy."

"Maybe you're right," the man called Feather said. He sounded thoughtful now. "Maybe I best go make myself useful."

"Do that."

Nick was amused at the woman's curt authoritative tone, but there was no way to laugh on the metaphysical plane. He was too busy shoving wild power through the glowing crystal.

He was aware of the warmth first. Her hand was wrapped around his. He could feel the pleasant heat of her palm seeping into his cold fingers. Then he realized that the entire left side of his body was warm. He could feel the curve of her hip pressed against him.

He opened his eyes and saw the narrow band of morning sunlight that had managed to slip between the drawn shades. When he turned his head on the pillow he saw Zinnia asleep beside him.

He did not know when he had finally finished wrestling the demons of his psychic energy. He only knew that at some point during the endless night he had at last achieved a state of calm exhaustion, thanks to Zinnia. She had held the focus until the storm had passed.

Even a full-spectrum prism should have burned out quickly in the face of the ceaseless waves of raw, high-class matrix-talent that Zinnia had handled last night. Psychic burnout was nature's way of protecting prisms from being overpowered and controlled by a talent whose energy level was higher than the prism's. The burnout was a temporary condition. Unpleasant, but not permanent.

But Zinnia had not burned out. She was every bit as strong as he was. Nick smiled at the thought.

Her lashes fluttered. For a few seconds she seemed disoriented. Then her eyes cleared. "You're awake."

"And reasonably sane, thanks to you."

She pushed herself up to a sitting position. "My God, you scared the living daylights out of me."

"Believe me, you couldn't have been half as scared as I was." He reached up to run a hand through her tangled hair. "I have never been so glad to see anyone as I am to see you right now."

"Do you feel all right?"

"Never better." He smiled. "Which is pretty amazing, considering the fact that I spent the night in the company of a genuine psychic vampire."

She halted half on and half off the bed. Her eyes widened. "Are you calling *me* a psychic vampire?"

"I'm calling you mine, Zinnia Spring." He pulled her back down on top of him and kissed her deeply.

When he released her, she smiled at him. But there was a wistful sadness in her eyes that worried him almost as much as the winds of chaos had.

"Zinnia?"

"Don't move. I've got to call Dr. Ferguson."

The door opened just as Zinnia stabbed a call button. A middle-aged woman in a badly wrinkled medical jacket walked into the room. She looked weary, but when she saw Nick sitting up in the bed, her dark brown eyes brightened with satisfaction.

"Welcome back to the physical plane, Mr. Chastain. I'm Dr. Ferguson." She moved toward the bed. "You had us worried there for a while. But Miss Spring assured us that you were keeping yourself busy elsewhere."

"Very busy." Nick rubbed the stubble on his jaw. "What day is this?"

"The morning after the ball," Dr. Ferguson said with a quick surprising chuckle. "You and Miss Spring will be thrilled to know that you're in the papers."

"Because of the attack in the garage?" Zinnia asked.

"Not exactly." Dr. Ferguson held up a copy of *Synsation.*

Zinnia groaned. "Oh, no, not again."

Nick studied the picture of himself sprawled on the floor of the Founders' Club lobby. In the photo Zinnia knelt anxiously at his side. Rexford Eaton stood over him, fists clenched. Daria and Bethany wore expressions of angry dismay. A ring of well-dressed spectators stared in shock.

"Take your time," Dr. Ferguson said. "I've got to see to another patient." She looked vastly amused as she left the room.

Nick read the first paragraph of the story.

> Life in High Society. Things went from bad to worse for Nick Chastain last night. Following this bruising encounter with one of the Scarlet Lady's old flames, he wound up in the hospital after a mugging in the Founders' Club garage. No word on the extent of the damage, but rumor has it one of the attackers hit him with a dose of crazy-fog. Wonder if things were a trifle more civilized in the Western Islands?

"Now, don't get excited, Nick." Zinnia touched his shoulder. "You're still recovering. You need to stay calm."

Nick smiled with deep satisfaction. "Why should I get excited? Cedric Dexter finally got it right this time."

"What do you mean?"

He tapped the paper with one finger. "I mean that with this photo, I now have grounds for a protracted lawsuit that will drag Rexford Eaton through the courts for months."

Zinnia narrowed her eyes. "You goaded him on purpose last night, didn't you? You knew Cedric Dexter was skulking around the lobby?"

"Saw him when I went to get your coat." Nick scanned the next paragraph of the article. "I suppose it was too much to hope that Dexter would have gotten a description of the two muggers."

"Feather is looking for them." Zinnia's brows snapped briskly together. "Nick, about this lawsuit. I really don't think it's a good idea. I appreciate that you want to get some revenge on Eaton and Daria and Bethany for what they did to me, but a long court battle will cost a fortune."

"I can afford it."

"You always say that. But some things aren't worth the price and this is one of them. Let it go, Nick. That picture is punishment enough for those three. It'll take weeks for them to live it down."

She was probably right, he thought, but he was reluctant to give up his newly hatched scheme. On the other hand, the last thing he wanted at that moment was an argument with Zinnia. The melancholic expression in her eyes a few minutes ago still worried him.

"I'll think about it," he said.

He was still pondering the look in Zinnia's eyes a few hours later when the door of the hospital room opened with a sharp bang. A vision in black leather, studs, and chains stalked toward the bed. Short, stark white hair bristled. Boot heels rang on the tile. Dark eyes glowered ferociously.

Nick put down the notepad he had been using to make a list of instructions for Feather. "Clementine Malone, I presume?"

"Damn right." Clementine propped one booted foot on the nearest chair and braced her forearm on her leather-clad thigh. "I think we'd better talk."

"About Zinnia?"

"Yes. About Zinnia. She works for me and I look out for my employees. I've tried to stay out of this, but now things have gone too far. What in five hells are you up to, Chastain?"

"I enjoy her company. What makes you think I'm up to anything other than the obvious?"

"Bat-snake shit. You're a matrix." Clementine scowled. "Matrix-talents are anything but obvious. The stronger they are, the more secretive, devious, manipulative, and downright sneaky they get."

"We've gotten a bad rap."

"Sure. And I'll bet you refund to your customers all the money you take from them at your casino, too."

"I didn't say I was stupid."

"No one's accusing you of stupidity. What are your intentions toward Zinnia?"

"My intentions?"

"I know you're registering on the sly with a match-making agency. And I know Zinnia's registration is inactive because she was declared unmatchable. Which pretty much means that you don't plan to marry her."

"Do you always leap to conclusions?"

"Come off it, Chastain. Zinnia says you want a wife from a wealthy upper-class family. Her clan used to meet that criteria but it doesn't anymore. It's fallen a long way since the bankruptcy. Besides, even if everything were hunky dory in all the other departments, I doubt that the two of you could be matched. Everyone knows the agencies never match high-class talents and full-spectrum prisms."

"I hear it happens occasionally."

"Try hardly ever." Clementine's mouth curved with disdain. "Zinnia says you've got a plan to buy respectability."

"It's a good plan. What's more, it's working."

Clementine gave him a mocking sneer. "The daily photos in *Synsation* are part of your master plan?"

"Minor setbacks," he assured her. "They won't be allowed to get in my way."

"Doubt if anything much gets in your way." She took her foot down off the chair and planted her hands on her sturdy hips. "So we're back to the basic question. Where does Zinnia fit into your matrix?"

"I'm going to marry her."

Clementine gaped at him for a few seconds. When she closed her mouth her teeth snapped together. "Are you crazy?"

"I think maybe I was for a while. But I'm not anymore."

"Have you told Zinnia that you plan to marry her?"

"No. And I'd appreciate it if you'd keep your mouth shut until I can deal with that end of things."

"Why in hell would she marry you?"

"She says she's in love with me," Nick said.

"I was afraid of that. But it doesn't make any difference. She would never marry someone who wasn't a good match. And she's unmatchable."

"I'm in love with her."

"I think we're talking lust here, not love. And maybe you like the fact that she can handle your talent, too." Clementine snorted. "Easy to see how a matrix could mistake that for love."

"I know the difference now," Nick said steadily. "There's nothing like looking into the face of chaos to help a matrix make a few obvious connections."

"Think so?" Clementine looked distinctly skeptical. "There's still the other problem. You and she are hardly likely to get matched. Especially given the fact that Zinnia's registration isn't even active."

"Don't worry about it. I've got a plan."

The ringing of the phone awakened Zinnia. She opened her eyes and glanced at the bedside clock. Nearly four in the afternoon. She had been dozing most of the day since she had returned from the hospital that morning. The long night had exhausted her physical as well as psychic energy, but she sensed that she was recovering swiftly.

She listened while the answering machine picked up the call.

"Zinnia? This is your Aunt Willy. I have been trying to reach you all day. Why didn't you tell me that Mr. Chastain was a member of the Founders' Club? You never mentioned that you were going to the annual charity ball. By the way, I wonder if Mr. Chastain ought to consider a lawsuit against that dreadful tabloid and Rexford Eaton, too. Give me a call as soon as you get in."

Zinnia heard the new note of respect in her aunt's voice. So it was *Mr. Chastain* now, was it? Maybe Nick was right. Maybe one could buy respectability. A single photo of him inside the Founders' Club, even though it showed him stretched out on the lobby floor, and Aunt Willy was starting to think he had possibilities.

Zinnia got off the bed and headed for the shower. The phone rang again just as she was about to step into the bathroom. She paused on the threshold to listen.

"Zin? It's me, Leo. I just got back from the hospital. Nick is chomping at the bit. The doctor says she wants

*to keep him for another day or two for observation, but
I have a hunch he's going to check himself out soon. I
called to see how you're doing. Guess you're still
asleep."*

Zinnia hurried across the room and scooped up the
phone. "Hi, Leo. I'm awake. Just about to take a
shower."

"Feeling better? I was worried about you last night.
You looked as if you'd been dragged through a West-
ern Islands jungle after you finished focusing for
Nick."

"Nothing like having a younger brother when you
want to know the truth. I'm recovering fast. Almost
back to normal. How's Nick?"

"Like I said, getting ready to check himself out in
spite of the doctor's orders. Clementine was visiting
with him when I got there."

"Uh-oh."

"I think they'd had what might be called a heated
discussion about you just before I arrived. But they
looked like they'd called a truce when I walked into
the room."

"A truce?"

"I heard Nick say something about having a plan."
Zinnia winced. "Not a good sign."

"Zin? Level with me. What's happening between
you and Chastain?"

"I don't know."

"You're in love with him, aren't you?"

"Yes."

Leo was silent for a moment. "Think he's in love
with you?"

Zinnia clutched her robe tightly and sank down
into a chair. "The last thing he said to me before the
crazy-fog got him was that he loved me. But I'm sure
he only said it because he thought he was going
insane. He was facing what, for him, was the ultimate

horror. I was the last human being he saw before he walked into chaos."

"In other words, you think the drama of the situation had a profoundly motivational impact on his decision to declare his love," Leo said dryly. "The final farewell before the great battle, et cetera, et cetera."

"I think we can assume that, yes." Zinnia reached for a tissue to blot the sudden dampness from her eyes. "Perfectly understandable."

"It's also perfectly understandable that he might actually be in love with you."

"I don't fit the profile of the woman he intends to marry. And he's not exactly my ideal mate, either. It's one thing to have an affair with a matrix, but what intelligent woman would marry one?"

There was a short loud pause on the other end of the line. "An affair?"

"That's all it can ever be."

"Do yourself a favor, Zin. Don't make any snap decisions here, okay? You've been through a lot during the past twenty-four hours. Give yourself some time to calm down and regain your sense of balance."

She sniffed into the tissue. "Okay."

"Take care. I'll check back with you later."

"Thanks, Leo." Zinnia put down the phone. For a long time she gazed morosely at the Early Exploration Period seascape on the wall.

After a while she crumpled the tissue, tossed it aside, and got up to take her shower.

She did not hear the phone ring a third time because of the noise of the pulsing water and the closed door. But when she walked out of the bath half an hour later the answering machine was in the midst of recording another call.

"Miss Spring? Newton DeForest here. Say, I did some checking in those old files. The ones I have stored

*down in the family crypt. I was surprised to find that I
did have some information on the financial aspects of
the Third Expedition. Not much, but if you would like
to take a look at it—"*

Zinnia snatched up the receiver. "Hello? Professor
DeForest? Hang on." She punched buttons madly
until the answering machine clicked off. "Sorry about
that. What were you saying?"

"I have a brief note taken from an old interview
with a New Portland University clerk here. For some
reason, I jotted down the fact that a company by the
name of Fire and Ice Pharmaceuticals had expressed
an interest in underwriting the Chastain expedition.
The firm went out of business years ago, however. Is
this the sort of thing you were looking for?"

"Oh, yes. Yes, indeed."

"I may have a few more bits and pieces here
somewhere. Not a lot, but you're welcome to what
little there is."

Zinnia glanced at the clock. Five-fifteen. "Would
you mind very much if I pick it up this evening?"

"I'll be waiting for you, Miss Spring. If I don't
answer the door, come on around the back. I'll be in
the garden. I like to use these long summer days to get
in a little extra pruning. My dear little blood-creepers
grow so quickly."

Chapter
22

* * * * * * * * * *

Nick looked up from his notes when he sensed the hulking figure in the doorway of the hospital room. "Come on in, Feather. It's safe. Zinnia went home to get some sleep."

"Too bad." Feather ambled into the room. "I was going to make my report to her."

"What report?"

"She didn't like me being here in the same room with you last night so she ordered me to go make myself useful." Feather's shaved head gleamed in the glow of the overhead light. He came to a halt beside the bed. "She sent me off to find the twin-snakes that jumped you in the garage."

Nick had a vague memory of an argument that had been waged across his bed sometime during the night. "Any luck?"

"Yeah. Kind of interesting. One turned up in the morgue."

"Don't look at me. I didn't put him there. The last thing I remember, he was on the floor of the garage but he was still breathing."

"He was still breathing when he and his pal got away during the confusion before the cops arrived, too," Feather said. "But he had a real unfortunate accident later. They found him in an alley in Founders' Square about five this morning."

"What happened?"

"Someone stuck his own knife in his chest. The official verdict is that he was just a dealer who got into a quarrel with one of his crazy-fog clients."

"He was carrying far too much crazy-fog to be a street dealer or a fog-head."

"Yeah, that's what Miss Spring said, too. Y'know, she's prickly as a cactus-orange, but she's got a brain on her shoulders." Admiration gleamed briefly in Feather's eyes. "So we have to assume someone paid two street toughs to dose you with the stuff."

"And later that same someone killed one of them to make sure he didn't talk. What about the second man?"

Feather shook his head. "No sign of him so far. I've put the word out that we want him and we're paying top dollar for information. My hunch is he'll turn up in the same condition as the other one."

Nick glanced down at the notes he had been making. "Two more connections in the matrix. Whoever sent those men after me knew that I was a matrix and probably had a good idea of what a heavy dose of pure crazy-fog would do to my kind of talent."

"Shit synergy. You mean whoever is behind this wanted to drive you insane?"

"Yes." Nick mused over that for a few seconds. "But why go to all that trouble? Why not just kill me instead?"

Feather's mouth twitched. "You're a hard man to kill. Easier to hit you with a batch of crazy-fog. Safer, too. The police would probably spend a lot of time looking into the murder of a guy in your position. There'd be a whole bunch of dumb speculation about gangster connections and stuff. Be all over the newspapers for days."

"But it would be easy to label what happened last night as just an unfortunate accident that occurred during a routine mugging. The police wouldn't have any reason to dig for a murder conspiracy."

"Right."

"Okay, the logic makes sense," Nick admitted. "But I think there's something else I'm overlooking in the matrix."

"No offense, boss, but you always think there's more to a situation than meets the eye. Some things are just what they look like."

"Not in this case." Nick hesitated.

"Jeez, boss, don't go gettin' paranoid on me now."

"The bottom line here is that I didn't have these problems before I started trying to get my hands on the Chastain journal a few weeks ago."

"If you ask me, you didn't have any of these problems until you met Miss Spring."

Nick looked at him. "She saved me last night, Feather."

"I ain't arguin' about that. Point is, would you have needed saving if she hadn't walked into your life?"

"Now you're the one who sounds like a conspiracy buff. Concentrate on finding the other knife man."

"Don't worry, I will. Hey, almost forgot." Feather reached into his pocket and drew out a small notebook. "Finally located one of the clerks who used to work in the budget offices of New Portland University thirty-five years ago. Name of Mrs. Buckley. Retired to a little farm in Lower Bellevue."

Nick swung his legs over the side of the bed. The movement caused a flicker of lightheadedness. He froze, but the sensation vanished quickly. He drew a deep breath of relief and stood on the cold floor.

"Did this Mrs. Buckley remember anything about the funding arrangements for the Third Expedition?"

he asked as he yanked at the tie that secured the hospital gown.

"She didn't handle that project. Said the clerk who processed the paperwork for it died a long time ago. Heart attack or somethin'."

"Yet another astonishing coincidence." Nick tossed the gown onto the bed. He was still a bit unsteady but everything felt relatively normal.

"You okay, boss?"

"Yes." He made his way to the small closet and opened it. The formal black shirt, jacket, and trousers that he had worn to the ball hung inside. They were badly wrinkled and there was a lot of garage-floor dirt on them but he was not feeling too concerned about presenting a respectable appearance at the moment. He reached for the shirt. "Did Mrs. Buckley have anything useful to tell us?"

Feather chuckled. "Turns out she was having an affair with the clerk who handled the Third Expedition arrangements. He talked a little about it after they got word that it had been canceled. She believes he told her that a chemical or pharmaceutical company of some kind had agreed to underwrite the venture. She thinks he said that the company wanted to remain anonymous in order to avoid publicity."

"A chemical or pharmaceutical company." A tingle of adrenaline shafted through Nick. It had a remarkably steadying effect. The familiar sense of rightness told him that the coordinates in the matrix were starting to form a complete pattern at last. He paused in the act of buttoning his shirt. "Yes. That fits. Did she give you a name?"

"She couldn't remember it exactly, but she thinks the word *fire* was in there somewhere."

Nick felt more points in the matrix begin to connect. He stepped into his trousers. "Did you check the—"

Feather held up a hand. "Hold it right there, boss.

301

I'm way ahead of you. I checked the phone books, the tri-city-state registry of corporations, and the lists of all business-license holders in New Vancouver, New Seattle, and New Portland. There are no chemical or pharmaceutical companies with the word *fire* in their corporate names."

"The company probably disappeared along with everything else that has to do with this thing." Nick buckled his belt. "We'll have to go back to the phone books and the corporate registries of thirty-five years ago."

Feather scowled. "Where the hell you gonna find those?"

"The public library, where else?" Cold amusement flowed through Nick. "Even the most obsessive matrix-talent on the planet would have found it impossible to destroy the microfilm records of every library in the tri-city-states."

"Never thought of that."

"Maybe whoever is behind this didn't think of it either." Nick considered that more closely. "Especially if he moves in the corporate world. He would have been focused on covering his tracks from the business and financial angles. Even a matrix makes mistakes."

"You're sure whoever's behind this is a matrix?"

"Zinnia's right. It has the feel of a matrix scheme." Nick yanked his jacket off the hanger. "I'll start with the main branch of the New Seattle Public Library downtown."

Feather surveyed the crumpled black tuxedo. "You going to go back to the casino and change first?"

"No time."

"What do you want me to do?"

"Find the second mugger. By now he probably knows what happened to his friend. He'll be running scared. Check New Portland and New Vancouver and all flights leaving for the Western Islands. Check the freighters, too."

"I've already got people on it."

Nick shrugged into his jacket as he headed toward the door. "I don't know what I'd do without you, Feather."

Feather reached into a pocket and pulled out an object. "Guess this means you won't be needing this, huh?"

Nick glanced at the deadly little blade lying on Feather's broad palm. It was small enough to smuggle into a hospital room but sharp enough to cut the plastic tubing that led to a piece of vital equipment, or anything else that a man facing insanity might want to slice. His wrists, for instance.

"No." A soul-deep shudder went through Nick. "I won't be needing that. And for the record, you can cancel all previous instructions relating to it."

"Glad to hear it. I never did like that part of my job description."

Zinnia knocked a third time, but there was still no answer.

"Professor DeForest?" she called loudly.

Still no response.

"Great. I guess this means the gardens." She had hoped that she would not have to take another tour of the maze.

She walked reluctantly around to the back of the old house and crossed the stone terrace.

The innocent-looking trellised entrance to the vast garden maze loomed at the bottom of the steps. She glanced around, wishing that Newton would appear.

There was no sign of the chubby-cheeked horti-talent.

Zinnia walked cautiously to the gate of the dark maze and stepped just short of the feathery leaves that had woven themselves through the latticework.

"Professor DeForest?"

"Afraid he's busy at the moment. But I'll bet I can help you."

"What?" Zinnia whirled around. She stared at the wiry man who was striding toward her across the terrace. There was something familiar about his voice. And about the way he moved.

"Took you long enough to get here," the man said.

Zinnia did not like the swift way he was closing in on her. She assessed the situation quickly and knew at once that there was no way she could get past him if she chose to make a run for the house. He must have sensed her thoughts because he gave her a cruel grin.

"Not like last night, huh? You haven't got that damned matrix to help you this time. How's he doing by the way? Swinging from the chandeliers yet? Or did he try to cut his own throat or take a hike across a busy freeway? We weren't sure how the fog would get him. Kind of an experiment, y'know?"

"You were one of the men in the garage." The one she had hit with the trash-can lid, she realized.

But he was not wearing his mask this time. In the light of the fading sun she could see his haggard angular face very clearly. The fact that he was allowing her to get a good look at him worried her more than anything else. He obviously did not expect her to be in any position to go to the police with a description at some point in the near future.

"Name's Stitch. Pleased to meet you." Stitch's pale eyes glittered with malice. "Look forward to spending a little quality time together before he gets here."

"Who?" Instinctively Zinnia stepped back a pace, past the feathery leaves that guarded the maze entrance. At that moment the terrible garden of carnivorous hybrids seemed preferable to falling into this man's clutches.

"Never mind. You'll find out soon enough. Come on out of there, now. I got a score to settle with you.

My head hurt all night on account of that trash-can lid. I'm gonna make sure you do some hurtin', too."

"Stay away from me." Zinnia took another step back.

"You don't want to play in that garden. I hear it's some kind of maze. If you get too far in, you'll get lost. Be dark in another couple of hours. You don't want to be wandering around in there after the sun sets. No telling what you might find."

Zinnia took one last look into Stitch's vicious eyes and made her decision. Nothing in the maze was as nasty as this creep. Thanks to her earlier visit with DeForest, she knew what awaited her in the garden. If she was very careful, she would survive it. She did not even want to think about what Stitch intended to do to her, let alone what the mystery man had planned.

She dropped her purse, whirled, and ran several steps down the nearest green corridor.

"Damn bitch. Come back here."

The leafy canopy overhead thickened rapidly within a few feet of the entrance. By the time she reached the first intersection it had blotted out most of the waning sunlight.

Things sighed and rustled in the foliage around her. It seemed to Zinnia that there was an air of hungry anticipation in the small disturbing noises. Feeding time at the plant zoo.

She kept her hands close to her sides and watched where she put her feet. The important thing was not to touch anything, she told herself. She must not provoke any of the little green monsters.

"I said, come outa there. *Aaah.* What the hell? Bat-snake shit. I'm bleedin.'"

Zinnia realized that Stitch had run afoul of one of the plants. She wondered if the experience would cut down on his eagerness to pursue her.

"Goddamned matrix whore. You're going to pay for this."

Stitch's footsteps resumed. He was moving faster, more recklessly now. Zinnia could almost feel the rage that was propelling him forward.

"Shit." Stitch's voice rose. "What is it with these damned plants?"

She edged deeper into the unpleasant maze. Glancing down, she saw that she was not leaving any footprints on the thick, eerie green moss that carpeted the floor of the maze. Stitch was no doubt using the sound of her own retreating footsteps as a guide.

She tried to walk more softly but she soon discovered that it was nearly impossible to move both quickly and stealthily at the same time. At least it was impossible for her. She had a feeling that Nick would know how to do it.

She inched past a row of barbed leaves and caught a glimpse of something that could have been a green tongue.

A slithering sound overhead made her flinch. She peered into the shadows. A thick meaty-looking vine curled down from a matted stretch of leaves. It appeared to sway slowly, as if in response to a light wind.

But there was no wind. Not even a breeze.

The vine swayed closer. There was something almost hypnotic about the way it swung gently across the width of the narrow corridor. It had uncurled to a point about three feet off the ground.

Back and forth. Back and forth. The longer Zinnia watched it, the more harmless it looked. It was just an ordinary vine. She could brush past it easily.

No. She must not touch anything, she reminded herself.

She froze in place, aware of Stitch's approaching footsteps.

"Where are you, you stupid woman? If you go any deeper, you won't be able to find your way out. Then what will you do?"

Slowly Zinnia sank down to the ground and crawled under the questing vine.

The ropy vine descended a few more inches in response to her presence but she managed to scoot beneath it without touching it.

"All right, bitch. You win. I'm not going to follow you any farther. *Five hells.* Damn this stuff."

Zinnia whirled. He was too close.

Stitch came around a corner, nursing a bleeding arm. He stopped when he saw her standing on the far side of the swaying vine.

"Well, well, well." Stitch's small eyes brightened with malevolent excitement. He started forward more quickly. "There you are. Come on, we're going to get back out of here before we get lost."

"We're already lost, hadn't you noticed? Don't come any closer." Zinnia stepped back. "I'm warning you. Some of these plants are extremely dangerous."

"I'm not afraid of a few thorns." He rubbed a hand on his pants. The motion left a streak of blood on the fabric. "And this'll slice anything in this damn maze to ribbons." He held up the long-bladed knife.

"Don't count on it." Zinnia turned away from him and walked gingerly down another green corridor.

"Damned fucking bitch." Stitch lunged after her.

Zinnia heard a soft deadly swoosh.

Stitch's ear-splitting scream froze the blood in her veins. There was a terrible thrashing in the bushes behind her. The dreadful screaming halted abruptly on a strangled note.

Zinnia swung around, searching for the entrance to the corridor that she had just exited. But all she could see was a wall of green. She knew that she was only a few steps away from Stitch, but she was completely lost and disoriented.

"Stitch?"

There was no answer.

She waited a few more minutes but there was no further sound.

After a while, she turned and walked slowly down another green-walled corridor. DeForest had told her that the maze was designed to funnel anyone who entered it straight to the grotto. If she got that far without running afoul of one of the plants, she could sit on the stone bench and wait for Nick.

She did not doubt for one minute that he would come looking for her.

A few minutes later she stumbled, unscathed, into the clearing that surrounded the grotto. The stone bench was there, just as she had remembered. It would make a cold perch for the night, but at least it was a safe spot to spend the next few hours while she awaited rescue.

She did not see Newton DeForest until she started to sit down.

A scream rose in her throat.

Newton floated face down in the grotto pool, enmeshed in a net of fibrous water plants.

Even as Zinnia stared in horror, several more tendrils snaked out from the shrubbery that clung to the rocks. They drifted across the surface of the water until they reached Newton. When they reached the body, they twined themselves around his legs.

Demented DeForest was feeding his plants one last time.

Nick gazed at the enlarged frame of the micro-filmed edition of the New Portland Corporate Registry and felt the last connections click into place. Fire and Ice Pharmaceuticals, the company that had committed to underwriting the Third Expedition through the University of Portland had gone bankrupt a few months after the expedition was supposedly canceled. But that was not what interested Nick the most.

What fascinated him was the name of the CEO of Fire and Ice.

It had taken him a while to find what he needed but his hunch had been correct. Not even a matrix could successfully wipe out all records of a large business that had existed as recently as thirty-five years ago.

The public librarians of St. Helens took their profession seriously. They could give matrix-talents lessons when it came to one type of obsession, Nick thought. They were a passionate lot when it came to the preservation and storage of information. All kinds of information.

It was more than an obsession for librarians, it was a sacred trust. The First Generation colonists had learned the true value of information storage and retrieval the hard way. Shortly after the Curtain closed, stranding them, they had seen their only hope, their computerized databases, start to disintegrate along with everything else that had been manufactured on Earth.

The colonists had known that without the advanced technology of the home world, they would need the ancient skills of a more primitive time in order to survive. The secrets of those old crafts were buried in the history texts stored in their computerized library.

A scriptorium had been set up to copy as much basic medical, agricultural, sociological, and scientific data as possible before the computers failed. Teams working with rough handmade paper and reed pens had labored around the clock for weeks in a frantic effort to record the most essential information before it disappeared. Everyone had understood that the more that was lost, the less chance there would be for survival.

Technologically, the colonists had been thrown back to a period roughly equivalent to the late eighteenth century on Earth.

When the Founders had crafted their vision of a society that would be strong enough to ensure their survival, they had embedded two values most deeply into their design. The first was the value of marriage and family. The second was the value of books.

Librarians, Nick thought with a sense of keen appreciating, had been zealous in honoring the Founders' trust. Because of their commitment to hoarding every scrap of information, including old phone books and corporate registries, he now knew the identity of the person who had murdered his parents.

None of the library patrons bothered to glance more than twice at the sight of a man dressed in wrinkled formal black evening wear running through the book stacks toward the door.

Half an hour later when he broke the lock of Zinnia's loft and slammed into the apartment, Nick was no longer basking in the rush of satisfaction that had hit him in the library. He was fighting a rising tide of fear.

Zinnia was supposed to be home, resting. But she had not answered the door.

He walked quickly through the airy apartment. The bed was rumpled. The towels in the bath were damp. She had been here earlier but now she was gone.

He paused by her desk and picked up the phone to dial Leo's number. Then he noticed the flashing light on the answering machine. He punched the button.

There was a hum and then a click. *"Zinnia? This is your Aunt Willy . . ."*

Nick hit the FAST-FORWARD button.

Another hum and a click. *"Zin? It's me, Leo . . ."*

He pushed the FAST-FORWARD button again.

Hum. Click. "Miss Spring? Newton DeForest here. Say, I did some checking in those old files . . ."

"Five hells." Nick ran toward the door.

The connections in the matrix were shatteringly obvious now. Zinnia was not a hapless bystander who had been caught up in the elaborate web of events surrounding the Chastain journal.

She had been the target of the killer all along.

She had to be here. But she was not responding to his psychic probe.

Nick stood at the entrance of the dark maze. Everything in the matrix was designed to draw him into those twisting corridors of grotesque foliage.

He sensed the hunger of the gently rustling plants. He knew that Zinnia was somewhere inside. He could see her purse on the ground near the first turning point. Farther on a bit of khaki cloth dangled from a long sharp spine. A piece of a man's shirt.

Someone had chased Zinnia into the maze.

He shoved the flashlight he had brought with him into the pocket of his tuxedo jacket. He did not need it yet. The sun would not set for another hour. He walked cautiously into the evil green maze.

He was immediately engulfed in a deep perpetual twilight, thanks to the heavy canopy of vines and leaves. An innocent yellow flower caught his attention. He did not see the toothlike thorns inside until he glanced down into the heart of the bloom. A large half-dissolved insect floated in a sticky pool at the bottom.

He went forward, careful not to brush against even the most innocuous-looking leaves. He slipped through the dark halls the way Andy Aoki had taught him to move through the jungles of the Western Islands.

He let his senses expand to full awareness. His matrix-honed instincts for spatial relationships kept him centered in the passageways.

He turned and went along another corridor. Something slithered near his foot. He glanced down and saw a small vine creeping toward the toe of his shoe. He stepped over it and continued on to the next intersection.

It did not matter which way he chose to go, he decided. Zinnia had told him that the design of the maze was such that anyone who entered it ended up at the center.

At each twist and bend in the path, his stomach tightened at the possibility of what he might find around the corner. He told himself that the maze was not deadly so long as one was careful. DeForest had given Zinnia a tour. He had explained to her that as long as she did not provoke the plants, she was safe.

But Zinnia had been fleeing from someone when she had entered earlier. She would have been scared. Her thoughts would have been on escape, not on protecting herself from the foliage.

He rounded another corner and saw the body. It dangled from a vine that was twisted around its throat. Dozens of small spongelike flowers had descended from the canopy and attached themselves to the corpse. They were swollen and dark. They throbbed as they dined.

For an instant Nick could have sworn that his heart stopped. Then he realized that he was looking at the body of a man, not a woman. The person who had chased Zinnia into the maze, no doubt. What remained of the torn khaki clothing matched the scrap of fabric he had seen at the entrance.

There was something familiar about the khaki, he thought. Then he made the connections and realized that he was looking at the second knife man.

Nick got down on his hands and knees and crawled beneath the gently swaying body. His hand brushed against an object lying on the moss. A sheath-knife. He picked it up, closed the sheath, and dropped it into the pocket of his black trousers.

On the far side of the body, he stood and continued

along the corridor. He tried another psychic probe. Still no response from Zinnia. She was alive, he thought. She had to be alive. He would know if she were not. And she was here somewhere in this damned maze. Why wasn't she responding?

He moved more swiftly now. The fear that Zinnia might be lying unconscious or hurt somewhere in one of the green corridors briefly overrode his old cautious habits and his natural sense of timing. The sleeve of his black jacket brushed against a leaf. A rustling sound alerted him to his mistake.

Instinct took over. He leaped forward, barely avoiding two long blade-shaped leaves. The leaves snapped together with a sound that was uncannily reminiscent of a pair of scissors.

A moment later the gurgle of water bubbling over rocks caught his attention. The grotto. He was near the heart of the maze.

He walked around the last corner and saw Zinnia. She was not alone.

Duncan Luttrell stood a short distance away. He had a gun in his hand. His mouth twisted in amused disgust at the sight of Nick's rumpled tux.

"We've been waiting for you, Chastain," Duncan said. "You're a trifle overdressed for the occasion. But, given your notoriously bad taste, I suppose that was only to be expected."

Chapter
23

* * * * * * * * * *

Nick." Zinnia shot to her feet as he walked casually into the clearing. She started toward him.

"Don't move," Duncan ordered.

She halted. Relief and fear soared through her. Nick was here. But now they were both trapped. "I knew you would find me. But I wish you hadn't. Duncan has gone crazy."

"Sit *down,* Zinnia." Duncan's voice vibrated with sudden rage. "Now. Or I'll kill Chastain where he stands."

She whirled around, fists clenched. "If you do I'll never give you what you want."

"Yes, you will." Duncan smiled thinly. "Because I will make certain that Chastain dies very slowly if you don't. I'm sure those plants that are munching on what's left of DeForest would welcome dessert."

Nick stopped beside a large, dark purple-green plant that rustled expectantly. He ignored the shrubbery and spared only a passing glance at Duncan. His whole attention was focused on Zinnia. "You may as well do what he says. Have a seat. We'll probably be here a while."

She searched his face. In the eternal twilight of the maze it was impossible to read his expression. But, then, it had never been easy to tell what Nick was thinking, she reminded herself. He could be as enigmatic as the sea. Slowly she sank back down onto the cold stone bench.

"He's got your father's journal." She looked at the neatly wrapped package that lay beside her on the stone bench. "He stole it from poor Morris Fenwick and then murdered him. He had already hired Wilkes to create the duplicate and a fake note for Polly and Omar to find. He thought if you accepted the fraud, you'd stop looking for the original."

"I know." Nick looked at Duncan. "And you tried to implicate my uncle in both the murder of Fenwick and the forgery."

Duncan's empty hand swept out in a what-can-you-do gesture. "I tried to put you off the scent or at least distract you by leaving one of your uncle's cuff links at Wilkes's house."

"How did you get the cuff link?" Nick asked.

"Oh, that was simple. He and I were meeting regularly to discuss business. I made certain that he lost one link after he'd had a few too many scotch-tinis. I really did not want to have to kill you, Chastain. I was afraid it would draw too much interest, not only from the police, but from your circle of lower-class associates."

"His associates, as you call them, are not nearly as low class as yourself, but you'll certainly get their attention if you kill him," Zinnia said fiercely. "You'll never get away with it."

"I've found a way around that little problem," Duncan murmured. "By the time anyone finds his body in this charming country garden, there will be very little left. It will be assumed that he and Demented DeForest argued about the fate of the Third Expedition and both of them ran afoul of these damned meat-eating plants."

"It will never work," Zinnia said.

She was hoarse from repeating the words. She had been saying them over and over for the past hour while they waited for Nick.

Duncan had been just as certain as she that Nick would show up eventually. She had deliberately refused to respond to the familiar probe of Nick's strong talent in an attempt to discourage him from entering the maze. But he had found her, anyway. Typical matrix.

Nick looked at Duncan. "Your father went to a lot of trouble to rewrite history. He murdered several people and he faked the bankruptcy of his own company in an effort to blur his tracks. But even a paranoid matrix-talent couldn't wipe out every piece of evidence that related to the Third Expedition."

The flash of rage that had appeared in Duncan's eyes vanished as if it had never existed. He assumed his familiar warm, charming, open-faced expression. "My father certainly tried hard enough. Got to give the old bastard credit. In all the years I knew him, the only thing he ever cared about was that damned journal. He didn't even bother to come to my mother's funeral because he was so busy working on it."

"Why didn't he get rid of DeForest years ago?" Zinnia asked.

Duncan chuckled. "There was no reason to do that. In his own bizarre fashion, Demented DeForest made an unwitting contribution to the plan."

"He helped turn the truth into a legend," Nick said.

"Precisely." Duncan smiled. "Thanks to his silly theories about alien abductions, no serious scholar ever paid any attention to the subject. It became the kind of story that only the tabloids covered."

"Which was just what Marsden Luttrell wanted," Nick said.

Duncan nodded. "The Third Expedition was receding very nicely into the mists of legend on schedule. But unfortunately, things got complicated after my father jumped out that window a year ago. The Chastain journal disappeared within hours of his death. It was stolen by his mistress. She apparently guessed that it had value, and she decided to make her fortune with it. Sold it to a book collector in New Portland."

Zinnia raised her chin. "I suppose you murdered her, too?"

Duncan chuckled good-humoredly. "She very wisely disappeared before I realized what she had done. I spent months and a great deal of money searching for her, but I still hadn't found her by the time the New Portland collector had a stroke and died. Morris Fenwick was called in by the family to evaluate his book collection. Fenwick found the Chastain journal and knew he had something important."

"But he didn't know how important it was, did he?" Nick said.

"Of course not," Duncan scoffed. "He couldn't break the code. He didn't even realize that it was encoded. But he knew that the family-history angle would be of great interest to a Chastain."

"So he contacted me." Nick moved slightly, causing another sigh of anticipation in the leaves of the nearby shrubbery. "He also notified my uncle, Orrin Chastain. The rumors must have started up immediately."

"Yes." Duncan pursed his lips in mild disapproval. "By the time I heard them, Fenwick had already made arrangements to sell the journal to you. He refused to turn it over to me."

Zinnia narrowed her eyes. "So you threatened him.

You forced him to give you the journal and then you murdered him."

"I really couldn't let him live." Duncan sounded dryly apologetic. "He knew too much, you see."

"You mean he had read enough of the journal to know that your father was the sixth member of the expedition team." Nick watched Duncan with expressionless eyes. "And he knew that the expedition had not been canceled. It had departed on schedule."

"So you figured that out, did you?" Duncan gave him an approving look. "Very clever. Dad thought he had erased all traces of the fact that there had been a last-minute addition to the team."

"He tried." Nick's eyes were the same hard green as the grotto plants. "Marsden Luttrell murdered my father and the other members of the expedition team, as well. What kind of poison did he use?"

"Do you know, I never thought to ask him," Duncan said. "One of his own creations, no doubt. Something slow-acting and extremely subtle, I imagine. He was always tinkering in his lab."

"Poison?" Zinnia's mouth fell open in shock. "He poisoned the expedition team?"

"Marsden Luttrell was the founder of Fire and Ice Pharmaceuticals," Nick explained. "He was a brilliant chemist. He funded the Third Expedition through the University of New Portland. Anonymously."

"Oh, my God," Zinnia whispered.

"The legal agreement was that his company would have first crack at developing commercial products from any promising botanical specimens that were discovered," Duncan said. "Nothing odd about the arrangement. Just business as usual."

"Not quite," Nick said. "Your father was a matrix."

Zinnia winced. "So much for business as usual. Matrix-talents never do anything in the usual manner."

"That was especially true with Marsden Luttrell."
Nick kept his gaze on Duncan. "He had probably
been getting increasingly flaky for years, but he must
have been a full-blown paranoid by the time he
funded the Third. It's amazing that he was able to
conceal his mental state from the university officials."

"I doubt they would have cared, even if they had
guessed that Dad was getting a little weird," Duncan
said. "After all, money is where you find it and the
university needed the cash very badly for the venture."

Nick looked thoughtful. "Marsden was so paranoid
by then that he convinced himself that he had to join
the expedition in order to protect his investment. He
didn't trust anyone."

"Least of all your father," Duncan retorted. "He
suspected that Bartholomew Chastain was a strong
matrix. He figured Chastain would plot to steal or
conceal any valuable discoveries."

Zinnia frowned. "When Luttrell showed up at the
last minute in Serendipity, Bartholomew Chastain
had no choice but to accept him on the team."

"No choice at all," Duncan agreed. "After all, Dad
had paid for the whole damn expedition. He gave the
orders."

Zinnia took a deep breath. She wondered if it was
her imagination or if the air in this section of the
garden was becoming thick and heavy. It occurred to
her that the plants were not the only predatory species
in the vicinity. She was sitting on a bench between
two very dangerous carnivores, one of which, the one
who appeared the most normal, was clearly crazy.

The only thing she could think to do was buy time.
Fortunately, Duncan seemed quite willing to talk.

"What's the big secret?" she asked. "What did the
Third Expedition find that was worth so many lives?
Was it a botanical discovery?"

"Actually, Dad did bring back a rather interesting

plant specimen," Duncan said. "He spent a lot of time working with it after he returned. He synthesized one of the active compounds. He was certain that it held the potential to allow him to use his talent without the assistance of a prism."

"But instead, it just made him crazier," Nick said.

Zinnia looked from one to the other. "What are you talking about?"

"Crazy-fog." Nick did not take his gaze off Duncan. "Marsden Luttrell fiddled with it until it finally put him over the edge. He took too much of the stuff one afternoon about a year ago and walked out a window which happened to be twenty-two stories above the sidewalk."

"It was his mistress's bedroom window," Duncan explained. "He had spent the day with her, working on the journal and dosing himself with fog. That's why she was able to grab the damned book and get away before I learned what had happened."

"But Marsden Luttrell killed himself a year ago," Zinnia said. "The police and the newspapers claim that crazy-fog only recently became a problem on the streets. Where has it been for the past thirty-five years?"

Duncan winked. "Dad never saw the real potential for crazy-fog. The crazy old coot kept it for himself. All he could think about was finding a way to decode the Chastain journal without using a prism. He was so paranoid by that time that he was afraid to even create a focus link with another person."

"But you saw the financial implications of crazy-fog, didn't you?" Nick said. "After your father's death, you started producing it in large quantities and selling it to drug dealers."

Zinnia stared at Duncan. "That's how you financed the recent expansion of SynIce and the development of your new generation of software, isn't it?"

"Indeed." Duncan gave her a patronizing smile.

"In business, money is blood. You get it from any source you can."

"You arranged for those two men to attack Nick with crazy-fog last night," she accused.

"I knew what a large dose of the stuff had done to my father," Duncan said. "I assumed it would have the same interesting effect on Chastain. But something must have gone wrong. No matter, I'll take care of tidying up the loose ends tonight."

Zinnia clenched her hands around the edge of the bench on either side of her thighs. "I still don't understand. You said your father tried to use the crazy-fog to decode the Chastain journal. So the drug wasn't the big discovery that the Third Expedition made?"

"No, of course not." Duncan glanced at her, impatience simmering in his eyes now. "The fog was only a means to an end as far as my father was concerned. What he wanted was the real secret that Bartholomew Chastain concealed in his journal. And that is what I want, also. What I'm going to get very soon."

"What was that secret?" Nick asked in his softest voice.

"The location of the alien tomb," Duncan said.

Nick said nothing.

Zinnia was flabbergasted. "Alien tomb? You're saying that the Third Expedition discovered an alien burial site?"

"Yes."

She spread her hands. "I don't believe it. You sound like Demented DeForest."

"Why do you find it so impossible to believe, Zinnia?" Nick said seriously. "Lucas Trent discovered those alien artifacts that are now housed in the museum. It stands to reason there might be other relics scattered around the world. Why not a whole tomb?"

"In point of fact," Duncan said, "your father didn't

believe that the structure was intended as a burial site. He thought it was probably meant to be a sort of temporary storage facility for the aliens and their equipment. His theory was that the Curtain had opened and closed more than once in the past, you see."

Zinnia sat very still on the bench. "And the aliens came through during one of those earlier openings? When the Curtain created a gate between their world and St. Helens?"

"Precisely. And when it closed, they were stranded, just as the First Generation Founders were a thousand years later," Duncan said.

Nick shifted slightly. Leaves rustled nearby. "But instead of adapting to St. Helens and learning how to survive on this planet, the aliens decided to try to hibernate until rescue arrived."

"But it never came," Duncan concluded. "The equipment that was supposed to keep the aliens alive failed. Chastain figured it had simply run out of fuel after several hundred years. Whatever the case, the alien tomb is a treasure trove waiting to be opened."

"Who knows what might be inside?" Zinnia tried to adjust to the vision of a tomb full of alien machines.

Duncan laughed softly. "I see you're beginning to get the full implications. Weapons, incredibly advanced technology, medical and scientific data that could make a fortune for the company that controls it. The list of possibilities is endless."

"It might contain nothing more than a few mummified bodies and some pieces of equipment made out of the same weird alloy as the artifacts that Trent found," Nick said prosaically. "Interesting, but not especially profitable. Not worth so many lives."

Duncan's expression transformed itself from good-humored to enraged in the blink of an eye. "My father believed it was worth untold millions. I'm stronger than he ever was. I'm going to do what he was unable to do. I'm going to find the location of that tomb."

Zinnia looked at him. "I don't understand. Why did your father spend thirty-five years trying to decode Bartholomew Chastain's journal? Marsden Luttrell was a member of the expedition. He was there when the tomb was discovered. He knew where it was."

"Ah, therein lies the crux of the problem." Duncan shook his head. "Unfortunately, Bartholomew Chastain was alone when he discovered the tomb. He left the expedition camp early one morning to do some surveys. He was supposed to return by nightfall. But he didn't show up until late the following day."

"What happened?" Zinnia asked, desperate now, to keep Duncan talking.

"The team was organizing a search when Chastain walked back into camp with the story of the tomb." Duncan's jaw tightened. "But he refused to give anyone else the coordinates. He said he would turn the information over to the university officials and no one else. He claimed the discovery was too important to be left in the hands of any one man."

Nick's brows rose. "My father obviously had a few suspicions about Marsden Luttrell at that point."

"Apparently." Duncan shrugged. "Dad was furious because Chastain would not lead them back to the tomb or give him the coordinates. Dad had a real problem controlling his temper. There was a violent storm that night. Things were chaotic for a while. Dad took advantage of the confusion to slip the poison into some portion of the food supply. They were all dead by the time breakfast was over the following morning."

Nick gazed at him with an unwavering stare. "In the process of covering his tracks, Luttrell also killed my mother."

"And a number of other people over the years,"

Duncan said, unconcerned. "It's surprisingly easy for a good chemist to kill, you know."

"But all the killing didn't do him any good," Nick said. "Because Bartholomew Chastain had encrypted the information that referred to the location of the tomb."

Duncan's eyes darkened with sudden rage again. "Not just the location of the tomb. The whole damned journal is in code."

"Typical matrix," Zinnia whispered.

"My father was a strong matrix," Duncan snarled. "But he was unable to break Chastain's code for thirty-five years because he was too paranoid to employ a trained prism to focus his talent. But I'm not going to make the same mistake."

"What do you mean?" Zinnia asked.

Duncan's eyes glittered feverishly. "I have my prism. A very special one who can work well for long hours with a powerful matrix-talent."

"I'm not going to help you," Zinnia said.

"Oh, but you will, my dear. Because if you don't I shall begin putting holes in Chastain. I shall start with his legs so that he won't be able to move. I expect the blood will soon excite the plants. It will be interesting to see what comes creeping out of the bushes to nibble on him."

Nick looked bored by the conversation.

"No." Zinnia leaped to her feet for the second time. "You can't do that."

"Chastain lives as long as you oblige me with a focus," Duncan said.

She looked into his friendly open face and saw the madness in his eyes. She knew that he had no intention of allowing Nick to live while she focused for him. For one thing, even a powerful matrix such as Duncan would find it impossible to do three things at once. He would not be able to maintain the psychic link for an extended period, unravel a complex code, and keep an eye on another very clever matrix at the same time.

It was easy to second-guess Duncan's real plan. He intended to try his hand at playing psychic vampire. As soon as she gave him a prism he would try to jump it and hold it captive.

And based on what her friend, Amaryllis, had told her about her own experiences with a real-life vampire named Irene Dunley, it was conceivable that Duncan could do just that if he was sufficiently powerful.

She recalled the way Nick had impulsively tried to seize the prism she had instinctively created for him that first night in the casino. His psychic strength had been almost overwhelming but she had not burned out as did most prisms when faced with an aggressive talent.

She had struggled and Nick had released her before they had engaged in a serious contest of psychic power. He had never again tried to force himself on her. But she shivered at the thought of what might happen if Duncan, who might well be as strong as Nick, made a similar attempt. The result would be a kind of mind rape that she could not bear to contemplate.

"At least I now know why you've been so friendly and considerate for the past month and a half, Duncan," Zinnia said. "How did you find out about me?"

"It was very simple. I made some discreet inquiries." Duncan smiled briefly. "I discovered that Psynergy, Inc. offered a very special prism service for matrix-talents. Naturally I didn't want to contract through the agency. But once I knew who you were, it was easy to strike up a relationship. Do you know, Zinnia, I had hoped we would be something more than friends."

"You mean, you hoped that I'd have an affair with

you. You thought you'd be able to manipulate me more easily that way."

"It would definitely have made things less complicated," Duncan agreed. "But you kept me at a distance, even when I hinted that I might be open to the notion of a non-agency marriage. Then Chastain came along and charmed you straight into his bed."

"It wasn't quite that simple," Nick said.

Zinnia groaned. "Thanks."

"I still can't imagine what you see in such an encroaching upstart, Zinnia," Duncan said. "The man has no family, no class, and no taste. He actually thinks he can buy his way into respectable society. Last night I realized that you were enthralled with the bastard which meant he had total control over you."

"Not exactly." Nick looked fleetingly amused. "I doubt that anyone could ever control Zinnia."

Duncan scowled at him. "Not only did you possess the one prism in town who could help a strong matrix decode the journal, Chastain, you wouldn't give up the search for the book. In spite of your tacky nouveau-riche pretensions, you're a matrix and that means you can think logically. I'm sure you understand that my alternatives are extremely limited."

"They're limited, all right," Nick agreed.

"Stop it," Zinnia said fiercely. "I won't help you decode the journal under any circumstances, Duncan."

Duncan said nothing. He merely smiled, took aim at a point just below Nick's belt, and started to squeeze the trigger.

"No," Zinnia shouted. She hurtled forward, putting herself between the two men.

Duncan relaxed his grip on the trigger. "Change your mind?"

Zinnia wanted to scream with rage and panic. "You bastard."

"Your lover is the bastard. I'm a respectable businessman." Duncan's face tightened. "Just give me a prism. This will end as soon as you focus for me."

"Liar."

"Do it, you damn stubborn bitch," Duncan roared.

She felt the sudden flicker of a psychic talent probe. There was a foul quality to it that made her recoil instinctively. She could not define the nature of the wrongness, but it was so strong that it seeped from the metaphysical plane to the physical plane. No wonder Duncan had hidden his talent from her.

"It's okay, Zinnia," Nick said softly. "Give him the focus. The same way you did for me that night in your apartment."

"But, Nick, he'll try to take control. What if he succeeds?"

Duncan laughed.

"Just do it, Zinnia," Nick said very quietly. "Exactly as you did it for me."

She stared at him helplessly while frantically trying to decipher the hidden message in his words. She had given Nick a strong clear focus that night. It was, he had told her later, the first time he had ever had such a perfect prism. *And he had gotten a little drunk with the pleasure of his own power.* She had a vivid memory of him staggering slightly as he attempted to regain his balance.

She stared at Nick with sudden comprehension. He wanted her to use the focus link to distract Duncan. If she could disorient and dazzle him with a brilliant prism for a few seconds, Nick might be able to take him.

She had to move quickly before Duncan began to suspect a trap. His eyes were already narrowing.

She bowed her head, trying her best to look like a beaten woman. "All right."

"An excellent decision, my dear." Duncan sent another slashing probe of noxious psychic energy out onto the metaphysical plane.

Zinnia remembered the truly crazy matrix she had focused for once at the beginning of her career with Psynergy, Inc. She had never forgotten the deeply unpleasant nature of her client's psychic energy. But the colorless throbbing talent that Duncan produced was a thousand times more unwholesome.

She sank her nails into her palms and resisted the urge to draw back her own power. She concentrated desperately on creating the most compelling, most intriguing, most enthralling prism Duncan had ever seen. Last night she had brought Nick back from the edge of chaos with such a promising prism. Perhaps this evening she could push Duncan over that edge.

Duncan leaped for the prism with a wild crushing swath of raw power.

Zinnia screamed as the focus link was forged. Claws of colorless darkness seized the prism, imprisoning her on the metaphysical plane.

"Do what you did to me the first night in the casino, Zinnia." Nick's voice came out of the night.

She wanted to tell him that she was frozen. She could not move, let alone struggle. But she could not get the words out.

"Damn it, Zinnia, do what you did to me."

Nick wanted her to twist the focus. She could not fight Duncan now that he controlled the link, but she might be able to shift the focus just enough to distract him, maybe even hurt him.

"Damn, but you're good, Zinnia." Duncan sounded altogether thrilled with himself. Perhaps even a little drunk. "This is exquisite. I can only imagine how good the sex would be under such circumstances. No wonder you seduced her, Chastain. When we have finished our business with the journal I shall have to give her a try, myself."

"Don't hold your breath," Zinnia managed to say aloud.

"Yeah," Nick echoed very softly. "Don't hold your breath, Luttrell."

Duncan ignored them both and hurled power savagely through the prism. "Incredible. Absolutely incredible. I'm going to enjoy this even more than I had anticipated. But now I'm afraid that I must get rid of Chastain. I have you so I no longer need him, do I?"

She knew that it was crunch time. Duncan was preparing to shoot Nick. She had to do something and she had to do it now.

She threw every ounce of psychic energy she possessed into twisting the power of the focus. For an instant she feared that nothing had happened. Then she saw a slight skewing in the energy pattern.

"What's this?" Duncan was enraged. "What are you doing? Stop it."

Zinnia twisted harder.

"No," Duncan shouted.

Zinnia opened her eyes. Duncan was swinging around toward her, raising the gun. The madness mingled with the fury in his eyes. She found herself looking down the barrel of the pistol. She was pouring so much power into fracturing the prism that she did not have enough strength left over to scream.

Nick's voice cut through the gathering darkness. "Kill her and you'll never find another prism that can handle your talent, Luttrell. You'll never decode the journal."

Duncan's mouth opened and closed. Rage and frustration and the effects of his tortured power paralyzed him for a few seconds.

Zinnia saw a dark shadow move soundlessly across the clearing.

It was Nick. He only needed a couple of heartbeats of time.

Duncan shook his head as if to clear it. He started to turn back to the real threat, but it was too late.

Nick smashed into Duncan. The impact sent both men sprawling onto the green moss. The gun flew out of Duncan's hand and landed in the pond with a small splash.

Duncan lost control of his psychic talent as his instinct for physical survival took over. Raw power cascaded aimlessly across the metaphysical plane. Zinnia seized the opportunity to shut down the prism in the blink of an eye.

The thud of fists against flesh made her flinch. Duncan reared up above Nick. She saw a blade gleam in his hand.

"He's got a knife," she shouted.

"Damn Chastain bastard." Duncan drove the blade downward toward Nick's throat.

Nick blocked the thrust with his arm. Duncan shouted in mindless rage and raised the knife a second time.

Nick rolled to the side. Thrown off balance, Duncan staggered.

Nick was already on his feet. He drove a fist into Duncan's chest, sending the other man reeling back against the rocks that surrounded the dark pond. Nick closed in quickly. He landed another savage punch.

Duncan groaned and collapsed against the rocks. Nick loomed over him.

The hulking shrubs trembled. A thick green frond unfurled and stretched lovingly toward Nick's leg. Zinnia saw the hidden spines.

"Nick, get away from the pond."

He leaped back just as the frond struck with the speed of a twin-snake. The spines sank deep into Duncan's leg.

Duncan screamed.

More fronds lashed out, securing Duncan with their spines. He stopped screaming quite suddenly. He jerked. His head fell back. A great shudder went through the huge plant. The fronds convulsed once, hurling Duncan into the pond.

He landed facedown next to DeForest's body, quivered once, and then went still. The plants seemed to sigh as they reached for the new feast with hungry green tentacles.

"Oh, my God," Zinnia whispered.

Nick pulled her into his arms, turning her away from the sight of Duncan's body. "Are you all right?"

"Yes." She buried her face against his elegant black shirt. "Yes, I'm okay. What about you?"

"I'm fine but this tux will never be the same. Come on, let's get out of here."

Zinnia raised her head. "How are we going to do that? We're at the heart of the maze. We'll have to wait until someone figures out where we are and how to get us out of here."

Nick grinned as he released her to scoop up the package that contained his father's journal. "Give me a break, lady. I'm a matrix. I could find my way out of this maze with both eyes closed and one hand tied behind my back."

Chapter
24

* * * * * * * * * *

I hope you know what you're doing." Zinnia eyed a little blood-creeper that lurked in the shadows.

"Have faith." Nick moved confidently down a shadowy green corridor. "And don't touch anything."

"Believe me, I won't." Zinnia hastened past a wispy green leaf that seemed to want to play with her hair. "How did you figure out the secret of the maze?"

"I picked up the pattern when I entered." Nick turned a corner and chose a new avenue as if he held a map. "No great trick to it. After all, it had to be simple enough that a non-matrix like DeForest could find his way in and out easily."

"That's true, I suppose." Zinnia scurried past some large blooms with red throats.

"The underlying design is based on the plants. The more innocuous ones are toward the front of the maze. The nastiest are in the center. I recognized most of them."

"But these are hybrids."

"Yes, but they were all hybridized from Western Islands jungle plants. I grew up in the islands, remember? One thing you learn real early is how to recognize the plant life."

"Oh." She hugged herself to avoid touching a trailing vine. "I can hardly believe that Duncan was behind everything that happened."

"I know." Nick ducked under a web of leaves. "He seemed like such a nice man."

"Not funny. He did seem like a nice man." Zinnia frowned. "But it's no wonder he never let on that he was a matrix. One glimpse of his talent and I'd have known the truth. He was as evil as his father must have been."

Nick looked at her over his shoulder. "Evil?"

"I suppose the syn-psychs would say he was sick or insane, but I can tell you that from what I saw on the metaphysical plane a few minutes ago, Duncan was bad to the bone. The evil infected everything, even his talent."

"Interesting."

"Do you think he was telling the truth about the alien tomb?"

"We'll find out once I've had a chance to decode the journal." Nick paused. "I might need a little help. It could take a while."

"I doubt it if you'll need the assistance of a prism. Your brand of matrix-talent is probably very similar to your father's. I suspect you think the same way he did. His code will probably seem quite obvious to you."

Nick threw her another dark glance. "So much for subtlety."

She was startled to see that his jaw was rigid. "What's that supposed to mean?"

"I'll try to make this a little more direct. Will you marry me, Zinnia?"

She came to an abrupt halt midway down the green passage. "Huh?"

Nick stopped. "You heard me." He turned back to

333

face her. His face was an enigmatic mask except for the fierce determination that burned in his eyes. "Look, I know you think I'm a risk."

"Risk?"

"I've got no family, no class, and no taste. But I've got a five-year plan to change all that."

"Yes, I know, but—"

"I can't offer you the assurance of a marriage agency recommendation, but I'm a matrix. That means that once I have a goal, I stick with it."

She swallowed. "And just what is your goal?"

"I intend to love you for the rest of my life."

Zinnia fought back tears. "Oh, Nick. Are you certain? Are you sure you're not just feeling grateful because I helped you survive the crazy-fog attack last night?"

"I was in love with you before you saved my sanity," he said roughly. "I've been in love with you since the first night I met you. Five hells, woman, I've been waiting for you all of my life."

A great lightness swept through her. She wondered that she didn't float right off the ground.

"Oh, *Nick.*" She threw herself into his arms. "I love you, too."

He wrapped her close and kissed her the way he did everything else, with full commitment and attention.

Something slithered in the greenery. Nick broke off the kiss.

"Damn."

Zinnia stepped back. "What's wrong?"

"One of the plants just took a bite out of my jacket." Nick scowled at a drooping leaf. Then he surveyed the ripped sleeve. "Look at that hole."

"Don't worry, you can afford a new one."

He laughed and grabbed her hand. "You're right. I can. Let's go. I want you very badly, but I'm not about to make love to you here. No telling what part of me the next plant will go after."

Zinnia smothered a grin as she followed him down one last corridor. They turned another corner and she saw the entrance of the maze. A small crowd was gathered on the lawn.

"Looks like we've got an audience." Nick towed her through the trellised entrance.

Four people turned to stare. Zinnia recognized Feather and Detective Anselm immediately. A third man was busy squeezing into what appeared to be a fireman's protective coveralls. A huge set of pruning shears lay on the ground beside him.

"Boss." Feather trotted forward. Relief flared in his eyes. "You okay?"

"I'm fine."

"When I couldn't locate you, I went to Miss Spring's place. Heard DeForest's message. Figured you'd heard it, too."

"Good thinking, Feather. Thanks."

Detective Anselm scowled. "What's going on around here? Feather called me up about fifteen minutes ago and told me that if we didn't move we'd have a couple more murders on our hands."

Before Nick could answer, the fourth man stepped out of the shadows of a large tree. He raised a camera.

"Hot synergy." Cedric Dexter snapped the photo. "Great shot."

"Mr. Dexter," Nick said very softly. "I want to have a word with you."

Alarmed, Zinnia seized his torn coat sleeve. "Now, Nick, take it easy."

Nick gave her a beatific smile. "Don't worry. Mr. Dexter and I understand each other perfectly. Isn't that right, Dexter?"

"Uh—" Cedric took a nimble step backward. "Just doing my job, Mr. Chastain."

"Sure," Nick said. "And because you did such a professional job at the ball last night, I have a scoop for you."

Cedric looked distinctly wary. "A scoop?"

"You do have a recorder with you, don't you?"

Cedric brightened and dug a small object out of his pocket. "You bet. I never leave home without it."

Two days later Nick sat at the black desk in the gilded chamber and signed the last page of a fat legal document. He did not bother to look up when the door opened.

"What is it, Feather?"

"A lot of folks to see you, boss. You want I should have 'em escorted off the premises?"

"Don't bother, they'll only come back later. I may as well get this over with so that I can get on with my life." Nick finished scrawling his name and put down the pen.

Orrin charged into the room waving a copy of the *New Seattle Times.* His wife, Ella, was close on his heels. They were followed by two people Nick had never met.

Feather caught his eye. "Mr. Stanley Spring and his lovely wife, Wilhelmina, sir. Said it was important."

"What is this all about?" Orrin demanded as he came to a halt in front of the desk. He shoved the paper toward Nick. "It says here that you're going to make a large investment in Chastain, Inc."

Nick studied the headline in the business section. *Casino Owner to Fund Expansion of Chastain, Inc.* "This is old news. That headline was in *Synsation* yesterday."

"*Synsation* is just a cheap scandal sheet," Ella snapped. "No one pays any attention to it." She stabbed a beringed finger at the headline. "But this is the *Times.*"

Nick leaned back in his chair. "It must be true, then. Assuming my money is good enough for Chastain, Inc., of course."

Orrin scowled. The expression did not hide the reluctant hope in his eyes. "Are you serious about this?"

"Yes."

Ella nodded, apparently satisfied. "I told you he would do his duty by the family, Orrin."

"We'll have to talk," Orrin muttered. "There's a lot to go over. This will change everything."

"I'll have my secretary schedule lunch at the Founders' Club tomorrow," Nick said.

Orrin blinked. "You want to have lunch with me at the Founders' Club?"

"I'm told that I'm still a member in good standing," Nick said. "Apparently the club management has decided to overlook that little scuffle the other night at the ball. I understand that the Eatons and Miss Gardener did not want a fuss made."

"Very gracious of them under the circumstances," Ella said.

Nick was amused. "Very smart of them, you mean. For my part, I have graciously decided not to sue Eaton. Will there be anything else, Uncle Orrin? Aunt Ella? I'm a little busy at the moment."

Ella frowned at the papers on the desk. "The story in the *Times* says you plan to sell the casino."

"That's right. I'm starting a new career."

"What sort of career?" Stanley demanded quickly.

"I'm going to become a business consultant." Nick steepled his fingers. "My fiancée informs me that since I have a certain aptitude for making money, I might as well let other people pay me to show them how to do it, too."

Wilhelmina eyed him with open speculation. "What about this expedition you're funding in conjunction with the University of New Seattle and the New Seattle Art Museum?"

Nick looked at her. "The Fourth Chastain Expedition will depart in three months. The goal is to locate a large collection of alien artifacts that my father discovered thirty-five years ago."

Stanley's brows shot up and down several times. "My nephew, Leo, says he's scheduled to join the team."

"His training in Synergistic Historical Analysis and his strong psychometric-talent will prove invaluable in dating the relics." Nick paused meaningfully. "And having his name on the monographs and books that will be written after the team returns should do wonders for his future career at the university."

Orrin clasped his hands behind his broad back and began to pace in front of the desk. "You're throwing a lot of money around here, Nick. The investment in Chastain, Inc., funding the expedition, and now you say you're starting a new business."

Nick smiled politely. "I have a great deal of money to throw around, Uncle Orrin. Don't worry, I won't go bankrupt with these projects. The sale of the casino will net several million."

Wilhelmina exhaled deeply. "Very true. Very true." She turned a steely gaze on Orrin and Ella. "We're planning a large wedding for Nick and Zinnia, you know. It will be the event of the season. I look forward to seeing you both there."

Orrin looked taken aback. "Well, I suppose, that is, I don't—" He broke off and glanced at his wife for guidance.

"We wouldn't miss it for the world," Ella said firmly. She traded looks with Wilhelmina. "Can we assume that this is an agency match?"

"My fiancée has always insisted that she would only marry if properly matched by a first-rate agency," Nick said smoothly before Wilhelmina could respond.

"I see," Ella murmured.

Nick examined each face in turn. They all knew

that the presence of the legitimate branch of the Chastain family at his wedding would set the seal on the acceptance of the bastard into both clans.

"I'm glad to see that no one has a problem with that," he said finally. "If there are no more questions, I have some business to deal with here."

"We're on our way," Stanley said quickly. He took Wilhelmina's arm and steered her toward the door. "Business consultant, eh? That sounds interesting, doesn't it, dear?"

"It has a certain cachet," Wilhelmina agreed. "He'll be dealing with some very influential people in town."

Orrin snorted. "Business consultant? Hope you know what you're doing, Nick."

"I always know what I'm doing, Uncle Orrin. I never work without a plan. By the way, I'll want to see your five-year plan for the future expansion of Chastain, Inc. before I hand over the investment cash."

Orrin flushed. "Giving orders already, I see. I don't care how much money you put into the company, I'm the CEO of Chastain, Inc., and don't you ever forget it."

"Don't worry," Nick said. "The job's yours, Uncle Orrin. All I want from you is to see your smiling face and the faces of all the rest of my dear relatives at my wedding."

"Now, see here, you can't just go about making demands," Orrin huffed.

Ella took Orrin's arm. "We will all be at the wedding," she said in ringing tones as she marched him to the door.

Nick watched them leave. When they were gone he heard the soft whir of the secret panel mechanism. He turned to see Zinnia lounging in the opening, arms folded. He felt the now-familiar leap of happiness.

"You heard?" he asked.

"Everything." She shook her head, smiling. "You're

amazing, you know that? I'm beginning to believe your plan just might work. Five years from now no one's even going to remember that you once operated a casino and had no legitimate family connections. All anyone will care about is that you're the wealthy business consultant who funded the Fourth Chastain Expedition."

He grinned. "Who says you can't buy respectability?"

Epilogue

* * * * * * * * * *

The scent of passion hung in the air of the darkened bedroom, hot and intoxicating. Nick inhaled deeply as he eased himself into Zinnia's snug inviting heat. She wrapped her arms fiercely around his neck. Her leg shifted, pressing against his thigh.

"Nick." She kissed his throat and then set her teeth delicately against his bare shoulder.

"I love you," he said. "I love you so much." The words that had once been incomprehensible to his logical matrix mind were now the most important in the language.

There were other things he wanted to say to her, but they would have to wait. As always, when things got this intense between them, he could no longer think logically, let alone speak coherently. All he could do was feel.

And what he felt was indescribably satisfying. For the first time the matrix of his life was complete. Zinnia was his true mate, the other half of himself.

He sent out a questing tendril of talent. A perfect crystal-clear prism formed on the metaphysical plane.

He hurled a wave of power through it at the same moment that he felt Zinnia's body tightening around him.

Psychic energy fused for an instant with physical energy. In that split second Nick looked into chaos and saw that there was a pattern there, after all. A fabulous, glorious, indescribably beautiful pattern. He would never comprehend it completely, but that no longer mattered. It was enough to know the design existed and that he and Zinnia had a place in it.

The vision was gone in the next heartbeat. He did not try to recover it. He had glimpsed it and he would never forget it. He knew that Zinnia had shared it with him.

Her passionate response brought him back to the pleasures of the physical plane with a sweet vengeance. Nick heard his own exultant shout echo in the moonlit room. He lost himself in the shimmering matrix of happiness.

The phone rang half an hour later, just as Nick was about to drift off to sleep. "If that's your brother wanting to talk about the expedition plans again, I swear I'm going to wrap the phone around his neck."

Zinnia chuckled and settled closer against his side. "Don't worry about it. The machine can take the message."

Nick threaded his fingers through her hair. "I wasn't about to answer it."

There was a click and a familiar voice came through the answering machine.

"Mr. Chastain? Hobart Batt here. I understand you can be reached at this number. I want to let you know that we've got our match."

Zinnia sat straight up in bed. "What is that little twit talking about? If he thinks he's going to set you up with an agency date, he can go jump in the bay."

Nick smiled. "Take it easy."

"You were absolutely correct about Zinnia Spring being a perfect match for you, Mr. Chastain. Per your request, I reactivated her old paperwork and there's no doubt about it. The syn-psych profile harmonizes extremely well with yours."

"What?" Zinnia got to her knees and crouched over Nick. Her eyes gleamed in the shadows. "You never told me that you finished the registration process. And you paid Batt to reactivate my paperwork?"

"Couldn't resist," Nick said.

"There are always some unknowns when one is dealing with a matrix-talent, of course. We went with your own estimate of class-ten-plus for you. Most unusual. But our records show that Miss Spring's form of paranormal energy is quite unique also. It was one of the things that made her impossible to match four years ago. From what I can tell, it appears that it will compliment your strong matrix attributes in some peculiar fashion."

"Peculiar." Zinnia grimaced. "Well, I like that."

"Hey, I happen to like peculiar," Nick assured her. "Especially in red."

"I hope you're as delighted as I am that we've found you a suitable match, Mr. Chastain. I wish you the best of luck."

There was a discreet pause and then Hobart cleared his throat.

"Can I assume that you are entirely satisfied?"

Nick stretched out a hand and picked up the receiver. His fingers brushed against the set of gold cuff links he had left on the bedside table earlier when he had undressed. The cuff links had been a gift from Ella. Each was inscribed with an elegant *C* and the initial *B. "Your father's,"* she had explained.

"This is Chastain, Batt. Consider your debt to Chastain's Palace paid in full."

"Thank you, Mr. Chastain." Gratitude and relief vibrated in Hobart's voice. "You know, this is my second match between a very high-class talent and a full-spectrum prism in recent months. Most counselors don't see even one such match in their whole careers."

"Is that a fact." Nick stroked Zinnia's thigh.

"I'm starting to wonder if we've been functioning under some false assumptions concerning the synergism between strong talents and powerful prisms," Hobart continued in a chatty tone. "The phenomenon of psychic energy in humans is so recent and it's evolving very swiftly. We may have a lot more to learn than we realized."

"You may be working under some false assumptions, Hobart, but I know exactly what I'm doing." Nick hung up the phone and started to pull Zinnia down into his arms.

She splayed her fingers across his chest. "Hold it right there, Chastain. What would you have done if it turned out that my old marriage-agency records did not spell out a good match between us?"

He smiled into her laughing, loving eyes. "I would have altered the records through the computer until they did show a perfect match. I'm a matrix-talent, remember? I've always got a plan."